Francis Selwyn and The Murder Room

〉〉〉 This title is part of The Murder Room, our series dedicated to making available out-of-print or hard-to-find titles by classic crime writers.

Crime fiction has always held up a mirror to society. The Victorians were fascinated by sensational murder and the emerging science of detection; now we are obsessed with the forensic detail of violent death. And no other genre has so captivated and enthralled readers.

Vast troves of classic crime writing have for a long time been unavailable to all but the most dedicated frequenters of second-hand bookshops. The advent of digital publishing means that we are now able to bring you the backlists of a huge range of titles by classic and contemporary crime writers, some of which have been out of print for decades.

From the genteel amateur private eyes of the Golden Age and the femmes fatales of pulp fiction, to the morally ambiguous hard-boiled detectives of mid twentieth-century America and their descendants who walk our twenty-first century streets, The Murder Room has it all. **〉〉〉**

The Murder Room
Where Criminal Minds Meet

themurderroom.com

T0352279

Francis Selwyn (pen name of Donald Thomas) (1926–)

Donald Thomas was born in Somerset and educated at Queen's College, Taunton, and Balliol College, Oxford. He holds a personal chair in the University of Wales, Cardiff, now Cardiff University. His numerous crime novels include two collections of Sherlock Holmes stories and a hugely successful historical detective series written under the pen name Francis Selwyn and featuring Sergeant Verity of Scotland Yard, as well as gritty police procedurals written under the name of Richard Dacre. He is also the author of seven biographies and a number of other non-fiction works, and won the Gregory Prize for his poems, *Points of Contact*. He lives in Bath with his wife.

Mad Hatter Summer: A Lewis Carroll Nightmare
The Ripper's Apprentice
Jekyll, Alias Hyde
The Arrest of Scotland Yard
Dancing in the Dark
Red Flowers for Lady Blue
The Blindfold Game
The Day the Sun Rose Twice

As Francis Selwyn

Sergeant Verity and the Cracksman
Sergeant Verity and the Imperial Diamond
Sergeant Verity Presents His Compliments
Sergeant Verity and the Blood Royal

Sergeant Verity and the Swell Mob
Sergeant Verity and the Hangman's Child

As Richard Dacre

The Blood Runs Hot
Scream Blue Murder
Money with Menaces

Sergeant Verity and the Blood Royal

Francis Selwyn

An Orion book

Copyright © Donald Thomas 1979

The right of Donald Thomas to be identified as the author of this work
has been asserted in accordance with the Copyright, Designs and Patents
Act 1988.

This edition published by
The Orion Publishing Group Ltd
Orion House
5 Upper St Martin's Lane
London WC2H 9EA

An Hachette UK company
A CIP catalogue record for this book is available from the British Library

ISBN 978 1 4719 0425 7

www.orionbooks.co.uk

For Carol

IN CONFIDENCE

WILLIAM CLARENCE VERITY, Sergeant, 'A' Division (Private-Clothes)

Born 8 November 1832, Redruth, Cornwall, eldest son of Luke Verity (deceased), tin-miner and Wesleyan class-leader

Educated Hebron Chapel School, Redruth

Married Arabella Sophy, daughter of Julius Stringfellow, cabman, Paddington Green, 8 August 1857

Issue William Albert Verity, born 24 May 1858
Victoria Sophia Verity, born 3 September 1859

Previous employment Page and footman to the Dowager Countess Linacre, Royal Crescent, Bath, 1844–49; private, 23rd regiment of foot, 1849; corporal, 1852; sergeant, 1854; present at battles of the Alma, Inkerman, and the Redan; invalided to England and discharged, 1855

Divisional Record Sergeant, Metropolitan Police 'A' Division, 3 January 1856; Private-Clothes Detail, 1 October 1856; South Eastern Railway bullion robbery inquiry, July 1857; suspended on suspicion of complicity, 19 July 1857; suspension lifted, 30 July 1857; seconded Provost Marshal's office, Calcutta, September 1857–December 1858; Kaiser-i-Hind diamond inquiry, 1858; services hired by Jervis family following death by shooting of Lord Henry Jervis, May-July 1860; present at attempted sinking HMS *Hero*, July 1860

Paraded   Twice for assaults upon members of the public; twice for insubordination; eight times for private reprimand by Inspector H. Croaker, officer commanding detail

Current Duties   Assigned to bodyguard of HRH the Prince of Wales during tour of Canada and the United States, by request of HRH the Prince Consort. Inspector Croaker's obedient and humble reservations as to the officer's fitness for this duty are herewith appended.

H. Croaker, Inspector of Constabulary

21 August 1860

SUSPECTED PERSONS   1249/Dacre/1857

Not to be taken from the file

VERNEY MAUGHAN DACRE

Born   12 May 1825, only son of Charles Delaune Fox Dacre, of Faring Abbey, Gloucestershire, and Carlos Place, London, W. (deceased)

Educated   Collège Louis-le-Grand, Paris, 1837–1843
Trinity College, Oxford, 1843–1844

Commissioned   19th Lancers, October 1844; Lieutenant, May 1845; Sikh Wars, Chillianwallah, etc., 1845–46; half-pay, 1846

Clubs   White's, Beargarden

Criminal Convictions   None

Died   26 July 1857, Albemarle Street, London, W. Verdict of self-destruction while of unsound mind returned by coroner's inquest

On suspicion   (see also subject-file: perjury, extortion, forgery)

(1)   Robbery of five cwt gold bullion from South Eastern

Railway ferry-train, ex-London Bridge for Folke-stone, 16 July 1857

(2) Murder of Charles Baptist Cazamian, railway guard, between 17 and 20 July 1857 (post-mortem report appended)

(3) Inflicting grievous bodily harm with a horse-switch on the naked person of a young woman known professionally as 'Miss Jolly', 24 July 1857 (medical report under ref. *Jolly*)

Remarks Lieutenant Dacre remains the most dangerous and determined criminal with whom the Private-Clothes Detail has dealt. Contemptuous of his own safety and that of others, he combined scientific ingenuity and moral ruthlessness. His unique skill with locks and safes led to the removal of five cwt of gold from a sealed bullion van and double-locked safe with no indication of the method used. His delight in cruelty is shown by the manner of drowning his accomplice Cazamian and by the evident amusement afforded him by the whipping of Miss Jolly.

1

THE JUDAS CAPER

I

The English Lieutenant lit a long El Sol cigar and stared broodingly across the dark river gorge to the Loudoun heights of Virginia on the far side. At some distance behind him one of his servants held the reins of a pair of sleek geldings, their hides the colour of dark smoke. The animals stood between the shafts of an open carriage, a swan's-neck Pilentum in olive green, the most elegant four-wheeler that Clapps of Boston had ever built. In his cream suiting and dark silk hat, his gold-topped cane under his arm, the Lieutenant seemed as much out of his element as the freshly-painted carriage. The Pilentum and its owner summoned up images of the procession of fashion in Pall Mall, the first day's racing at Royal Ascot, the shimmering brilliance of the Marine Parade at Brighton.

Down to the tips of his white, fine-boned fingers, the Lieutenant appeared as a man born to command others. Even when murder was necessary to his schemes it was carried out, as a rule, by other men. He brooded now on the destruction of a creature who was no more admirable than himself. Under the circumstances, each would have rated the other's life cheaply enough. The young officer's lips moved in a thin quiver of distaste, blowing the first mouthful of acrid smoke into the autumn dusk. On either side of him the woods of the Maryland height were already stripped to black skeletons of their summer glory.

Tall and narrow as a clock-case, he stood with his back against the trunk of a holm-oak, crossing one foot over the other in a manner which instantly conveyed the leisured boredom of a Hussar dandy. He smoked with a petulant impatience, his free hand brushing compulsively over the limp blonde whiskers which adorned his spoilt face. That face was a study in arrogant self-possession. Its one physical

3

flaw was betrayed by the manner in which the Lieutenant from time to time touched a silk handkerchief to the corners of his pale blue eyes, which seemed to water gently but without respite. The complaint was trivial but incurable. Certainly there was no softness in the tears. The pale blue eyes had watched men die and women scream without reflecting the least emotion beyond an occasional brightening of satisfaction.

The bare cliffs fell away before him to form a magnificent river gorge, where two streams joined as they emerged from their mountain courses and began to cross the broad tidewater plain. Between them, as they converged, an ugly little town stood on a tongue of land. In the late autumn twilight, the two principal streets were easily picked out by the yellow glimmer of regularly spaced oil lamps. Equally distinct were the lights burning on the great iron span of the covered bridge, raised on stone piers, which carried the Baltimore and Ohio railroad across the Potomac, on its way to Washington.

The Lieutenant raised a pair of small field-glasses to his eyes and scanned the shabby conglomeration of railroad offices, hotels, stores and eating-houses which made up the main street of the little town below him. He turned slowly, taking in the drab sequence of warehouses and machine-shops, the tall brick chimney, the terrain of railroad tracks, puddles and mounds of iron pipes. At last his gaze came to rest on the iron span of the bridge, and then he slid the glasses back into their case. From the deep pocket of his long coat he took a small bag of wash-leather. Its weight moved to the metallic shuffle of coins as he shifted his grip. The Lieutenant patted it impatiently, his eyes still watching the railroad bridge.

'Dammit, Charley Temple,' he said softly to the man he could not yet see, 'a fellow that don't care for five thousand chinkers ain't to be trusted with a fourpenny bit in the china dog kennel!'

His drawl and intonation would have sounded almost as odd in London as on the Maryland height. It was the voice of 1809 rather than 1859, echoing the slangy supercilious tone of a Regency buck rather than the conscientious precision of a sober Victorian gentleman. With his way of saying 'goold' for 'gold', 'vartue' for 'virtue', or 'faller' for 'fellow', the Lieutenant hinted at long acquaintance with the stubbornly preserved exclusiveness of mess-rooms in fashionable cavalry regiments, select club-rooms in St James's or Piccadilly, and the hunting aristocracy of the Pytchley or the Quorn.

The mimic thunder of hooves on leaf-mould reached him from the lower slope of the woods. A bridle path led upward from the river bank, at the nearer end of the Baltimore and Ohio bridge, almost to the spot where he stood. The Lieutenant pitched away his cigar and stepped back into the shadow of the holm oak.

'Well now, Charley Temple!' he said to himself with a soft satisfaction. 'Well now!'

He never doubted that Charley was moving as quickly as the need for silence allowed. Stealing another man's slave, a fancy-girl at that, was not in itself a hanging matter. But selling her across the state-line to a new master in a free territory was a bad business for an old rascal of Temple's reputation. Always provided, of course, that he was brought to justice for it.

The Lieutenant heard the crackle of brushwood under a man's tread and then saw through the twilight the figure of Temple leading two horses behind him. Bearded and grizzled, the old trader's face combined the sanctimoniousness of a gospel-preacher and the cunning of a horse-thief. Of the two girls mounted on the horses, Jennifer's Asian or Indian beauty made her a slave by colour as much as by descent. Her sheen of black hair lay in a pretty tangle between her shoulder blades, her high-boned olive-skinned face and almond eyes warm with a challenging sexuality. She straddled the horse in tight denim breeches, the slight fullness of her hips and seat suggestively displayed.

It crossed the Lieutenant's mind that the owner of the Richmond whorehouse would have more reason to pursue

5

Temple with a posse of ruffians for the theft of the second girl. Maggie was a slave in practice, but not in theory. She was a pale-skinned, hazel-eyed young woman, the curtains of her blonde hair sweeping loose to her shoulders. She had, of course, been broken to the bondage of the brothel as completely as Jennifer. The limit of her ambition to be free was merely that she should be traded with the Asian girl, to whom she owed her only attachment in the world.

The Lieutenant stepped out of the shadow and greeted these arrivals. Temple helped the two young women to dismount.

'Dammit, Charley,' said the young officer genially, 'ain't you got a way for keepin' a fellow at a stand by the hour together? May I be cursed if it's short of nine o'clock now!'

Temple twisted his mouth and spat accurately to one side.

'You know a quicker way across that river, mister, you're sure as hell welcome to try it.'

The Lieutenant laughed good-naturedly at this rebuke. It cost him nothing. He patted the wash-leather courier bag.

'Take the chinkers, old friend. Count 'em and see you ain't been robbed. I shall have a minute or two close with the young Khan doxy. If she answers true to form, the dealing's done. I don't choose to stand idling where dogs and trackers can find us.'

'Not a whimper, not a yelp,' said Temple confidently. 'Hear 'em a mile off on a calm night.'

He took the bag of coins, loosing the string at its neck. Taking up a dark lantern and opening its shutter, the Lieutenant crossed the path to Maggie. Her golden blonde tresses had a childish look in the way in which she wore them loose to her shoulders. In the oil light he surveyed the hazel eyes with their dark lashes, the pale firm features and the outline of her nineteen-year-old figure. She was a little too short to be a beauty, though her body seemed to him coltish rather than stocky. As he turned her chin to and fro, the Lieutenant promised himself that the young woman would prove to be an earner in a thousand before he had done with her. In this matter, at least, his expertise was universally acknowledged. A blush warmed her pale face at his voice.

'You may top and tail your tawny Jenny to your heart's content, missy, my word upon it. Only remember, if you please, that all pleasures have a price and a bill of reckoning.'

As the Lieutenant had promised, it was Jennifer's sullen, tawny skinned appeal which formed the greater attraction. He led her aside and questioned her expressionlessly for several minutes, his thumbs braced against the gold-topped stick which he held across his chest, as though he might strike her with it at the least provocation. Instead, he handed it to her and watched the Asian girl draw a square with it upon a smooth patch of damp earth. Within the four furrows she traced out a design, hardly speaking or looking up at him as she did so. The Lieutenant surveyed the completed pattern, put two more questions to the girl, and nodded at her replies. Then he turned back to the carriage once more, twirling the stick in his fingers like a band-master.

'This is all a great bore, Charley Temple. Count the chinkers, old fellow, and have done. Take the gold and leave me the horseflesh. They shall put themselves about for my profit or taste the back of Lucifer's knuckles otherwise. I don't choose to catch God's own plague out here!'

Temple glanced up at the impeccable arrogance of the young man.

'All done,' he said ungraciously. 'Five hundred tens.' Then his face relaxed and he came towards the Lieutenant, extending his hand as though in a sudden gesture of goodwill to seal the bargain. The young man laughed and ignored the proffered hand.

'Dammit, Charley,' he said reasonably, 'I ain't that anxious to have the rings filched off m' very fingers! Be off with you, y' damned old scoundrel!'

Joseph Morant-Barham, more familiarly known as Joey

Barham, heir to the heir of Earl Barham, stood in the shadows of the trees, a dozen yards from the beginning of the Baltimore and Ohio bridge. A frown of concern marked the fierce young subaltern's face, its black moustaches and sun-reddened cheeks suggesting several years of service in one of the Indian regiments. The frown was caused by the sudden reappearance of Charley Temple, riding his own horse and leading the mare on which one of the two girls had been carried half an hour before. Morant-Barham had not expected to see him return so soon and he felt a pang of apprehension in his throat at the thought that the plan was about to miscarry. But he underestimated his own ability as well as that of his partner. Joey Barham had laid his information well, and the men to whom he had given it were not about to lose their advantage. Apart from which, it was not in the nature of plans laid by his partner, the English Lieutenant, to miscarry.

The hooves of Charley Temple's horse woke the first echoes of the planking which formed the surface of the bridge on either side of the railroad track. With a hollow resonance, the sound rang back from the iron trellis-work whose span enclosed the sides. Before him, Charley Temple must have seen a safe and open road to follow home. Even Morant-Barham thought the bridge was deserted, his apprehension rising as Temple trotted his horse close to the Virginia end. He was almost across when a murmur of voices rose in the stillness of the evening and several horsemen cantered forward from the shadows which had concealed them, beyond the far end of the bridge. The murmuring came from twenty or thirty men on foot who now rose from the ground on either side of the further embankment and pressed forward behind their mounted leaders. Charley Temple, encumbered by the horse he was leading, hesitated a moment too long before attempting to wheel round and ride for the Maryland bank.

It hardly sounded as though he were in any danger. The tone of some of the voices calling his name was more that of his saloon companions recognizing their crony. Morant-

Barham caught the derisive greeting.

'Charley Temple, you goddam horse-thief! Where away so fast, Charley?'

The bonhomie of the crowd on foot would seriously have worried Morant-Barham, had it not been for the silent resolve of the leaders mounted on horseback.

'That's him!' said one of the followers impatiently. 'Rode across the slave-line with a dark-skinned girl not an hour since and come back without her! Whether she's stole from whorehouse or Bible School makes no odds.'

'It ain't the first time, Charley Temple,' said one of the riders. 'You had this coming to you a long while!'

The softer, more assured voice was the one which caused Temple to panic. At the best he could hope for a back laid raw by the whips of the riders, but the coiled rope on one of the saddle-bows suggested that the best was too much to hope for. He turned his horse about, spurred hard for the Maryland side of the bridge, and bowed his head over the animal's neck. But somewhere in the darkness of the mob which followed him, the first shot rang clearly in the cold air. Morant-Barham watching from the shadows had waited his chance, never expecting that the confusion would provide one so propitious. Joey Barham had unslung his rifle at the first sight of Temple. The gun was a Baker muzzle-loader, proved by the British army in the Crimea as the most accurate of its kind. Temple was going to pass within ten yards of him but Morant-Barham knew there would be time for only one shot.

When the moment came, several of the pursuers were firing after Temple, though without much hope of hitting him at such range and speed. It was the riders who would overtake and bring him to justice in the end. Before that happened, Joey Barham knew he must finish the business. Revising his plan and his aim, he sighted down the barrel of the Baker at a more distant gap in the iron trellis-work of the bridge, the last which Temple might pass before the leaders of the mob seized him. With the assurance of a marksman, he stood very still, shutting out from his mind

9

the shouting and confusion, watching the lamplit space between the girders with as much detachment as if he had been observing a theorem in geometry.

He aimed low, at the chest rather than the head, knowing that it would offer a fuller target. Charley Temple's shape flashed briefly behind the further struts and then came into full view. Morant-Barham, in a long five seconds, followed steadily with his aim and then, just as steadily, brought an even pressure to bear on the trigger. The rifle barked, deafening as a cannon at such range, and left Joey's ears singing with the shock. But Charley Temple had thrown up his arms in a pantomine gesture of despair and was now at the feet of his hunters. No one, in all the uproar, would question that a lucky shot from one of the pursuers had brought him down. Joey Barham kept very still among the trees, not even attempting to reload the rifle for his own defence. Then his heart seemed to stop and his throat to tighten as he heard someone on the bridge say with mingled impatience and amusement: 'Why, the cunning old rat ain't even dead yet!'

There was no more that Joey could do, but Charley Temple was in safe hands. While he shrilly and blasphemously protested his innocence, his body arching convulsively with a fear that was greater than pain, half a dozen men had hoisted him level with the iron parapet of the bridge. Morant-Barham looked for a rope round the scraggy neck as they lodged Temple above the swirling waters of the Potomac, but there was none. With a great communal howl they heaved him over, the body falling spread-eagled through the air while a stutter of small-arms fire opened on the moving target.

Joey Barham slung his rifle on his back and prepared to move gently away through the woods. Temple had hit one of the stone piers and was lying there motionlessly. Then, to Joey's surprise, the old thief raised his head, shook it, and began to crawl awkwardly like a broken insect. There was a yell from the men on the bridge, partly of hatred and partly of delight at finding that their vengeance could be further prolonged. Another patter of shots followed. The body on the stone pier jerked spasmodically under the impact of several bullets and then, at last, lay still.

Almost at once, there was a stillness in the crowd and Joey Barham was able to hear the crunching tread of a regiment on the march, approaching the far bank. Charley Temple's assassins scattered wildly, running in every direction as the yellow oil light caught the first flash of blue uniforms. Since John Brown's attempt on the national armory at Harper's Ferry, a militia company had been kept permanently on the alert. Even the mounted brothel bullies and the mob which followed them had barely time to despatch Charley Temple. But they were keen to set an example to other traders and emancipationists alike. They made it time enough.

A militia captain had halted his men on the far bank and was rapping out orders to various details. As the company broke up into smaller units, each with its allotted duty, Joey Morant-Barham turned away. He walked softly through the Maryland woods, climbing the obscure path by which he had come. His horse was still tethered to the trunk of a silver birch, not half a mile from the road which led across the narrow neck of Maryland and into Pennsylvania. His rendezvous with the Lieutenant, an hour later and five miles further on, was easily kept. The Pilentum stood by the roadside, its dark hood raised and its carriage-lamps flickering.

The Lieutenant listened to Morant-Barham's account of the tragedy at the Baltimore and Ohio bridge. Then the young officer whinnied with laughter at the extent of the old man's folly.

'By God, Joey! What a fellow will do for five thousand yellow boys! Ain't it justice, though, truly speaking?'

'And the girl?' asked Morant-Barham, unamused. 'What of her?'

The Lieutenant rested a polished boot on the foot-board of the carriage and sighed.

'Joey, Joey, there was never a word of a lie in it. When

11

she was fifteen the cove that owned her left Richmond for Philadelphia. By a stroke of fortune the missioners never got to her and the young fool never took her liberty. Our Miss Jennifer chose a full belly before starving in freedom. For a year or more, the cove put her naked up chimneys to clean 'em. She worked for him and he pleasured her, until she fancied herself in love, Joey! Then he gave up the sweepin' concern and took her back south. Cured her of love by selling her to a bawdy-house. Ain't remarkable she should look a bit surly, old fellow, is it?'

'And the rest?' asked Morant-Barham. 'Is it bono?'

The Lieutenant laughed.

'Oblige me, Joey, by giving a fellow a little credit! When our Khan doxy was a sweep, she was in a state that might have been black or white, boy or girl. She was put up chimneys in the great buildings of Philadelphia and the small. She mayn't drawn builder's plans of the main rooms, but there ain't nothing she couldn't tell you about chimneys. Now, Joey, I know enough of ground plans. While you were galloping after us just now, Miss Jennifer drew a sketch in the dust of the one thing lacking.'

'Oh yes?' said Morant-Barham nervously.

'She has cause to remember it, Joey, from torn skin and raw joints. The stacks and flues of the United States Federal Mint.'

Joey Barham whistled appreciatively.

'And the locks? Vault doors and strongroom?'

'Come now, Joey,' said the Lieutenant reasonably, 'a man must do something for himself. Where's the sport in it all otherwise?'

'A million,' Morant-Barham said thoughtfully, 'a million in gold!'

The Lieutenant frowned.

'Hold hard, Joey! I ain't Charley Temple to be bought and sold cheap. More than two million but perhaps not three. And no one to know that it's been done.'

Morant-Barham chortled and the Lieutenant turned to another topic.

12

'Joey, old fellow, take Miss Mag and ride the horse with her a bit. I've a mind to put the tawny doxy on her back in the carriage. Curse Charley Temple, but these Newgate japes do leave a fellow feelin' frisky!'

2

Department of the Treasury
Pennsylvania Avenue
Washington
District of Columbia

18th of November 1859

Captain Jefferson Oliphant, of the United States Treasury, presents his compliments to Inspector Henry Croaker, of the Private-Clothes Detail, Metropolitan Police, London. Captain Oliphant presumes, on the basis of their meeting two years ago, to solicit Mr Croaker's advice in a matter of some delicacy and confidentiality.

Mr Croaker may have read, in the latest exchange of intelligence, of an unfortunate incident at Harper's Ferry, Virginia, where pro-slavery feeling was already roused by the attack of Captain John Brown and his conspirators on the national armory. Captain Oliphant refers to the subsequent murder by lynch law of a known thief and trader in slave-women, Charles Temple, alias Samuel Edge. Having stolen a young woman, Jennifer or Jenny Khan, from her master, Temple sold her across the state-line to a brothel trader in Maryland. Being watched secretly, he was seized upon his return, gravely wounded by a shot during the struggle, and thrown to his death from the Potomac railroad bridge. A company of militia arriving soon after put the mob to flight and recovered Temple's body from the stone pier of the bridge.

13

Captain Oliphant has since had occasion to interview Major Eliot, the first officer to reach Temple's body. Though mortally injured by the fall and by loss of blood, Temple was still conscious and lived for several minutes longer. During this brief period, he swore repeatedly that he had been betrayed by the man for whom he had stolen the young woman. She was not bought for her physical beauty but for having in her head the plan of one of the great bank-vaults of the United States.

Captain Oliphant cannot see how this could be the case. Yet Temple's dying words were emphatic and urgent. He was also in possession of five thousand dollars in gold coin, a sum far in excess of the price generally paid for a 'fancy-girl' used for immoral purposes.

Finally, Temple named the villain who had betrayed him and was to employ the girl's information. He was, in Temple's words, a disgraced British army officer, Lieutenant Verney Dacre, late of the 19th Dragoon Guards.

When Captain Oliphant had the pleasure of meeting Mr Croaker in London, during the autumn of 1857, Lieutenant Dacre's name was often mentioned. He was then credited as the intelligence of the great bullion robbery on the South Eastern Railway of London. Five hundredweight of gold at twenty-two carat had disappeared while held under maximum security and had then not been accounted for.

Though Temple's story of a plot against an unspecified bank-vault must be treated with caution, Mr Croaker will appreciate the concern of the United States Treasury if Lieutenant Dacre were at large in this country. At the same time, Captain Oliphant understood that the bullion crime had been brought home to Dacre by the pertinacity and zeal of Mr Croaker himself. He further understood that Dacre had taken his own life by shooting himself, almost in the presence of the arresting officers, and that a coroner's inquest was held upon him.

Captain Oliphant would be immeasurably obliged if Mr Croaker were able to confirm the view of the Metropolitan Police that Lieutenant Dacre died in 1857 and to state briefly the circumstances of his demise.

In conclusion, Captain Oliphant offers to Inspector Croaker his best respects and begs to remain Mr Croaker's obedient servant.

Inspector Henry Croaker
Metropolitan Police 'A' Division
Scotland Yard
Whitehall Place
London, W.
England

3

Metropolitan Police
'A' Division
Whitehall Police Office
London, W.

2nd January 1860

Inspector Henry Croaker, of the Whitehall Police Office, presents his compliments to Captain Jefferson Oliphant and is in receipt of Captain Oliphant's communication of the 18th of November last.

At the outset, Inspector Croaker must say how deeply he deplores the late incidents at Harper's Ferry, Virginia. Ever an enemy to social unrest in all its forms, Inspector Croaker views most strongly the wholesale evils which must result from conferring arbitrary freedom upon those whose status and education ill-equip them to receive it.

In the matter of Lieutenant Verney Maughan Dacre, late 19th Dragoon Guards, Mr Croaker is happy to assure Captain Oliphant that this officer cannot now be in the United States, having been certified dead by a coroner's inquest in 1857, upon Mr Croaker's own information. Mr Croaker must emphasize that Lieutenant Dacre is not, in law, a criminal, having no indictment or conviction against his name. However, Mr Croaker sees no injury to protocol in revealing those details of Lieutenant Dacre's death known to 'A' Division, Metropolitan Police.

Strong evidence, implicating Lieutenant Dacre in the bullion robbery, had been amassed by the following month. Sergeant Albert Samson of the Private-Clothes Detail, under Mr Croaker's orders, confronted Lieutenant Dacre at the latter's rooms in Albemarle Street, London, W. Also present was Sergeant William Clarence Verity of the detail. This officer was not on duty, however, and therefore not to be credited with apprehension of the suspect.

Sergeant Samson questioned Lieutenant Dacre and was then obliged to go down to the street and send for a constable to carry a message to Scotland Yard. During his absence a shot was heard. On returning to Lieutenant Dacre's room, he found the suspect sitting in his chair, still dressed in the same russet suiting and yellow waistcoat. He had evidently shot himself through the mouth with a Manton duelling pistol which then lay in his lap. The wound was extensive, at such close range, devastating the skull and causing severe general injuries. Of the manservant, Oughtram, there was no trace, though immediate search was made by way of an internal door in the room, leading below stairs. Oughtram eluded all pursuit by the constabulary authorities, who sought him as a witness to the tragedy. There was, of course, no evidence implicating him in the bullion theft.

Mr Croaker therefore takes the greatest satisfaction in assuring Captain Oliphant that Lieutenant Dacre died three years since in Albemarle Street. This has been legally established by a coroner's inquest. In addition, Mr Croaker is prepared to add his own formal assurance of the fact to Captain Oliphant, upon the authority of his own constabulary rank and reputation.

In conclusion, Mr Croaker remains, etc.

Captain Jefferson Oliphant
Department of the Treasury
Pennsylvania Avenue
Washington
District of Columbia
United States of America

Captain Oliphant handed the letter across his desk to Sergeant Thomas Crowe, who stood plain-suited on the far side. The Captain folded his hands behind him and walked slowly to the tall sash window. He stared, without noticing the view, down the long tree-lined avenue towards the unfinished dome of the Capitol building at the far end. His eyes rested briefly on the litter of builders' scaffolding and blocks of stone. Then he turned back and took the sheet of paper which Crowe had finished reading. Captain Oliphant glanced at it again and then looked up at his subordinate with an audible sigh.

'Right!' he said softly. 'I guess this tells us everything we need to know. Take Stevens. And take Hamilton. And go out there, and find Lieutenant Dacre!'

2

BLOOD ROYAL

4

Beyond the rippling surface of Plymouth Sound at full tide, placid as an inland lake, the waters of the English Channel glittered like copper tinsel in the dying summer day. The storm clouds, gunpowder grey, which had hung over the Western Approaches earlier in the afternoon, had passed overhead harmlessly and had now almost vanished beyond the Dartmoor slopes.

Packed closely on Plymouth Hoe and on the high ground of the Citadel, a crown of men and women murmured as though in long expectation. Just out to sea, beyond the breakwater, the ships of the Channel Squadron lay at anchor in two lines. The wooden hulls, with their rows of square ports on the gun decks, their black shapes topped by acid-yellow and by the creamy-grey billows of their sails, were indistinguishable at this distance from the ships which had sailed with Nelson to Trafalgar, or with Lord Howe on the Glorious First of June. The setting sun was behind their sails, suffusing them with a reddish gold, concealing the short squat funnels which rose by the mainmast and indicated the new power of Her Majesty's fleet.

The crowd was made up of grave-looking men in long-tailed coats and tall hats; women in broad crinolined silks and triple flounces, the patterned stripes running vertically down the dresses, since Paris had decreed that horizontal bands were now irrevocably out of fashion. There was a score of red-coated and gold-braided gunners from the Horse Artillery battery at Mount Edgecumbe, gaping lantern-jawed at the scene with their tunics unbuttoned. The gunners were vastly outnumbered by the parties of sailors in their dark broad-brimmed hats, the royal blue of their short jackets, and their white breeches. Bearded and sun-freckled, they watched the pageant before them with

21

professional curiosity. At a trestle table set down on the grass of the Hoe, a row of frock-coated and bare-headed men with papers before them waited philosophically. These were the reporters of the London dailies whose accounts would be telegraphed within the hour for the next edition of *The Times*, the *Globe*, or the *Morning Post*.

It was a little after seven o'clock when the murmuring in the crowd rose in intensity and a flurry of hands pointed and gestured. Rounding Great Mew from the east was a paddle-steamer, a trim little vessel with its dark hull and white paddle-boxes, its two buff funnels. In the stillness of the evening and the quiescent sea, the rhythm of its wheels carried as an audible *pat-pat-pat* to the watchers on the Hoe. Two flags flew from its mastheads. One was the White Ensign with the Cross of St George boldly marked. The other, recognized with a cheer by the onlookers, was the Royal Standard of England, the gold lions on their scarlet ground streaming bravely in the evening light.

Conversation on the Hoe was obliterated by the sudden outburst of a Royal Marine band.

> *Come, cheer up, my lads, 'tis to glory we steer,*
> *To add something new to this wonderful year . . .*

This in turn was submerged in the booming of royal salutes from rival batteries, like so many clocks striking the hour in competition. The battery of the Citadel set off first, in reverberating billows of white smoke, then the Horse Artillery guns of Mount Edgecumbe. But most splendid of all were the salutes of HMS *Hero*, accompanied by the *Ariadne*, *St George* and *Emerald*. Beflagged and dressed overall, their cannon smoke rolled from one gun-port after another with successive precision. At the same time there was a well-drilled movement in the rigging. The crews who had manned the ships' yards brandished their hats and roared three cheers for the *Victoria and Albert*, as the royal yacht dropped anchor in the Sound after her voyage from Osborne.

An ornamental barge, rowed by sailors of the fleet,

pulled out of the inner harbour and began to negotiate the armada of little yachts and pleasure vessels which filled the Sound. It drew alongside the gleaming black hull of the royal yacht and a file of senior military and naval commanders was helped over the paddle sponson, followed by the Mayor, the Recorder of Plymouth in wig and gown, and the city fathers with their address of welcome.

In the crowd itself, every pocket spy-glass was trained on the *Victoria and Albert*. The Prince of Wales was not only on board but must show himself sooner or later. The young man's father, the Prince Consort, was also on board and might, perhaps, be glimpsed. It was said that Her Majesty, too, had come to see the eighteen-year-old heir to her throne on his way to the New World.

The last of the evening sky faded, somewhere over the Cornish moors. Riding-lights and the oil-lit squares of open gun-ports illuminated the Channel fleet at anchor. On the royal yacht itself the grand saloon showed a curtained brilliance. Then the ornamental barge returned to shore with its cargo of dignitaries. The admiral's barge from HMS *Hero* crossed the harbour to the *Victoria and Albert* to take on its precious cargo and ferry him back to the towering hull of the flagship. The crowd began to drift from the Hoe and the ramparts of the Citadel. Late that night, the paddles of the royal yacht went astern, bearing the Prince Consort back to Osborne. In the dawn light, to the thunder of salutes from the Citadel and Mount Edgecumbe Park, the *Hero* put to sea under full sail and with smoke trailing from her black stumpy funnel. The ports were closed for safety over her ninety-one guns as she passed with her escort, the *Ariadne*, between the two lines of the Channel Squadron. Then, taking the lead, she remained at the head of the mighty fleet until the watchers on the ramparts saw that the last sails had dipped below the western horizon.

The novelty was more than a passing wonder. Eighty-four years earlier the American colonies had won their freedom from the mother country in bitter battle. Now the young man who would one day be king of England was undertaking the first royal pilgrimage to the land which his great-grandfather had lost.

Sergeant William Clarence Verity, of the Metropolitan Police Private-Clothes Detail, sat on his wooden travelling-box among the sooty brickwork and granite-rimmed breakwaters of Liverpool's Waterloo Docks. To one side of him, barefoot girls with dirty legs and women nursing babies at the breast, huddled with their shabbily dressed menfolk. The surplus population of England awaited shipment by steerage to the new cities of North America. At the opposite end of the quay, protected from proletarian intrusion by a pair of stalwart dockyard policemen, groups of gaily-dressed women in pink or turquoise silks, and spruce family men with trim whiskers, chattered and guffawed self-confidently. Many of them clutched little tins of 'The Sea-Sickness Remedy', thoughtfully purveyed by Thomas Thompson, chemist of Liverpool.

Sergeant Verity, in rusty and threadbare frock-coat, shiny black trousers and tall stovepipe hat, glowered at them all. His pink moon of a face, black hair flattened and moustaches waxed for neatness, grew a shade redder with portly indignation.

'It ain't right!' he said furiously. 'It ain't never right. And you know it, Mr Samson!'

Sergeant Albert Samson, red-whiskered and pugilistic, turned his eyes reluctantly from those of a dark and dimpled pauper-girl with whom he seemed on the point of reaching a distant understanding.

'There's a lot in this world ain't right, but what happens just the same, Mr Verity.'

He spoke with the nonchalance of one unaccustomed to letting other men's troubles bow his spirit. Verity swung round on his lacquered box.

'I *saw* it, Mr Samson! In Superintendent Gowry's office. It was signed "Albert", in the Prince Consort's own hand, plain as I sit 'ere! He chose me for guard to the young Prince of Wales for the American visit. Mr Samson, 'e been gone a week, so have the rest! And 'ere I am!'

'You was needed for the Volunteer Review in Hyde Park,' said Samson cheerily. 'The detail was short-handed as it was.'

'Mr Inspector-bloody-Croaker!' said Verity through his teeth. 'He was in the room when I saw that letter. Sick as the kitchen cat he looked when he knew it was me and not 'im that was asked for!'

Sergeant Samson looked noncommitally across the chocolate-coloured waters of the Mersey, surveying the little boats and barges, with their wine-red or ochre sails. Busy paddle-tugs fussed round the red-funnelled Cunarder at her moorings, where smoke and steam already seeped from her in thin drifts. Samson clapped a hand on Verity's shoulder.

'Well, my son, you're going now, ain't yer? With me to see you safe and snug on board!'

Verity was not so easily placated.

'It ain't the point, Mr Samson! If this boat should get itself delayed now, I'll be at the other side just in time to meet 'em all coming back. I was to 'ave gone from Plymouth in the flagship. Mrs Verity, and her old father, and the whole boiling of Stringfellows was coming special to see the show. A right fool I been made to look!'

'Draw it mild, old fellow,' urged Samson sensibly, seeking the gaze of the barefoot girl again. Verity snorted.

'It's Mr Croaker behind all this, don't think I don't know it! I tell you, Mr Samson, I gotta eye for 'im. Let him put one foot wrong, that's all, and I'll have him – by his privates!'

'Here!' said Samson, in genuine alarm. 'Don't you go talking like that round Whitehall Police Office. Not unless you want Mr Croaker to have you by your whatsits, and dangle you so high your feet won't even reach down to touch old Lord Nelson's statty.'

Having delivered this advice, he resumed his survey of the girls, while his friend brooded in silence. Presently Samson looked about him. His eyes brightened.

25

'I just got to run a little errand, old fellow. Shan't be 'alf a twinkling.'

'Huh!' said Verity, still nursing his indignation.

Scowling, he looked round at the huddle of ragged men and women waiting to be ferried out to a wallowing pauper ship. They had been joined by a group of Irish emigrants, soaking wet after their crossing from Dublin on the little packet-steamer with its open decks. The sounds of a fiddle and a hand-organ filled the warm August afternoon. A mellowing sun fell on granite wharves and the brick walls with their placards for lodging houses and their fading government bills, headed by the words 'Notice to Emigrants – Cholera', issued by the Colonial Office.

Even in his indignation and misery, Verity had been vaguely aware of Samson's overtures to the barefoot girls. But there was no sign of Samson among them. As an after-thought, Verity glanced towards the brightly-dressed women and the elegantly suited men at the other end of the quay, where they waited for the first-class tender to take them out to the Cunarder for New York. His eyes widened and his cheeks bulged as though with a sudden eruption of wind.

'You gone ravin' silly, 'ave you, Mr Samson?' he said softly and incredulously.

Samson was standing on the edge of the group, in close proximity to a girl in pink silk, her bonnet worn fashionably well back from her face, showing her features in the latest style.

'Jolly!' said Verity with throaty indignation.

There was no mistaking, even at this distance, the warm gold of her complexion, the slight seductive slant of her almond eyes, the dark hair combed back from the clear slope of her forehead. Even without a facial view, he would have recognized that neat little figure, the delicate whorls of her ears, the slim grace of her neck, the straight slender back and the trim young legs. Her very walk gave her away. Her legs were perhaps a little too short, causing her to move with quick, diminutive steps, producing a swagger of

26

her rounded hips which was both absurd and at the same time cheekily provoking.

The thought that Samson, with his predilection for taking a series of 'common law wives', should have chosen this one filled Verity with dismay. Miss Jolly's appearance on the scene had been the unfailing prelude to murder, extortion, robbery, and the most grievous forms of bodily harm. He struggled to his feet and stood by the travelling-box, gesticulating with the entire length of his plump right arm.

'Mr Samson!' he roared. 'Mr Samson! If you please!'

A few of the fashionables turned to look briefly at the red-faced man who was making all the noise. He was standing at the embarkation point reserved for servants of first-class passengers and it was necessary to assure themselves that it was not one of their own domestics who was causing the disturbance. Samson approached self-consciously. The girl followed at a distance, recognizing Verity and halting just close enough to exchange glances. Miss Jolly's face was inexpressive as the Sphinx, except for her eyes which met Verity's with the stony immobility of distaste.

Verity addressed his colleague in a furious whisper.

'Mr Samson, you lost your marbles, 'ave you? You any idea, 'ave you, what'll be done to you at the Whitehall Office for this little a-moor of yours?'

'Yes,' said Samson impassively, 'I got a very good idea.'

Verity became persuasive.

'Mr Samson, I ain't never interfered in your private business, you know that. I'll allow that Fat Maudie might be a good sort – only except her language being a bit Billingsgate and on the loud side. Whether you married her Church of England fashion or not is between you and her.'

'You leave Fat Maudie alone!' said Samson sharply. 'She never done you harm!'

'All right, Mr Samson, but this one here is another matter. She been a notorious criminal and the only reason

27

she ain't gone to the gallows is her singing Queen's evidence
sweet as a linnet every time she was caught.'

'Be quiet,' said Samson wearily.

' 'ave you forgot,' Verity hissed, 'how many of the kings
of the swell mob she been spreading her legs for? You forgot
how she helped to empty the night ferry to Paris of half a
ton of gold, and kill two men, and still twist her pretty neck
out of the noose? You forgot how a few weeks ago she was
party to blackmail in that Bond Street stew? She'd have
lured the poor young Prince of Wales there, if we hadn't
stopped her! Imagine him photographed gaping, while
Miss Jolly's bare backside was wagging at him over the
footlights!'

'Be quiet!' said Samson threateningly, and Verity was
quiet. 'I ain't left Fat Maudie, not even for this tight little
tit. I met her here from the Euston train to see her safe on
the boat.'

'What boat?'

'New York packet, same as you. But seeing as she'll be
first-class and you'll be with the superior servants, it'll save
you the distress of having to associate with her.'

'Hang on!' said Verity triumphantly. 'Hang on! This
got a real ripe smell about it! Two weeks since, this little
bitch was working out her time in Mrs Rouncewell's wash-
house, down the Elephant and Castle. And now, all of a
sudden, here she is! Dressed up like a fourpenny hambone
and going to New York in a first-class state-room. Who's
behind this bit of villainy Mr Samson, eh?'

'Superintendent Gowry,' said Samson coolly, 'and perhaps others more important even than him. She been
brought here especial on the train by the police matrons. I
shouldn't wonder if they didn't have a bit of a time with
her in that carriage!'

'Mr Samson!'

'Well, yer asked, all right? I was to meet her off the train,
and now I'm to see her on the boat and see she don't get off
again before it sails. Orders. All right?'

'But why, Mr Samson? Why?'

28

'Going to be adopted by a kind old Yankee couple.'

Verity stood thunderstruck at the revelation.

'Mr Samson! How could you be so stoopid? How could any of you?'

'Whatcher mean?'

'Three years back, Mr Samson, she was brought to England from India to be adopted by a charitable old pair. The same story. And what happened? Half a ton of bullion vanished into air from a sealed railway van with double-locked safes. A man was shot by a firing party for a crime he never committed. There was bodies in the river and me suspended and accused of murder! And that little bitch had her dainty hand deep in the game.'

'Excuse us,' said Samson coldly. He turned back to the girl and began to propel her rapidly towards the other first-class passengers who were now descending the granite steps to board the little steam boat which would carry them to the Cunarder at her moorings. Verity almost danced with exasperation as he stood helplessly by his wooden box and shouted after his colleague.

' 'ave you lost your reason, Mr Samson? All of you?'

The whole business was so monstrous that he could hardly begin to grasp it. Perhaps, he thought cynically, the authorities had decided to solve the problem of the almond-eyed girl and her criminal activities by shipping her off to New York, giving London a respite from her talents. The first-class tender puffed its way out to the liner and the expensively-clad passengers went aboard. Samson returned with it and sauntered towards Verity again. Conversation on the subject of the girl was now largely precluded by the presence of a dozen or more male domestic servants and their luggage, gathered at this point of embarkation.

'Now,' said Samson in his most business-like manner. 'Got everything, 'ave you? Got your beef tea? Got your pepper? You no idea how a good dose of pepper in the soup do help the sea-sickness.'

'I *have* been on a boat before, Mr Samson,' said Verity with all his plump dignity. 'From 'ere to 'indoostan and back. And to the Rhoosian war before that.'

'Right,' said Samson chirpily, 'off we go then.'

Verity and the rest of the group were to go out in the baggage tender. This was a small, snorting steamboat, now moored at the foot of the granite steps. It was piled high with the luggage of the first-class passengers, to which the boxes of the servants, and Verity's own, were being added by the porters. When this was done, the servants, followed by Verity and Samson, filed down the steps and went aboard. The little boat bucked and rocked across the anchorage towards the red-funnelled Cunarder, whose tall stack was smoking bravely in preparation for the departure. Verity looked back once, wistfully, at the outline of the Coburg Dock and the Adelphi Hotel diminishing with every throb of the little steam-boat's engine.

The dark hull of the liner towered above them, sailors standing by the lower deck opening to take the luggage in over the paddle-sponson as it was handed up from the ferry. Packing-cases, portmanteaux, carpet-bags and lac- quered boxes were going aboard from hand to hand in steady procession. The captain, holding his speaking- trumpet ready, stood on the paddle-box above and watched. Then the smartly-dressed officers were helping the occu- pants of the boat up over the little platform of the sponson. Someone shouted, 'Ring the bell! Now for the shore! Who's for the shore!'

Samson held out his hand.

'Safe journey, old chum. There and back.'

Still torn between indignation and sentiment, Verity took the hand in a firm grip.

'Let's hope it will be,' he said piously, and turned to step up on to the sponson. He hardly had time to make his way in and climb to the upper deck, when the paddle-wheels throbbed under him and he heard the hiss of the wake as the dark waters of the Mersey were churned to a dingy froth. Far away, almost level with the Coburg Dock, the ferry boat looked like a child's toy on a great pond. But there was a figure in the stern, Verity could see, which was still, unmistakably, that of Sergeant Samson staring searchingly out to sea.

The voyage, however safe, was not a happy one. Behind the little door of the servants' cabin, well aft and deep down in the hull, were two horsehair slabs, on one of which Verity's box had been left. The cabin would normally have held a pair of manservants, but the workings of the official mind required that a police officer should mix only with his own kind. At first he was glad of the extra space, but as the empty days and restless nights passed with agonizing slowness, he would have been glad of almost any man's company. He thought affectionately of Sergeant Samson.

Apart from the narrow berth, the only other adornment of the cabin was a looking-glass with a small bull's eye mirror above for shaving. Other than the cabin there was nowhere to go except the saloon, and the after-deck, which was permitted to passengers of his class but which reeked of soot and smoke blown back from the funnel. The saloon was long and narrow with windows at intervals down the sides. It reminded him of nothing so much as the interior of a hearse. A few mournful looking stewards warmed their hands over a stove at one end, beyond the long dining-tables and the racks fixed to the low roof to hold the drinking-glasses and cruet-stands securely, in the event of rolling seas and heavy weather. A group of cadaverous footmen were playing whist, but the cards would not lie on the table, obliging the players who took tricks to keep them in their pockets.

Day and night, Verity lay on his horsehair slab and listened to the tramp of boot heels on the deck above. Late on the fourth afternoon, the distant sounds of a ship at sea grew louder. Every plank and timber creaked. There was a more violent movement from time to time, accompanied by clattering on the decks above and the gurgling of water in and out of the scuppers. The ship rolled and pitched until, without warning, she lurched to one side and the sea burst through the deck skylights and slopped down into

31

the cabins below. Miserably, Verity resigned himself to a
night of storms.

By the next morning he had made his resolve. He must
find the girl, confront her in her state-room and frighten
or coax the truth from her. Light-headed from sleeplessness
he struggled to his feet and went up to the top deck. He had
guessed that in such weather as this it would be deserted
and that it would be easy enough to pass the barrier and
gain the first-class promenade, forward of the funnel. He
stepped out on to the wet planking, the sea still running
high and the horizon like a black hoop. The first lifeboat
had been smashed like a walnut shell by the gale. Part of
the paddle-box planking had been torn away, leaving the
iron struts of the wheel exposed as it whirled its spray about
the deck. The funnel itself was encrusted by white salt, the
storm-sails set, the rigging knotted, tangled, wet and
drooping.

There was no one to be seen. Verity strolled forward, as
nonchalantly as the conditions would allow. He passed the
barrier and moved casually towards the first companion-
way which led down to the state-rooms. A burly figure
suddenly materialized in what he had thought was the
empty doorway.

'You ain't first-class!' it said.

'Stop a bit,' said Verity reasonably.

'No one been out this way this morning,' said the
man, 'so anyone trying to go down must have come from
elsewhere.'

'I got a special reason, a matter of business.'

A second large man appeared behind the shoulder of the
first.

'What business?'

With a sense of triumph, Verity produced his warrant-
card and held it where they could both see.

'I'm from Scotland Yard,' he said proudly, 'Private-
Clothes.'

'I don't care if you're from Buckingham Palace,' said the
first man, 'you're not first-class. You don't *look* first-class.

And you could have stole that card anywhere!'

'I'm a police officer!' said Verity with indignation.

'Not here you aren't,' said the man and closed the companionway doors.

For six more days, Verity lay on his horsehair slab and thought.

'Even Mr Croaker ain't soft enough to fall for the same dodge twice,' he said to himself. 'Then why the mischief is she sent?'

He lay there thinking of the girl's past. Even her real name was a mystery. She was known professionally as Miss Jolly from the cant term for a 'jolly' as one who brought trouble in her wake. Her apprenticeship had been picking up Pall Mall clubmen in Waterloo Place and taking them to her room in Panton Street. Then her trim gold figure and dark odalisque eyes had given her a second income, doing harem dances before coster audiences at a penny-gaff. Her true proprietor, however, was Lieutenant Dacre, the cracksman of the famous South-Eastern Railway robbery, whom she helped to spirit away almost half a ton of bullion from its sealed van. She scuttled about her business like a frightened little mouse, knowing that she might hang for his murders if he were ever caught.

Then her sneering master imprisoned her in his Langham Place bawdy-house, promising her the living death of a closed brothel in Marseille. She had escaped briefly, disguising herself as a boy in tight trousers and cap. They caught her easily, bringing her to the soundproof room of the Langham Place house. Her master watched, calmly snoking his cigar, as his two bullies stripped her of the trousers and bent her forward over a rocking-horse. Verity had later seen the leather switch. He had heard with a shudder the account of her screams and gyrations. He had even glimpsed the tapestry of fading weals across the smooth coppery cheeks of Miss Jolly's bottom.

But in the agony and shame of the thrashing, the almond-eyed young slave had planned her implacable revenge to destroy her sardonic tormentor. Her brief moment as a pretty angel of destruction had been awe-inspiring. Verity had no illusions as to her dislike of him, though he had done nothing to compare with the cracksman's whipping of Miss Jolly. Yet the malice in the dark eyes suggested that she might find supreme satisfaction in deceiving superior officers for the pure pleasure of destroying him.

After many more days and nights of such conjectures, he stood on the deck on a misty morning and saw a sloping shore on either side, with neat white villas among immaculate turf and trees. Presently this Arcadian view gave way to the grey institutional walls of a prison and an asylum. Then, under a cloud of drifting smoke, there appeared a profusion of buildings with an occasional church spire rising among them. They were approaching a river estuary, crowded with a forest of masts and with ships of every size under way. Several ships of the Cunarder's size were making their way cautiously through the teeming cross-traffic of the noisy steam-ferries, laden with passengers, coaches, horses, wagons, baskets and boxes. The clinking of capstans and the ringing of bells from other ships were now clearly audible. They were so close to the shore itself that Verity caught the hum and buzz of the city, the sound of a steam-whistle and the barking of dogs. Unlike his companions at the ship's rail, he hardly seemed to notice the bustling panorama of New York under the warm September sky.

'She may have made fools out of them,' he said softly to himself, looking towards the first-class promenade-deck, 'but if she 'opes to make one out of me, she ain't half going to be disappointed!'

5

It was to be so easy. Standing among the wooden shanties of the oyster-bars on their tumbledown wharf, just beyond the

Cunard mooring, Verity had an uninterrupted view of the first-class passengers as they disembarked. There was no chance that Jolly could escape from the ship without showing herself. Verity had been surprised to discover that he himself was one of the first off, being met and ushered ashore by a self-conscious official of the shipping line who had handed him his instructions. He was to report to Captain Smiles of the Prince of Wales's staff at the Astor Hotel that evening. He would then accompany the Captain to join the royal party during the closing stages of the Canadian tour, before the Prince crossed into Michigan.

The day which lay ahead of him might seem too short a time in which to prove the girl's villainy. Verity, chuckling to himself, knew that he would find it long enough.

'If she's out for flash cads and draggle-tails,' he said to himself, 'she'll have to show it from the start.'

He was distantly aware that he ought to be paying more attention to the New World in which he had just arrived. But the New York waterfront, though warmer, seemed to him remarkably like Wapping Stairs, the streets lined with dirty, unpainted buildings and choked by heavy drays and baggage wagons. The ramshackle oyster-bars and the little drinking-shops with their grimy, uncurtained windows would have graced London's riverside equally well.

Presently a pink bonnet and dress appeared. He knew without further inspection that it was her. She crossed the quay with quick, taut hip movements and rapid little steps. This brisk little swagger showed, through smooth silk, Miss Jolly's buttocks twitching lasciviously against each other at every step, touching and parting rhythmically. He exhaled a wistful sigh. Even her movements were unmistakable. And now, of course, she was not alone. Her hand rested with ill-practised nonchalance on the arm of a tall, slimly-built young man with a sun-reddened skin, auburn whiskers and ginger hair.

'Charitable old couple!' chortled Verity, and he almost skipped after them, pom-pomming a little tune as he shadowed them effortlessly. He had a fleeting mental

35

image of Inspector Croaker, sullen and downcast at the appalling error at which he had connived, and the white-whiskered noble old face of Superintendent Gowry, tears filling the rheumy eyes as he took Verity's hand in a manly clasp and thanked him again for the revelation of Miss Jolly's scheme.

They were the easiest quarry he had ever known. The tall ginger-haired young man was visible as plainly as a church steeple in the crowds by his tall bottle-green hat. Miss Jolly's pink silks flashed in the openings of the throng. If she had decided to vanish into the obscurity of the great metropolis, she had chosen almost the worst way to do it. But then Verity remembered that she would think he was still on the ship, obliged to wait while the first-class passengers disembarked.

'Very neat, miss!' he said admiringly, brushing a fleck of perspiration from his black moustache. He had no idea that it would be so warm in America. They crossed from Canal Street to West Street, with the single-storey market buildings, open at the front and designed more like Venetian temples than stables or warehouses. Everywhere there were men in straw hats and white overalls, two-horse street-cars and private traps with canvas canopies, jostling along the broad cobbled highway. Behind the warehouse buildings the columns of black smoke from funnels along the waterfront dimmed the hot September sun.

Verity was uneasily aware that he ought to make contact with someone, to get a message to Captain Smiles perhaps, or to locate a responsible officer of the New York police department and seek assistance. He saw a police officer, in belted dark-blue tunic and a hat like a solar topee, directing the confusion of horses and conveyances with his nightstick. But to stop now would be to lose the quarry.

The midday heat grew more oppressive. Verity could feel the coarse suiting clinging wetly under his plump arms and down the length of his spine. They turned a corner and he stood in amazement at the length of the street before him. He knew, beyond question, that this

was what had been described to him as Broadway, as rich
and gaudy as Regent Street but much longer. The wide
thoroughfare was a stream of hackney cabs and street-cars,
large-wheeled tilburies, gigs and phaetons, the sun sparkling
on their green and yellow paintwork. Verity stared in
astonishment at a smart olive-painted Pilentum bowling
past with its dark-skinned driver and its footman in nankeen
breeches and frogged-coat riding behind.

Resolutely, he took up his pursuit of Jolly and her escort.
The pavements on either side were now bustling with
young women in silks and satins but he had never before
seen so many dainty parasols, such gaudily-lined cloaks and
hoods, so many fluttering ribbons and tassels. The men, in
their long-tailed coats of blue or russet, looked drab by
contrast. Bright red-brick houses and glittering shops
stretched away in an infinite perspective, interrupted only
by an occasional church spire or the massive fortress-like
block of a new hotel, green blinds drawn against the heat
of the afternoon sun.

Verity walked in his habitual lumbering manner, one
hand lying in the palm of the other behind his back, as
conspicuous among the men and women of fashion as if
he had been a performing bear. Several of those who passed
turned their heads as he walked by, with grins of amusement
or frowns of disapproval that such a figure should be
allowed to mar the elegance of the passing show.

He stopped suddenly, and then drew aside to take
advantage of the cover offered by one of the trees lining the
carriageway. Miss Jolly had gone alone into a shop which
occupied the ground floor of what might have been a
gentleman's town-house with a tall mansard roof. Her
companion waited outside at a little distance. Peering
cautiously round the trunk of the tree, Verity saw from the
windows of the shop, as well as its faded gilt sign, that it was
a jeweller's.

'Oh, my!' he sighed happily, 'Oh, my eye! Ain't this
prime?'

He knew exactly what was going to happen next. After

37

ten minutes or so, Miss Jolly emerged in company with the jeweller, or his assistant, who was seeing her courteously on her way. Her neat young features were unusually animated by smiles and widening of her almond eyes as she explained, evidently not for the first time, that the jeweller's admirable stock had not, alas, quite the trinket which she fancied. The man bowed and retired. Miss Jolly bustled towards a milliner's window and began a long contemplation of its display of Paris modes. In the warm afternoon, she presented a still odalisque profile, the features sharply defined, the brows arched high over the expressionless Turkomen eyes.

In London, Verity assured himself, the dodge would never have lasted this long. Perhaps the New York jewellers still had a lesson to learn. Now, as he had expected, the girl's accomplice entered the shop, holding in his hand what looked like a cheap watch for repair. No, thought Verity, the New York merchants had never suffered this dodge before. A London jeweller would have been out on the pavement by now, bawling his misfortune at the top of his voice.

The young man came out of the shop, following the girl along the pavement, though they now walked separately, as though unknown to one another.

Verity watched them as they approached a second jeweller's about two hundred yards further on. Miss Jolly opened its door demurely to the accompanying tinkle of a little bell.

' 'ere!' said Verity aloud. 'They're bloody going to crack every jeweller's in the town! Wait till they get this news back at Whitehall Police Office! Charitable old couple adopting her! Stoopid ain't the word for it!'

His plump cheeks flushed more deeply with his sense of self-righteousness as he strode to the door of the first shop. The elderly, slightly-built jeweller stood behind one of his glass-topped display-cases in the cool, dimly-lit interior. Verity looked round the shadowy premises as the door closed behind him, and made his first American acquaintance.

'You got this place laid out like a villain's paradise, my man!' he said sternly. 'It's no wonder you just been robbed!'

The little man gazed at Verity, mild and uncomprehending, over the rim of his glasses.

'Robbed?' he murmured in that gentle twang which Verity had now begun to identify as the American way of speech. 'Robbed, sir? To be sure, sir, you are most certainly mistaken.'

'Wax,' said Verity, running his fingers quickly under the ledges of the show-cases, where the glimmering stones huddled in their dark velvet nests. 'Oldest dodge in the business. Young person comes in, slaps a dab of it under here, asks to see jools. Slips one under and presses it into the wax, then goes off. Nothing on her, no sign of her being the robber. In comes her magsman with a cheap watch for repair, hands it over, runs his fingers under the ledge and goes off with wax, sparkler, the lot!'

'And who might you be, sir?' asked the old man, coming forward nervously. 'Not the city police department, surely?'

'Metropolitan Police, Scotland Yard,' said Verity proudly. 'I'm in pursuit of that young person in the pink silk. She's an English girl.'

'Miss Jolly?' queried the little jeweller. 'Indeed, she said as much in conversation.'

Verity paused in his search and stared.

'She gave you her real name?'

'It would seem, sir, that dissimulation is not one of her vices,' said the little man, observing Verity with the first faint signs of scepticism.

'Her vice,' said Verity indignantly, 'is the wax under the counter dodge. Where the mischief is it? Course, you wouldn't be familiar with such things, not having met the London sharpers.'

'My dear, sir!' the jeweller inclined his head in mild reproof. 'We are all too familiar with such artifices. Mr Myrtle!'

39

As the old man raised his voice, a square of wooden panelling at the rear of the room slid back and a young man's face peered through it.

'Glass,' said the jeweller for Verity's benefit, 'painted glass. It gives a view, sir, of any customer in the shop without the disagreeable knowledge for them that they are under our surveillance. I guess, sir, our ways are not so different from yours.'

'But she gone into another jeweller's just up the street,' said Verity insistently.

'When a young lady cannot be suited at one emporium, sir, it is frequently the case that she visits another.' The little man turned to his assistant, 'Mr Myrtle, did you observe the lady in the pink silk just now?'

'Every second, Mr Liddell, and the gentleman who came in after. Most respectably they both behaved.'

The jeweller turned to Verity with a little shrug.

'You see?' he said gently. 'And you may be sure that we check the items exhibited to customers with great care. There was nothing missing from the tray which the young lady examined. Have you found your wax by the way?'

'No,' said Verity shortly, 'I ain't. P'raps they twigged your apprentice there behind the panelling. I'd best be getting up the street to the next premises. All things considered, Mr Liddell, you came off very fortunate in this affair.'

The little jeweller bowed and held the door for his visitor.

Above Broadway, the sun now seemed bright as a furnace and hot enought to blister the smartly painted sides of the passing carriages. Jolly was sauntering with her pink parasol open and her accomplice was just emerging from the second shop. The girl began to thread her way across the road, her eyes on a third establishment whose narrow front stood between a saddler's and a hat-shop.

'She got the cheek of Old Nick!' said Verity furiously, dodging through the crowd to the shop which the girl and her companion had just visited.

The interior was less like a shop than an elegantly

furnished drawing-room with curved chairs and sofas, padded by cerise velvet and ornamented by ivory inlaid on rosewood. It was presided over by a pudgy young man with large ears and features, bearing the deformities of the prize-ring and bare-knuckle contests. His black hair was parted in the centre of his forehead, as if in careful imitation of a Norman arch. He looked at Verity as at one who had no legitimate business on his premises, fingering his thick gold watch-chain with its seals and key as though it might have been a weapon.

'Metropolitan Police, London,' said Verity breathlessly, waving his warrant-card. 'I got reason to think you might a-been robbed a few minutes ago by a young person in pink silks and her accomplice who was here just after. . .'

'You are mistaken, signore,' said the pudgy man, his eyes as blankly threatening as wet stone. 'No goods are missing. None have left their cases.'

'You Eye-talian, are you?' inquired Verity suspiciously.

'I am a ceetizen of the United States,' said the dark man, resting a heavily-ringed hand on his flowered waistcoat and glaring. 'I am honoured by the visit of Signorina Jollee who ask for what I have not, and the young gentleman who come to ask if she have been and gone.'

Verity began running his hands under ledges of tables and chairs.

'You got wax under here somewhere,' he said desperately. 'You must have. I daresay they mightn't have robbed you now, but they must a-left the wax ready for when they come back.'

'The lady and the gentleman stand only 'ere,' said the jeweller. 'You see? The little table. Turn it over. No wax! All right, eh?'

Verity's plump face quivered, as though he might be about to weep with frustration.

'She give you her real name!' he muttered uncomprehendingly. 'And you swear her fancy man never left you a watch to mend?'

'To you,' said the jeweller, 'I do not 'ave to swear. The

41

gentleman inquired only if his lady had been and gone.
There was no watch!' He moved heavily towards Verity,
almost jostling him towards the door, his boots creaking
as ominously as the cracking of one set of knuckles in the
palm of his other large hand. Verity looked at the sharply-
filed stones set in the heavy rings of the jeweller's fingers.

'I hope, for your sake, you're right and you ain't been
robbed,' he said at the door, mustering his portly dignity
to have the last word.

The olive-skinned jeweller leant forward, the perfume of
Eau de Mille Fleurs enveloping Verity like a cloud. The soft
Italian intonation was almost a caress in his ear.

'I hope so, signore, *for your sake–* '

Then the man stood in his doorway, glaring through the
glass until the plump, insulted sergeant had disappeared
from sight.

For the rest of the afternoon, Verity shadowed the girl
and her accomplice as unobtrusively as a wraith. Twice
more he entered jeweller's shops with growing furtiveness,
only to find that nothing was missing and that no in-
criminating blobs of wax were to be found under the ledges
of tables or display-cases. Each time, Jolly had given her
real name.

'It don't make sense,' he said irritably to himself. 'It
don't make any sort of sense at all. First time I ever heard
of villains trying to look as if they was going to commit
robbery – and leaving a real name – but never doing anything! P'raps she wants to get herself apprehended.'

He looked longingly at the great blocks of clean ice
being carried into shops and bar-rooms, the stacks of pine-
apples and water-melons displayed for sale. They passed
shops which sold French calf-boots or gold birdcages, art
galleries which looked like the drawing-rooms of gentlemen's houses in Piccadilly, offering for sale paintings by
Titian, Rubens and Raphael. Jolly paused at H. S. Beal's
Daguerrian Rooms, as though thinking of having a dollar
portrait done of herself.

'She gone silly!' Verity gasped. 'I never heard of a pretty

thief advertising herself like that before!'

But the girl entered and came out again a few minutes later. By the next day, her face would be staring from Beal's display of the photographer's art, for all the world to see.

Verity lost count of the jeweller's shops. There were at least a dozen which the couple visited, perhaps as many as twenty. In the autumn dusk he followed them back, past the trees and fountains of Washington Square. The panes of shop-fronts glowed with the light of gas lamps, the bells of street-cars jangled in the cooler air, and the newsboys hawked the evening papers with sharp, discordant cries. Verity glimpsed hotel interiors through plate-glass windows, the marble-paved lobbies with lamps and columns, travellers from the West stretching their legs on the divans of lounges and reading-rooms. The vestibules of theatres were already illuminated, their swinging doors of red leather studded with brass nails swung open to reveal coloured bills and photographs of actresses.

In an hour or so more he would have to break off the pursuit and report to Captain Smiles. To have reported what he had so far seen would merely have earned him a reprimand and an instruction to mind his own business for the future. But now they were turning east. Hurrying after them, Verity saw them arm-in-arm again, approaching a shabbier neighbourhood. He saw a street sign which identified it as Second Avenue. Soon they were among large, decaying houses of red brick with faded green shutters and matching first-floor balconies with roofs of painted tin. Jolly and her escort paused at the corner, where the canopy of a grocer's shop extended over the pavement to posts fixed in the kerbstone. A fly-blown card offering 'Table Board' was lodged at an angle in the adjoining window. A strong odour of smoked fish and the thick fragrance of molasses wafted from behind the piled baskets of vegetables under the grocer's wooden canopy.

Jolly and the tall young man were engaged in some final and earnest conversation. Then the girl moved quickly, flitting across the rutted street, between the leaning lamp-posts and the ash-barrels to the large shabby house on the far side. She pulled the bell beside the heavy door, which opened in a moment. As she scuttled inside, the man who had escorted her turned and strode away. Verity, unable to watch both of them, chose the girl. He was unlikely to force the truth from the young man, but he had frightened a confession from Jolly twice in the past and had no doubt that he could do it again. He crossed the street with a determined stride and approached the door of the decayed red-brick house with its green verandah. On the wall to one side of it was an engraved metal plate, 'Asylum of the New York Magdalen Female Benevolent Society'.

'It never is!' said Verity confidently. 'Not after what I've seen this afternoon. Bloody thieves' kitchen, more like.'

It was not the easiest of buildings to enter unobserved. Standing back, he looked up at the verandah. There was a light in one of the windows looking on to it, but the other was in darkness. A glance at the darkened ground-floor window revealed that it was barred on the outside but to a man intent on climbing, the vertical iron rails were as good as a ladder. He looked up at the overhang of the verandah, and he knew that it could be done. Whistling softly to himself he walked slowly away for a few yards, waiting until the street should be empty. There were two men in the grocer's store, but they were intent on weighing and packing goods. His chance came in a few minutes and for a space of thirty seconds or so he was sure that he would be unnoticed.

For all his bulk, Verity's agility was as remarkable as his strength. With hardly a sound, he stepped on to the sill of the ground-floor window, pulling himself up so that he could clutch the highest bar. There was an awkward manoeuvre as he stood on the higher bar with nothing to hold him against the wall but his own weight, until he could reach up and seize the first metal strut of the verandah rail, where it joined the wall. Hanging for an instant by one arm, and then by two, Verity kicked his feet up until he could cross them round a further strut. Praying that the metalwork had not rusted from its fixtures, he put his strength into the gripping of his feet on the bar, and snatched himself up, hand over hand, until he was diagonally against the verandah rail and could pull himself over its ledge. It had not been an elegant display of acrobatics, but it had been quick and almost silent. With a final heave, Verity's capacious trouser seat and plump legs disappeared over the rail and on to the floor of the verandah itself.

Cautiously and silently he got to his feet. Somewhere in the rooms facing him, the meek and contrite women of the New York streets shed tears of repentance on the shoulders of a sisterhood of mercy. So, at least, the brass plate by the street door proclaimed to the world. He was still standing there, judging the best and quietest means of entry when, from behind the lighted curtain of the left-hand window, a slurred male voice said, 'Ah, shit! Don't you whore-pokers never deal nothing but twos and threes?'

There was gruff, pleased laughter from two other men, one of whom said, 'Make a call, soldier, and stop talking from ya ass.'

Verity's spirits rose with delight. The asylum for fallen women was about to prove richly rewarding. Combined with the story about Jolly being adopted by a charitable married couple, there was every chance that it would have Inspector Croaker out of Whitehall Police Office and back in the artillery.

As a preliminary, he crept to the lighted curtain and peered through a chink where it had not quite closed. His view was restricted but he could see the back of a man sitting in his shirt-sleeves and the dark hair of a second man on the other side of the table. The shirt-sleeved man belched and fluttered a card down on the table.

'Deuce!' he said.

There was a groan of disgust from someone who remained out of Verity's view. Blue-green cigar smoke rose, funnelling upward, above the man whose back was towards him. Glass clinked against glass and there was a splash of liquid.

The dark head turned and a yellow squirt of tobacco juice shot into the china resonance of a spitoon. The shirt-sleeved man threw down his hand of cards with a light patter.

'Ah, shit!' he said monotonously.

Silent as a shadow, Verity drew back and moved gently to the next, darkened window. It was closed, but fastened by nothing more than a rather loose casement-latch. He took out his carefully-oiled clasp-knife and slid the blade between the jamb and the window-frame. It was child's play. The loose catch lifted easily and the window swung open. He slid soundlessly into the darkened room. The glimmer of light from the street lamps showed it to be a poorly-furnished sitting-room with heavy mahogany upholstered in horsehair. Verity sniffed the air. Whatever the truth about the New York Magdalen Asylum, it certainly had the familiar smell of such institutional buildings, a steamy carbolic vapour concealing the grosser scents.

Cautiously he opened the door and stepped out on to a tiled landing with narrow flights of stairs, their bare wood stained the colour of treacle. Below him, the building seemed to be in darkness, but a brass oil lamp was suspended over the well of the stairs and there was a glow of light from the next floor up. A single step creaked loudly under his weight as he moved quickly in that direction, but the noise of the card players in the other room more than covered the squeal of wood.

The next landing was identical, except that there was a slit of light under one of the doors. From beyond it, Miss Jolly's voice came softly and melodiously in high-pitched song.

> '*Oh, the man that has me must have silver and gold,*
> *A chariot to ride in and be 'andsome and bold . . .*'

Verity tried the door. It was unyielding. He inspected the vertical chink of light and saw that it was held on the inside by a tiny bolt.

> '*His hair must be curly as any watch-spring,*
> *And his whiskers as big as a brush for clo-thing!* '

46

He crept back across the landing to the point which would give him the longest run.

'Oh she was beautiful as a butterfly, and proud as a queen . . .'

Then he launched himself across the landing at the thin panelling of the door.

'Was pretty little Polly Perkins of Paddington Gre-e-e-n!'

The last note of her song rose, shrill and prolonged, as the fastening splintered under Verity's weight. The broken door flew back against the wall and rebounded harmlessly.

'Right, miss,' he said sternly. 'Now let's have an end of this little caper!'

Then he paused. The room was as he had expected. Its bare distempered walls were patched by damp, their yellowness blotched by brown and draped with old cobwebs towards the high ceiling, like shot-torn regimental colours hanging in the vault of a garrison chapel. Miss Jolly was in the furthest corner, cowering and immobilized. More precisely, she had just stepped into a tin bowl of steaming water, her pink silk and a flurry of white underwear lying scattered on the uncarpeted floor. Her dark hair was pinned high on her head in the shape of a tall helmet or miniature bee-hive. Her trim gold thighs showed a sheen of moisture, where she had begun to wash herself.

Oddest of all, she was still wearing her plum-red silk corset, with its array of straps which might have done credit to a rifleman's webbing. Verity looked at it in astonishment. The wasp-waisted creation was far more suggestive than total nakedness. It covered her neat breasts but only to mould them more sharply and prominently. At the front, it ended in a narrowing v-shape between her thighs, as though deliberately leading the eye to the dark thatch of hair. At the rear, it was cut shorter, arching up over her slim brown waist as if in a calculated display of Jolly's coppery hind cheeks.

She saw that it was Verity, her alarm changing to in-

47

dignation in the dark feline eyes. With a gesture of outrage, however, she covered herself with one hand in front, the other shielding her behind.

'Now, miss,' he said with quiet insistence, 'don't scream, and don't do nothing that's going to make this worse for you!'

Her eyes brightened, as though he had suggested the answer to her problem. With no more urgency than in her song, she raised her voice and emitted a soprano monotone.

'Ah-h-h-h-h-h-h!'

'You'll get such a seeing-to if you don't stop that!' said Verity furiously. 'All I want is answers to some questions!'

She stopped, her sharp little nose and lynx eyes a study in scepticism. Then she pitched her voice an octave higher.

'AH-H-H-H-H-H-H-!'

There was nothing for it now but to get out while he could. At least he had evidence enough to unmask the New York Magdalen Asylum. That should be a start. There were heavy steps on the staircase. Verity wrenched back the curtains and discovered, to his surprise, that the window had been screwed immovably into its frame. With burly determination he turned to face the adversaries who stood between him and the stairs.

There were two of them, one he was sure was the man who had sat in the room below with his back to the window. The other he saw, with a rush of gratitude, wore the tunic of a New York policeman.

'All right, all right,' said Verity, inviting amiability, 'there ain't no cause for aggravation here. I'm a police officer too!'

He felt for his warrant-card and held it out to the man in the dark blue tunic.

'Metropolitan Police, London, Private-Clothes Detail,' he said proudly.

The man in the tunic had a very large freckled face. It creased in an ecstasy of longing, as though he could have loved Verity for this latest revelation.

'See?' said Verity hopefully. 'An officer of the law.'

The big man kneaded one fist in his other palm.

'You'se a peeler!' he said gratefully. And he hit Verity with all his strength, the bare knuckles striking into the right hand side of the jaw and mouth, sending the plump sergeant sprawling. Miss Jolly gave a little squeal of apprehension and delight. No one even looked at her as she stood, clutching herself, in her tin bowl. Verity sat up, tasting blood and feeling a numbness which paralysed half his mouth, as though some terrible injury had been inflicted.

'N'lissn-me, lissn . . .' he mumbled foolishly, ' 'm plice-offser . . .'

'A peeler!' The eyes of the man in the tunic were almost moist with gratitude. 'Murderer of Ireland's patriots! Robber of the poor! Defiler of Irish maidenhood . . .'

Verity scrambled to his feet.

'You got the wrong man!' he said helplessly. 'I never been there!'

'Assassin of Robert Emmet! Butcher of Wolfe Tone!'

' 'oo?'

The man in the tunic turned to his companion.

'Let's finish the bastard before the others come up.'

The two of them moved forward. From her bath, the girl watched, her almond eyes shining with excitement.

'Right!' said Verity with a confidence he did not feel. 'You bloody asked for it!'

He stepped to one side, where the girl's clothes had been discarded and he stooped down in a swift movement of retrieval. In his hand was the 'cage' which she had worn under her crinoline, a series of descending wire hoops suspended by strips of material to spread the dress outward. He ripped the largest hoop from its stitching and let it spring open into a length of steel, long as a rapier and as lethal as a razor. Whipping the air with it, he advanced towards the policeman and the card-player, who now backed prudently in the direction of the door.

In his mind, Verity planned the route. Down the stairs, into the darkened room, out on to the verandah, and jump.

49

There was no time for anything more elaborate. He had just decided on this when there was a slithering sound to one side of him. Across the floor shot the remains of the crinoline cage, tossed by the girl so that it landed just at the feet of the card-player. In a moment more both his adversaries would be armed as he was and his last hope would have gone. As the card-player stooped cautiously, Verity's quivering steel described an arabesque in the lamplight and lashed the man across his hand. To Verity's dismay, the weapon was far more effective than he had imagined. The card-player screamed and fell backwards on his knees, his head bowing up and down in agony, as if in some absurd obeisance. Blood was spattering on to the wooden boards like heavy drops at the beginning of a thunder-storm.

'Oh God!' wailed the man, his voice rising again to a shriek. 'Oh God in heaven, I'm maimed!'

There was nothing for it but to finish the business quickly. Verity threw down the rippling wire and advanced on the man in the tunic. He dodged the repeated blow to his jaw, lowered his head and butted his antagonist in the face. The Irishman fell back a couple of steps, blinking away tears of pain, his face now distorted by sudden anxiety. He snatched at Verity's hair, exposing his under-jaw to the force of Verity's right fist which snapped the man's head back with a nauseating click of bone. He followed this by getting the Irishman's head under his arm, 'In Chancery', and running him full tilt into the wall. The skull and the plastered wall met with a crack, the Irishman slithering limply to the floor.

But now there were three more burly figures in the room. Verity threw himself on the first, the man staggering under the impact and sitting heavily on a wooden chair which crashed like matchwood under their combined weight. Only Verity got up again. He faced his remaining opponents his face glowing and his bull-neck flushed.

'Lost yer taste for it, then?' he croaked derisively.

One man jumped at him, and Verity threw him off with his powerful shoulders. He was gathering himself to rush the other man when suddenly a shimmery and agonizing deluge bowed him, choking and blinking. He knew instantly that he had made the mistake of forgetting the girl and being deaf to her soft, barefoot approach. The harsh, perfumed carbolic of Miss Jolly's bath-water was in his throat as he fought for breath, and its sharper agony streamed in tears from his eyes. A numbing blow to the back of his skull brought him to his knees in a drunken daze, so that he was hardly aware of what happened next. Their boots were hammering his spine, but he could barely feel it, the first pain having anaesthetized him to the rest by its numbing impact. Of all that was said by his attackers, he heard only one sentence, treasuring it against oblivion.

'You fat Irish bastud! You got the wrong one!'

The wrong one. Verity lay half-stunned on the floor of a wagon. Remember, he told himself, the wrong one. Above him was night sky, the tops of buildings, and what looked like balloons illuminated internally by candles and bearing inexplicable messages. 'Bowery Street Rooms.' 'Bespoke Tailors.' 'Oysters in every style.' For the first time since he had entered the Magdalen Asylum, he though of Captain Smiles. He tried to sit up, but his hands were cuffed behind him and the effort was too great.

'Smiles!' he bleated hopefully. 'Captain Smiles! Prince of Wales's orders!'

A boot toed him hard under the lower rib, driving the breath from him.

'Bastud!' said someone in the darkness.

At last the wagon stopped and they carried him unceremoniously out, his head hanging backward. A massive granite building with squat pillars, suggesting the portico of an Egyptian temple, rose above him. The tall rectilinear windows, heavily barred, ran almost the entire height of the façade. As the men who were carrying him passed into the shadow of the first hall, their steps echoed lingeringly along the bare vaulted passageways. Then they were in a long narrow interior which rose like the nave of a lofty cathedral. There were several iron platforms along its sides at varying

51

levels, and iron bridges which crossed from one side to the other. The men dragged Verity to what looked like a small furnace-door. There was a rattle of keys, his wrists were uncuffed and he was dumped down heavily in a pool of water on a stone floor.

The door closed and the keys rattled again. As though from a great distance he could hear voices, plaintive, weeping, angry and cursing by turns. From time to time there was the slow measured tread of a man walking the length of the hall outside. Then, like iron castanets, keys rattled the length of the platform and stairway railings. Verity recognized the gaoler's inveterate habit of drawing the bunch of keys along the iron struts, as though to comfort himself as well as his charges by breaking the sepulchral silence of the long night. He was assisted in this by a woman's voice, wailing and eerie, and by a man's drunken song. Verity knew little about the prisons of America but he was evidently in one of the most impressive. At least, he thought, it was no worse than that.

When the first light of the autumn morning lit the small barred window of the cell, it was grey as all light in that place. Working himself up to peer out, Verity could see that all the windows looked out on to a narrow yard, the pitiless prison walls rising so high that the sun never slanted into the cells. In the centre of the yard was the gallows without either a platform or a drop. Presently a slow procession crossed to the structure and a small pinioned man was stood beneath it with the rope round his neck. Verity watched in horror as the preparations were made. The man was left standing on the ground, while his executioner walked behind the gallows and released a cord. A weighted sandbag, at the top of the gallows, plummeted to earth with a soft thud, jerking the pinioned man off his feet and swinging him into the air. He hung almost still, after a few spasmodic struggles, his head inclined as though in acknowlededgement of his fault.

Verity clambered down, his body shaking uncontrollably,

and sat on the stone floor of the bare cell. Presently he heard a woman howling from the yard outside, the last desperate sounds from the throat of the creature who had been wailing the night before. He pushed his fingers into his ears and prayed.

It was half-way through the morning before anyone came to him. Then the door of the cell was opened by a uniformed gaoler who stood back to allow a smartly dressed little man in. The visitor was hardly larger than a dwarf but his hair was plastered flat and his dark eyes gleamed with the zeal of one accustomed to command.

'I,' he said bitterly, 'am Captain Smiles.'

Verity's coat and trousers were still stiff with damp from the deluge of Miss Jolly's bath-water. They hung shapelessly upon him. He pulled himself up in a parody of parade-ground attention.

'Sir!'

'I have been woken early this morning,' said Smiles peevishly 'to learn that a sergeant of the Prince of Wales's bodyguard, who should have reported for duty last night, is being held in the Tombs Prison!'

'Is that a fact, sir? Is that where this is, then?'

'Damn you, sir!' shouted Smiles, making Verity jump with the explosiveness of his anger. 'What the devil do you mean by it? Within twelve hours of landing in New York, you have burgled a house of charity, menaced a naked young woman, almost severed the right hand of a United States government clerk, savagely beaten a New York City police officer and committed criminal damage to civic property!'

'Wasn't like that, sir, with respect, sir. That Miss Jolly is a young person of bad reputation and the story of 'er coming to be adopted by an old couple is gammon, sir.'

'How dare you traduce a brave and selfless young woman?' hissed Captain Smiles, his trim dark head thrusting like a game-cock.

Verity's face creased with incomprehension.

'Brave and selfless, sir? 'er? She and her fancy-man been

53

setting up every jeweller's in the city! I had a list, till they emptied my pockets. There was Hancock's, though, and Hunt and Roskell's, and a big new place called Ball and Black's.'

'And where is this fancy-man?' asked Smiles contemptuously.

'He gone off, sir. But he was there, with her. I saw him and I'd know him again!'

'You will forget the matter, sergeant. You were mistaken. Do you understand me?'

'Yessir,' said Verity with ill-suppressed indignation. 'One other thing to say, sir.'

'Well?'

'That Magdalen Asylum where they got Miss Jolly. It ain't nothing but a thieves' kitchen. It's full of heavy swells gaming, drinking shrub, smoking cheroots, and fouling the air with their slum talk, sir. And that little minx looked as though she'd took her things off and was ready to spread her legs for all of 'em in turn, sir!'

'Sergeant!'

'That's 'ow it looked, sir, with respect, sir. And that Irish bully'd have killed me if I 'adn't done it to him first, sir! Being Irish wasn't any excuse for what he tried to do, sir!'

Captain Smiles cocked his head on one side, bright-eyed as a little bird, and looked up at the dishevelled sergeant.

'I shall not waste time with you,' he said flatly. 'Indeed, but for some service which it seems you performed for the Prince of Wales a month or two since, you would already be on your way home. Now you may choose. Your conduct last night will be overlooked, provided that you forget the entire incident.'

'And if I can't forget, sir?'

'Then,' said Smiles reasonably, 'you are to be sent home on the orders of His Royal Highness. And make no mistake, if that happens, your service with the Metropolitan Police will be at an end.'

'Don't seem to have much choice, sir, do I?'

Captain Smiles shrugged as Verity persisted.

'Ain't I to be told anything, sir? There *was* a fancy-man. And she been putter-up to robbery and blackmail at home, sir! All the world knows it! And I've seen whore-houses that looked more like Magdalen Asylums than that one! And why was I the wrong one?'

'Curiosity killed a cat, sergeant.'

'Yessir. Just as you say, sir.'

Verity's flushed jowls and dark eyes were as close to glowering as he had ever been in the presence of a superior officer.

'Come along, then,' said Captain Smiles impatiently, leading the way with a bandy-legged swagger, down the gloomy passageways and into the sunlit slums of New York.

6

The smooth-skinned young man with his mild blue eyes, carefully-flattened fair hair, his heavy mouth and jaw disfiguring an otherwise pleasant face, stood on the edge of the flat rock and gazed in awe at the sight before him. On every side of him there rose a long incessant roar, which seemed almost to be emitted from the deep centre of the earth. The broad river, smooth and wide, flowed swiftly on, each rock and islet diverting the current in a recoiling feather of spray. Presently the first foam appeared on the eddies, and there were whirlpools that made the youth's head spin until he had to look away from them. Torn, and jagged, and roaring, the broad torrent poured and throbbed over rocks and stones in mounds of spray, like loosely-driven snow. In the mad onward rush of the stream, trees tumbled over and over, their branches rising from the surface briefly, like the arms of drowning men.

Soon there appeared a line of breakers between dense foliage, the writhing and hissing of a cataract, enough to make the very banks quiver with its vibration. The tumbling waters emerged at last on to the brink of a sheer and mighty precipice, extending in its thunder far away into the western sunset. Into the cauldron of spray beneath, the mighty curtain of green plunged smooth as oil or polished marble. As the sun dipped behind the hills on the American shore a great gauze-like mist rose higher from the seething waters below, making the very rocks and pine woods seem like a stage magician's vision hovering in the air. The young man and his companions stood, as though in the presence of a divine revelation, before the majesty of Niagara.

He alone stood forward from the rest. Behind him was a group of older men. One of these, a grave-looking figure with a fair beard closely-trimmed, approached the young man and spoke softly.

'Mr Blackwell's Bengal Lights, sir. They will be best seen from where we stand now.'

The youth nodded, as though his heart were too full for speech. There was a moment's delay, and then from the cliff below them and from behind the very curtain of waters sweeping into the abyss, a silver magnesium brilliance blazed out across the dark chasm. From the party on Table Rock and from the crowds on either bank there was a gasp of wonder. The great falls of the Niagara had been turned into a shimmering surface of crystal glass, in which the droplets of the spray became a cascade of diamonds, and the seething foam shone white as a river of phosphorus.

At length the Bengal Lights began to sputter and die, but only to be rekindled in deepest red. The Niagara seemed a torrent of blood or a river of fire in the night. In its deep natural drama the transformation scene held the great crowds in silent veneration. Then, at last, the two hundred torches guttered and died, one by one.

The eighteen-year-old Prince of Wales stood for a long time alone gazing at the darkened scene from the edge of the rock, while the trimly-bearded Duke of Newcastle, Secretary-of-State for the Colonies, and the other officials of his party stood behind him in respectful attendance. Behind them were several young officers of the Prince's staff.

Further back still, in the shadows, stood Sergeant Verity, his large boots planted firmly apart, one hand resting in the palm of the other behind his back. It was the approved stance for a Private-Clothes officer on surveillance duty of this kind.

The grandeur of the occasion had moved him so deeply that there was a lump in his throat. He had never seen anything to approach such a display. Just before his departure for America he had taken Bella to Mr Grieve's Stereorama at the Cremorne Gardens, on his rest day. All the others in the jostling crowd of the canvas booth had sworn that it was just like being in the Alps or on the shores of the Italian lakes, so vivid were the scenes. Yet he had thought it only a clever toy. The glory of Niagara illuminated was the union of man and nature, so sublime that one might shed a manly tear in admiration. Such a tribute would have been absurd in a penny show at the Cremorne.

The young Prince walked alone and thoughtfully along the path which led back to the grounds of Clifton House on the Canadian bank of the river. Among its trees and gardens were several picturesque cottages. One of these accommodated the Prince himself, while the others were taken up by the Duke of Newcastle, General Bruce, who was the Prince's Governor, Dr Acland the Royal Surgeon, and the dark plump figure of Lord Lyons, the British Ambassador to the United States. These dignitaries followed their young master at a distance, talking with bright self-consciousness. Verity strode heavily behind. He had learnt by instinct that there was a point which was close enough for him to be an effective bodyguard, and yet not so close as to make his presence intrusive.

A single illuminated banner streamed somewhere over the falls 'God bless the Prince of Wales!' It seemed tawdry after the grandeur of Mr Blackwell's Bengal Lights. Verity watched the young man bid a pleasant good-night to his elders and enter the neat white cottage. Then Verity himself took the first watch. He marched smartly three paces forward from the door and came to attention with a ceremonial precision, though he was in private clothes and there was no one to see him. With equal exactitude he planted his feet 'at ease', his hands folded behind him. His pink jowls were set and his black eyes narrowed as he scanned the darkness ahead of him, with scowling suspicion, promising damnation to the Queen's enemies.

He was relieved by the Canadian guard at 2 am, but at first light he woke and crept out almost furtively to look again at the majesty of the great falls. His swelling emotion was marred by only one regret. This was Bella. To have had her with him, and to have stood before such grandeur, side by side, would, he imagined, have been a foretaste of standing before the greatest throne of all.

By the afternoon, he had resumed his duties as bodyguard, drab and inconspicuous among the elegantly-suited members of the official party and the peacock splendour of the royal equerries Major Teesdale and Colonel Grey, resplendent in scarlet and gold with the white plumes of the British General Staff. The Prince and his followers had ranged themselves on a graceful little suspension-bridge, a web of white-painted iron which seemed thin and delicate as a net. The bridge was almost two miles below the falls, above a splendid ravine between whose cliffs the rapids of Niagara roared and surged in their narrower channel. Dark pine trees stretched like a forest on either side but in the gorge below the little bridge the blue water formed its menacing whirlpools.

It was a place of fascination and of horror. The victims of the falls, suicides or accidents, were borne to the great whirlpool below the bridge. Their bodies were, bizarrely, stripped naked by the current but rarely damaged otherwise. Forced down by the thrust of the current, the naked corpses, as well as fragments of trees and rock, would be whirled round for months together before a shift in the river's flow released them at last into the calm waters of Lake Ontario. Verity shuddered at the thought of the horror beneath his feet as he stood at a distance on the little suspension-bridge and awaited the pleasure of the rest of the party.

Their eyes were all on the slack rope which hung between the two cliffs of the rapids, just upstream from the bridge. Like so many other visitors to the place, they had come to satisfy a morbid excitement by seeing Blondin walk. Verity was 'not particular' to see it, as he had confessed to the Canadian sergeant with whom he shared guard duties, but now that he was on the bridge he found that he could not take his eyes off the slack rope.

From the American side of the gorge there appeared a slightly built man, modest and serious in his demeanour, dressed in woollen fleshings and wearing what looked like a leather kilt, as though from a sense of decorum. On either bank the crowds waited expectantly.

Blondin approached the rope, which was stretched almost directly above the sickening vortex of the whirlpool. He slid his slippered foot along the cord, as though testing its surface. Then, with arms held waveringly outward, he moved forward with neat, gliding steps. The slackness of the rope meant that he was walking down an incline which appeared perilously steep. Verity glanced at the whirlpool and the grisly dance of the dead within its spiralling waters. If Blondin should fall, he thought, nothing would save him in the rapids and the downward suction. It was not the death which horrified him most of all but the long moment of agony, while the hapless victim and the onlookers gazed mutely at one another.

When he looked up again, the acrobat was almost at the bottom of the sloping cord, where he paused. There was a gasp from the crowd as Blondin's feet flew upward from the rope, and he turned a vigorous somersault, regaining his balance easily. In the stillness, Verity could hear the voice of the young Prince, tormented by the peril in which the man had put himself, whispering, 'No! No! For God's sake don't do it again!' But Blondin now turned sideways on the rope and began to cartwheel leisurely in a star-pattern of extended arms and legs. There was no sound of applause or appreciation from the crowd, only a deep and ghastly silence. Verity had no idea of how long the performance lasted, but at length Blondin moved forward, leaning towards the Canadian bank as he climbed the upward slope of the cord, just as he had held his body backward when descending the slope on the American side. In a moment more, he had set foot firmly on the Canadian cliff. There was an instant of indecision, followed by a patter of stunned applause. The royal party exhaled audible sighs of relief.

Presently, Verity was aware that the acrobat was being brought on to the bridge to be introduced to the Prince. The young visitor had recovered from his nervousness, though perhaps his ready laughter was now a sign of the shock he had felt. Blondin, light-footed and deferential, approached and bowed deeply. The young Prince congratulated him and then, with a lightness which robbed his words of their effect, said, 'For God's sake, let that be the end of the performance.'

Blondin spoke softly and rapidly. His words were inaudible to Verity but the effect on the Prince was unmistakable. His eyes brightened as though at a challenge. Blondin meanwhile began to make the motions of a man pushing something with his hands and gestured toward one end of the bridge, where a wooden wheelbarrow stood beside his few items of equipment. Then the young Prince laughed again.

'Very well!' he said with amiable aggressiveness. 'If you're game, then so am I!' He took a step forward, as if to accompany the acrobat.

Verity watched with growing unease. But already a glance had passed between the grave, bearded figure of Newcastle and Major-General Bruce with his fine white moustaches. They advanced on their young lord and spoke with quiet vigour. The Prince's amiability faded into sullen resignation. Blondin waved an arm as though inviting someone else of the party to be his passenger. The Prince's companions now looked stonily at the tightrope artist who had made so indecorous a proposal. Then one of the smartly uniformed staff officers turned suddenly and looked at Verity.

'By Jove!' he said brightly. 'But ain't we got a man here for it? The hero who saved the *Hero*, eh? What? The Alma and Inkerman, eh? Beat the Russians? Rescued pretty little chits from the Sepoy mutineers, what? Nothing to him to cross a rope in a barrow! Ha?'

Verity stood horrified at the proposal. Now they were all looking at him, the royal party in amusement, and Blondin with calm optimism. He thought of Bella and the children. It was mad, absurd. He could refuse to associate himself with such folly and no one in the world would blame him. But though they would never speak the thought, they would wonder if, after all, he had been afraid.

'I ain't afraid to go, sir!' he said, his plump cheeks flushing and his legs trembling. The others continued to look with amusement but the young man, for whom he cared more than for all the rest of them, turned his eyes on Verity and spoke softly.

'Good for you!' he said admiringly. 'Good for you!'

The acrobat laid a hand lightly on the shoulder of the plump sergeant and urged him gently towards the wooden barrow. It was just big enough for him to sit in with his knees hugged up to his chest and his feet inside. Blondin moved him easily and Verity was abruptly aware that the solidity beneath the wheel had gone. The entire barrow seemed to be swaying wildly and perilously. They were on the rope.

He must not look down. The instinctive fright of his reaction would be enough to make him dislodge the hair-breadth equilibrium of the little wooden conveyance. At first he kept his eyes closed, feeling only that they were going down and down, as the incline of the slack rope drew them to the centre of the rapids. From time to time he felt Blondin pause, legs weaving to retain his balance and the barrow heeling over sickeningly. Once, in his secret terror, Verity knew that the angle of the wooden side was such

61

that another inch or two would throw him helplessly to his death. He turned his weight the other way, sweating with fear, and felt the man behind him pull urgently against this.

'Keep still!' breathed the voice of his invisible companion. 'Quite still, or we shall both be overset!'

There was no panic in the words but a vast and controlled confidence. Verity crouched motionless and slowly opened his eyes. They were far out from the cliff now, still descending the slack cord toward the centre. Below him the blue waters dimpled and gurgled in their menacing vortex, at what seemed an enormous distance. A wider ring of angry froth swirled the trapped logs and branches into the suction of the liquid green chasm. From the direction of the falls a rising wave, spreading dark and terrible from cliff to cliff, roared down upon the gorge in a headlong tumble of spray. Swallowing a rising sob of fear, Verity raised his head to train his eyes upon the safety of the American shore. As he did so, a gust of wind, following the direction of the stream, lifted his tall stove-pipe hat from his head and carried it gently away. He watched, sick with dismay, as the dark high-crowned hat circled easily as a bird, down to the waiting river beneath him. At the first touch, the waves smashed it over and over, into the churning rim of the whirlpool. The beaten and shapeless remains flew faster and faster round the successive circles until they reached the spiralling centre where they paused inexplicably for an instant, before being thrust down from the sight of the onlookers.

Verity's cheeks still quivered uncontrollably with alarm. He and Blondin were level with the royal party on the bridge and he heard a half-admiring and half-derisive cheer. But his eyes were on the American shore now. For the first time, he began to believe that he would not, after all, die in the horror of the whirlpool below. And he had been braver than any of them, except the Prince. Now that it was almost done, he assured himself, he would do it again any time he was asked.

Confidence was swelling in his breast when he saw the

tall stranger on the American bank. The man was scanning
the royal party through a pair of field-glasses. His other
hand lay against his belt. The cloth of his coat, at that point,
betrayed the outline of a holster whose size and shape
suggested one of the new Colt revolvers. Then, as Blondin
wheeled him closer, he could see clearly that the tall young
man was Miss Jolly's escort on her tour of the Broadway
jewellers' shops. The pattern of villainy changed in Verity's
mind. Miss Jolly, as an agent of death and assassination,
might gull the American police authorities. Her accomplice,
the marksman of a hundred organizations who hated
England's royal blood, would somehow be placed where he
could fire without missing his target. And all this through
the girl's double-dealing. The sum paid for the death of
the Queen's heir would be an ample reward.

At any moment, Verity feared to hear the *twing-g-g-g* of
shots overhead, which a man might mistake for the sound
of large stinging insects unless he knew better. When he
had been in camp with the 23rd Regiment of Foot before
Sebastopol, the sounds had been followed by half a dozen
of his comrades falling back with blood pumping from their
shattered breasts or the ghastly sockets of their eyes.

'Dear God!' he said softly. ' 'is Royal Highness!'

At the centre of the dainty suspension-bridge, the young
Prince stood, eager and smiling at the performance on the
rope. Verity twisted his head and shouted.

'Sir! Get down, sir! Get down!'

An air of puzzlement clouded the Prince's expression.
Only the mirth of the well-fed staff-officer acknowledged
the cry.

'Hero, eh? Find this a bit stiff though! Can't take it
without blubbering a bit, eh, what? Told you, by Jove!'

There might even be an assassin in the trees, with a
marksman's rifle, for whom the tall young man merely
acted as range-finder. By now, Blondin had almost reached
the far bank with his passenger. Verity set his eyes grimly
on Miss Jolly's accomplice.

'Right, Captain Smiles!' he said aloud. 'So he don't

exist, don't he? We'll soon have a see about that, sir!'

His jaw was set with intimidating ferocity as the barrow jolted on to the turf and the spectators applauded Blondin's arrival on the safety and solidity of the cliff-top. Verity pushed himself out of the barrow and parted the grinning crowd.

'One side! Mind yer backs! Quick-sharp!' he barked sullenly.

Miss Jolly's tall young escort wore a hat of grey felt, moccasins and deer-skin trousers. A bullet-pouch and a knife, as well as the revolver holster, were shaped by the fall of his jacket over his belt. He was lowering the field-glasses and turning away as Verity bounded towards him.

'No you don't, my fine fellow!' Verity's words, like thunder, drew the attention of the entire crowd on the American side. The tall young man paused for what was, in his circumstances, an injudiciously long moment. Verity ran forward and leapt, throwing all his weight on to the man's back and knocking him sprawling. The stranger was stunned by the unexpected impact. Verity had had no time to discard his equipment before surrendering to Blondin's orders. He snatched the handcuffs which still hung at his belt, snapped the first one on the man's right wrist, wrenched the arm behind his back, and clicked the other steel cuff onto the left wrist.

Gathering his breath for a moment, he then jerked the prisoner to his feet and propelled him with blows of his knee toward the party on the little suspension-bridge. Captain Smiles, smooth and expressionless, awaited him.

'Sir!' said Verity smartly. ' 'ave the honour to report that there was going to be shooting at 'is Highness from the cliff, while I was taken across. This person 'ere was using field-glasses as if to give out the aim, sir. And another thing, sir. He's also the fancy chap that was going the rounds of the New York jewellers as Miss Jolly's accomplice. He's the one that you and the others said you'd never heard of, sir! With respect, sir. There might be a marksman in them bushes on the bank, sir. If this one in custody can be made to talk quick, sir, we could have the name of the marksman out of him before that party does a bunk. Sir!'

'Take those handcuffs off him, sergeant!'

'Sir?'

'Get the bloody things off! Or did you leave the keys in England?'

'No, sir.' Unhappily, Verity took the little key from his belt.

'You fat, officious fool!' said Captain Smiles bitterly.

'Sir? 'e was spying on His Royal Highness most suspicious, sir. And he'd got a hand on his gun.'

'There was no spying! No marksmen, no assassins! Damn you, you idiot!'

'Then what about 'im, sir? With respect, sir.'

'Him? Oh, yes,' said Captain Smiles miserably. 'You have just arrested Captain Thomas Crowe of the United States Marine Corps, assigned by his own government as a bodyguard to His Royal Highness during the American stages of the tour. In short, he is to be your partner!'

'But 'e can't be, sir! It don't make sense!'

'He not only can be, sergeant, he *is!* '

Verity, his face downcast and lowered, swallowed hard.

'Dunno what to say, sir,' he mumbled wretchedly. 'I couldn't a-made a worse mess of all this if I'd tried deliberate!'

The hurricane lamp hung from the central pole of the little tent, casting a white glare on the table where the two sergeants sat. Verity assembled the dark brown flagons of Buttery's County-Bottled Allsopp, like riflemen to be drilled. He handed Crowe a regulation-issue canteen and took a bottle in his pudgy fist. He tipped a generous pint into Crowe's canteen.

'You'll 'ave another sup, Mr Crowe,' he said encouragingly, 'consequential on the unfortunate affair this afternoon. Makes me feel better about it, being able to stand you chummage now.'

The night seemed filled by the steady roar of the falls and

the cataract. Crowe raised the corner of the metal canteen to his mouth.

'Mr Verity,' he said gently, 'it's forgot.'

Verity's cheeks filled abruptly with wind as he put his own canteen down. He wiped his moustaches appreciatively on the back of his hand.

'Now there, Mr Crowe, we 'ave to disagree. I can't forget what I don't understand.'

Crowe spread out his hands, his high thin face a study in honest bewilderment.

'Folks can't always be allowed to understand, Mr Verity. Not you, not me. I guess I can't tell you anything you don't know already.'

'There too, Mr Crowe, we have to disagree. True, you wasn't trying to assassinate the young Prince, after all. I acted in 'aste there, Mr Crowe. But I never saw wrong in New York, did I? And what I saw was you and that little bunter Jolly setting up the wax-under-the-counter dodge all the way along Broadway. That randy little piece never done the law a good turn, Mr Crowe, only once when a cracksman tanned Miss Jolly's bum for her and she peached on him out of spite.'

'Did you hear that a jeweller was robbed?' asked Crowe mildly.

'No, Mr Crowe, I never did. Not hear it for a fact, that is.'

'Then I guess you never saw robbery being put up, did you?'

Verity tilted his head back, his thick flushed throat pulsing rhythmically at the descent of half a pint of dark ale. He put down the canteen.

'And that house you saw her to, Mr Crowe, that was a Magdalen Asylum, was it? You know it never was! Now, Mr Crowe, you and me is going to be working together. It's time I was told something of all this.'

Crowe's lean sun-browned face was a study in innocence.

'A police refuge,' he said quietly, 'that's what it was. You sure did pick the worst house in the city to burgle, Mr Verity.'

'But they was expecting someone, Mr Crowe. I was the wrong one. They said so. 'oo might they have been waiting for?'

Crowe shrugged.

'Sure don't know, Mr Verity.'

'And why was Miss Jolly there, if she hadn't been arrested?'

'Safekeeping,' said Crowe equably. 'When a young woman volunteers her services, they like to keep her safe and decent.'

Verity's dark eyes bulged with indignation.

' 'er *services!* Mr Crowe, you got any idea, 'ave you, what her services been in the past? There's men dead a-cos of her services. She's a right tight little villain, she is! You don't want to listen to 'er nor trust 'er!'

'You really don't take to her at all, do you, Mr Verity?'

'Mr Crowe, I gotta know what all this is about. We shall have the devil to pay if that little bitch starts trouble here.'

'What I know,' said Crowe firmly, 'is that I was to meet her from the boat, show her the town a bit, and then deliver her safe to the police house that evening. And I never asked why.'

'There's more to it, Mr Crowe. There got to be.'

'Then you'd better ask your own people or ours,' said Crowe wearily. 'If I knew the whole story, which I don't, I sure as all hell wouldn't get my ass kicked from here to Washington and back by telling you!'

'Your *what*, Mr Crowe?'

'My ass,' said Crowe, suddenly becoming self-conscious.

'Oh!' Comprehension began to dawn in Verity's eyes. 'Cor, 'ere, ain't you got a funny way of saying things in this part of the world? Don't think I shall ever understand the 'alf of it.' He beckoned Crowe's head forward across the table, as though to ensure that they would not be overheard. 'We say arse, Mr Crowe. Ass is a sort of donkey.' He sat back with a brief nod of intellectual authority.

Crowe stretched out his long thin legs. Then he yawned and got to his feet.

'An ass is what you sit on,' he said firmly, 'and being a king or a commoner makes no odds as to that. Being a commoner, however, it is also liable to get other folks' bootprints on it when you don't mind your own concerns. Not that your Miss Jolly wouldn't be a tight little wriggler, I daresay, if a man had her under his instruction.'

Verity bade his guest good night and watched him move leisurely away across the turf with his long, loping stride. He had met few Americans and none whom he felt would typify their race. Yet in Thomas Crowe he found a new friend, despite the Marine's laconic dourness, and an invaluable guide in the unfamiliar ways of the American continent.

Some ten minutes later, Verity walked out into the night air. In his mind there was a confusion of trails, none of which led to any conclusion. At least if there was some ingenious conspiracy afoot, he was sure that Crowe was as much a victim of it as he was. But what had they said to Crowe, what orders had been given him to account for his complicity with Miss Jolly in the matter of the Broadway jewellers? To what purpose was the girl allowed to appear to be robbing the shops without actually doing so? As for Jolly's lynx-eyed beauty, for whose benefit was it displayed in a new and strange country? Verity stood, scowling in thought, before the iron fretwork of the white suspension-bridge, where Blondin's rope still hung slackly across the swirling rapids.

3

CRACKSMAN

7

Verney Dacre tucked away the blue silk handkerchief in the pocket of his fawn-coloured summer jacket. Even in September the stateroom of the Philadelphia Packet, now approaching New York, was warm enough to warrant a linen coat with matching waistcoat, cream trousers, and a cambric cravat in pink stripes. His lavender gloves and round silk hat lay with his cane on a small occasional table of pale mahogany. Behind him, the wake of the paddle frothed and rushed past the curtained window. Before him, the remains on the dinner-table consisted of an empty bottle in its silver ice-bucket, a pile of smoke-grey oyster shells, and a scattering of silver cutlery.

The stateroom panelling was of rosewood and bird's-eye maple, the wood polished, and gilded along its cornices. Cut-glass handles adorned every door and cupboard, while the velvet of the sofa and lounging chairs was a rich port-wine tone by comparison with the lighter cerise of the carpet. A pair of handsome pier-glasses flanked the door which communicated with the retiring room.

Ignoring Joey Morant-Barham, who reclined with his feet on the sofa, trailing greenish-grey smoke from his cheroot, Dacre opened the communicating door an inch or two. Maggie had straightened the white satin of the bed-cover and had begun to dress herself. She had on her short white vest and a pair of close-fitting pants in light blue cotton, enclosing her from waist to ankles. Dacre's eyes narrowed in curiosity at the sight of her on all fours, brushing at the thick carpet. The blonde curtains of Maggie's hair fell forward, almost hiding her straight firm features. She scrubbed at the carpet with her hands, moving backward on knees and palms. With a whore-master's instinct, Dacre stood behind her and assessed the

71

appeal of her figure in this posture. Her lack of height gave a slight heaviness to her hips and buttocks, which made him wonder whether she might not have dropped a cub on the sly. Presently she clawed up from the pile of the carpet a bright yellow circle, like a small wedding-ring. Dacre knew it for a 'hollow' half-dollar lately coined in this form. No doubt it had dropped from his pocket during his earlier enjoyment of her. He quelled an urge to treat Maggie like the thieving little shop-girl she might once have been. A fellow who was to have millions of such coins had better mind that business first. Moreover, experience had taught him not to strike a woman until she was of no further use to him. He closed the door on her and turned the key. The wash of the paddle-wake against the hull was ample security against Maggie hearing the conversation in the next room.

'They'll have us berthed in an hour, Joey Barham,' he said sternly. 'So give your best attention to this for a while.'

He unfolded a drawing in his own hand and spread it on the littered table. The square building with its central courtyard had been adorned by marks and shapes representing the contents of its rooms and the massive doors behind which they lay.

'Charley Temple's legacy and Miss Jennifer's confession,' he said softly. 'Just half a promise of being set free with Miss Mag as her bride and the Khan doxy couldn't talk fast enough. Now, put your mind to one door, plated steel with a time-lock, and one vault door of steel with a combination of numbers set to one in a million. This paper shall turn up treasure or turkey, old fellow, according to how we play the game now.'

Morant-Barham suppressed both his dismay and his scepticism. He knew how uncertain Dacre's temper might be and, after all, the Lieutenant had lightened a ferry train of half a ton of bullion three years before. The United States Federal Mint was hardly more than a bullion train on a larger scale.

'Three months' reserve of gold, Joey,' said Dacre softly,

'and the one day in the century is next Tuesday as ever is.'

'There's a rope for us both if it don't go smooth,' said Morant-Barham peevishly. 'I ain't that partial to go in there until I know the rig.' With that he had pressed his opposition as far as he judged prudent. Dacre's lips curled in a smile.

'Trust me, old fellow, it shall go as smooth as oil on glass. And you shan't go in, Joey, only in the properest way. I must shift for myself in this, with you outside. Now, oblige me by attendin' to this paper.'

Dacre had meditated so long on the design of the building that he hardly needed to look at the drawing as he spoke. The Federal Mint at Philadelphia had been built in the form of a Grecian temple, at the corner of Chestnut and Juniper Street. Its four sides enclosed a central courtyard, and Dacre had paced out the dimensions of the place as one hundred and fifty feet by two hundred.

Gold bullion, arriving at the Mint, went neatly round the four wings of the building. It was received at the south portico on Chestnut Street. This wing contained the public vestibule, the Director's office, and a small coin-museum. The bullion passed the main steel doors, along an arched subterranean corridor to the weighing-room. Moving to the west wing, the gold was melted and refined. It was first melted in crucibles with three parts of silver. The refiner would then dip his ladle into the molten mass, skim off the gold and throw it into vats of cold water. The lumps of cooled gold were then passed to the corroding-house to be further refined. This was done by placing them in porcelain troughs of nitric acid, which were in turn set in boiling water. After six hours, the gold had lost most of its impurities and was reduced to a dull, dark brown gravel. This was placed in hydraulic presses to be compacted into 'cakes' or 'cheeses'.

Before beginning the coining process in the north and east wings, the cakes of gold were covered with charcoal to prevent oxidization and were again melted to be cast as ingots. The north wing housed the great rolling-machines

73

with their massive wheels which would flatten an ingot into a strip from which the planchets or blank coins could be cut. In convenient lengths, the strips of gold were passed through the steam-driven planchet-cutters in the east wing and the blank circles of gold were punched out. These were then stamped with the design of the coin, milled by hand, and their weights checked. After stamping and milling, they were passed to the stronghold in the east wing.

'Now Joey,' said Dacre reasonably. 'What we must have is finished coin from the stronghold. There's a million or two at least, all in bullion chests, waiting there to be shipped to banks and private clients of the Mint. Double eagles at twenty dollars a touch. Ingots is too deuced heavy, old fellow, you have my word upon it. And they need melting and getting rid of at a poor price. But with coins of the realm, Joey! Why, a chap might carry ten thousand dollars in his pockets almost! And a dollar will pay a dollar, devil-may-care where he got it from!'

'It ain't that I wish to be churlish,' said Morant-Barham, with a good-natured laugh to prove it, 'but how is all this money to be got?'

Dacre smoothed the plan flat.

'It's to be got in the course of one night, Joey. Between six in the evening, when the locks go on, and seven the next morning when they come off. There's a night-watch, but they ain't trusted near the gold. They're carrying guns, of course, but they can't get into the refining-shops or anywhere but the outside offices.'

'Why not?'

'Here,' Dacre's bony finger traced a line just behind the entrance vestibule. 'Short of a ton of gunpowder, a man won't get near the gold except through that door. Plated steel and weighs several tons. It ain't just locked, Joey. A fellow might soon come to terms with a lock. There's a devilish clever cove by the name of Sergeant who built this one and geared it to a clock. From six in the evening until seven in the morning, there's three inches of solid steel, tight as a curate's purse, closing the keyhole on the inside.

A fellow can't even chisel out the entire lock, for it's fitted from the far side of the door. At seven in the morning, the wheel that the clockwork keeps turning will move round so that the steel is clear of the keyhole. And then you may open it with a key. It ain't to be broke, Joey!'

'Then you'll never see inside!' said Morant-Barham peevishly.

'It ain't to be broke, Joey! But no more am I! Now, have the goodness to attend to me again. A fellow that *could* get past the time-lock might get to the refining-shop and the rest of the machinery. Not that he'd find gold there, unless he could scrape a peck off the crucibles. Between him and the stronghold wing stands another door with a lock that never saw a key. It's all numbers, Joey. A man that knows the seven figures he must turn the dial to can open it in a minute. Otherwise, he might as well go home and forget it.'

'And you know it, Dacre! You must, by God!'

Dacre shook his head.

'I don't, Joey. No one knows it. The man who closes the lock may choose any figure in a million and may alter it every time he closes the lock. Once it's shut, he must either tell you what the secret is, or you must break into his skull for it. It's a lock that is never set except by the Director himself or his private secretary.'

'Then you must rack it from them!' said Morant-Barham furiously.

Dacre laughed.

'If you suppose, Joey Barham, that I shall do anything of the sort, y'are most monstrously misled. I trade in masterpieces, old fellow. When this crib has been cracked, there's not a soul who shall know when or how. Not a lock forced, not a door scratched, not a man spoken to in ill-temper. That's the art of it, Joey. After the time-lock and the figure-lock, however, there's nothing but a Double Treasury lock in the door of the vault, and one of Mr Yale's cylinder locks on each of the bank boxes. If I ain't sprung that lot in five minutes, Joey, then I deserve to be hung.'

'May I be damned if it's to be done!' said Morant-Barham, sitting down heavily on the sofa again. 'There isn't a way past that time-lock. The night ain't long enough for you to try every setting of the figure-lock, even if you'd nothing else to do. And if you found it in the end, they'd change it before the next night! Where's the good of being able to open vault doors and cylinder locks, when you'll never so much as see them? I don't mean to cavil, old fellow, but it *can't* be done – any of it!'

'Joey, Joey,' said Dacre gently, as if he were soothing a crying child, 'ain't that the beauty of it? It *can't* be done! You might go to the Treasury or the police tomorrow and tell them the tale. They'd laugh in your face. It can't be done, old chum. And that's why I shall do it. By God, I ain't come this far without knowing what needs doing in the matter. The Khan girl's plan was a gift from the gods, and damned if they ain't given me one other.'

'You've a partner inside?'

'Just you and me, Joey. One week from today!'

'Time-locks that can't be broke?' said Morant-Barham sceptically. 'And a figure-lock that must be set at one in a million?'

Verney Dacre brushed his fair whiskers gently against the flush of excitement in his spoilt, petulant face.

'Joey, Joey,' he murmured to himself, 'I'm through those locks already, as sure as I stand here!'

Morant-Barham lay on the sofa in the stateroom as the steamer carried them past the Battery and towards their landing. He listened to the details of the plan, sometimes gasping, mouth gaping with delight, sometimes sniggering with sheer pleasure at the neatness of it. He thought that even if the gleam in Dacre's eye bordered on derangement, there was after all a way through the time-lock and the figure-lock, as the scheme unfolded. Once the cracksman had mastered the locks and was in that part of the building where even the most trusted officers of the night-watch could not follow, he was master of the place until morning.

And when Dacre described the means by which the entire contents of the gold vault might be shipped effortlessly out of the Federal Mint, Joey Barham rolled hopelessly about the sofa, roaring and tearful in an ecstasy of mirth. His scepticism had gone. It *could* be done – every last half-dollar of it, Joey thought.

Dacre left him and slipped into the adjoining room. Maggie was still in her short white vest and close-fitting cotton pants, though now she was standing before a long mirror, shaping her hair on top of her head, as though trying a selection of styles. She let it fall, so that it hung in a blonde tail behind her, down to the level of her shoulder-blades. Dacre knew that the next few minutes were as important in his plan as any time which might be spent in manipulating a mere lock. Maggie was a pet English-born acquisition, a common shop-girl whom he had drilled until she was the most expensive young whore in the house which he operated in New York. There was a sulky petulance about her but she had learnt not to show it to the man who was virtually her master. Not that Dacre had so far broken her lips for her, but Maggie maintained a romantic attachment to another girl of the house, 'Tawny Jenny', and Dacre had left her in no doubt that Jennifer, with her Indian beauty, would suffer for the blonde girl's sins.

He stood behind Maggie, holding her jaw firmly with one hand, keeping her face to the mirror so that he could watch her expression as he spoke. With his other hand he undid her pants and let them fall, so that she stood only in the short vest. Maggie stood tense but still, knowing that she had little choice in the matter.

'Now, miss,' said Dacre softly, 'you know what must be done?'

'Yes,' she said, in a low soft voice with the hint of a Celtic lilt, 'I know. I've been told often enough.'

Dacre's hand caressed the pale satiny warmth of Maggie's bare hips.

'Y' love Jennifer, do y' not? There ain't much doubt, to

77

judge by the way you sniff that young Bengali bitch's tail half the day and most of the night!'

The anger in Maggie's eyes was quickly subdued.

'Very well,' Dacre continued. 'Now, Miss Jennifer ain't exactly a free agent in the matter, having cost me money to buy in the South and bring here. And if you think you may walk off the premises with her, miss, you shall find that Cowhide and Lucifer will contradict you both.'

'I never meant that,' said Maggie, hardly audible.

'So y' say, so y' say, miss.' Dacre's hand lightly mapped the fair-skinned smoothness of Maggie's body, stroking over the marble-whiteness of her twenty-year-old belly whose childish flatness had gone and whose first firm outward curve was just perceptible. He brushed the little growth of fair hair at her thighs. The girl lowered her hazel eyes but moved slightly in response. He lifted his hand, touched the side of her waist, and weighed the full ovals of Maggie's bottom. Again she arched backward to him, as if in submissive compliance.

'Now, miss,' said Dacre gently, 'it's no secret that you'd rather have your Jenny doing this for you than me or any man. And tonight you shall decide. When you see your beau, Captain Moore, tonight, you shall give your message and give it well. If he comes to you at a run next week, as he will if you bid him properly, you shall be free. And Tawny Jennifer shall go with you as bride or groom, and a purse of gold for you both.'

Maggie was arching and pushing herself into his palms now, showing an innocent delight and eagerness to redeem the promise.

'But, Miss Mag,' said Dacre with a hint of paternal affection and warning, 'if the message ain't given the right way to Captain Moore, and if he don't come at a run, then things must go otherwise with you and your Jennifer. A fellow like me can't afford losses on all sides and must sell up to pay his way. Now, a Khan girl may be a Moslem beauty but Jennifer's shade of tawny makes her a slave in states not far from here. And that's where she must go, Maggie, to earn her price on the auction block. Now, she may find a kind and loving master who buys her, or she may find a cruel one who delights in what can be done behind closed doors. But whichever it is, she and you must part. It ain't that I wish it, but needs must if you lose Captain Moore.'

Maggie drew forward from his caressing, prepared to turn and push herself into his arms.

'Promise us we may go,' she whispered, 'Jenny and me together, when it's all done. You shall have whatever you ask from us.'

'Then I can't make it plainer, Maggie,' he said gently. 'What must be done is best for all of us. You and I, and your handsome Jenny.'

Well trained in her profession, Maggie began to arch and round her broad young bottom restively against Dacre. Turning in his embrace, she raised her lips to him, so that he caught the warm sweet taste of her mouth, her lips themselves as sensuous as the velvet of a flower petal. She slipped down, kneeling at him in a lascivious gesture of submission, while Dacre brushed back the veil of her blonde hair and held her face between his hands.

Presently they moved toward the bed with its white satin cover, the girl drawing her master after her by his fingers. As she did so, Maggie held her free hand behind her to excite him further by coyly shielding what they both knew she must reveal fully in a moment more. Maggie's stockily seductive figure, the blonde curtains of her hair, were shared with a thousand working-girls in shops and mills. Dacre knew that it was he, as whoremaster, who had endowed her with talents to ensnare men of wealth and intelligence. She even managed a slight blush, beside the bed, as she took the white singlet, the only garment she wore, and pulled it well up above her waist, her eyes watching Dacre to seek his approval for this display. He patted her forward, watching her scramble onto the white satin and then turn on her back to receive him.

Dacre had enjoyed her a dozen times before. Now, as

then, he explored Maggie's secrets fully, hearing her murmur at the cool metal caress of his ringed fingers. As their bodies closed together, he observed the dreamy wandering of her eyes, the fluttering of Maggie's eyelids as they opened and closed, shutting at last in a secret reverie as her body matched the movements of his own.

'Why, Mag,' he said, when it was over, 'y' may have chosen a handsome young Khan girl for a sweetheart, but damme, there's more to you than a sapphist, ain't there?'

She turned her head aside, as though from a blow. Then she reached and touched him, as if to lure him down upon her once more. Her voice was soft as she sighed, 'Please!' Dacre laughed.

'Oh no, Miss Maggie! You ain't forgetting what's to come tonight I trust! A doxy may have a taste, but she ain't to make a glutton of herself before the main serving!'

She turned round towards him, shaking back the long golden tresses from her face, and her eyes were so hard that he really thought she might try to strike him with her trim little fists. Dacre laughed, almost good-naturedly, to take some of the sting out of his jibe. He got up and attended to his appearance.

'And there again,' he said ambiguously as he was about to close the door behind him, 'you ain't to forget your tawny Jenny either.'

The lights of the city were close on both sides of them by this time, and Morant-Barham was crushing out his cigar as Dacre returned to the stateroom. Thinking of the two girls and their eventual disposal, Morant-Barham said anxiously.

'It ain't for me to argue the matter, but a lot has to be taken on the trust of Maggie and the Punjabi bitch. They mayn't know much about the caper, but once we're gone they could tell enough for a fellow to find himself in the wrong box.'

'Never a word,' said Dacre, picking up his gloves and stick.

'But young Maggie won't do this except on a promise of

a purse of gold and having the Khan girl for her own, free
and away.'

Morant-Barham's sun-reddened face with its black
moustaches was a study in youthful scepticism. Dacre
adjusted his silk hat in the pier-glass.

'Joey, old fellow, I'm damned if after all you haven't
lived this far and never learnt the first rules of a gentleman's
conduct.'

'Meaning?'

'Meaning,' said Dacre, 'that I never met a man of sense
who believed that promises to a whore were ever obligations
of honour. And now, my dear boy, we'd best see to the
night's business.'

8

The night's business, like most of Lieutenant Dacre's other
commerce, was carried on close to the notorious Five Points
area of slums and alleys, between Broadway and the river.
It reminded him more than anything else of the Seven Dials
rookery in London with its lowering tenements, overflowing
gutters, and narrow ill-lit footpaths. It was a disagreeable
area and Dacre's visits to it were rare as his visits had been
to the Langham Place house in London. For the most part,
he left it in the capable hands of Joey Barham, ably assisted
by Cowhide and Lucifer. No one who knew the well-dressed
young lieutenant with his house in Westchester county
would have imagined that this could be his source of
revenue. They would have found it still harder to imagine
why a man who had no need of the revenue should follow
such a trade. Verney Dacre's weaknesses were few, but he
admitted to himself that there was a real satisfaction to be
found in the prostituting of young women. Like many
philanderers, he hated his young victims quite as much as
he loved them. In his narrow breast and his bitter blood,

he felt a savage delight at the debasement of Maggie, Jennifer, and their entire sisterhood. It surprised him that the American nation should, just then, be making such a caterwaul over slavery. A man that could enslave his victims regardless of laws and institutions was the only sort of fellow for Lieutenant Dacre.

In company with Morant-Barham and Maggie, he passed through the narrow ways of the Five Points, the gaslight flaring on the stagnant pools of the choked gutters and the slimy condensation of the cobbles. Coarse and bloated faces scowled at the elegant young men from their narrow doorways. In the succession of decaying taverns, coloured prints of Washington, the American Eagle, and Queen Victoria, showed dimly in the oil-light through the small grimy panes of the windows. A pock-marked girl, about thirty years old, covered with bruises and her upper lip swollen, whined for their attention as she slouched against one of the doorposts. The room behind her was packed with sailors from the nearby wharf, the loud din of the place overlaid by shouts of merriment and the tinkling of a guitar.

The narrow passage opened into a decaying square of houses, their exterior walls blotched by damp and patched against collapse by pale areas of rendering, as though the very fabric had become diseased. Wooden stairs, damp and rotting, led up the exterior of the buildings to the higher floors, where the fugitives from tavern and grog-shop huddled by candlelight. Dacre swung his stick and looked about him.

'Ain't it a regular break-down, though?' he said languidly.

The walls beyond the square bore designs of ships, forts, and flags in coloured chalk. A sign directed the pleasure-seeker to a flight of stairs leading down to a large, smoky basement, where it was just possible to glimpse pairs of negro girls dancing together and awaiting their customers. Outside the place, a dark-haired little man with a barrel organ was grinding out a sentimental song, accompanying a girl of fourteen or fifteen. She was dressed up in clothes that were ten years too old for her, a crinoline and mantle, a straw hat with a flame-coloured feather in it, the entire outfit worn and shabby. Her voice was coarsened by street singing, but it was still strong and appealing.

'The older woman snuffed it,' said Morant-Barham for Dacre's benefit. 'Now he takes his daughter round singing, dressed in her mother's clothes.'

Dacre gave a short hum of disapproval. Maggie, dropping back a pace, fumbled in her pocket, drew out the hollow half-dollar, and slipped it quickly into the girl's hand. Dacre caught the movement, however, and exchanged with Morant-Barham a look of hopelessness.

By now, he was almost on his own territory, where the alleys became less shabby and more gaudy, opening out into courts and little squares which were close enough to Broadway to have been once fashionable and picturesque. Albion House, or the Albion, was as plain-fronted as a prison, except for its one plate-glass window, through which the hesitating customer had a glimpse of the 'Introducing Parlour' with its chandelier and polished floor.

At the opening of the square, towards Broadway itself, Dacre was pleased to see that two of the girls, Pauline and Sue, had been carefully placed. The two young women worked as a pair, Sue with her soft pale body and cropped blonde curls acted the slut. Pauline with a firmer body, dark eyes with long lashes, cropped dark curls, and pretty snub-nose, played the refined whore. Any man who accepted their invitation was accompanied to their room by both of them. He was then made to pay extra either for the privilege of one girl leaving or for having them both at once. Occasionally, he would pay to see Pauline and Sue as one another's lovers, an act which they performed with stupefying lack of conviction.

The most important clients were, of course, received by appointment. Even so, there was a little knot of men at the plate-glass window, which was protected on the inside by a wire mesh. The plain façade of the house was some

83

indication that it had been built to keep eager intruders out and reluctant girls in. Dacre glanced at the coarse, laughing faces, peering through the glass, and then saw Maggie's features tighten in ill-concealed anger.

The men with their caps and pipes were watching Jennifer. She was an object of curiosity both for her Asian beauty, which was rare in the Five Points, and for the sullen challenge with which she dismissed their gaze. Her high cheekbones gave just a slight upward slant to the outer corners of her dark, deeply expressive eyes. The features of her olive-toned face were straight and firm, sloping to the prominent jawline of her type. A sheen of black hair, combed from its central parting, ended in a pretty tangle between her shoulder-blades.

The attraction was that several of the girls were performing tableaux, in tight, coloured fleshings, for the benefit of the clients in the room, who surveyed the young actresses and then made their choice of bedfellow. Outside, the impecunious voyeurs gloated over the sight of Jennifer, the nearest beauty. Like Maggie, the Asian girl was hardly tall enough to carry the softness of breasts and slight heaviness of hips with true elegance. The voyeurs, pop-eyed at her shape in clinging dark blue tights and white bodice, hardly cared. There was a general shifting in the group of men. Some tried to catch the girl's eye, to show her their interest in the soft fall of breasts, the bow of her thighs, the smooth triangle of her lower belly. Others showed her their boisterous amusement as the display required her to turn her back to them and stoop.

Dacre paused, coolly observing the effect of this final derision on the dark contempt with which Jennifer treated her uncouth admirers. Her eyes moved uncertainly and her glance wavered. Soon she avoided the gaze of the laughing onlookers when her performance brought her to face them. Dacre was aware of Maggie's soft anger at his side.

'Stop them! Stop them! Make them go away! Make them leave her!'

'Damme,' said Dacre, smiling over Maggie's head to

Morant-Barham, 'your Jenny had best learn humility, Mag, as a moral principle. If the missioners never taught such lessons, it's quite the best thing she should learn her place from these fellows.'

The door opened at his touch. Like sentries at their posts, Cowhide and Lucifer guarded the threshold. Lucifer, stout and clean-shaven, was Dacre's 'foreman'. He stood in a shabby green evening coat, fair hair cropped short on his large round head, an almost feminine softness in his yellow face. His dark eyes promised a capacity for inflicting suffering equal to any of his master's orders. Cowhide was instantly recognizable for what he was, by the width of his shoulders, the straining of his jacket across chest and back. The slack jaw and wandering eyes held the supreme recommendation of being able to impart pain or death without the distraction of imagining his victim's ordeal.

Dacre's hand brushed back Maggie's almost childlike curtains of blonde hair. He stroked the pale silken skin of her warm neck.

'Now, miss,' he said gently, 'remember what's to be done. If it ain't acted well, you may wave goodbye to your tawny bitch. And if that happens, you know the road she must follow!'

At the centre of the house was a small room, hardly ten feet square. It was furnished with two wooden dining-chairs and a little table. The floor was bare of carpets and there was no light except for the lamp which Dacre had brought with him. In the four walls, there were thin strips of glass, covering chinks that were narrower even than those through which an archer might have fired an arrow from a mediaeval fortress. Morant-Barham moved softly from one to another of these spy-holes, surveying the bedrooms by which Dacre's private apartment was surrounded.

'You might tell a fellow,' he said resentfully.

'Keep a watch, Joey. And listen for every word.'

The spy-holes had never had such use as this evening. Dacre had uncovered those on one wall. They looked upon

85

a room with a fine, ornamental bed covered in maroon silk.
The chairs and sofa were also silk, candy-striped, while the
walls were papered in Regency pillaring of white and gold.
The shaded lights, arranged so that they appeared to
spring upward from the pillars of the design, were golden
torches, held by naked nymphs who earnestly contrived
to embrace one another as well as the phallic lamp. The
gilt-framed pictures upon the walls were almost evenly
divided between representations of men making love to
women, and women making love to one another. The place
of honour among the objets d'art was taken by a copy of
Hiram Potter's sculpture of the Grecian Slavegirl, chastely
naked in her manacles.

Maggie, in linen drawers and bodice, sat on a velvet-
topped stool before a mirror. Jennifer, still in the dark blue
tights and white top, was busily clearing a small occasional
table. She picked up two empty glasses and a long-opened
bottle of Moët et Chandon. Hiding these behind a chest,
she then opened the table drawer and tidied into it a
cylindrical douche and a thin rod. As Dacre and Morant-
Barham looked into the room, there was a light tap at its
door. Dacre motioned Morant-Barham to silence and
closed the shutter on his lamp so that it should not illuminate
the glass spy-hole. At the same time, Maggie and Jennifer
were hastily assuming their places for the performance.
Maggie sat on the stool in her underthings, gazing soulfully
into the glass, while Jennifer stood behind her, the bed-
slave of a blonde young mistress, combing through Maggie's
pale gold curtains of hair.

Almost soundlessly, the door opened to admit Willson
Moore, tall and earnest in his blue evening-coat and fawn
breeches. Everything about him seemed to breathe whole-
someness and decency, from the cleanly-cropped red curls of
his head to the sober boots of a working gentleman. His
pale face was lightly freckled and might almost have been
better placed on a boy of ten than on a man of thirty. He
moved as one on the threshold of a great moral adventure.

At the same time, nothing could have been more calculated to bind Willson Moore to his blonde young mistress and her tawny slave than this present cameo. Maggie, catching his reflection in the glass, rose and turned, covering the bust of her bodice with crossed arms, as though taken unawares by her lover's early arrival. But she hurried towards him, her voice low and lilting rather than raised with excitement.

'Willie! Oh, Willie, thank God you're here! I thought of so many things! Of such dangers you must pass!'

Her face was hidden from Dacre and her words muffled as the young giant folded her in his arms.

'Why, Miss Maggie!' he said presently. 'I guess you thought they'd stop me! I guess you thought them bullies on the door might keep me out! I'd surely like to see·'em try. You wasn't born to be a slave, my sweet. You shall be saved from here any day you choose.'

'Oh, Willie!' The little blonde was running her hands over him from shoulders to hips. 'Oh, Willie! I'm not worth the trouble I've caused you!'

'You!' said the young man gallantly. 'Miss Maggie, you're worth more trouble than there is in the whole world! If next week is the week, you have only to name the day or night. I will be in New York, and I don't care if they invest this building with the United States Marine Corps. I will carry you out of here and you shall be free!'

Maggie had coaxed him toward the bed, on which they now sat.

'Not free, Willie,' she said with her gentle Celtic lilt. 'I shall be yours, to do as you please with. And if Jennifer is my slave, then we shall both be yours. You shall command us as you please.'

Willson Moore swallowed visibly at the prospects which passed before his inner vision. The darker-skinned girl, who had been standing obediently to one side, now stepped forward.

'Take the captain's coat, Jennifer,' said Maggie firmly, 'and hang it in the dressing room.'

Jennifer helped Willson Moore off with the blue evening-coat. As she did so, she raised her modestly lowered eyes and looked directly and meaningly into his own. Then she took the coat into the far room, out of sight of Dacre and Morant-Barham.

'Willie,' said the blonde girl softly, 'Willie, I want you to take this and keep it for both of us. It's not safe with me any longer. If they find it . . .' She tugged at the waist of her bodice and produced a tiny purse.

'I can't, Miss Maggie!' His pale face creased with honest anxiety, 'I can't take money from you like a pimp. . . '

'*Keep* it for me, Willie. Till next Tuesday.'

'Tuesday?' he said quietly. 'That's the day, then?'

She nodded.

'But, Willie, promise me not to tell a soul. Tell no one that you're coming to town, nor that you're to be away. These men, my love, they have friends and spies. There are policemen who are in their pay. On Tuesday, there will only be two of them here. I've got a friend, Willie, who will kick up a row enough to keep them occupied for ten minutes. Then you must break us out, Jenny and me.'

'You shall be fetched out, Miss Maggie, if I have to burn down this house of abomination!' The fierce young lover almost glared at her in his determination. 'And it shall be the day you choose.'

Her hands were busy in his red curls.

'Oh, Willie! Don't fail us. The secret won't keep for another time. You may find us both gone to the same place.'

'What place?' he asked, pulling from her.

'You don't get the town news, my love. There's two men in the Tombs prison, waiting to be hanged, Hicks and Sanchez, for dealing in girls – white and tawny – and using torture and murder. When a girl gets difficult, as they call it in these houses, they send her far away. She has no comfort but her tears, Willie, and no hope but death.'

Willson Moore slipped on to his knees before her.

'Miss Maggie, I swear that they may cut my heart out before I'll let such a thing happen to you, or to little Jennifer.'

The dark-skinned girl, who had prudently remained in the dressing-room during this conversation, now returned.

'Jenny, my love,' said her blonde mistress, 'put this purse into the captain's coat. And, Willie, make sure you count the notes after you go. Count the notes, my love.'

As Jennifer walked back to the dressing-room, out of sight, Dacre cupped his hands over Morant-Barham's ears.

'There's a screw loose, old fellow, I'll swear it. Get Lucifer to send his best light-foot little thief into that dressing-room from the far side door, fetch that purse from the feller's coat, and see what's in it!'

The two girls were giving Willson Moore a foretaste of his bliss to come. As Maggie, lying on the bed, raised her hips and divested herself of the white linen drawers, Jennifer acted the part of their lover's valet. His voice trembled slightly as he turned excitedly to his blonde mistress.

'Miss Maggie,' he gasped, 'there ain't no objection, I guess, to your handsome brown-skinned Jennifer taking off those navy tights and posing where we both might admire her?'

Maggie's answer was to draw her lover down upon her. As the couple embraced, however, the young Asian woman wriggled the dark blue fleshings off and stood proudly beside them, her sturdy young hips smooth and firm, her golden thighs like those of an Eastern goddess. She turned slowly, offering first her soft warm belly to the caresses of master and mistress, then the statuesque hind-cheeks. In an ecstasy of admiration, Willson Moore planted several re-sounding kisses on the tawny body, before Maggie absorbed all his energies.

Verney Dacre watched the easy fool and his two girls with a faint sneer of contempt on his lips. He despised Willson Moore for his honest stupidity, but he felt a vindictive relish at the manner in which he was certain that the two young women had betrayed themselves. Morant-Barham returned with a scrap of paper, extracted by Pauline or Sue from the purse in the blue evening-coat. He slid the shutter of the lamp back by half an inch, trusting his own body to block the light from the spy-hole.

Willie. We are watched, my love. Tuesday is a plan of theirs. We must act sooner. Be in the square before the house on Monday and we will try to come to you. Don't come in or let them see you. They plan to rob you but we will beat them. If we are not with you by ten, Monday night, go to the police department. The man who is here did murder a girl with Hicks and Sanchez. Willie, my love, I can't say this as anything might be overheard. Your devoted girl, Maggie.

Dacre's face tightened, not in anger but in a thin grimace which was his nearest approach to a smile of satisfaction. He motioned Morant-Barham out of the little room which spied so effectively on the others.

'Joey, old fellow, would you say that Lucifer and Cowhide are chaps who might like Maggie and Jennifer all to themselves, under lock and key? If they were assured that no tales would be told afterwards, might not they do the thing very finely?'

Morant-Barham looked uneasy.

'Come now, Joey,' Dacre continued, brushing his fair moustaches thoughtfully, 'a man can't let his stomach turn at the first skirmish. There ain't but one choice for those two doxies now.'

He walked down the deep pile of the stair-carpet, the ground-glass lamps of the gas-pillars harshly illuminating his way. He spoke to the two bullies. A broad grin creased Cowhide's mulatto face. The feminine pallor of Lucifer's expression was quickly animated by the eagerness of bright little eyes. Clean and wholesome, Willson Moore took his innocent departure.

Neither Maggie nor Jennifer had bothered to dress. It was now the tawny Asian bed-slave who lay on the silk covers, her fair mistress toiling over her with fingers steeped in scented oils. Maggie's blonde hair almost brushed the Moslem girl's nudity as she worked the oil over the responsive breasts, belly and thighs. She turned her patient gently over, massaging the golden indentations of the spine lingeringly, reaching the cool double-swell of the rump, her hands moulding and stirring the olive-skinned cheeks of Jennifer's bottom.

Cowhide and Lucifer burst in without ceremony, causing Jennifer to roll over and Maggie to draw away. Dacre unfolded the paper in the blonde girl's face.

'There ain't further explanation needed for what must happen now,' he said contemptuously. 'You shall both go into the keeping of Lucifer and his man. You shall serve them in a very private place until the present matter is over. You shall deny them nothing. And when I have the leisure, by God you shall answer to me!'

Jennifer maintained her dark-eyed defiance of the men, but Maggie's eyes showed that she recalled too easily the scandals of Dacre's conduct in Langham Place with Miss Jolly. Cowhide escorted Jennifer through a doorway to an inner room. Maggie, following in Lucifer's grasp, turned to implore the man who had so lately been her bedfellow. Dacre dismissed her with a glance.

'See to it the door is stopped tight,' he told Lucifer, 'and the house ain't woken by caterwaulin'.'

The closing panel muted a wail of depair.

'Here's a pretty pickle!' said Morant-Barham uneasily.

'Why should y' say that? We might have swung for those two whores, Joey. But they ain't to be croaked, not even to be hurt. They shall stay fast in there till no harm can come from them. Then, Joey, when the dodge has been pulled, you shall have your Khan doxy and Mag too if you choose. They won't be needed further, old fellow. Ain't you seen Willson Moore, private secretary at the Mint, and God's own fool if ever there was such? Ain't he happy? Then keep those two bitches tight, here and in Philadelphia, and you shall have them both.'

'They won't be snuffed, then?'

'Joey, Joey! I ain't a complete fool! There's no cause to snuff 'em when there's no harm they can do. And suppose the case should alter and we must show Mag as bait, we should curse ourselves for hanging her a week earlier!'

'If Willson Moore don't play . . .' said Morant-Barham, taking up that line of thought.

'Play, Joey? He shall play and never know it. When Captain Moore takes one step from Philadelphia to New York, the trap is sprung.'

'A dishonest fellow would have served us better than that canting fool. A villain can be used, and bent, and made to pull weight.'

'Ah, well,' said Dacre philosophically, 'if you care to think so, you may. When you've eaten more vittels, however, you'll find that it ain't villains who trap easiest. There's no easier game than a cove that thinks himself honest.'

In order not to rouse Joey Barham's anxieties one upon another, Dacre reserved his other revelation until noon on the following day. They were at lunch in a private room of the river-steamer which carried them up the Hudson to Verney Dacre's modest Westchester estate.

'Joey, old fellow, it's best you should know the whole account. It seems the police-fellers over here know that I'm alive still, after all that London nonsense. They take it *au sérieux*.'

Morant-Barham, on the far side of the table, spat a mouthful of ham back on to his plate.

'What?'

'Lie easy, Joey, there's not proof of it. They think it, and they expect to go to work one day and find all the bank-vaults in America empty!'

'How should you know what they think?'

Dacre took a long swill of hock and seltzer.

'First, Joey, His Royal Highness, the Prince of Wales is guarded by a London policeman, a fat fool who stumbled on the dodge with the railway bullion in England. It seems he had a fight with a New York constable, and a paragraph in the papers to show it.'

'What's that to you?'

'Hold hard, Joey. It might be no odds for him to be here.

But there's a girl who was once mine, a Miss Jolly. After Harper's Ferry and Charley Temple not dying sweet as we hoped, Miss Jolly is fetched to New York. She's seen by the putters-up of burglaries going the rounds of jewellers' shops and looking as if she might be giving them the run. But she gives her real name and nothing is taken. She has her likeness snapped and framed in the window of a Broadway studio. Now, Joey, even in New York, a story like that is round the parish in a few days.'

'Is it her?'

'Oh, yes, old fellow. A speaking likeness. Smallish-built and trim. Golden skin, dark hair worn straight back and lacquered, eyes a bit on the slant and brown as Miss Jennifer's. A sharp little nose and a randy walk.'

Morant-Barham chanced another mouthful of ham. He spoke through it.

'I still don't see, old fellow, what it is to us.'

'This,' said Dacre fiercely. 'I am here as a fugitive because of Miss Jolly. She was mine, and I ploughed her every way. Then she crossed me after the gold robbery. I had two bullies then as well. In my presence, they took her things off and horsed her. Then they took their turns with the rod and raised a few dozen welts across Miss Jolly's backside.'

'I still don't see . . .' Morant-Barham began, but Dacre's glittering eyes silenced him.

'When they had done with her, Joey, I should have swung her. That was my mistake. The little whore got loose a few days after and sang the whole bloody cantata. Now they think I mayn't be dead and there's a trap set for me, with that randy little piece as the bait. They know I must have her for my revenge. And I will!'

He handed Joey Barham a printed paper.

GENTLEMEN'S RELISH!!!

By Private Auction on Saturday the 13th next
Aboard the FIDÈLE steamboat, now mooring at ST LOUIS!

TWELVE FANCY GIRLS!

(Light and quadroon)
Thro' Private Treaty of a Gentleman's Creditors!
UNDER THE HAMMER OF MONSIEUR VIGNIE
OF THE NEW ORLEANS ROTUNDA!
(Whole bids and unreserved)

At two o'clock in the afternoon, punctual
'MISS JOLLY'
A Feast for all Choice Spirits
Broken in by an English aristocrat – Two thousand
dollars refused in private negotiation! – Light-
coloured – Petite – Beauty of the Orient – Every
Man's Fancy in Reality – Will sell again high!

At half-past two o'clock exactly:
NABYLA
All the Perfumes of Arabia
High-stepper – Jewel of the Harem – Ready-trained . . .

Morant-Barham's sunburnt features creased in a fierce
frown.

'They might know you're alive,' he said firmly, 'but it's
plain as day they don't know exactly where and they don't
know what you plan. If they had an idea about Philadelphia, they'd never wait until afterwards to stage this
slave-girl caper.'

'They shall know in good time,' said Dacre, almost
dreamily.

Morant-Barham put down his knife and fork.

'Know? Know what?'

'Joey,' said Dacre patiently, 'emptying the vaults is one
thing. But it ain't the greatest pleasure a man can have.
If the world can't know that I did it, then to me the thing's
not worth trying. Where's the charm of passing doors that
can't be opened and emptying the gold vaults of the Federal
Mint, if it's never to be known who worked the miracle?

By God, Joey, can't y' see the joy of it! Walkin' free in the eyes of the whole world of prigs – and not a law that can harm us. There ain't a work of art in the world, Joey, that can touch such a cracksman's masterpiece as this! There ain't the pleasure in any woman's body that a fellow would trade for such delight!'

Dacre's narrow blue eyes burnt with a glacial fire, his thin frame and spoilt face consumed by enthusiasm. Morant-Barham observed a tactful silence, working with his knife and fork. At length he said casually: 'Then you shan't go near the trap where Miss Jolly lies as bait?'

Dacre blinked, as if breaking his own trance, and looked at his companion with sharp surprise.

'Oh, but I must keep the rendezvous, Joey. When their vaults are empty, I must steal the bait from their trap too. I wouldn't miss their auction for a second mint of bullion!'

'Why?' Joey Barham's hands beat petulantly on the table. 'Why? To put it all in chancery for a slant-eyed little whore!'

'Ah!' said Dacre gently. 'It ain't that. First, however, she *did* cross me, Joey, and there ain't a pleasure sweeter with her than vengeance. This time, she shall have her skin taken off in such ways as shall make her bless the man who lets her taste the noose at last. But it ain't that, my dear fellow. The exquisite part is in letting them bait the trap, taking the prey, and showing them that they've been twice beaten!'

'The risk,' Morant-Barham muttered. 'It don't excuse the risk!'

'A fellow that's in rut don't excuse himself, Joey. Did you ever excuse yourself when you topped and tailed that young Khan bitch? Did you beg pardon from blonde Maggie when you stoked her to extinction? Believe me, Joey, you must see it that way for me. I'm in rut for that gold! I'm in rut for skinning that little bitch Jolly! And I'm in rut for the world to know what I have done! And it may cut its guts on envy before it shall be able to lay a hand on my shoulder over it!'

95

9

The two British staff officers were distinctly recognizable by their scarlet tunics, gilded epaulettes, and the white plumes of their cocked hats. A small crowd had gathered outside the Chestnut Street entrance of the Continental Hotel, the newest and most splendid of its kind in Philadelphia. It rose, massive and Italianate at the corner of Chestnut and Ninth Street like the fortified palace of some latter-day Medici. Its ground-floor façade, however, was graced by finely-wrought cast-iron arcading, which supported the balconies of the first-floor rooms. In the September sun, several of the little shops and ticket offices, which occupied the street-level, had pulled out their awnings.

The crowd had been attracted in the first place by the smartly painted Clapps two-wheeler, glossily panelled in royal blue, which stood awaiting the two officers at the hotel entrance. It was one of several such vehicles seen in the city of late, its doors bearing a small and discreet emblem, embodying a gold crown and three white feathers above the words *Ich Dien*. The two officers lowered their heads gingerly and entered the closed carriage. As the two-wheeler pulled out into the traffic, where the horse-drawn buses on their iron rails occupied the centre of the broad avenue, the little crowd settled down again. Sooner or later one of the smart carriages would return to the hotel bearing the young man whom they had all waited so long to see. They had already had one extra stroke of fortune in seeing Colonel Dempster and Major Morant enter the carriage. The mere equerries of a Prince warranted some attention in themselves.

As these thoughts passed through the minds of the watchers at the Continental, Colonel Dempster was removing his cocked hat and addressing his companion.

'Now, Joey, breathe deep, mumble if you must speak at all to them, and have the goodness to leave the rest of the business to me.'

Morant-Barham sniggered nervously as the two men sat in unaccustomed silence, the light catching their wine-coloured sashes, and the golden fringes of their epaulettes jigging at the movement of the carriage-wheels. The large fortress-like stores of Philadelphia, with their canvas awnings and plate-glass, shone like marble in the sun.

Verney Dacre's heart raced with the exhilaration of it all, and his pride swelled within him at the perfection of the design.

'If a fellow was to ask the Federal Mint for a peck of bullion,' he had said a dozen times, 'damme, they might want our pedigrees longer than your arm. But who ever heard of pedigrees being questioned when a fellow asks for nothing, except that the Mint should be pleased to take a present of gold with his best compliments?'

Morant-Barham had agreed the ripeness of the scheme, and indeed he saw now why men spoke of Verney Dacre as they did. There was nothing to raise the least suspicion or question, quite the reverse, unless a man were so churlish as to suspect a free gift of royal gold, or so unmannerly as to refuse a Prince hospitality who had just been the guest of President Buchanan himself, and had been cheered by tens of thousands in the nation's streets.

It was no more than half a mile from the Continental to the marble temple which housed the Mint. The two-wheeler stopped at the Chestnut Street portico with its six Ionic pillars and its grand pediment. Verney Dacre, in colonel's full-dress, marched stiffly up the steps, followed by Morant-Barham, smartly returning the salutes of the two military guards at the door. Once inside, Dacre tipped his cocked hat forward from his head and lodged it ceremonially under his left arm. They now stood in the semi-circular vestibule, confronting a frock-coated man in his late fifties. Dacre brought his heels together and gave a slight bowing inclination.

The older man made his own nod of acknowledgement and extended his hand.

'James Ross Snowden, sir, Director of the United States

97

Federal Mint. My private secretary, Captain Willson Moore.'

'Servant, sir,' said Verney Dacre smartly, his words more clipped than ever in a parody of his normal speech. 'Colonel Villiers Dempster, 10th Prince of Wales Hussars, Master of Horse to His Royal Highness. Major Morant, Royal Horse Artillery, attached to His Royal Highness's staff.'

There was further inclining of heads and an exchange of formal greetings. Snowden led the way, between two lines of admiring subordinates, along the vaulted passageway to the marble staircase at the end of the south wing. Verney Dacre felt a swelling joy at the realization that his map of the building was proving accurate in every detail. At the head of the marble staircase, as he had expected, were the handsome double-doors of Snowden's office, in light polished oak. The interior was lit by tall windows opening on a wide and sunny prospect of Chestnut Street, the carpet deep crimson, the leather chairs in autumnal bronze. Even the wide partners' desk and the cabinets were precisely at the point indicated on Charley Temple's plan.

Dacre was filled by a surge of exultation which swept aside all sense of fear, or even of self-preservation. His blood raced at the thought that the gold would be his, followed by the exquisite satisfaction of having the satiny, copper skin off Miss Jolly for her treachery. What more could a man of sense ask for? He took the monocle which hung on its black lace, screwed it into his eye, and played his part with vigour. Drawing himself up, tall and slim in his scarlet and gold braid, he addressed Snowden.

'I have th' honour, sir, to be commanded by His Royal Highness, Albert Edward, Prince of Wales, – aw – on th' occasion of his visit to Philadelphia, to – aw – present to the United States Federal Mint a gift in recognition of the strong – ah – binding affiliation 'f two peoples' trade and manufacture. Major Morant, oblige me, if you please!'

Joey Morant-Barham stamped forward to attention,

holding a plain oak box, rather larger than the size of a brick. Dacre took it from him and stamped about to face Snowden. He opened the lid of the box to reveal a fourteen-pound gold ingot with an ornamental edging and a carved inscription.

ROYAL MINT

23 VICTORIA R.

24 CARAT

Presented to the United States Federal
Mint by His Royal Highness Albert Edward,
Prince of Wales, on the occasion of his
reception at Philadelphia, the 9th of
October 1860, in the Directorship of
James Ross Snowden, Esquire

The metal glowed a deeper shade, like burnished copper, in the maroon velvet lining of its box. Snowden, though prepared to receive the gift, was moved almost beyond words by the discovery that his own name had been coupled with that of the Prince for all posterity. Dacre listened politely to his full-throated appreciation, still letting his eyes wander over the handsomely furnished room. The bait had cost him more than a thousand dollars, or rather it represented almost all that remained from the great bullion robbery on the South Eastern Railway in 1857. But, he told himself, a fellow that angled for two or three million was not to begrudge such a bauble. Especially when he had every intention of stealing the bauble back, once the main business was concluded.

Presently Snowden was escorting his two visitors volubly to the little museum of coins which, as Dacre's map had promised, lay along the corridor from his office. In the central courtyard of the Mint, the air was heavy with the hot mineral smell of molten gold. Dacre caught a breath of it in his nostrils and his heart beat faster at the memory and the promise. In the little museum, Snowden fluttered from cabinet to cabinet, displaying his treasures.

99

'And here, sir, we have the widow's mite, the very coin of which the Bible speaks – a mighty rare specimen. . . Here the Greek republics, Aegina, Athens . . . and here, sir, is Darius, and there Alexander. . .'

Dacre peered down from his height at the insignificant flakes of metal and made the replies which might be expected of him.

'Very fine, sir . . . aw, exquisite, damme . . . deuced fine, though, ain't it, Morant?'

They came to the end of the cabinets and he assumed command of the conversation.

'Y'have a noble city here, sir. A man might go far and never see such agreeable buildings, nor meet such crack society. Crack society, sir. The Prince has long been determined for Philadelphia, sir. Regrets only that he must travel incog as Baron Renfrew in your country, by Her Majesty's wish, of course.'

'We shall be honoured by his presence under any title, sir,' said Snowden, his wire glasses gleaming as he turned a sharp, birdlike face to Dacre. 'We regret only that His Royal Highness has not leisure enough to visit us at the Mint and see our little acquisitions.'

'Regrettable, sir,' said Dacre, mournful and sincere. 'But he shall hear of it, sir, from me. Never fear that. Indeed, I have a commission to execute on his behalf in which it is possible you might incur His Highness's obligation.'

'I should be glad to know of it,' said Snowden hopefully.

Dacre looked about him, as though anxious not to be overheard.

'You must know, Mr. Snowden, that in the course of such a tour, with the good-will and the ceremony, many gifts are given and received by His Royal Highness. As he leaves Washington, for Philadelphia, then for New York and Boston, the sealed boxes must accompany him. Tomorrow night they must rest in Philadelphia, the gifts and the presents. In Washington, where we have our Embassy, they were no embarrassment. In Philadelphia, we have nowhere but the Prince's suite at the Continental

Hotel. Truth, sir, there is nowhere the six boxes might lie safer or more convenient for that night than in your own vault. . .'

'Why, Colonel Dempster!' Snowden regarded Dacre with that faint, smiling disparagement which might have indicated that Dacre should either have known better than to ask, or should not have hesitated to put the request.

'It is an imposition, sir,' said Dacre humbly, 'aw – imposition, damme.'

'No!' Snowden shook his head, 'No imposition whatever, sir!'

'You must make whatever restrictions are usual, sir,' said Dacre firmly. 'You are not to be put to inconvenience in the matter. His Royal Highness is positive as to that. For my part, it is only to see the boxes delivered to you under seal tomorrow morning, and to obtain them from you again on the morning after.'

'Name your wish, sir!' said Snowden earnestly. 'Only name it!'

'The Prince asks only one other,' Dacre looked about him again cautiously. 'It is that you alone and your most trusted lieutenants should know of this matter.'

'Our stronghold is safe enough,' said Snowden, taken aback.

'To be sure it is, sir, but the boxes must come and go. There might the danger lie. If all the world were honest, sir, I should not have to ask this. But it ain't, damme. It ain't at all.'

By this time, the three men were walking back down the marble staircase. Dacre had expected to be led politely off the premises but to his delight Snowden was obviously intent on showing off the security in which the royal treasures might be kept. Returning to the circular vestibule at the main entrance, they turned inward, following the sunken passageway to the secrets of the Mint itself.

The great steel doors were there, just as the plan had indicated. Painted in the pale grey of an ironclad, they stood open with an armed and uniformed guard at either side. The thickness of the steel was impressive, Dacre allowed that. He even glimpsed the little keyhole, no more than an inch high, which was shuttered by the steel plate and its time-lock from dusk until dawn. If anything, he had under-estimated the strength of these main doors. Once they were locked, almost airtight, across the vaulted passage, a ton of gunpowder might do no more than pit their surface. Behind him walked Morant-Barham and Willson Moore, the former replying with hums and murmurs to Moore's attempts at conversation.

They passed the weighing-rooms, where the bullion was entered in the records of the Mint. Another metal door opened at Snowden's touch and they stood before the searing brilliance of the furnaces in the refining shop. Four of these were set into the opposite wall, like square, open ovens, molten gold simmering on top of the crucibles inside, above its deposit of silver. The refiners in their shirt-sleeves stood at each furnace with long-handled dipping-cups, scooping out the liquid gold and tipping it into zinc vats of water, like sparkling fire. Dacre's eyes filled at the white heat of the ovens, whose flames roared in concealment behind the ventilation grill. Yet through the haze of tears he noted the two furnaces which were unlit and knew that Charley Temple's informant had not misled him.

Beyond the refining-shop, with its hot metallic air, the corroding-house was laden with steam from the porcelain vats where the golden granules hissed in hot nitric acid. The fumes, which rose in a bright golden fog, were collected by an overhanging metal 'umbrella' and drawn into the upward draught of the chimney. Several men, in leather jerkins and hats to protect their hair from the fumes, stirred the bubbling acid with long wooden pokers. To one side of this, set back in a narrow recess, was a chimney-hatch, giving access to the flue. Dacre, nodding and making agreeable comments on Snowden's description of such ingenuities, gave his mind to plotting the intricacies of the next day.

After the refining process, the Mint assumed the character

of any other engineering works. There was a casting-shop'
with a smaller, arched furnace, bricked into the wall,
where the gold was melted again and poured into the empty
upright moulds of the ingots, which stood in rows on low
trolleys to receive the precious fluid. Beyond that was the
great expanse of the rolling-room, with its massive mill
powered by two broad iron wheels on each side, large
enough to have driven a ship. Dacre watched in fascination
as the brick-like ingots were drawn in by the broad-rimmed
iron wheels and pressed into long slim strips of metal,
thin enough for the coins to be punched from them.

The muffled thunder of the steam-driven rolling-mill
gave way to the metallic chatter of the coining shop, where
men who looked like clerks sat on high stools at what
seemed to be church organs. Into the base of these, where
the keyboard might have been, they fed the thin strips of
gold, using their free hand to regulate the mechanical
punch of the stamp. The metallic clatter and the trickle of
blank coins into boxes rattled endlessly about the great
shop. Finally came the subdued female murmur of the
weighing-room, where the punched coins were checked by
thirty or forty girls, each sitting at her little table with a
pair of scales before her.

Snowden led the way to the far entrance of the room,
through which no one but he and his confidants ever passed.
Another steel door, as massive as those at the vestibule
entrance, stood before them. This one was closed across the
arched passageway and boasted no keyhole. There was a
single knob projecting from the centre of the door, let in
from the far side so that its screws and edging were inacces-
sible to any burglar. Dacre looked politely away as Snowden
clicked the knob round, first one way and than another.
He took hold of a bar across the door and, with an effort,
opened it.

Inside this door was the stronghold, a dozen or more
bullion boxes bound with iron bands and bearing a stamped
seal across their locks. In one wall was an iron door with a
large inset key-lock.

'Depending on the size of your boxes, sir,' said Snowden doubtfully, 'they might be fitted into the vault itself. But if they can't fit, would you find our stronghold here to be satisfactory?'

'More than that, sir,' said Dacre effusively. 'Why, sir, the jewels that lie in your stronghold shall be safer than in the Tower of London.'

'Without disrespect to your Tower, sir,' said Snowden with a polite smirk, 'we like to think such things may be as safe here.'

He led the way back through the various processes of coining and refining. Before the main steel doors, he paused while two uniformed guards patted him down in a rapid search. Director of the Mint he might be, but it was more than their jobs were worth to let him know that any man could leave the vaults with the contents of his pockets unchallenged. Dacre and Morant-Barham submitted to the same indignity, followed by Willson Moore whose honest, lightly freckled face coloured slightly at the very thought of being suspected.

'You see, sir?' said Snowden cheerfully. 'Even I am not my own master here. Merely the servant of the Treasury Department. And now, sir, I bid you good-day. I regret that I cannot be here tomorrow to receive you myself, but Captain Moore will attend to all your needs. I shall do myself the honour of waiting upon you when you return to collect His Royal Highness's treasures.'

Verney Dacre brought his heels together and ducked his head.

'Servant, sir!'

Morant-Barham imitated the same parody of acknowledgement. The two men took their leave, striding smartly and in step down the approach of the Grecian portico.

Inside the carriage, Dacre threw off his plumed hat, rolled back against the dark buttoned leather, and threw up his fists with a cry.

'By God, Joey! We're in! Devil take me if that crib ain't as good as cracked already! Huzzah for Charley Temple!

He never knew the turn he did us, but it's every inch the
way his doxy showed it to be, walls, flues, drains, the whole
damn show!'

'I do hope so, old fellow,' said Morant-Barham, his sunburnt cheeks flushing under his dark whiskers. 'I don't
even care for standing in the beastly place. Gives a man a
mouth that's dry as a whore's cranny for a pull of hock-and-
seltzer.'

Dacre crowed in his delight.

'Dammit, Joey, but ain't it a prize? Did y' never see such
yaller goold? Damn great lumps of the stuff, big as a dray-
man's skull? The smell and the touch of it! I don't care, old
fellow, if I must be hanged for it. I can't cry off now, no
more than you could jump off your handsome young Khan
bitch when you know you must spend or be damned! There
ain't a whore in the world that can pleasure a man in his
mind with such beauty!'

For all his flushed excitement, it seemed that Morant-
Barham was by far the cooler of the pair, Dacre's eyes now
glittering with an almost insane zeal.

'Joey,' he said, the whisper almost a hiss of madness,
'come tomorrow, y' may have to black your face if the
worst happens. It ain't likely but y' may. I think, however,
I was right. I'm in already. What I've got under the seat of
this very cabriolet shall melt steel doors and burst time-
locks in two. Damme if it shan't tell one number in a million
on the figure-lock, and have the last gold coin out of the
stronghold and into our pockets!'

'Oh?' said Morant-Barham sceptically. 'And what might
you have there?'

Dacre reached down under the seat and gave an energetic
tug. He handed to Morant-Barham a bundle of three old
and rather dirty sacks.

By the time they reached the Florentine fortress of the Hotel
Continental once more, all Morant-Barham's ill humour
had vanished and he was roaring with delight at the scheme.

'Whores in hellfire!' he bellowed, deeply flushed, eyes

105

swimming and mouth agape. 'Ain't it a tickler? Dear God, Dacre, old fellow, they're on the hip and they don't know it!'

The two men composed themselves in order to step out into the sunshine as tall, slim and dignified staff officers, marching briskly under the hotel canopy and disappearing into the cooler and darker interior. It was left to Cowhide, as coachman, to drive round the corner, strip the transfer of the royal insignia from the door panels, and return the carriage to the livery stables.

Dacre and Morant-Barham strode quickly across the blue-carpeted lobby of the great hotel, where travellers lounged on gilt sofas behind the *New York Herald* or the *Pennsylvania Chronicle*, gaining the broad flight of stairs with their polished mahogany rail and the ascending pillars of the gas-globes at either side. Such comings and goings had grown so frequent in the Continental itself that they were already less noticed. The two men strode up the curving stairway to the third floor, where 'Colonel Dempster's suite' lay at the end of a carpeted passageway and behind two sets of doors.

Lucifer, his pale effeminate face watching anxiously through the crevice of the doors, opened them at their approach. Neither he nor Cowhide was privileged to share the details of Dacre's plan. They knew only that it had something to do with bleeding Captain Willson Moore of his fortune by blackmail, which necessarily involved confronting him at his place of work. The suite at the Continental was, in effect, a length of one corridor, sealed off from the rest and self-contained behind its locked double doors. In its rooms, Maggie and Jennifer languished, under the constant care of Lucifer and two minor accomplices of the slave-dealer Hicks: Raoul and Bull-Peg.

Dacre hardly paused to look at Lucifer, striding on into his own rooms with Morant-Barham, stripping off the uniform and tossing its items on to the bed. Lucifer hurried after him.

'Well?' snapped Dacre, stripped to his shirt. 'Don't I pay my way, then?'

He tossed a small purse of gold coins to Lucifer, who caught it fumblingly.

'Keep it,' said Dacre, more civilly. 'The poor mark had nothing more in his pockets. He shall bleed rich, however!'

Lucifer shook his head.

'It ain't that, captain, it ain't that at all. Only he sent a note to you here that was given in not five minutes ago.'

Dacre snatched the envelope from Lucifer's hand and ripped it open.

Captain Willson Moore presents his compliments to Colonel Dempster and does himself the honour of looking forward to receiving Colonel Dempster's visit and instructions tomorrow in the forenoon. Captain Moore, standing engaged the latter part of the morning, would take it as a particular personal obligation if Colonel Dempster should find it convenient to call upon their mutual concerns before eleven o' clock.

Dacre crumpled the paper in his hand in an ecstasy of triumph. He swung round upon Morant-Barham, his mouth distorted in a rictus of delight, and contempt for Willson Moore.

'The honest little sprat!' he snorted. 'Damned if he ain't took the bait and pin right into his gut! Only ask the desk-boy downstairs, Joey. I swear y' shall find a feller that would be in New York tomorrow night, to save young Miss Maggie from perdition, must be away from here at eleven in the morning to catch his train!'

Joey Morant-Barham smacked one fist into his other palm, joining Dacre's laughter.

'Trust me Joey – and see if it don't all go smooth as milady's rump!'

Later that evening, Dacre drew on his gloves. Morant-Barham opened a door to the room where the assistants of Lucifer and Cowhide kept watch. Raoul was sleek and swarthy, Bull-Peg a pink and white giant whose skull was smooth as an egg. To these rooms, in private suites with private servants, no hotel flunkey ever penetrated. Dacre

107

had chosen this one as a luxuriously furnished cell.

While their guards sprawled in a pair of cane chairs, Maggie and Jennifer lay on the two beds, staring into space. Morant-Barham came, as usual, before setting off with Dacre. He hoped to be remembered by the girls, when they came into his possession, as the friend who had protected them during the time of their greatest danger. To make escape doubly difficult, both young women had been left with no clothing but their white singlets. Maggie lay on her side, knees drawn up and her back to her warders, hands pressed together between her thighs. Jennifer was on her belly, her head resting on her folded arms. The manner in which her singlet was pulled up at the back betrayed Lucifer's vindictiveness after the attempt to betray Dacre to Willson Moore.

Morant-Barham's heart beat faster at the sight, and at the knowledge that in a few days more the girls would both be his. Even now, as he stood between the beds, both girls turned inward towards him. He spoke softly, promising them safety from any malice by their guards, and that when they were his he would be the lover of both, as they should continue to be lovers themselves. He took Maggie's pale hand, which she gave easily and limply, and led it to stroke Jennifer's face. The Asian girl, in a frenzy of hope and reliance upon him, took his own free hand and kissed it eagerly. Morant-Barham vowed softly to them that he would not only allow their mutual affection to blossom, he would encourage it by every means. Maggie, in return, promised herself as his woman, while Jennifer whispered pledges of love in its more exotic forms, which almost stopped Morant-Barham's breath at the thought of them.

'Dammit if you ain't the luckiest of all,' said Dacre at the head of the stairs, 'dammit if you ain't!'

Morant-Barham gave a modest laugh. Dacre, at the hotel entrance, clapped on his tall hat and glanced at the street bunting which proclaimed a royal visit.

'Right and tight, Joey! And now, seeing there ain't a jewel more precious in the world than loyalty, let's show these fellows that we ain't to be outdone in the matter!'

Like many thoroughfares in Philadelphia, Juniper Street had lately been disfigured by the drab wooden telegraph poles which marched in two ranks down either side. The telegraph, which had linked Boston to New Orleans, was a mixed benefit. On the occasion of a royal visit, however, the citizens had quickly used the poles to suspend ribbons and banners of welcome. These were mingled with other displays proclaiming the imminent triumph of Lincoln and the Republican party in the Pennsylvania poll, whose result was to be proclaimed on the very evening of the Prince of Wales's arrival.

As the autumn dusk began to gather on the day before, the workmen of the city were still occupied in the last preparations, with bunting and ribbons in red, white and blue. Two men, on either side of Juniper Street, were engaged in hoisting a bold canvas banner so that it might swing between two of the poles. Its trite good wishes GOD BLESS THE PRINCE OF WALES! were mirrored on a thousand other strips of canvas and in the thumping rhythms of the brass bands who prepared for His Highness's welcome with the now familiar song.

On the more westerly of the two poles, the workman in his dark clothes was high above the deserted roadway, which seemed an oasis of calm by contrast with the brightly-lit and fashionable pavements of Chestnut Street no more than twenty or thirty yards away. He made fast the end of the banner. Only at this height was it apparent that the banner was not a single strip of cloth, as might have been supposed, but a double-sided slogan which was in effect a long canvas cylinder. Nor was it held by mere cords, a stout strip of wire being stitched under its upper surface, running from post to post.

Verney Dacre finished his adjustments. Holding his position by the pressure of his knees on the post, he drew out a fine, spidery wire, which disappeared into the recesses of the canvas tunnel. The wire was weighted at its free end

109

with a cloth-bound ball of wood, about the bulk of a large apple. The telegraph pole stood several feet away from the guttering of the building on that side of Juniper Street. The roof itself, enclosed by a low parapet was not quite flat, having a slight tiled slope running to either side. For aesthetic reasons, however, this departure from classical form was easily hidden by the little parapet from those who viewed the building at street level. Beyond the peak of the roof rose an even more unclassical chimney. But it was hardly four feet above roof level on the far side of the tiled expanse. This ensured that it too was concealed from street level, though its presence was betrayed by a steady column of smoke in a changing variety of colours.

Making allowances for the awkward twist of his body, Dacre aimed with care and with great gentleness. A fool would have been too vigorous, he told himself, and would have spoilt the game. He lobbed the padded ball and heard it land softly, just on the far slope of the roof, where it ran down and bumped gently in the hidden gutter. It was not as he had wished in every detail, but it would do. The thin wire between the ball and the canvas banner would hardly have been visible on the brightest day at ten feet, let alone at twenty feet in the middle of the night.

Gingerly, he descended the post and found Joey Morant-Barham waiting for him on the far side. Dacre gasped, as much with the relief of tension as from any exertion.

'The bird's in the coop, old chum! Dammit, Joey, I shall be in no end of a wax if it's all as easy as this! Where's the fun if a fellow ain't stretched over a furlong or two?'

'Should you like to stand here and come to smash?' said the younger subaltern sourly. 'Or shall we get the business done?'

Dacre laughed at Morant-Barham's sudden fierceness, following him to the far side of the road. On this side, Juniper Street remained what it had been for more than fifty years, a row of ramshackle tenements still overlooked in the ostentatious rebuilding of the prosperous 1850s. As the main thoroughfares of the city had grown in importance, the old houses of the little streets had become motley apartments for clerks, artisans and decayed gentlefolk. The occupants of each floor, with their brawling families and whining children, lived on threadbare carpets or bare boards, indifferent to the welfare of their neighbours. Dacre might have bought out any household in the district, but he had contented himself with the upper and attic floors of the present house. In the two lower storeys and the basement, the crowded families shrilled and squabbled. As he and Morant-Barham climbed the bare communal staircase, a woman's voice shrieked wildly.

'Have a care! The boy's on the stairs with the dog again!'

They saw no dog and no boy before they reached their own floor and Dacre closed the door behind him.

'The window, Joey! See where we stand!'

From the lower of the two rooms which they occupied, the banner was slightly above them and several feet further down the street, as well as being a yard or more out from the wall of the building.

'That's as near muffing it as any cove might come!' said Morant-Barham nervously.

Dacre leant over the sill, stretched, and caught the wire where it wavered in mid-air.

'May I muff it as well next time, old fellow. The rest is held by nothing but a loop of cord on that post, which a flick with a pole might dislodge. And if it don't, Joey, tie a taper to the pole and burn it off! It ain't likely to catch the canvas alight but if it should, you shall have it at arm's length and may quench it at leisure.'

'Well, old boy,' said Morant-Barham softly, 'I do hope so!'

'It looks like enough a banner, don't it?' Dacre inquired. 'May I be shot if there was ever so fine a thing as loyalty for filling a man's purse. And now, open the basket over there, Joey, like a good fellow. I swear I may be famished if I don't get a glass of cham and a wing of chicken soon.'

111

The wagon which moved slowly down Chestnut Street in the early sun looked more like a pauper's hearse than any other form of conveyance. It was long and dark with frosted designs upon its windows, even the two black geldings which pulled it moving at a funeral pace among the brightly-painted carriages and the lumbering horse-buses on their central rails. Morant-Barham broke the silence with a nervous, braying laugh.

'To think that a fellow might crack such a crib with three old sacks for his jemmy! They ain't likely to believe it, Dacre, not even if it was to be told them in a yard of letterpress.'

Dacre remained tense and moody.

'It ain't sacks, Joey, it's what rules a man's head and eats his heart. Don't I tell you that the picks to the finest locks are always made of flesh and blood? And a man that will be master of that must make slaves for himself, whether the law wishes it or not.'

He nodded cursorily at a muddle of posters, plastered one on top of the other on a derelict wall, the name LINCOLN standing out from the blur of words in bold black type.

'Ain't Maggie as much my slave as the handsome young Khan bitch?' he inquired. 'And must I have a law to make it so?'

Morant-Barham sat in silent disapproval of this reference to Jennifer. Presently, Cowhide reined in the horses. His two passengers, both dressed in black suits and silk hats, got down from the coach and walked in step up the approach to the portico of the Mint. The military guard at either side of the door stared impassively, but alert, at the black vehicle with its precious cargo.

Willson Moore, his auburn curls uncovered and his anxious face creasing into a sudden smile of relief, welcomed them. Dacre bowed in the same clipped parody of his normal manner as he had used the day before.

'Why, sir,' he said, 'may I be damned if I remembered to ask Mr Snowden about the gold key yesterday.'

'Key, sir?' Captain Moore's young face was a study in shifting impatience.

'Damme, sir, for the box with the royal ingot. Ain't it got a key?'

With almost unceremonious speed, Moore led them up the marble staircase to the offices and sent for the box.

'Deuce take it,' said Dacre with every show of vexation, 'no key. Never fear, sir, one shall be fetched for you tomorrow. It ain't in your curator's charge, by chance? A fellow can hardly open the casket without it.'

Moore swung round and questioned the man who had brought it.

'Very well, sir,' said Dacre conclusively. 'No key. Be sure, sir, I shall have it for you when I come tomorrow.'

They moved back downstairs, where two blue-uniformed guards had now taken up position at the rear of the wagon with a low trolley. Dacre gave a command to Cowhide and, like the hearse it resembled, the wagon was opened at the back.

'Six boxes, sir,' said Dacre to Moore. 'You are to make such stipulation as you wish about 'em. They are sealed, sir, but the Prince is positive the seals must be broke open if you choose.'

'Mr Snowden left no instruction as to that,' said Moore, nervous and hasty.

'To be sure, sir, nor he did to my knowledge.'

The first two boxes, the size of coffins and black-lacquered, were lifted down gently on to the trolley. They bore the familiar gold crown and white plume on their glossy sides. The new brass locks were sealed over with blood-red wax which bore the same impress. Dacre and Morant-Barham followed the Mint porters and the trolley up the planks which had been laid on the shallow steps. Willson Moore walked self-consciously at their side. At the semi-circular vestibule, Moore merely acknowledged the

113

guardians of the open steel doors and his party passed between them. To enter the Mint was comparatively easy in this way, but even for Moore himself there was no way out except through search and scrutiny. The trolley was wheeled aside into the weighing-room, the first of the two royal boxes being lifted on to the flat surface of the weighing pontoon.

'We are,' said Moore, 'under obligation to the Treasury Department in this rule. All that leaves or enters must be checked and weighed.'

'And so it must, sir,' said Dacre good-naturedly, 'for your safety and ours are one, sir. Be rigorous, sir! Be rigorous as you can! You shall hear no complaint from us, by God!'

With the weights entered, the trolley resumed its way through the refining-shop, corroding-house, melting-shop, past the great rolling-mill, through the planchet, stamping, and weighing-rooms, to the door of the stronghold itself. Dacre was exultant at the discovery that every stage of manufacture seemed to be working with the routine of the previous day. The steel door of the stronghold loomed before them, massive and closed. Only the almost conical knob projecting from its surface and controlling the million-number combination offered a way beyond. Dacre paused.

'Aw – Major Morant, if you please! We will withdraw somewhat. It ain't for us to spy on Captain Moore at his lock.'

Moore gave a laugh of inattention as he put his hand over the knob.

'Have no fear, sir, I might change the number to any other in a million every time I close the door. Why, sir, if a man were to forget and turn it to the wrong place the whole building would know.'

'You don't say, sir?' said Dacre with polite indifference. 'And how might that be?'

'Why, sir, the moment he turns beyond the setting, he triggers a bell that you might hear the length of Chestnut Street.'

Joey Barham's face turned to Dacre's, his expression

showing an ill-concealed consternation. Dacre's spoilt, petulant features seemed only to grow more weary of the entire conversation.

'Aw – damn fine, damn fine,' he murmured laconically, 'ain't it, Morant?'

Morant-Barham thought it anything but fine, knowing that the last chance for private consultation over such matters with Dacre was now gone. Willson Moore turned the knob back, clicking through its final selection of one figure from the last ten. Then he took the bar and swung the door open. The porters wheeled the trolley in, lifted the black-lacquered boxes and laid them reverently in one corner. Willson Moore remained at the stronghold with Morant-Barham while Dacre accompanied the porters and the trolley back to the wagon. He submitted to the patting appraisal of the guards on his way out and saw the third and fourth boxes loaded. He accompanied them to the weighing-room, saw them entered and signed his agreement to the weight which had been recorded. He let the porters proceed ahead of him while he did this, since the boxes were entirely secure in this area, behind the main steel doors. A man who had been admitted this far, and was obviously a gentleman of some importance, attracted little attention. He could not have got in without official sanction, and he would not get out unsearched in any case.

Dacre followed slowly after the trolley, letting it turn the corner beyond his view. He strolled through the refining-shop, where the gold was ladled from the white heat of the furnace crucibles and tipped like a stream of sparkling fire into the vats of cold water. Beyond this room he came to the long corroding-house. Down one side, under an overhanging metal canopy, were the porcelain vessels, standing high as a man's waist, containing nitric acid heated by the steam which rose from the troughs below. The rows of vessels were set back in a long recess, like an alcove running down one side of the shop. The men who worked in there, their long wooden pokers stirring the brightening lumps of gold in the acid-baths, kept well back from the acid-laden steam as it

115

was drawn into the chimney-draught above them.

Once Dacre passed the end of this recess, where the door stood open between the corroding-house and the right-angle bend of the passage as it led to the melting-shop, he was out of sight. It hardly seemed to matter. There was nothing in that short stretch of passageway but another recess, no more than a couple of feet wide, with the metal chimney-hatch, just big enough for a sweep's boy to enter, where the cleaning of the flue was carried out.

Holding his breath, Dacre took from his pocket a large steel bodkin and applied it to the slot in the hatch. It opened easily, revealing the dark shaft of the flue from which the mingled fumes of sulphur and sharp corrosive of nitric acid drifted in the wind. He put the metal hatch down gently and drew from under his shirt the strips of sacking. He was still wearing his grey morning gloves, which he stripped off for the next part of the operation. The flue was hardly more than eighteen inches across at this point and as he wedged the tight bundle of sacking into it, he could feel that the ventilation was blocked and that the draught of warm fumes had died away. Working speedily, he replaced the hatch-cover, drew on his grey gloves again to conceal the black soot on his fingers, and walked smartly after the porters and the trolley.

He had guessed the dimension of the flue from the size of the hatch, and he was uneasily aware that the next part of his plan must be accomplished in a period of some three to five minutes. He cursed himself for not having timed the porters to see how long it was between leaving the stronghold with the empty trolley and returning with a new load as far as the weighing-room. That was the time he needed.

Their movements seemed infinitely slow, as they wheeled the empty trolley back to the wagon for the last two boxes. Dacre followed them in again, dreading the first cries which would announce the destruction of his hopes. The weighing of the boxes seemed an eternity, the pen of the clerk crawling like the track of a wounded beetle on the page. But the porters had once again gone on ahead of him with their load, and still there had been no cries. Dacre passed through the refining-shop and the corroding-house to the little recess with its chimney-hatch. He dared not stay too long, and he wondered for the first time whether something had been displaced by the force of the draught. Could the mere fumes of nitric acid eat through sacking in so short a time? It was absurd.

He was suddenly conscious of a rising murmur from the corroding-house and then shouts.

'Smoke! Smoke! Make fast the doors! Make fast the doors and leave!'

He could smell it from where he stood, the poisonous acid which the trapped steam was bearing down into the corroding-house. He stepped from the recess and closed the door at the corner of the passageway, where it divided the corroding-house from the melting-shop.

'Doors closed! Doors fast!' he shouted. There was no danger to him from this. Even if they knew who he was, they would merely congratulate him on his presence of mind, but he remained out of sight. Best of all, though the door was metal, it was secured by a mere bolt, which allowed him to shut this part of the Mint off from the rooms which followed.

Dacre remained in the recess until all sounds of movement had ceased in the corroding-house. He had gathered from his investigations into the proceedings of the Federal Mint that the down-draught of nitric acid fumes was one of the most serious problems. Hence the easy access to the flue by means of the hatch. He opened the hatch and drew out the sacking. Replacing the metal cover, he moved quickly to the corroding-house itself. By holding his handkerchief over nose and mouth he was able to avoid some of the fumes, but his narrow chest was soon convulsed by uncontrollable coughing in the steamy atmosphere and his lungs seemed to be on fire. The way to the refining-shop was open but beyond that another iron door had been closed. For a precious moment he was alone. Because there was molten gold in the refining-shop and no time to remove it, they had

117

unknowingly sealed him into the area which was vital to his plan.

Dacre tossed the sacking into the first furnace, where it burst at once into bright fire and drifted upward in the renewed draught. He threw his silk hat after it, and his frock coat after that in a tight bundle. The clothes burnt more slowly but in a minute more they were flimsy lengths of ash, disintegrating further at every shift in the flow of air. Finally, he tore off his shirt and hurled it after the rest.

Absurdly dressed in black trousers, boots, grey gloves and a black doublet, he seemed a cross between a Victorian gentleman and an Elizabethan executioner. But these were the clothes of his true profession. He added a final touch by drawing from his pocket a black Balaclava helmet and pulling this woollen cap over his fair curls. He hesitated for a moment, torn between comfort and necessity. Then he unlaced his boots, throwing them one after the other into the brightest furnace, whose heat made his eyes swim at several yards' distance. He knew what he would suffer without them, but the accidental scrape or thud of them might mean the difference between a hangman's noose and the greatest triumph of the cracksman's art.

In the minute or so which it had taken him to prepare, the steam had begun to clear and his chest was no longer contorted by such fiercely-suppressed convulsions. He ran past the shining heat of four furnaces to the two at the far end, which were black and dead. He chose the furthest and, doubling his body, squeezed himself in backward. When he raised his head, his torso was upright in the shaft and his legs sticking horizontally out of the furnace opening. Cautiously, he worked himself upright and stood in the narrow shaft, feeling at every contact the soft flakes of soot, which seemed to have the crumbling texture of dry snow. Immediately above him, the shaft sloped away, behind his head. The shaft was so narrow that only a man of Verney Dacre's narrow build might have been able to enter it. It had, evidently, been built for child sweeps.

Making the most of the time before the doors were opened

again and the furnace workers returned, he worked awkwardly round and reached for the ledge above him where
the slope began. By the pull of his thin, gloved hands, and
the pressure of his stockinged feet, he hauled himself upward on his belly, into the long and stifling darkness.

Joey Morant-Barham regained the garret, high above
Juniper Street and looking out on the blank side-wall of
the Federal Mint. His throat was dry, his legs felt weak,
and there was a tension in his abdomen which would have
made the swallowing of food or drink an impossibility.

For all that, as Verney Dacre had promised, it had gone
smooth as oil. Indeed, the clouds of acid steam had cleared
so quickly that those in the stronghold had hardly realized
that the mishap had occurred and that they had been
closed off from the main entrance of the Mint for several
minutes, for their own protection. When Willson Moore
had led the way back, he was far too preoccupied with
the urgency of his own secret plan to question what was
told him. Cowhide had readily explained how 'Colonel
Dempster' had been caught in the worst of the acid down-
draught. His chest, weakened by pneumonia which had
seized him during the night-marches on Lucknow, in the
Sepoy Mutiny of '57, had suffered enough in the steam to
make him return at once to the Continental by private
carriage. He left his regrets, and a promise of attending
Captain Moore the next day at all events.

Joey Barham and Cowhide had separated as soon as they
were out of sight of the Mint portico, Cowhide returning to
the stables and Joey slipping quickly down Juniper Street
and into the door of the dark tenement.

It was almost half-past ten, when Willson Moore, his
honest face still hardened by a faint anxiety, walked down
the steps of the Mint into Chestnut Street. He carried no
luggage and seemed merely to be on some errand in the
street as Snowden's proxy. It would be easy enough to send
a message from the railroad depot, feigning a return of
summer fever and vomiting, which would excuse his

119

attendance at the Mint for the next day or two.

He had walked no more than fifty yards, when the olive-green cabriolet rattled slowly beside him at a walking pace and the head of a pale, effeminate-looking man peered at him through the open window.

'Cap'n Moore? Cap'n Moore, sir?'

Willson Moore stopped, looking at the round white face, and the hand with its cerulean blue envelope.

'You are Cap'n Moore, as they told me at the Mint? Cap'n Willson Moore?'

'Yes', said the young man suspiciously.

'And I guess you could prove it?' the round pale face creased with concern. 'I can't trifle with missy's safety by lettin' the wrong party read her letter.'

A sense of alarm welled up in Moore's throat.

'Miss Maggie?'

'First, sir, Miss Jennifer, the beauty of Asia. She brought this for you and is at the depot now. You must go with her, she says, or you shall never accomplish what you promise to do. You may ride with us, sir, if you be Cap'n Moore. If you ain't, I guess Miss Jennifer can tell us when we get to the depot.'

The pale man opened the carriage door.

'And who the devil might you be?'

'We, sir, have no connection with the devil, sir. Quite the other side. We like to think, sir, of being missioners of rescue and salvation to poor lost women. It ain't no odds to us, sir, if it's a black skin that must be brought safe across Ohio to sanctuary here, or a white skin that must be fetched from a house of abomination.'

Willson Moore reached for the envelope, but the pale man withdrew it.

'Oh no, sir! When Miss Jennifer tells us that you really and truly are Cap'n Willson Moore, you may read. Until then, you must excuse our suspicions. What may be nothing to you might be life and death to Missy Mag!'

The closed carriage tilted slightly on its springs as Willson Moore ducked his head and pushed his way in to sit beside the large pale man. The door closed with a heavy click and the vehicle jolted forward.

'I don't figure on an enemy following us here,' said the pale man, 'but we will, if you please take the precaution of crossing the river lower down, beyond South Street, and coming at the depot from the far side. Miss Jennifer gave us to understand that you and she must be on the train in an hour from now.'

They drove in silence, southward through drabber streets and then across the river bridge.

'There's nothing amiss with Miss Maggie?' Willson Moore asked as they passed the outline of the alms houses.

'No-o-o,' said the pale man. 'And when I *know* that you are Cap'n Willson Moore, you shall have all your questions answered. Till then, sir, you must excuse me in the matter.'

They took a circuitous route, turning at last beyond the edge of the town as if to drive back on their own tracks and surprise any vehicle which might have followed them. And then the coachman took them off the road and on to a track between trees, stopping suddenly in a grove beside a stagnant pool.

'What's amiss?' called the pale man to his driver. Grumblingly he opened the door and got down on to the soft turf. Willson Moore ducked his head again and began to follow through the door. It was while he was in this posture that the pale man, Lucifer, brought a nightstick down on the exposed nape of the young man's neck. Willson Moore fell with hardly a sound.

Bull-Peg, jumping down from the driver's box, seized the young man and lifted him while Lucifer spread out a blanket. They worked with cord, turning, looping and knotting, packing the body round with a dozen convenient rocks. Then they carried it between them, trussed into the outline of a mummy, to the edge of the pool. What seemed at a distance to be a green pond was, on closer inspection, a slowly bubbling morass, overhung by stunted and twisted trees which looked half-poisoned by the foul vapours. The two men braced themselves for their last exertion.

121

'He's stirring again!' said Bull-Peg urgently.

'He shall sleep long enough!'

The weighted shroud tumbled only a few feet through the air, smacking down on the verge of the shimmering depth. But the shape of the rocks tilted it, so that it rose like a vessel in its final plunge, slowly and inexorably carrying the half-conscious Willson Moore to the dark, brief horror of his last awakening.

Verney Dacre, his eyes stinging and his mouth furred by the inhalation of soot, clawed at the upward slope. The inner bricking of the shaft was corroded and broken so that at every yard the uneven ledges tore at his clothes. He paused, seized by half-suppressed convulsive coughing again, and spat the foul black dust from his throat.

The slope was bad enough, but he knew there was worse to come. Below him, the furnace was dead, but ten feet further up, the flues from the row of furnaces merged into the main stack, carrying the heat from half a dozen which were stoked to brilliant and sparkling fire. Upon the number and intensity of these would depend whether he could survive without more than acute discomfort, or whether he would be roasted alive, first his clothes and then his skin being peeled from him like charred paper in the searing draught.

There was not even safety in testing the heat before he began the long ascent of the main stack to the tiny rectangle of sky above. The degree of heat varied with the damping or stoking of fires. It had always been possible, he knew, that he would be caught by a sudden surge of flame as a fresh fire was lit or the dying embers of other furnaces rekindled.

He sobbed for breath and spat again. The elbows were torn from his clothes already and the soot was like a refined torment on the raw and increasingly bloody joints. His right foot slipped against decayed brickwork, tearing wool and flesh until he felt the light, crawling trail of running blood. With his teeth clenched in a snarl of determination, he wrenched himself forward, feeling that the sooty bricks

122

around him were now considerably warmer than his own body-temperature. A few feet beyond him lay what he had always expected to endure as the price of his masterpiece: the prospect of death, and of agony which would make death a blessing. At the best, he must suffer torment which made most men cry out for a chance to recant or to satisfy whatever demands their inquisitors made upon them. He knew that he would face it, and endure if necessary until the last shrieking paroxysm of death. He would endure because he was Verney Dacre, because he was more than lesser men, and because the masterpiece was greater than he himself.

The draught which touched him now, about the cheeks and forehead, was like the hottest wind which he had ever felt in India, upon the Maidan or at Cawnpore. He was emerging from his cramped tiny shaft into a round, barrel-shaped chamber at the foot of the main stack. It was several feet across with half a dozen flues entering it round the circumference of its base. The chamber itself was about four feet high, narrowing at the top to the two-foot opening of the main stack itself.

Even as he pulled himself into this barrel-shaped chamber, Dacre's eyes were closed by the scorching vapour from the other flues. Blinded, he put out his hand to save himself, touched a brick flue-entrance, smelt the burning of his chamois leather glove, and screamed at the red-heat across the palm of his hand. Crying out in the dark, he put the pain of his hand from his mind and snatched for the entrance to the shaft above him as he felt his feet swell and blister on the searing floor. Pulling himself up, his back pressed against one side of the stack and his toes at the other, he searched for finger- and foot-holds.

In his torment, renewed at every contact of the brick upon his branded palm or his blistered feet, he cried aloud. Yet the cry was both triumph and curse. In his pain, Verney Dacre shrieked victoriously against the slave mentality of his pursuers and confidants alike. He cried his contempt for religions of humility and creeds of brotherhood. The victory should be his. As he clawed at the brickwork, the blood slippery on his fingers, he shouted with laughter in his pain, with unalloyed delight at the thought of what was to come. For a hundred years men would remember this caper, and would admire. He pictured the vault, empty of its gold, and as his torn feet scrambled against the falling soot, his mouth widened in a smile. Men who had known Verney Dacre were apt to conclude that he was afflicted by a form of insanity which earlier centuries believed to be possession by a devil. Yet there was now a terrible clarity in his reaction to suffering.

He thought of Miss Jolly, picturing in the dark the sharp profile of a young Egyptian princess. She was to be a prize second only to the gold. In his clawing exultation, the foretaste of her retribution drove his own pain from his mind. Again, in the darkness, he remembered her curved over the rocking-horse at Langham Place, howling under the attentions of his two bullies. He cherished the image behind his closed eyelids. He too must suffer, perhaps as much as she. Yet he endured his agony for fame. This masterpiece must live for eternity in the history of crime. Miss Jolly would suffer in ignominy, bound like a slave, fed on her own tears of misery. In his exultation, he laughed aloud.

Through the watering of his eyes, as he tried to open them against the acid stinging of the soot, he saw a blur of grey light above him. It was small but closer than it appeared. He guessed that the places which he now found for his fingers and toes had been chipped out by the first chimney-boy to make the ascent. Even the air was growing cooler and the grey light faintly illuminated the inner surface of the stack. He clung to the sooty wall, his narrow chest heaving, and pulled slowly up the last ten feet.

The chimney opening, some two feet across, was almost the same dimension as the square stack. Dacre braced himself with feet and shoulders, just beneath it. As he had expected, iron bars at six-inch intervals were fixed across it and set into the bricks. After all, he thought, the courtyard of the Mint even contained a vat with a filter so that water from the refining process had the tiniest scraps of gold filtered from it before it was allowed to flow into the sewers. Men who were so scrupulous would hardly have left a main chimney-stack open. Indeed, they had taken a double precaution. There were two sets of bars, crossing one another to form a grill, and coated with cement.

Dacre snorted with delight. In their enthusiasm to secure the opening it had evidently not occurred to these worthies that the cross design meant reducing each bar to half-thickness where it crossed another. Better still, Dacre judged that under the thin protection of cement the bars would have been rivetted together at their crossing. It needed only two tiny, opposite cuts to reach the rivet-holes and sever the bars.

The file which he drew from the courier-belt next to his skin was more than equal to the task. The cement was flaked and loosened by the heat and fumes of the shaft, yielding easily at the first application of the steel file. Then it was a matter of mere patience, working gently and skilfully at the eight intersections until the bars, except for the twelve embedded stubs of iron, now projecting inward from the sides of the shaft, could be lifted clear. Dacre hung the freed grill gently on the projections at one side. They had been embedded so far and, no doubt, with so heavy an iron bolt anchoring them deep in the wall, that they were capable of supporting considerable weight. Dacre grasped two of them in his fists, releasing his purchase on the brickwork gradually until he felt himself hanging from the butts of the two bars with not the least sign of their yielding. The strength with which the guardians of the Mint had secured their treasure was now his to use.

He waited until a clock, somewhere over Independence Square, struck six. Then he raised himself slightly and looked cautiously over the top of the stack. The cloth-wrapped wooden ball lay in the gutter about three feet below, just where he had thrown it the night before. Over the pitch of the roof he could now see the telegraph pole

125

and the nearer curve of the banner. GOD BLESS . . . Beyond that there was a partial view of the tenement roofs, and the garret window, behind which Joey Morant-Barham shiveringly awaited his moment of glory.

Joey Barham watched the sky grow dark over Chestnut Street and the river. The noise was thunderous from the main thoroughfare and he thought at first that the crowds must be cheering the Prince of Wales on his way from the railroad depot to the Continental Hotel. He caught a glimpse of carriages with men standing on their roofs, moving slowly in procession with lanterns waving and placards brandished aloft. But there were shouts of disapproval and noises of a struggle. What sounded like shots but must have been firecrackers thrown under the horses' hooves followed this. Joey Barham saw the entire crowd surging and hurrying after the coaches. Somewhere a pipe band was playing *Yankee Doodle* with shrill spirit. Morant-Barham caught sight of two placards being carried on poles by followers of the procession: LINCOLN AND THE PRO- TECTIVE TARIFF! FREEDOM IN THE NEW TERRITORIES! From the general jubilation of the crowd he guessed that the expected Republican victory in Pennsylvania had now been confirmed. The confusion was welcome to him. Under its cover the arrival of the Prince of Wales would be a tame affair, and the precise arrangements not generally noted.

As twilight came, he went down to the lower room and opened the window. Verney Dacre had been right. With the aid of his gold-topped stick, Joey was able to unhook the loop of cord holding the banner on the telegraph post and draw the end of the canvas round toward the window by the thin wire attached to it. The banner would look lopsided to the few passers-by who bothered to glance down Juniper Street but that would hardly concern them. He pulled the wire harder and from within the tube of canvas a further length unfolded and stretched toward him. By the time that he had drawn it as far as it would go, the banner formed a canvas tunnel, ten or twelve inches high, running from the telegraph post on the far side of the street into the room where Joey Barham stood. He looked into the darkness and waited.

In the deep silence of the heavily-draped boudoir, where he was alone with the two girls, Bull-Peg surveyed Jennifer, moist-eyed. Like a Moslem Venus, she lay on the bed with her back to him. Her head, propped on her hand, was half-turned towards him. A little gold-coloured chain, the sole ornament of her nudity, circled her waist. Bull-Peg slipped his fingers under it at the base of her spine, feeling her warmth against his knuckles. Stroking and patting, the naked pugilist had no time to look into the opposite mirror, which reflected the motionless hatred in the girl's dark eyes, as she looked away from him, receiving his caresses in silence.

I I

Verney Dacre waited until the last flush of daylit cloud began to die from the western horizon. Blue-black, the night above the city reflected only a shallow gas-lit glow. It was a little after eight o' clock. He pulled himself up, lying awkwardly over the coping of the chimney, feeling the fragments of stone and brick on the ledge as they shifted and scattered in a thin rain of dust. The wooden ball wrapped in cloth lay in the gutter beyond his reach. Using his long steel file, he was able to pat it towards him, until he could curl his fingers round the soft shape.

He lifted it slowly. Any break or dislocation now in its precious thread would destroy his scrupulous plan. He slid back until he found toe-holds which would keep him upright in the chimney with the rim of the stack at breast-height. Then it was a matter of infinite patience, pulling gently towards him the thin wire which connected the

127

wrapped ball with the end of the banner. As on Joey Barham's side, the wire pulled out a further length of canvas
which had been folded back into the double banner. When
Dacre had drawn it fully out, he was holding the end of a
canvas chute which ran from his vantage point, down over
the roof of the Mint below him, across Juniper Street in the
banner of welcome to the Prince of Wales, and into the
opposite window, where Morant-Barham waited. Dacre
let out a long breath of tension.

Now that the canvas was unfurled at its full length, there
was something else at his disposal. It was the end of a thin,
strong rope, whose length ran backwards and forwards
several times within the banner, making some two hundred
feet in all. At regular intervals of about twelve inches,
wire had been twined into the hemp thread and bent to
form convenient hooks, which might carry two or three
pounds weight each. Dacre made one end of the rope fast
to a row of three iron stubs, the remains of the iron grating
where it had been set into the wall. Then he dropped the
rest of its length into the dark tunnel of the shaft and began
to ease himself down cautiously, hand and foot.

The fires had been out for almost three hours, and though
the black and foul brickwork held some residual warmth,
the danger of being caught in a searing blast of air was now
over. Verney Dacre faced only the perils of capture and the
hangman's noose, which must inevitably follow. But he was
more than prepared to encounter such hazards as those.
Lucifer and Cowhide would surrender him to save themselves, at the first sign of trouble. He had never thought
otherwise. 'A fellow ain't to peach on his chum,' Morant-
Barham had insisted stoutly. Yet Dacre counted on Joey's
desertion of him too. Indeed, he could have borne it all,
the noose, coarse and slack above his unbuttoned collar,
the prison chaplain's blathering. He could have borne it
with a smile of delight if he knew that the stolen gold was
irretrievable and that, somewhere, Miss Jolly was howling
naked under the attentions of Bull-Peg and Raoul.

Dacre paused in his descent. Though it was long past

sunset, there was light coming from below him, its rays faintly illuminating the rough chimney walls. It was not the light of fires but the harsh brilliance of gas. It was nothing to him. He had expected that the workshops and vaults of the Mint would be lit during the night, even though none of their guardians could get beyond the time-lock. There might be secret windows or gratings which gave a view of these areas and he made a mental reservation as to the need to detect them. The sight of an intruder in the sealed rooms would presumably have a brigade of troops surrounding the building at once.

On this occasion, Dacre made no attempt to follow the flue down to the furnaces of the refining-shop, where he had entered it. There was another branch of the chimney shaft, broader and easier, which left the main column higher up, about fifteen feet from its top. This broader shaft led to the furnaces of the rolling-shop, much closer to the stronghold door with its figure-lock. By using this route he shortened the distance over which the gold must be carried, and diminished the chances of being spied upon.

Carrying the rope with him, Dacre slithered down the broad shaft, his clothes snagging and tearing on the rough surfaces. By the time he reached the opening, he had paid out some fifty feet of rope, while three-quarters of it still remained in a coil. He laid this down in the dark opening of the boiler furnace and looked about him.

He was between the massive upright ovals of the iron coining-presses, which stamped the designs on to the blank gold planchets, and the empty weighing-room with its forty or so tables, all deserted, and the double-pan scales upon each standing idle. Having calculated his route so carefully, he had only to cross the weighing-room and pass down a few yards of the opposite passageway to come to the great steel door of the stronghold with its single conical knob. Yet in that distance, of about forty feet, there might be a grill or concealed window through which he could be spied on. It would be pure chance, since the guards beyond the wall would hardly bother to look more than once in half an hour.

Yet Verney Dacre was conscious of putting his neck, however willingly, into their noose. There was only one answer. He moved quickly to the long brass chain controlling the weighing-room lights and pulled gently upon it. The great central 'gasolier' faltered, flared suddenly, and then subsided to a dying glow of red mantles. It was a risk but, as Dacre reflected, a man who feared risks would hardly be in the vaults of the Federal Mint at dead of night, with the gallows as the price of failure. If the guards had a spy-hole, they would see only that the gas had gone out or that someone had forgotten to light it before leaving the weighing-room. They might call out a regiment of dragoons on the strength of this, but Dacre chose to think otherwise.

By stopping the flue and driving the acid fumes back into the corroding-house, he had got beyond the outer door with its time-lock. Now, as the second stroke of the cracksman's masterpiece, he was about to open the heavy steel door of the stronghold with its million-combination lock. He had watched and heard Willson Moore opening the lock that morning, but of course Moore was able to reset the lock automatically to any other combination when he closed it again. Dacre had not been there at the closing of the door and in any case he was sure that neither he nor Morant-Barham would have been permitted to listen to the sequence of clicks as the lock was reset. And yet, as he crossed the room towards it, Dacre had not the least doubt of his ability to open the lock and the door as quickly as Willson Moore had done that morning.

The secret was simple. The lock itself was one of the most intricate that James Sergeant of Rochester had ever devised. Yet Dacre knew that when the lock was set, the routine of the Federal Mint would require that two men, the Director as well as his private secretary in this case, should know the combination. When James Snowden had closed the stronghold the day before, he must have set it to a number known to Willson Moore. Only in this way could Moore open it to receive the 'royal treasure' in Snowden's absence. After that, Moore could have reset it to any number, since both men would be at the Mint on the following day and Moore could tell Snowden what the number was.

But, thanks to the snare which Dacre had set and Maggie had baited, Willson Moore knew that he would not be at the Mint on the following day, having promised to rescue the young woman from the house of abomination in New York. Being unable to reveal this to his employer, and knowing that Snowden must be able to open the stronghold to retrieve the Prince's alleged possessions, Moore would have only one possibility open to him. He must set the lock to the combination already known to Snowden and refer to the fact, in any note of apology, without actually giving the figures. To have written down a new set of figures in a note which must pass through other hands would have been an unpardonable lapse of security. When he closed the stronghold door that morning, Moore must therefore have left the lock on the same setting as when Dacre and Morant-Barham watched him open it. So, at least, Verney Dacre reasoned.

Moving forward in darkness, he felt for the door ahead of him, the cold flat steel of its surface with the milled conical spindle of the lock. His strong bony fingers closed over this and he began to turn it slowly to the right, as he had seen Willson Moore do. He felt the metal click as the spindle passed over the first notch of the tumbler. There was no indication as to whether this was the correct setting for the first number. If Willson Moore was to be believed, the only indication was when the would-be cracksman turned the spindle beyond the notch of the setting and triggered an alarm bell. It was not a refinement which Dacre had met before and it seemed peculiar to the security system of the Mint.

He turned further, counting the clicks until the spindle engaged the sixth of the ten notches. Then he let out a long gasp and realized that he had been holding his breath throughout the process. The engaging of the sixth notch felt no different to any of the others. But if his reasoning

131

about Willson Moore was right, it must be the chosen setting. With great care he now turned the spindle to the left to engage the second chosen number. Only with each of the six figures in the right order would the door open. That morning he had counted five clicks on the second rotation as he made polite and inane conversation.

He reached the fifth notch and though there was still nothing to indicate whether this was right or wrong, he heard no bell and no alarm. Six again to the right, faltering once when he thought he heard the spindle engage but knew that he must turn it once more to match Willson Moore's pattern. Still there was no alarm. Four to the left. Nine to the right, expecting at any moment as he approached seven, eight, and the final setting to hear the air burst into a clanging resonance. But the silence about him was complete as in a tomb. Three to the left, the last one, the clicks seeming incredibly far apart.

Dacre stood upright with a long breath. Despite the chill of the rooms at night, the black dust of his face was grotesquely streaked white by several rivulets of sweat. He took the bar across the steel door and pulled it towards him. The door held fast. It was not that his strength was too little, he could feel the door still securely held by its massive and concealed iron bolt.

The absurdity and injustice of it struck him equally. He knew that his logic must be right, and even if he could clear the lock of the setting he had just chosen, there was no hope of finding one other combination from a million possibilities. Yet he was sure of the setting which he had seen Willson Moore use in opening the door that morning. His teeth were set with rage, when suddenly he relaxed, guessing that in his confusion he had forgotten to turn the spindle once more to the right to draw back the bolt. That must be it, surely.

The milled metal turned easily in his grasp, he took the bar and felt the heavy door move slowly. There was no need to pull it wide, a couple of feet would be space enough for what he required. The stronghold was a vast blackness

132

before him. He realized with relief that it was unlit because there were no spy-grills into it, and nothing which he did there would be seen. Evidently, its builders had decided that any breach at this point in the massive walls must endanger the inner vault.

Dacre closed the steel door behind him without locking it. Then he felt his way forward to the corner where the six boxes had been stored that morning. He had taken great care over the order in which the boxes were loaded and as his hands examined the gloss of lacquered wood in the darkness, he knew from certain marks carefully made upon it that the first coffin-shape he had come to was the one he wanted.

He broke the wax seal and, fumbling at his belt, found the little key for the lock. The lid creaked open and his hands touched the metal shutter of a dark lantern and felt the rattle of sulphur-tipped matches. In a moment more, the rising glow of the oil lamp cast its wavering tawny light upon the walls of the stronghold. With a savage satisfaction, Verney Dacre thought that his enemies had delivered themselves into his hands. The power of the time-lock and the million combinations had fallen to his first assault. Before him in the open box lay the tools of his trade. The vault door in the stronghold wall was secured only by a Yale Double Treasury Lock, so sure were the authorities that no burglar would ever negotiate the time-lock and combination-bolt. The Double Treasury Lock would have deterred any cracksman of average skill, but Verney Dacre looked at it and chuckled.

The lock presented a steel surface, approximately a foot square, with two keyholes. It was only to be expected that this final door, behind which lay the treasure of the Mint, should require two keys to open it, each held by a different man. Dacre was acquainted with the inner working of a Double Treasury Lock. The massive bolt was held closed by the enormous pressure of a steel bit. Two levers on pivots slotted into this bit and, in turn, maintained it in position. Each lever was controlled by three interlocking cog-wheels.

The first cog-wheel, in each case, could only be moved by the turning of the correct key in the lock. When this happened, the first of the pivot levers was freed. When the second was freed as well, by the second key, the steel bit yielded to the weight of the bolt and the door was unlocked.

As a further precaution against unauthorized copies being made of the keys, the keys and locks could be altered easily. Each key consisted of a shank and the two extreme teeth. The remaining teeth of the key were held in place on a screw and could be rearranged or altered in number according to any adjustments of the lock. Dacre was undismayed. He took from the open box a key of just such description with an assortment of teeth. In the normal way, a burglar might have 'smoked' the lock, inserting a length of carbon-smeared wire to measure the distance of the tumblers. But any trace of carbon or soot in the mechanism would reveal the trick when the authorities began to investigate the theft. Moreover, a lock as sophisticated as this one required more subtle measurement.

Dacre had followed the career of James Sergeant, locksmith extraordinary, with considerable interest. The year before, he had given his attention to imitating Sergeant's achievement in the construction of a micrometre, designed for mapping the interior of a closed lock. Dacre had never seen Sergeant's device but he knew enough of it to believe that his own resembled it in general appearance. It had a watch-face as dial, the single hand controlled by two interlocking cogs on the face itself and measuring the distances of the lock, where the shaft of a key would enter, down to a hundredth of an inch. Sergeant claimed to have measured the ten-thousandth part of an inch. Dacre was less exacting.

From the outer cog there projected a thin probe, more slender than the barrel of a key, with a single tooth at its far end. Dacre eased it into the first opening of the Double Treasury Lock, the movement of it turning the little cogs and the hand on the watch-face until it met the obstruction of the first tumbler. He made a mental note of the reading. Turning the shaft on its side and then upright again, to

134

negotiate the tumbler, he eased it forward until it encountered the next tumbler. Again he noted the reading.
By the end of his investigation he had determined the
position of the five tumblers which must be raised to turn
the key and open the lock.

Next he took his key and fitted it with the smallest teeth,
all of the same size. None of them even encountered the
tumblers. He worked up, one size at a time, until one of the
teeth raised the lever of the first tumbler. He could tell which
one it was, partly by the feel of the key as he turned it and
partly by the bright scratch-mark on the tooth of the key
where it had scraped its carefully-polished surface against
the other metal.

Keeping that tooth in place, he increased the size of the
others until all five matched the tumblers of the lock. Last
of all, he turned it and felt the wheels of the lock move. It
was still impossible to open the vault door, until the second
lock had been treated in the same way. Dacre worked,
silent and intent, hearing occasionally a distant sound
which might have come from as far away as the street or as
close as the outer corridor of the Mint, on the far side of the
fortress-like wall. The vault door set into it was about five
feet high and Verney Dacre guessed he would be lucky if he
could so much as stand upright in the interior.

He turned the second makeshift key and felt the door set free
by the opening of the bolt. The yellow lamplight shone into
a space which looked more like a sepulchre than anything he
had ever seen. Like the coffins of the dead, though large
enough only for dead children, the locked boxes of finished
coin awaited despatch to the banks of New York or Washington, St Louis or Philadelphia itself. Each one was secured by
Linus Yale's inset cylinder lock. As Dacre told himself, a man
who had come this far could hardly afford a glance at the
chests of mere silver coin, assembled to one side. A fellow
must pay his way in gilt. Somewhere else, in another
stronghold and another vault, there was no doubt a stock of
uncoined gold and unstamped planchets, but even these
were nothing in comparison with the treasure before him.

Dacre had promised Joey a couple of million in coined gold, not believing in so much but hoping to keep the youth's spirits high. Now, as he surveyed the bank boxes, counting twenty-eight of them, Dacre swore that he must have spoken truer than he could have known. Golden Eagles at twenty dollars a touch! Two or three thousand dollars in each pound's weight! Twenty-eight boxes with thirty pounds or more in each! He cursed aloud in his joy!

The boxes had not yet been bound with steel bands and sealed across the lock with the Mint's stamp. That would happen when they reached the weighing-room on their departure. But the weight they now held would already have been checked, and Dacre knew that it must not alter.

First he examined the locks, and once more confronted the skill of Linus Yale. Each box had its individual lock, opened by a flat metal key. Instead of the conventional tumbler mechanism, the entire lock turned with the key to open the box. But the edge of the flat key was a mass of peaks and indentations, indicating an array of pins of different lengths, all of which had to be lifted simultaneously to free the lock. To have picked twenty-eight such locks would have taken even Verney Dacre a very long time. But he had twice dissected such a device, bought for the purpose, with the loving care which a student of anatomy might have given to a choice cadaver. The locks would not be closely examined again until they reached the banks. That being so, he could open them in a few minutes.

Returning to his array of tools, Dacre chose a craftsman's drill and fitted a small diamond-headed bit to it. He crouched before the first box with its black-painted lock-plate. The chosen point was quarter of an inch above the slit of the key opening. The tip of the drill was no more than a millimetre in size. Supporting himself on one knee, his left elbow steadied on his other thigh, Dacre wound the drill against the metal plate with all his strength. The stark pattern of veins and sinews in his face and neck, the racking pain in his wrists, bore witness to the exertion. But it was at this point that a tiny hole drilled through the mechanism

would cut through the pins holding the lock closed. Once
they had been defeated, a plain flat strip of metal inserted
in the lock would turn it and open the box.

One after another, he attacked the boxes, disguising the
holes afterwards by rubbing in soft black wax. The bit
squealed against the last metal plate and, as if in response,
he heard a shout close by, hardly further than the other
side of the wall. Dacre froze and listened. The shout came
again, and then a braying laugh. He let out another long
breath, knowing that it was probably two or three drunk-
ards in the street, making their way raucously home. How
the sounds carried to him he could not tell. There must be
ventilators and grills, as well as the system of flues. He was
conscious, above all, of the ease with which any sound of
his own might be heard.

The boxes, their lids standing back, revealed the canvas
bags of coin. Before going further, Dacre went to his own
box and took out a pair of clean gloves which fitted tightly
over his hands. He drew a double pair of stockings over his
feet and wiped any traces of soot from the handles he had
touched. Then, from the same box, he chose a pair of brass
scales and a pile of large bags in coarse stout canvas, the
colour of cooked gruel. It was as he was doing this that he
heard, far off, the chimes and strokes of midnight. It was a
shock that he had been absorbed for so long with the locks
and he knew that he must work desperately against time
to complete the task that remained.

Opening the other five 'royal' boxes with his key he
shone the lamplight on shifting piles of pale grey lead shot.
This could be added, little by little, to make up exact
weights. But for the bulk of the weight which must remain in
the bank boxes, he looked to the Mint itself. He thought
first of the iron fire-bars in the furnace-rooms and then, as
a possible addition, the spare five-pound and ten-pound
weights which stood to one side of the weighing-room.
He took several of the canvas bags and went in search of
this ballast. Even if the spare weights and bars were missed
in the morning, the first supposition would be that they had

137

been moved for an official reason. What man, after all, would break into a Mint full of gold in order to steal iron bars?

His first stroke of fortune had come in noticing that the bank boxes were marked with their weight, as were the bags of coin inside them. This made it easier and quicker to compute the amount of ballast needed to replace the gold. Dacre worked rapidly with scales and balance. He was surprised, despite himself, to find that some of the boxes had sixty or seventy pounds weight of gold coin and, by his guess, would hold a hundred thousand dollars or more in value. Dark and glowing in the rich oil-light, the coins trickled softly into the lined scale-pan. From there, Dacre poured them into the open 'royal' boxes, into the lined pouches waiting to receive them. By the time that he had exchanged the exact weights and closed the black-lacquered boxes, it had taken him more than an hour to accomplish the labour. In that time, working with the speed of a man who sensed the minutes passing all too vividly, he had packed the contents of almost nine bank boxes into his own.

Twice more, Dacre went back to the furnace, the boiler, the weighing-room, searching for whatever ballast came to hand. At length he had emptied the remaining bank boxes, filled them to their previous weight with ballast and lead shot, and closed them once more. He locked the vault door with his makeshift keys, locked and sealed his own boxes, keeping back the seal to stamp the wax of the last one, having replaced its weight with coin. On the floor around him lay the small cloth and leather bags of the bank, heavy with coin and each seeming about the size of a large grapefruit. First wiping the sweat away where it gathered on the woollen rim of his Balaclava helmet, Dacre began scooping up these smaller bags and thrusting them into his own canvas sacks. Much of the weight of the coinage had gone into his black-lacquered boxes, but there were still more than two hundred of the pouches and bags, swollen with their two-pound weight of Gold Eagles. The latest figures for the Mint showed a production of eight million dollars in gold coinage every year. The rules of the Treasury required that a three-month reserve should be held in the vault. As Dacre dragged the first of the laden sacks toward the furnace shaft, he knew that this computation confirmed his guess. Two million dollars in gold.

One after another, he dragged the loaded sacks across the weighing-room floor, knowing that this would obliterate any exact marks of the steps he had made. The amount of gold was more than he had imagined, its weight far greater. The nine sacks were too heavy to lift, perhaps because Dacre's thin, nervous body was shaking with fatigue as he pulled the last one to the dark, open furnace. He could have sworn that each seemed to hold more than a hundred-weight and yet it was absurd that he could have moved half a ton of gold in this manner, let alone the amount now lying in the black-lacquered boxes. Almost dizzy with the labour and the exhilaration, he closed the steel door of the stronghold, turned the spindle of the combination-lock to the left, and heard the heavy bolt slam home.

The long coil of rope was where he had left it, in the empty furnace opening. Dacre took the first of the smaller money bags from the sack and impaled it on one of the wire hooks with which his rope was equipped at twelve-inch intervals. He worked with the fury of demonic possession, racing to finish his labour of darkness before the first light of day should put an end to his hopes. Even with the rope uncoiled and every hook sunk into the canvas or leather of its respective pouch, there was still more gold left in the sacks.

Abandoning the remainder for the time being, Dacre entered the black, sooty shaft, crawling upward on his side toward the vertical drop of the main chimney. He towed the laden rope after him, yard by yard, until he had gathered it at last just where the slope from the rolling-shop furnace joined the main upward shaft. Leaving the rope, he worked his way up the main chimney until he was once again level with its opening, looking out over the roof where the canvas tube of the banner fell away to the window on the far side of Juniper Street.

139

It was still dark, darker indeed than when he had first gone down to open the vault, since most of the gas lights had long been extinguished. Gently he pulled the rope upward, feeling the growing resistance as the weight of the money-bags began to rise clear of the side-shaft. At the worst, there would be no more than fifty or sixty pounds weight at any one time in the vertical drop of the main chimney. He saw the first pale shape of a canvas pouch rising towards him and seized it, tearing it from the wire hook. It was the work of a second to rip it open, tilt the seething mound of Gold Eagles into the tightened canvas chute, and listen to the hissing sound of their descent towards the window where Morant-Barham stood.

As a final precaution, Joey was to receive the coins in a sieve lodged in a bucket of sand. Their arrival would make hardly a sound. Dacre paused a moment, long enough for them to be sieved out, then ripped open the second bag and disposed of its contents in the same manner. There was no time to do more than drop the empty bags into the chimney. They would not have moved easily in the canvas chute, and by falling directly to the bottom of the main stack, they would lie directly above the melting-shop furnaces and burn up within a few hours.

One after another, Dacre emptied the bags and shot their coins into the canvas gulley. His limbs ached as he braced himself in the narrow chimney opening. But he knew, from the angle and tautness of the canvas banner, that the coins were rolling and slithering down its incline like water in a channel-pipe. He worked till his nails bled and his hands throbbed with the cold. It must have been two o'clock by the time that he began to pull the rope upward, and a clock had struck three in the chill air before he felt a sudden yielding and knew that he had come to the last twenty feet or so of its length.

There was no way of warning Morant-Barham that things had not gone quite as he intended, that the amount of gold required a second descent. Throwing the slack end of the rope before him, Dacre began to ease himself down once more inside the main stack.

This time, at least, there were fewer money-bags to be hooked to the rope, yet in his exhaustion he seemed unable to match the passing of time. When the last bag was attached, he crawled once more into the sloping furnace shaft, holding the large empty sacks. At the joining of the main vertical shaft he tossed these down so that they might burn up the next morning with the discarded money-bags. Then, once more, he began to draw the rope up after him, coiling it at the joining of the two chimneys. With infinite weariness, he pulled himself up the main shaft for the last time, lodged himself at its top, and hauled on the rope.

It was, ironically, almost the last of the money-bags, which eluded him. His numbed and aching fingers hardly tried to catch it. From far below him, echoing up the shaft, he heard the clatter of spilling gold as the coins burst from their bag. Dismally, he realized that they might have gone in every direction, scattering into all the rooms of the Mint which had fire or furnace openings. Equally, they might have fallen down into the dark chamber where the flues converged and where they would melt slowly and un-detected.

In any case, it was out of the question to go back. It was some time after four in the morning and at any moment the first light might streak the sky behind him. Dacre disposed of the last coins. He pulled himself up, thrusting the rope into the canvas chute, and sat on the chimney edge, his feet dangling outside the shaft. He was safe, at least insofar as he could not be seen from the street, a black figure against a black sky. And there was one final task to perform.

When Dacre had filed through the grating bars, he had done it carefully at a slant, so that it was possible to lodge the severed grating back in place upon the stubs which projected from the wall. Once it was in place, he took from his belt a leather pouch which had been part of the equip-ment waiting for him in the first lacquered box. The grey and gritty paste stuck to his fingers as he smoothed it over the bars, replacing the mortar where he had chipped it

141

away. In a few days more, blackened by furnace smoke, the chimney grill would look, on casual inspection, as though it had never been touched. It was not a necessary precaution, but Dacre shivered with laughter at the neatness of it. When the hue and cry was raised, the authorities would be compelled to admit that there appeared to be no means, short of supernatural agency, by which he could have entered their Mint. And yet, as the missing gold would prove, he had entered it nonetheless.

Dacre detached the canvas banner from the blackened stack and moved on his belly over the roof slates, until he was at the parapet above Juniper Street. The road and its sidewalks were dimly lit and deserted. Four feet away from him rose the telegraph post, to which the banner was also attached, with a drop of some forty feet between him and it. He knew that it was an absurd risk in his present state to jump for the post, hoping that he could cling to it. In any case, there was no need. He wound the loose length of the banner round his waist, and tied it with the rope. Then, gripping it like a rope at the level of his chest, he launched himself outward and downward, feet poised to contact with the post.

He swung so easily that he thought, after all, he might almost have done it in a jump. He released the canvas round his waist and waited for Joey to let go the garret end of the banner. As soon as he saw it begin to slacken, Dacre also detached the end which was tied to the telegraph post on his side. The long, loyal greeting drooped gently to the street.

He moved soundlessly down the post by the alternating grip of hands and knees. It was the work of a moment to roll up the canvas chute and, with it under his arm, to enter the street door of the shabby house. As he stumbled to the top of the stairs, he heard a bolt being drawn back in readiness. Joey Morant-Barham stared at the figure in the doorway, the features blackened beyond recognition, the dark trousers torn, the doubled socks and gloves showing a wetness that could only be blood.

'Well, old fellow,' he said mildly, 'I rather think we may have done it this time!'

Dacre's shoulders began to move. Then he cackled aloud, and then, tearing off the Balaclava helmet and throwing it on the floor, he shouted with laughter till the tears ran.

'Joey, my dear boy,' he sighed, as though with a final effort, 'let the day break as soon as they like, they ain't going to find a single coined half-dollar of gold in the entire bloody Mint!'

12

'Dammit, old chum,' said Morant-Barham, still in a daze of adulation half an hour later, 'but did you ever see such chinkers as these?'

He held up a twenty-dollar Eagle, raw and shining in its newness, circling it with thumb and forefinger to catch the gaslight on its bright gold for Dacre's benefit.

'The pull ain't finished yet, Joey,' said Dacre hoarsely, 'and if our bags aren't packed ready to leave this bug-trap in an hour more, we may both get an up-and-down jacketing from Lucifer on account of it.'

Stripped to the waist, Dacre was stooping over a tin bowl of steaming water, scrubbing at his face and hands to remove the traces of soot. Through the thin curtains of the brightly-lit attic, the first cold faintness of day was just visible.

'Nine sharp, Joey,' Dacre continued. 'That's our appointment to fetch the boxes from the Mint.'

Morant-Barham looked up from the carpet-bags into which he was scooping the loose coins.

'And the gold brick from their governor's office, dear fellow. How the mischief you shall get that back, I don't know.'

Dacre laughed through his wet hands.

143

'Open that bag of mine, Joey, and rest your eyes on what's inside! Ain't I been carrying that brick around in it since yesterday morning?'

Morant-Barham opened and exclaimed. Dacre dismissed the trick as hardly worth comment.

'Should you not wonder at my sending for the box in Snowden's office, and the nonsense with the key? Could you not see that there was a moment when they must all turn their backs while I held the casket? And did you not know that I should change it for another, easy as taking out a hunter to tell the time by?'

Morant-Barham snorted with laughter at the absurd deftness of the plan.

'They have a box which won't open,' said Dacre smoothly, 'and for which we shall give them a key last of all. And by the time they find a clay brick inside it, where they thought they saw a gold ingot, you and I shall be away, Joey.'

'Stop a bit,' said Morant-Barham reasonably. 'A man could never have walked in and out of the Mint yesterday with a gold ingot in his pocket, not with all the poking and searching every time he walked out.'

Dacre began to dry his face.

'Did I ever, Joey? Did you not see that from the office we must walk down to the wagon and the loading without going into the Mint proper? Was it not then that I slipped the little box into my own bag for you to bring back here? And ain't it been here ever since? The job's done, Joey, done long ago!'

Before dressing himself fully, Dacre walked through to the back window, which looked down into the dark, cobbled mews yard at the back of the houses. The wagon, its shafts empty, stood there in the faintly-lit dampness of early morning. Below the window, the drop to its roof was sheer. Joey Barham moved with hardly a sound, down the stairs and out at the back, until Dacre could see him standing by the vehicle some twenty feet below. Now it was all to be the easiest thing in the world.

Morant-Barham opened the back of the hearse-like wagon and presently, with the faint scraping of wood against wood, Dacre heard the rear portion of the wagon roof being slid open. They had taken great care in the positioning of the vehicle and now they were to be rewarded. As Dacre lowered the first of the carpet-bags with a doubled rope, it bumped gently and then disappeared neatly through the open roof of the wagon. He gave Morant-Barham time to load it in its place, then prepared for the second. It was full daylight, though the yard was still deserted, when the last of the boxes and bags had made its descent.

Dacre dressed himself in the full colonel's regimentals, gathered up his few remaining possessions in the room and stuffed them into his bag, then took a final look about him, drew back the other curtains, and made his way once more down the stairs. Joey Barham had closed the roof of the wagon and was preparing to cover over the ranks of carpet-bags and boxes which covered the floor of the vehicle, two deep. When this was done, he began to button on his staff officer's uniform with its wine-coloured sash.

'Two nags ain't going to shift this weight,' he said, shivering in the early chill.

Dacre remained unmoved.

'Which is why Lucifer is under instruction to bring four,' he remarked, as if the precaution were the most natural thing in the world.

They closed the back of the wagon and waited. It was almost eight o'clock when Lucifer arrived from the direction of Chestnut Street, leading four horses with the aid of a stable-boy. The greys were less elegant than the black geldings of the previous day but they were a good deal more powerful. Dacre looked up from his labour of sticking labels on the boxes to identify them as the baggage of various clients of the Continental Hotel en route for New York. Lucifer harnessed the four greys and the entire equipage pulled slowly out of the yard.

Turning into Juniper Street, away from Chestnut Street,

he followed Dacre's instructions, which were to drive in the opposite direction to the Mint, crossing the river to the north and coming to the railroad depot from that quarter. It had been Lucifer's task for several days to watch the delivery of luggage from the Continental, for shipment by railroad freight, and he was well-accustomed to the routine. Dacre and Morant-Barham dropped down from the wagon at a little distance, ready to support Lucifer, if necessary, as emissaries of the Prince of Wales to whose retinue the luggage belonged. Even this was not needed. The bags were entered, the dues paid, and the wagon turned back once again toward Chestnut Street and the Mint.

It was a few minutes after nine when they drew up at the main portico and the two uniformed officers stepped down. James Ross Snowden received them, as before, in the vestibule. After the formal greeting Dacre underwent the bizarre experience of revisiting the rooms in the calm of an official call, which he had left as a burglar, blackened and exhausted, several hours before.

He looked carefully but without exciting Snowden's interest, as they walked through the refining-shop and the corroding-house, for any sign of the fugitive coins which had burst from their bag. He saw nothing. In the rolling-shop the bars which he had taken from the furnace were still not replaced, though the furnace had not been lit and, possibly, the oddity of the missing bars would not be noticed for some hours. Here and there, on the weighing-room floor, he saw faint smears of soot, left by his own feet. Yet they could so easily have been trodden there by others who had come from the furnace areas that they, too, would pass unremarked.

At the great steel door with its million combinations, Dacre had his first misgivings, the sudden fear that he had not left all as it should be. At the same time, he tried to reassure himself that no suspicion would fall on him. How could he have penetrated the time-lock, the combination-lock, and the other defences of the building?

Snowden pulled the steel door open by its bar, and

Dacre's pulse became steadier. The interior of the strong-hold was just as it had been on the previous morning. Dapper and courteous, Snowden was at that moment apologizing for the absence of Willson Moore, delayed by some unavoidable circumstance, which the Director was careful not to specify further. Dacre heard his own voice keeping pace mindlessly with these pleasantries.

'Greatly disappointed to – aw – not to take leave of the gallant young officer. Trust if you – aw – he in London, dine as guest of Prince of Wales's Own and – aw – St James's Palace guard.'

The black-lacquered boxes were being loaded on to three trolleys and Dacre was delighted to see that they were all to be taken out in a single journey. At the weighing-room he watched with some anxiety as the coffin-like boxes were loaded on to the pontoon again to be checked. Either he had been scrupulously accurate the night before, or the clerks failed to be scrupulously accurate now. At all events, the weights were confirmed and the boxes wheeled out through the semi-circular vestibule to the steps and the waiting wagon.

Dacre turned to James Ross Snowden for the last time, taking from his pocket a small gold key.

'My promise to Captain Moore, sir, to obtain for you the key which belongs to the box containing His Royal Highness's token of amity. My humblest apologies, sir, that it escaped my notice the other day.'

Snowden warbled his gratitude and his pleasure at having made the acquaintance of so fine and distinguished an officer as Colonel Dempster. Verney Dacre brought his heels together and inclined his head a last time.

'Aw, servant, sir. Command me at any time. Beg to take leave. Major Morant, if you please!'

The marble floor of the vestibule rang with the footsteps of the two uniformed equerries, marching in time, as their straight backs disappeared down the steps. Then ducking their heads, they took their places at the rear of the wagon and the door slammed behind them. The liveried driver

147

cracked his whip, the grey horses lurched forward, and the polished wagon dwindled from sight in the busy perspective of Chestnut Street.

It was on the following morning, by the unimpeachable agency of the postal service, that the Director received a flat, unmarked package. It contained a black-framed portrait photograph of a youth with bright eyes and heavy jaw. The likeness, in similar versions to this, was widely displayed in shop windows and public places. This copy, however, was finer, and it bore an ink inscription upon its lower right-hand corner.

> *To James Ross Snowden, Esquire, Director of the Federal Mint, with the good wishes and personal acknowledgements of Albert Edward, Prince of Wales.*

13

British Embassy
CIPHER *Washington*

12th of October 1860

Lord Lyons presents his compliments to Lord John Russell and begs to furnish a further despatch in amplification of his telegraph of last evening.

The disaster at Philadelphia, which so unhappily coincided with the visit of the Prince of Wales to that city, has assumed a graver aspect. Captain Willson Moore, the private secretary to the Director of the Mint, has evidently absconded. Since he alone knew which numbers would open one of the vital locks, he must necessarily have been an accomplice in the robbery. The perpetrators, however, appear to have been two Englishmen who passed themselves off as equerries to the Prince of Wales, and who have robbed the Federal Mint of a sum estimated at one and three-quarter million dollars in gold coin.

148

Lord Lyons need not say how unfortunate it is that the name of Great Britain, and of His Royal Highness himself, should be associated with a crime of such enormity committed against the United States government and its people. This is especially the case at such a delicate stage in the relationship between the two countries.

It is greatly to be regretted that the crime should have appeared to be connected in some way with the election of Mr Lincoln and the likelihood of secession by those slave-states who believe that England will support them in the matter. It is consequently thought, if not said, by some of the United States government, that this was a blow aimed to undermine the financial strength of the Union in the event of civil war. There is natural resentment that it should have been the work of Englishmen. There are those who will even suggest that they were secretly the agents of the British government. Lord Lyons cannot too strongly emphasize the damage which is likely to result from this affair.

The United States Treasury, which has the investigation in hand, has undertaken not to make the robbery public knowledge for the next few days. This is in part to prevent harm being done to friendly relations between Britain and the United States, during the visit of the Prince of Wales, and in part to retain public confidence until the gold may be recovered.

The present state of the case is that the conspirators are known to have stayed in a suite of rooms at the Continental Hotel, where the Prince and his retinue were also lodged. There were some lesser accomplices and two young women, apparently held against their will. When the party left, these two young persons were quickly smuggled out in a drugged condition by the assistance of a hotel porter who was assured that they were fugitive slaves who must be got beyond the reach of Pennsylvania law to be safe from return to their masters.

The United States Treasury officials, on the basis of 'Colonel Dempster's' appearance and the mode of the crime, which showed great ingenuity, seek to identify him as Lieutenant Verney Maughan Dacre, late of Her Majesty's 19th Dragoons. Lord Lyons is in some difficulty. He understands that Dacre is credited with robbing the South Eastern Railway bullion train in 1857 but that Scotland Yard insists that he committed suicide while being arrested. Though desiring to assist the investigation in any way, Lord Lyons is reluctant to condone criticism of Her Majesty's servants at Scotland Yard or elsewhere.

The Treasury officials further suggest that there is one man, a detective sergeant from Scotland Yard, who investigated the 1857 bullion theft and, perhaps alone, could identify Dacre. He is at present one of those officers guarding the Prince of Wales and his transfer to the new investigation has been requested. Lord Lyons understands that the American authorities have some hope of recovering the gold at St Louis, Missouri on Saturday next, for reasons to which he is not privy.

Lord Lyons is once again in a difficulty, being informed that the detective officer in question is not well thought of by his superiors, and that he has frequently had to be reprimanded for wilful or insubordinate conduct, as well as for two assaults upon members of the public. At the same time, Lord Lyons must repeat that the recovery of the missing gold, by any means, within the next few days, is the one hope of averting a crisis in the affairs of our two countries, fraught with the most dire consequences.

Lord Lyons prays Lord John's urgent attention to this matter and begs to remain his lordship's obedient servant.

The Rt. Hon. the Secretary for Foreign Affairs
The Foreign Office
London, W.

PER DIRECT TELEGRAPH

OPEN CODE

Pembroke Lodge
Richmond
Surrey
13th of October 1860

Do as you think best – R

The Right Hon. Earl Lyons
Embassy of Her Britannic Majesty
Washington

4

NEVER CALL RETREAT

14

Sergeant Verity, in a new frock-coat, stood, bare-headed but at attention, to one side of the double doors which led to the opera box. At the far side, Sergeant Crowe, lean and sunburnt, brought himself up tall and stiff. Two footmen with powdered wigs opened the baize-lined doors and the young Prince passed rather self-consciously into the box with the grave, bearded figure of the Duke of Newcastle. The dark plump Lord Lyons accompanied the Mayor of Philadelphia and his guests. At the rear of the procession, Colonel Grey and Major Teesdale appeared in plain civilian evening clothes, as if to disclaim any association with the uniforms used by the bogus 'equerries' in the robbing of the Mint.

The two footmen stepped inside the box, pulling the doors to after them, and preparing to stand in attendance there. As Verity moved across to take up his position in front of the doors on the outside, he caught just a glimpse of the interior of the opera house. Above the ornate horse-shoe of the auditorium the arches of boxes rose in cream and gold upon their Corinthian pillars. The shallow dome of the ceiling was covered with fresco-work, its centre filled by the flashing prisms of a seven-tier crystal chandelier.

Drawing his eyes reluctantly from the scene of splendour offered by the Philadelphia Academy of Music, Verity stood himself at ease with stamping precision. Then, staring immediately ahead of him, he resumed a conversation from the corner of his mouth.

'Stoopid ain't the word for it, Mr Crowe! You could a-said something, one of you! 'oo was it that was dead in Albemarle Street, then?'

'A servant named Oughtram,' said Crowe softly. 'He thought he was changing clothes to help Dacre escape. He

153

must have sat in that chair, not thinking why his master needed the pistol, until Dacre fired it in his face. After that, you'd no more identify Oughtram than you could tell a hog that's been cut up small for the butcher.'

'And Mr Croaker don't know this?'

'Your Mr Croaker,' said Crowe with some feeling, 'is a mutton-headed fool who swears on his reputation that Lieutenant Dacre was seen dead!'

'Mr Crowe, if you please! Mr Croaker is my superior officer.'

'Your superior officer is a mutton-headed bastard then.'

Verity, in his dismay, turned his face to Crowe.

'Mr Crowe, I 'appen not to like Mr Croaker. But liking and respect is two different things. A man that don't respect those who are put in authority over him, is going to lose respect for himself in the end.'

Crowe peered at Verity with incredulity, then he looked away.

'My God!' he said quietly. 'You really believe that, don't you?'

'Yes, Mr Crowe, I do. And I ain't a man that has an ear for profanities.'

Crowe mouthed several obscenities for his own benefit, and there was a silence during several minutes of mutual reproach.

'I ain't no wish to offend,' said Verity at length, 'but if I'd been told that you'd heard he was alive, I could have helped. But no! I wasn't so much as told that the young person Jolly had been fetched here as bait for your people to catch Lieutenant Dacre. When I followed her into that police 'ouse in New York and they said I was the wrong one, I s'pose they were expecting 'im!'

'No one can prove it was Dacre that robbed the Mint,' said Crowe defensively.

Verity snorted.

'If 'e's alive, 'e did it! It got all the marks of his capers! Getting through locks that no mortal man could open, emptying vaults as if 'e'd waved a magic wand. There's no way that dodge could a-been pulled, and all the same it was. He could do it again tomorrow for all we know how to stop him! And if he was to walk in here now, you couldn't arrest him for the robbery, only for pretending to be 'is 'ighness's equerry. That's how I know it's Lieutenant Dacre that did it!'

'And how shall he be caught?' asked Crowe gently. 'He might be anywhere in America with his gold by tomorrow. By this time next week even the Treasury won't be able to keep the robbery a secret. If the tale is told, Mr Verity, there's to be bad blood between your country and mine.'

Verity chortled, almost as if in disapproval.

'But between you and me, Mr Crowe, there ain't to be bad blood. And it's you and me that must settle with Lieutenant Dacre now. So, first off, I don't care twopence where he and the gold are now, nor where they may be tomorrow. I got 'im, Mr Crowe! I got him!'

'How?'

'By knowing that he must be on the *Fidèle* at St Louis on Saturday! Mr Dacre may be a master cracksman but 'e's got a chink in his armour that you could drive a coach-and-four through! A cruel mania and a delight in torment-ing unfortunate creatures. That's what shall be his undoing. When Miss Jolly goes up for sale, 'e'll be there.'

'I guess he might, Mr Verity.'

'No, Mr Crowe. Not *might*. He *must* be. Without her, he'd a-got clean away with the railway bullion and been a swell the rest of his life. He can hate like no man you ever saw! It don't even matter that he knows she can't be a real slave-girl for sale. It don't matter that he knows she's the bait in a trap. He must have her if the trap kills him for it.'

'That simple, eh?' Crowe relaxed his stance still further and rubbed his long chin in thought. 'And the gold? When you have Dacre, do you have the gold?'

'No, Mr Crowe, I don't. Not actually have it, that is. But it don't follow that I mightn't find a way to it in the end.'

Crowe shook his head and drew himself up once more.

'Captain Oliphant and the people in Washington ain't likely to settle for that,' he said firmly. 'The United States gold reserves for three months have gone, and if they aren't found again in the next few days, our paper money won't even be worth a man wiping his nose on.'

Verity stood silent and thoughtful. Beyond the baize doors, the first act of *Traviata* was being performed as a prelude to *Martha*, the principal entertainment being put on for the Prince's benefit. A woman's voice, of the most thrilling beauty, was gently audible in haunting minor cadences of limpid purity. Verity listened, spellbound. Presently the song burst into an exultant *Di quell' amor, quell' amor, ch'è palpito*, in the full brilliance of the voice of the seventeen-year-old ingénue, Adelina Patti.

' 'ark at that!' said Verity wonderingly. 'Now that's something that is! I only wish Mrs Verity could 'ear it!'

He listened, entranced, to the remainder of the act, the soaring melody returning again at the end, a male voice taking it up distantly while the thrilling vivacity of Patti's cadenzas charged the finale with an electric excitement. The melody died away and there was a storm of applause from the auditorium.

'Well!' said Verity proudly. 'Well, now! I never thought to hear the like of such singing, not in this world anyhow.'

The two men waited out the period of their guard, until the main opera was over. Verity was about to open the doors of the box in preparation for the Prince's departure, when he paused, rigid at attention. From the crowded pit, from the galleries and boxes, came a familiar sound.

> *God save our gracious Queen*
> *Long live our noble Queen . . .*

To hear the anthem sung spontaneously in this manner, by those who did so out of affection rather than by duty of birth, moved him more than the brilliance of Patti's aria. The final notes were followed by a rising patter of applause, directed toward the box, where the young Prince of Wales acknowledged it with slight, self-conscious bowings of his head. Then the royal party moved sedately down the broad stairway to the fine lobby and the waiting carriages. The Prince walked with his hosts, followed by the Colonial Secretary and the Ambassador, Verity and Crowe walking watchful and inconspicuous at the rear.

As the carriages moved off, Verity turned to his American colleague.

'Well, Mr Crowe,' he said, his pink face radiating satisfaction, 'it's to be hoped, of course, that we shall have both the villain and the gold in a little while. But even if we don't get neither, you and I shan't hate one another. Your people and old England ain't on different sides! Not if this is anything to go by!'

The peace was short-lived. The railroad which bore them to St Louis ran through a tangled, marshy wilderness of thick undergrowth and trees that almost hid the day. Wooden viaducts raised the track above waterlogged soil where trees with scant foliage and tresses of foul weed leaned in disarray.

Verity shook his head.

'Some things I shall never understand, Mr Crowe.'

'Where the gold might be?'

'No, Mr Crowe, how you can have a free country and then, when we travels through that Richmond place, there's poor black souls being took to be sold as slaves. Abomination, Mr Crowe. City of the plain it might be. A man must be free, Mr Crowe.'

'Like you, Mr Verity?'

'Britons never shall be slaves, Mr Crowe. They taught us to sing that at Hebron Chapel School.'

'Well,' said Crowe, 'then I guess you must have to vote when election time comes round.'

'No, Mr Crowe, not meself, that is. Not actually vote, that is. Why, Mr Crowe, what should I be doing voting about things that only parliamentary gentlemen understand?'

'Ah!' said Crowe, as though satisfied by the explanation.

'But I guess you must have a fine house in England, and land, and a few servants.'

'No, Mr Crowe. A police officer don't indulge in such things. You oughta know that.'

'Yes,' said Crowe, 'but you must be pretty free, I guess, in your police activities. Your own master. No one to answer to.'

'Superior officer, Mr Croaker, Mr Crowe. Superintendent Gowry his superior officer. There 'as to be a method.'

'Ah,' said Crowe, understanding again. 'Well, Mr Verity, I will tell you what. You go right on home to England after this little matter is settled. And the next time you get a cross word from Mr Croaker, you tell Mr Croaker to patrol London Bridge with his nightstick up his ass. And when you've done that, you tell me. And I'll believe you're free.'

The next half hour passed in an injured silence.

Verity gazed on the slow and muddied waters of the Mississippi. Behind him a dome of smoke, like a huge mushroom, hung over St Louis and marked the city out to approaching passengers from many miles downstream. Before him, along the levee, a line of graceful steamboats was tethered, their quiescent power giving them the air of white, patient animals. The *Louisiana*, heavily-laden from Cairo, churned the river to a hissing froth as she turned her bow towards a gap in the line. 'I never thought *you* wanted men to be slaves, Mr Crowe, you know that.'

'Course you didn't, Mr Verity. Now, keep a bright lookout. Either he's on the *Fidèle* already, in which case we shall have him, or else he must pass this way to get to her. Whichever it is, if you're right, Lieutenant Dacre's number is up at last!'

The two men walked slowly along the warm pebbles of the levee and the long stone quay with its high brick warehouses. Clerks in their shirt-sleeves bustled between the open doorways and the line of tall steamboats. Drays with their teams of mules and dark-skinned teamsters stood piled high with cotton bales and logs for the ships' furnaces.

Among the cobbles of the streets, the dark mud steamed in the sun after overnight rain.

'I'd take a dollar,' said Crowe thoughtfully, 'I'd take a dollar for every time I rode west from here with another party of settlers for Laramie or Santa Fé, and I'd almost be a rich man!'

'That what you was doing in the Marines, Mr Crowe?'

Crowe's lean, brown face creased in a grin.

'It's what I did when I was sixteen, my friend, and I sure never thought of the Marines then! Guide and hunter for the parties on the Oregan trail. You won't find many grocery stores west of St Louis, Mr Verity, until you come down to the Pacific.'

'That a fact, Mr Crowe? And that's what you was doing when you was sixteen? When I was sixteen I was first footman to the Dowager Lady Linacre at the Crescent in Bath.'

'A servant?' asked Crowe suspiciously.

'Superior servant, we call it, Mr Crowe. The next year I went for a sojer, 23rd regiment of foot.'

Crowe shook his head, as though such a choice was beyond his comprehension. Presently he paused. A few feet in front of them a dispute had broken out between a humble looking man and a stout gentleman in tight-waisted coat and buff trousers. The stout man, to whom the humble youth had been trying to sell a copy of a tract was responding indignantly.

'Now you go to hell, sir! I've told you three times I don't want your confounded book! I own slaves, and I trade in fancy-girls. And I calculate to own a sight more of 'em if I can get 'em. I don't want any damn'd preachin' from you or any other gospel-driver. And if you bring that goddam tract near me again, it goes pitch into the river and you after it! See?'

Crowe turned away from the squabble and waved an arm as if performing an introduction.

'The *Fidèle*,' he said courteously.

Verity stared up at the steamer with its five decks rising the height of a house and the tall ovals of its paddle-boxes

159

at either side. The lowest deck was open at the sides, showing the machinery, the wood for the furnaces, baggage space, and even makeshift stalls for cattle. At the next level he could just glimpse the windows of huge saloons, bar-rooms, staterooms, and barber's shops, sheltered by the galleries which ran the length of the vessel. In the centre of the ship, just forward of the paddles, rose the two lofty smoke-stacks and the tower from which the steamboat was steered.

He followed Crowe aboard and gained the upper deck, where the covered way with its arched windows seemed more like an arcade or bazaar than anything which he had seen before on a ship. As they strode towards the cabin where Miss Jolly waited under guard to perform the role of decoy, Verity glimpsed fine promenades, domed saloons, balconies overlooking sunlit water, mysterious passageways, shops and state-rooms which seemed fit only to act as bridal suites.

Near the stern of the ship, Crowe stopped and knocked at the door of one of the humbler cabins. It opened to reveal two strangers, with the bulky look of Treasury agents of Crowe's stamp, Captain Oliphant, and a muscular woman. Apart from the woman's nationality, she recalled at once to Verity's mind his acquaintance Mrs Rouncewell, ex-police matron of the Elephant and Castle.

Behind this phalanx of protectors stood Miss Jolly, slim and upright, her dark Turkomen eyes watching Verity impassively. Standing in the cabin, with its ground-glass solar lamp and its table of white marble, he sensed that he and Crowe had interrupted something, though he could hardly imagine what. He looked again at Jolly. Her trim figure was oddly dressed in a red singlet and a pair of blue denim trousers in Genoa or jean cotton. The jeans were creased and baggy, totally at variance with the neatness of her normal appearance. The woman, whose name was Mrs Lily, spoke briskly.

'If she got to be dry again by two o' clock, I reckon we'd better do her now!'

'Shall we leave you, Mrs Lily?'

'No Cap'n Oliphant. I reckon this little piece would as soon you stayed to watch. Wouldn't you, honey?'

She chucked Miss Jolly under the chin and was flashed a dark glare in response. Verity shifted nervously from foot to foot. Then Oliphant and the two guards moved aside to reveal a tin bath, half-filled with water.

'Take a plunge,' said Mrs Lily reasonably, and Jolly stepped in with a grimace at the coldness of the water on her feet. She held the trouser legs well up.

'Sit down!'

'Not in my things!'

Mrs Lily's response was a hearty downward shove on the slim shoulders. There was a splash and water slopped on to the polished boards.

'And stay down!'

'Ugh-h-h! It's horrid!'

'Get them really soaked, honey. If the customers can see you without taking off your things, it'll be a lot easier on you in the saloon, believe me!'

'They're wet through!'

Verity stared, uncomprehending, until Mrs Lily's broad and powerful hands released their pressure on the girl's shoulders. Jolly sprang up with a cascade of water falling from her. She stepped from the bath, bow-legged in a pantomime of discomfort and let the older woman lead her to the far side of the cabin.

'Just here, honey, where the heat from the boilers goes up to the stack.'

Verity whispered in bewilderment.

'Mr Crowe?'

'Shrinkage,' said Crowe knowledgeably. 'Tightest tights you ever saw.'

'Ah!' said Verity, understanding at last.

Half an hour before the time of the auction, the shrunk denim had dried to a fit that was smooth as drumskin. The girl stood before the long wall-mirror and surveyed her

161

reflection. She drew in her cheeks, her mouth forming an 'Oooo!' of admiration, while her almond eyes widened and she rolled them in humorous envy of her own appearance. Then, more self-consciously, she drew one of her slim hands upward over the taut denim of her seat, the red-painted nails bright against the blue cloth.

Mrs Lily intervened, completing the last details of the fancy-girl's toilet. With unnecessary scrupulousness, she pressed the denim to a flawless fit round the hips and crotch of her protégée, administering a couple of final pats to the seat, either as a matter of fitting or a gesture of approval. She touched the crop of dark hair into place, where its cut just brushed the back of the singlet collar. Playfully, she lifted it and imparted a quick kiss to the smooth golden warmth of the bared nape. Jolly evaded her.

'Stop that!'

The older woman exhaled a sigh, wistful but resigned. Then the procession made its way to the grand after-saloon, the scene of the auction on the main deck. Verity's eyes widened slightly at the tight, purposeful swagger of Miss Jolly's quick little steps in the straining denim.

'Mr Verity,' said Crowe at his ear. 'That's the third time I've spoke to you!'

'Oh,' said Verity, 'is it? It never is, Mr Crowe!'

'Much you'd know if it was or wasn't, my friend!'

And then Crowe explained the trap which had been prepared for Dacre. The auction saloon was at the rear of the main deck. It could be approached only by the two open galleries at either side of the ship. At the after end of the ship, there was no means by which Dacre could escape with the girl, nothing but a sheer drop to the water thirty feet below. Once a man passed the plain-clothes guards on either of the two galleries leading aft, he was in a cul-de-sac and the trap had closed. Three doors opened from the auction saloon on to the gallery and the ship's rails. Two of these opened at either side and the third was the after door, which opened on to a larger space at the stern of the steamboat with several seats and tables.

162

'I guess it should hold him,' said Crowe hopefully. 'Once
he's in this part of the ship, he ain't going to leave without
your Miss Jolly. And unless she goes willing, there ain't a
way out except past the guards on either side. To make it
certain, however, the *Fidèle* casts off in five minutes more and
steams down river and back while the sale is held.'

'I don't care for that, Mr Crowe,' said Verity thoughtfully. ' 'e might push her over the back and have his own
little boat waiting. I'd sooner we was at St Louis.'

Crowe nodded, as though he found this perfectly
reasonable.

'However, Mr Verity, there's a dozen men on this boat,
all dressed to bid in the auction but standing in different
parts of the vessel. Each one a Ranger or a Marine that can
put a bullet in a man with a Colt's revolver at sixty feet,
every shot. Any little boat that gets near us is going to have
more holes in it then a Swiss cheese before it can come
alongside.'

Verity paused and faced his colleague.

'Mr Crowe, where Lieutenant Dacre is concerned, it'll
take more than twelve men with revolvers.'

Crowe patted him on the back.

'Come on now, old friend, your Mr Dacre ain't
immortal!'

'No,' said Verity, as if conceding the point with some
doubt, 'I s'pose he ain't.'

They entered the auction saloon, light and airy with its
windows looking out to the river on either side. It was
furnished with stools, settees, sofas, divans and ottomans,
all of them occupied by those who had come to attend the
sale. The majority of these dealers, young and old alike,
sported cream or buff suiting with sticks that were topped
in either silver or gold. There were a few swallow-tailed
coats in blue or green, and a few dark-suited westerners
with broad-brimmed hats. Among the hundred or so men
present, a few were playing cards in small groups while
others sauntered past the marble-topped tables looking for
an empty arm-chair. At the forward end of the saloon was

163

a small wooden platform raised eighteen inches or so above the floor. Upon it there stood a lectern and a bedroom screen whose panels were of crimson silk. Vignie, in his white linen suit and red cravat, stood with his gavel at the lectern waiting to begin the sale.

'Remember,' said Crowe to Miss Jolly, 'if there should be a winning bid and if Mr Vignie lets you go with the bidder, trust him. Mr Vignie will know him for one of our men. If not, you won't be let go.'

She nodded quickly and stepped on to the platform, where two of Vignie's men waited, as though they might be about to carry forward a selection of furniture to be auctioned off.

'Messieurs,' Vignie tapped the lectern with his gavel, the slightest suggestion of French intonation in his voice. The murmur of conversation in the saloon died away. 'Messieurs, we will now turn to the business of the afternoon, if you please. It is not for me to claim your attention. I see from your eyes that that has already been done by the young person who comes before you now, Miss Jolly, properly called "Gentleman's Relish".'

Vignie made an unambiguous motion to her, with some impatience, and Jolly began to walk irritably up and down the platform, her leg movements constricted by the tightness of the jeans.

'Rarely,' crooned Vignie, 'rarely has it been my chance to bring before you a creature of such delicate, almost Oriental charm. The property of a European gentleman whose greatest desolation in the ruin of his fortunes is that he must part with such a jewel. Observe, if you will, the fineness of her features, the fierce challenge of those dark eyes, the warmth of that golden tan. Notice the slim back and firm bosom, as she turns. Why, gentlemen, there's a breast for you!'

Verity nudged Crowe.

'There ain't a face here to match Lieutenant Dacre, but he must be 'ere somewhere. Tell you what, see if you can notice a man that might be crying, with silk to his eyes.'

'Crying?' asked Crowe doubtfully. 'What about?'

'Not about anything, Mr Crowe. The Lieutenant got this complaint of watering eyes. Has to keep wiping them. 'e can be clever as any cartload of monkeys, but that's one thing he can't disguise.'

Crowe surveyed the bidders as their eyes widened, their tongues passed over their lips expectantly, and their gaze followed Miss Jolly's every movement. Vignie had stepped forward now to demonstrate his commodity more persuasively.

'The legs,' he said suavely, 'observe, messieurs, their lithe firmness. The tight waist. Imagine, if you will, the warmth of the bare flesh against the silk sheets of your boudoir. Picture her, while you bid, as the nude Eastern damsel who waits upon your table, the warm silky gold of her body moulding itself to every call that a man might make upon his bed-slave. May I say a thousand dollars to start, messieurs? I dare not say less!'

Jolly surveyed the room with stony-eyed hostility.

'Where the mischief is 'e?' whispered Verity savagely, ''e gotta be 'ere, Mr Crowe!'

'Well, Mr Verity, I guess there ain't a handkerchief touching an eye in this whole roomful of sinners.'

The two sergeants looked about them again, as Vignie turned the girl round and round slowly to display her to the bidders.

'One thousand at the back of the room, do I hear? Only see the roundness of the dark hair touching just to the nape of the neck! Consider the slim back, and the rounder hips. ... Twelve hundred, then ... the wantonness of the backside, seen in a stoop. . .'

The girl's almond eyes and sharp features turned on Vignie with bleak hostility. But she bent at last, the trim seat of her jeans broadening, each of Miss Jolly's hind cheeks tightly and separately rounded. Then came a sharp rending of seams, and open-mouthed delight from the bidders at the sudden prospect of palest coppery smoothness.

165

'Gentlemen!' cried Vignie happily. 'May I say fifteen hundred?'

Verity had frozen into immobility.

'Mr Crowe!' he hissed. 'That's 'im! In the after doorway! And 'e ain't disguised at all!'

There was no mistaking Verney Dacre, the tall, narrow body with its languid posture, the spoilt face and the light-coloured dundreary whiskers. His cream suiting and tall matching hat were set off by a dark brown coat and gold-topped stick. He surveyed the room, his eyes passing over Verity and Crowe without appearing to recognize them. Crowe turned to the plain-suited guard accompanying them, as Dacre moved to withdraw from the doorway of the after deck.

'The stern entrance! Cover it with your revolver and let no one through, either way. Mr Verity and I shall go out through the two side-doors and round to the stern of the ship by the galleries. There's no way he can get past us, and no escape over the stern. One way or another, we've got him!'

The Marine Corps private in the plain suit strode to the after door, through which Dacre had disappeared. Verity and Crowe made for the two side-doors of the saloon with ample time to seal off Dacre's avenues of escape. Like Crowe, Verity felt the weight of a Colt revolver at his side, but it brought him little comfort. He had come to regard the rifle as his 'best friend' in the siege of Sebastopol. The close-range duel of revolvers was something with which he was unfamiliar.

He slipped out on to the open gallery and began to edge his way slowly round to the stern, where he would meet Samson coming from the other side to confront Dacre simultaneously. At least, he thought, no one had given the least hint of recognition when the cracksman appeared in the doorway. He and Crowe had been well prepared, but he had feared the girl's response at seeing her tormentor again. Fortunately, Miss Jolly had been bending over dis-playing the tautly rounded seat of her jeans to the bidders.

She had seen nothing of Dacre.

Following the curve of the saloon wall along the outer deck, he came to the open space at the stern, an oval area some thirty feet along. It was almost deserted, its seats and chairs empty. Close by the stern rail itself, however, there was a wooden seat, double-sided and with a tall back. In the event of shipwreck, it could be inverted to provide a life-raft, the back acting as a keel. Sitting on the far side of the seat, staring thoughtfully over the stern rail and with his back to the saloon, was the figure of Verney Dacre.

The excitement of such an opportunity made Verity's heart leap to his throat. He had not really intended to use the Colt, but now he drew the heavy gun from his belt. Staring at the back of the brown coat, the cream hat, and the clearly identifiable stick with its gold top lying to one side, Verity knew that even he could not miss the target now. Not that he intended to kill Dacre if he could help it. To take the cracksman alive would be the greatest feat in the entire history of the Private-Clothes Detail. In his imagination, voices addressed him as Inspector Verity, Superintendent Verity, Verity of Scotland Yard. . .

He was close enough now to see the wisp of Dacre's cigar, and he moved with the stealth of a shadow. Sergeant Crowe had appeared from the other side of the saloon's stern-wall. Verity mouthed the unmistakable shape of, 'We got 'im!' We got 'im, Mr Crowe!' He hunched forward towards his quarry. He was hardly ten feet from Dacre, who still stared out over the rail oblivious of danger, when Crowe shouted.

'Get back, Verity! Get back here!'

'That's all right, Mr Crowe. Keep yer gun on 'im, and leave this to me. Right, Lieutenant Dacre, sir, let's be having. . .'

With intense annoyance he was aware of an impact on the deck behind him, a skidding of feet, and a thump that drove the breath from his body and knocked him sideways against the ship's rail. Verney Dacre ignored all this and a sudden thought crossed Verity's mind, even while he was

167

still falling behind another upturned life-raft with Crowe's weight on top of him. Could the cracksman be dead, sitting so still, the poison in his throat or the bullet in his brain? He tried to raise his head and look. With a sense of deep injustice he felt Crowe's fist connect with the nape of his neck and he slumped in a daze on the planking of the deck. Before he could protest, his ears went deaf, there was a muffled roaring like the draught of a dozen blast-furnaces and a wave of heat to match. Like a storm of hail, fragments of wood pattered about him, and he heard something carry over his head and splash into the river far below.

'Don't they teach you nothing at Scotland Yard?' asked Crowe tolerantly.

Verity pulled himself up. The seat on which Dacre had been sitting was a burning ruin. The clothes were torn and blackened fragments, while the stick had vanished, probably as the object which had gone overhead and hit the river at some distance from them.

' 'e was sitting there!' said Verity indignantly. 'Smoking his cheroot!'

'Look!' said Crowe, stabbing with a bony forefinger. 'What was sitting there was the wire frame! And what was on it was his coat, hat, and a fair-haired wig with its block. Good enough for a rear view at thirty paces.'

'Mr Crowe, he was smoking a cigar!'

Crowe raised his eyes to heaven in supplication.

'Did it smell like a cigar to you?'

'Can't say it did, Mr Crowe. But then there was that ship smell everywhere, like what they use to get the moth out of clothes.'

'Naphtha,' said Crowe glumly. 'Goes up like the Fourth of July. Turns gunpowder into a bomb that might sink a cruiser. Takes a short fuse. That's what you saw smoking.'

'He might a-bloody killed me, Mr Crowe!'

'I guess that was the idea, old friend! It must figure somewhere in his scheme of things.'

Verity stared at the burning slats and the twisted section of the ship's rail, bent by the force of the explosion.

'If you 'adn't been 'ere, Mr Crowe . . . knowing about trapping and traps as you do. . .'

'Save it,' said Crowe briefly.

'I may save it, Mr Crowe, but I shan't forget easy.'

They looked about them, peering over the ship's sides.

'He's gone,' said Crowe philosophically. 'Clean gone.'

'But *how*, Mr Crowe?'

'Simplest way in the world, Mr Verity. You and I come out here and see what looks like Lieutenant Dacre on the far seat. We shan't take our eyes off him, shall we? We daren't for fear he's waiting with his pistol cocked. Forward we go, just in time to reach the dummy as it goes up with a bang and takes us too. And all this time, Mr Dacre is back near the wall of the saloon, hiding under a seat or whatever. As soon as we're walking to glory with our backs to him, he tiptoes round the side of the saloon and slips into the crowd. For a certainty he's wearing a different suit of clothes and looking a new man by now!'

The force of the blast had temporarily stunned the occupants of the auction saloon, but now there were sounds of growing confusion. Two of the windows had been blown in and several of the traders nearby had been cut by the glass. It was evident that the *Fidèle* was on fire, to a greater or lesser extent, and the doors were jammed by men trying to force their way out. The sight of drifting smoke and a ripple of flame redoubled the energy of the fugitives. Verity caught sounds of 'She's on fire! On fire!' and even 'Ship going down!' From high above them came a long, shrill blast on the ship's whistle.

In the pandemonium, he saw Captain Oliphant and the two plain-suited Marine privates emerge on the after-deck. Crowe spoke to his commander and Verity heard Oliphant's mild voice rise in a petulant wail.

'Gone? What do you mean, sir? What the devil do you mean? How can he have gone?'

The ship was steering for the quay again. In the panic, men were scrambling for the lower deck, ready to throw themselves ashore, or into the water if necessary, before the

Fidèle should blow up and sink. From somewhere deep down in the ship there was a booming sound, repeated no more than thirty seconds later. In the fight to get ashore, Captain Oliphant's dozen guards would be overwhelmed and the chances of catching Dacre at this stage were almost nil. Verity, finding the saloon doors blocked, kicked out the remaining fragments of glass from one of the shattered windows, and stepped cautiously through it.

The room was half empty but there was still a good deal of confusion. He shouldered his way to the platform where Vignie still stood, imperturbable among the chaos. He had brought the second girl, Nabyla, on to the dais. As the bill promised, she was a young Arab woman with dark, expressive eyes, her gloss of black hair waved to her shoulders. Her soft figure was carefully revealed in another red singlet and dark blue tights.

'Sir,' said Vignie reasonably, seizing the opportunity of Verity's approach, 'there's a prize for you! Beauty of the harem. The well-kept thighs, the proud Arabian features, and a rump like a young duchess. . .'

Verity glared at him.

'I ain't time for that, my man!' he said briskly. 'Miss Jolly! Where is she! Sharp's the word and quick's the motion! Let's have her back in safe-keeping!'

Vignie resigned himself to leaving Nabyla unsold.

'Safe enough,' he said wearily. 'Mrs Lily and Mr Verity took her away five minutes ago, when the noise began.'

'I'm Verity!' said Verity indignantly. 'And that's Mrs Lily over there!'

'No you're not,' said Vignie confidently. 'Not unless you're a pair of quick-change artists. Miss Jolly was signed for nice and regular. And a warrant-card was shown.'

'That's a warrant-card!' said Verity, flourishing it angrily.

'To be sure it might be. Or a passable imitation of one.'

Verity thought for a moment.

'What might these two persons have looked like? Fair and tall either of them?'

'Fair but short, both of 'em.'

'Not Dacre then. And Miss Jolly went, thinking she was with me?'

'Ah,' said Vignie. 'She went not knowing nor caring. I guess she overheard 'em say that the men who was to kill her were fighting their way in and she must be got out for her life. And you may ask anyone, sir, as to my instructions. In the event of such attack, I was to give her into the safe-keeping of the officers as soon as possible.'

There was no more to be done. Verity pushed his way back to the deck, where Sergeant Crowe was standing expectantly with his hat in his hand.

'How's the outlook?' he inquired.

'Blue as old stilton,' said Verity with fury, and strode toward Captain Oliphant.

15

'He's caught sure enough,' said Sergeant Crowe confidentially. 'There's a search on every road. No one gets on a train or a steamboat without being seen down to the drawers. Every street and every building is turned over. There'll be more of Oliphant's men in St Louis by morning than bugs in a plumtree.'

'He's out already, Mr Crowe. 'im and the rest of his villains, and Miss Jolly, and the other two young persons in his power.'

The two men stared out across the twilit river from the long quay. Parties of blue-uniformed guardsmen were moving from one steamboat to another in turn, searching the empty vessels.

'How?' asked Crowe reasonably. 'I guess I shall have the greatest respect for your Lieutenant Dacre before this caper is done. But even a mouse that can't show its identity couldn't get out of St Louis tonight.'

'Roads,' said Verity, 'carriages and carts.'

'Blocked,' said Crowe. 'Public requested not to travel except in cases of necessity. Kidnappers and killers await them. Hardly a market-cart passed through, and those that did were almost laid in pieces by the militia.'

'Railways, Mr Crowe.'

'Likewise, Mr Verity. No trains since Miss Jolly's abduction, but the depots and tracks are guarded. The first train that leaves in the morning is likely to be picked clean as a pin.'

'That leaves the river, Mr Crowe.'

'Well,' said Crowe patiently, 'no steamboats in either direction until tomorrow. Again, when the passengers come to board, there'll be an inspection of them and their bags which will make Judgment Day look like Aunt Dinah's barn dance.'

'There must be other boats, Mr Crowe.'

'Yes, Mr Verity. However, it ain't easy to get a dozen men with three struggling prisoners into a row boat, and just push off down a thousand miles of the Mississippi.'

'Private yachts, Mr Crowe? Pleasure steamers?'

'Yes, Mr Verity. A dinky little ship, the *Anna*, went downstream under private charter from the hiring yard beyond the quay.'

'That's 'im, Mr Crowe! Don't I know it! How the mischief else should he get a dozen villains, three unfortunates, and all his baggage out of here!'

'Thing is, Mr Verity, the *Anna* sailed at one o'clock and only stopped at one landing between here and Cairo. You and me saw Lieutenant Dacre and Miss Jolly still on the *Fidèle* after two o' clock. So unless he swam downstream at twenty miles an hour, towing her in his wake, he's not on the *Anna*.'

But Verity's eyes were bright.

'Hello,' he said. 'This got a ripe aroma about it! What instructions were telegraphed to Cairo and them other towns about stopping ships from St Louis?'

'To stop and search any ship which had left St Louis after

two o'clock. The ones that had left before were notified.'

'Including the *Anna*?'

'Yes,' said Crowe impatiently, 'but they can't be on the *Anna*. She'd cleared the landing twenty miles downstream by the time your Mr Dacre could have got Miss Jolly off the *Fidèle*, and the trap was already in place, on the roads and the railroad.'

' 'ow many of these little charter paddlers might there be, Mr Crowe?'

'Several,' said Crowe defensively, 'but the only other one to leave the yard today came upstream to the quay, on charter, to load supplies for tomorrow, and hasn't been anywhere since!'

'Her name, Mr Crowe?'

'The *Rosa*.'

'Sort of a sister ship, Mr Crowe?'

'If you say so, Mr Verity. But she did no more than leave the yard about three o'clock and come upstream a mile or so to the quay. She was coming towards the *Fidèle* not away from her! What use is that to your clever lieutenant?'

Verity sighed with a deep contentment.

'Mr Crowe. This afternoon, I was stoopid and nearly got blown to smithereens. You saved me and, in due course, I mean to show my gratefulness. There ain't a man I've ever met that was cleverer than you in such matters as traps and snares. But there's one trick that I might teach you yet. Now, we shall need two horses, I think, and a reply to all them telegraphs saying where the *Anna* might have passed.'

'Why?' asked Crowe simply.

'You show me the *Rosa* and I'll show you why, Mr Crowe.'

They found the paddle-yacht with its tall trim funnel, its white-painted sides and its paddle-boxes bearing the name *Rosa* in bold black capitals.

'Well?'

'Lovely paintwork, ain't it, Mr Crowe? Over the deck, if you please, and we'll lower ourselves down on the paddle-sponson on the far side.'

173

Crowe followed him, the two men clambering over the rails on the far side and letting themselves down on to the little platform by the paddle-box, the dark river-water sucking and lapping just below them.

'Just lean out, Mr Crowe, while I hold you steady, and read what it says on that paddle-box.'

Crowe embraced the sides of the box and leaned out over the water.

'*Rosa*,' he said presently. 'What else should it say?'

Verity thought about this for a moment.

'Half a minute, Mr Crowe. 'old on while I have a real stretch.'

Verity edged outward, relying on Crowe's weight to balance him against toppling into the muddy water. He reached out with his hand and patted the flank of the vessel affectionately.

'Oh, my!' he said softly. 'Oh, my eye! Ain't this a prime caper, though?'

He edged himself back gingerly on to the paddle-sponson, his face set with a plump smugness which displayed his total self-satisfaction. He confronted the gaunt, sceptical figure of Sergeant Crowe.

'Mr Crowe, 'ow far across might you think this river was? You being a hunting and guiding man. Half a mile?'

'Yes,' said Crowe. 'Not less.'

'And getting wider as it goes down towards the sea, Mr Crowe? Same as all rivers do?'

'Yes, Mr Verity. What in damnation are you on about?'

Verity glowed with gratification.

'What I'm on about, Mr Crowe is what I was on about before. Lieutenant Dacre, and his villains, and his gold, and the young persons what's to be foully abused and then beastly murdered, is through your guards and miles away by this time.'

Crowe's suspicion deepened.

'Who says so?'

'You do, Mr Crowe, telling me about the river. And my fingers do, too. Just look at 'em!'

174

'They got dirt on.'

'Paint, Mr Crowe, black paint from the name on the side. Still sticky.'

'Boats get painted, Mr Verity. Keeps 'em smart.'

Verity nodded, as though all this were perfectly reasonable.

'Yes, Mr Crowe. There ain't no reason why someone shouldn't paint *Rosa* and leave all the letters wet. But, Mr Crowe, the last one ain't wet. Just *Ros*. Now a man that wanted to change *Rosa* to *Anna*, or back again, wouldn't need to concern himself with the last letter of the name, would he? Whereas a chap who was smartening up the vessel would paint all the letters.'

'He might break off till the next day.'

'Mr Crowe! There ain't even an undercoat on it!'

'All right,' said Crowe, conceding the point. 'Give us the story.'

'Thank you, Mr Crowe. Now, at one o'clock, there was two vessels moored under the bank outside the hiring yard. The *Rosa* goes downstream with her name painted as *Anna* on the side facing this bank. Don't matter about the other side. They could hang a tarpaulin over it, and in any case, it's too far for a man on the opposite bank to see. What everyone on this side thinks they see is *Anna*, on her way downstream long before Lieutenant Dacre and Miss Jolly. After an hour or so, she turns, in a part of the river that's out of sight, and what everyone sees coming back is the *Rosa*, which is what it says on her other side. On the far side, where no one can see, there's a cove with black paint changing her to the *Rosa* on that side too. She comes right up to the quay here and moors, ready for tomorrow. No reason for anyone here to think she hasn't come upstream from the yard. After all, the *Rosa* ain't going anywhere. Lieutenant Dacre can't escape on her, so no one asks questions about her, all right?'

'And the *Anna* '

'Yes, Mr Crowe. The *Anna* is moored just out of sight of the quay, all ready and waiting for Lieutenant Dacre and the doxy, and his two accomplices. I'd bet the side of her facing the shore, when he's pointing upstream, says *Rosa*. Five or ten minutes after the snatch, they're all on board. Turn her round, facing downstream. She says *Anna* on the side that everyone can see. And that's a boat that Captain Oliphant tells the look-outs to let pass because she left too early to be used in Mr Dacre's escape.'

'They saw her pass Sulphur Springs Landing once,' said Crowe. 'How can she account for passing it a second time?'

'A man might do it by dark, Mr Crowe. More likely, he'd ground her, run her into a creek and hide her, even sink her. I daresay he's got twenty miles of a big river to do it in, and most of the banks not much better than a wilderness. If they should look for the *Anna*, it'll be much further downstream, having seen her pass Sulphur Springs. Neat, ain't it?'

'And when he's done with her?'

'I don't say he has. But if he has, he might have other transport waiting. A boat that was never near St Louis, perhaps, and can move freely. Or he might find his way past the landing at Sulphur Springs easy enough. After all, so long as they think the boat never went back as far as St Louis and couldn't have picked up anyone from inside your Captain Oliphant's perimeter, why should they care if the *Anna* was moored upstream for the night?'

'And just how did you figure all this out, Mr Verity?'

Verity emitted a faint chuffing laugh and his shoulders moved in slow rhythmical mirth.

'Mr Crowe, when you was trapping, didn't you never find that after a bit you'd start to think the same as your prey? Now, I been after Lieutenant Dacre quite a bit. He's clever, all right. But like all his kind, he's clever in the same way. Sort of personal style. First off, you think he's beyond catching. And then you begin to see things his way and you can guess, almost, what he'll do. It ain't just being clever that would help a man to catch him. It's a sort of instinct.'

'And now?'

176

'Well, Mr Crowe. Since the *Anna* ain't been past Sulphur Springs twice, she's somewhere between here and there. She won't move again till first light, and if Lieutenant Dacre means to abandon her and move by other means, he'll hardly contrive that in the dark either. Now, two horses, and you and me could get as far as Sulphur Springs soon after midnight. I'd rather drive than ride, meself, but I daresay I could sit out a five-mile-an-hour trot!'

Leaving a single paragraph behind, as his confidential explanation to Captain Oliphant, Sergeant Crowe led the way along the rutted highway which followed the western bank of the Mississippi.

'You couldn't a-done otherwise, Mr Crowe,' said Verity, gasping behind him. 'If we'd waited longer, day might break before we got started.'

Below them, the river shone in moon and starlight. They were beyond the outlying villas of St Louis, where magnolias clustered over gateways, beyond the orchards and the vines, now heavy with blue grapes. The black dirt of the road flew from their horses' hooves as they passed between fields of yellow stubble which seemed to stretch to an infinite horizon. Then the terrain grew wilder and more overgrown, the water-logged flats beside the river being cluttered by thick undergrowth and trees whose branches seemed to interlock. Once they saw the silver smoke of a steamboat rising in wisps through the pale starlight. But it was a massive five-decker ploughing its way upstream.

Somewhen after midnight, as Verity was once again closing his mind to the soreness of unaccustomed riding, he heard the rhythm of the hoofbeats ahead of him change, and realized that Crowe was reining in his horse.

'Mr Verity! What would you say to that?'

But still the river was wide and tranquil in the opalescent light. At its centre, there appeared a dark islet, if anything more overgrown than the banks on either side.

'Now,' said Crowe, 'I'll be damned if that ain't the fanciest sight I ever clapped eyes on!'

177

'Mr Crowe?'

'There,' said Crowe, 'on the far side of that island. Look again. Just hanging in the air like a drift of mist.'

' 'ere, Mr Crowe! Ain't you got a pair of eyes, though!'

'The big steamboats pass this side,' said Crowe, 'You couldn't ask for a quieter nor more private berth than over there. And if you set your heart on sailing first thing, of course you'd have to keep a pound or two of pressure up. And you can't do that when a boat's moored, unless you let out a puff or two of steam.'

'Couldn't be smoke from a camp-fire or cabin, Mr Crowe?'

Crowe laughed.

'Out there? Not unless a man grew so tired of life that he chose to end it by a dose of river fever. I daresay there's a few dead slaves there, who thought to cross the river and get free to Illinois. And that's a good enough reason for most folks to give it a wide sweep.'

They dismounted and led their horses down to the marshy river bank.

'It couldn't be poor souls trying to escape their bondage, Mr Crowe?'

'And helping the bloodhounds by sending up signals, Mr Verity?'

When the horses were tethered, Crowe cut a pair of stout switches from a nearby bush.

'Right, Mr Verity. Now, supposing this is Lieutenant Dacre's party, what do you aim to find?'

'Mr Dacre and Miss Jolly, first off,' said Verity, gazing out across the sluggish current. 'Then there'll be several of his villains, with a hired engineer and captain for the steam-yacht. All of 'em probably from the Hicks and Sanchez lot that traded in girls who was took to houses of debauchery elsewhere in America. And the ones on board are probably cargo for the same destination, with the sale price as the reward for the crew that gets 'em there.'

Crowe sat down and began to unlace his boots.

'In that case, my friend, if we can only find the poor

young things and cut their throats quick, we shall do them a
service. They treat 'em so nefarious in those places that
never a girl is allowed out alive to tell the tale. Mostly, the
girls destroy themselves, if they get the chance, rather than
face any more of it.'

'Watcher doing, Mr Crowe?'

'Never learnt to swim and keep your clothes dry, Mr
Verity? Tie 'em in a bundle to the stick, and hold it out
of the water as you swim. Boots'll be too heavy for that.
Fasten the laces round the front of your neck and let the
boots lie on your back. They won't stay quite dry, but
you'll be glad enough to have them the other side when you
need to kick a man's privates or jump on his neck.'

'Just as you say, Mr Crowe.'

Presently the absurdly contrasted figures, Verity pale
and plump, Crowe thin and tanned, approached the ripple
of the river flow.

'Don't wade more than you can help, Mr Verity. Strike
out as soon as you can. It's like a quicksand under here.
And don't let it in your mouth. It's more mud than water.'

Soundlessly, they entered the dark flood. Verity launched
himself forward as the water lapped his thighs, his clothes
fastened like a tramp's bundle to the switch. The current
was not as strong as he feared and by swimming slightly
upstream he found he was able to keep in Crowe's wake as
they crossed the river toward the islet. As a boy, he had
swum in the moorland pools and rivers of Cornwall. To
cover two or three hundred yards was an ordeal but not an
impossibility, so long as a man took his time.

For all that, it seemed a very long time. Once he nearly
lost the switch with his clothes tied to it, but at length the
dark jungle of the islet rose higher and higher above him,
blotting out the paler night sky. He tried to find a footing,
and touched a slime which stirred under his feet. But he was
almost there and, presently, Crowe's arm reached out to
him. He waded from the stream and sat down, wheezing,
gasping and trying not to cough. Crowe had shaken and
rubbed off as much moisture as he could and was dressing

179

himself again. Each man carefully undid the bundle of his clothing and drew from one of the boots his Colt revolver, which Crowe had insisted on carrying in this fashion to keep it dry upon their backs.

'Don't rely on it, however,' he breathed in Verity's ear, 'there's no telling that it ain't had a slop or two of river water.'

They set off through the tangled brush, Crowe leading the way and moving with the silence of a ghost. Verity followed in his footsteps, marvelling at the Marine's ability to sense which twig would and which would not give out a faint crack, like a distant pistol shot. By contrast, his own stealthy progress sounded like a wounded animal thrashing about in the undergrowth. Crowe turned once or twice and, even in the darkness, Verity was conscious of his friend's scowl of disapproval.

Nevertheless, they crossed the neck of the islet without incident and stood among the fringe of trees on the far side. The *Anna* rested at a slight tilt in the shallows, an anchorage from which the use of one paddle would quickly free her. She was about a hundred yards downstream and there was a broad plank running from her paddle-sponson to the muddy foreshore. The two sergeants paused but there was no sign of anyone either ashore or on the little ship, nor any sound except faintly from the vessel itself.

Crowe moved first, edging along the marshy bank to a point from which they could see the uncurtained windows of the saloon where these faced the shore. Verity followed, thankful that the lapping and gurgling of the current among the muddy inlets more than obliterated the sound of his own slithering footsteps. Presently Crowe paused, raising a hand silently to halt his friend.

Through the lighted windows there was a scene which suggested a dinner party, or rather its aftermath. Several men, all of them unknown to Verity, were sitting in their shirt-sleeves at a long table with glasses before them and cards in their hands, the blue-grey cigar smoke rising in irregular clouds. There was no sign of either Dacre or Jolly.

A girl whom he had never seen before was standing naked by the table, filling the men's glasses when told to do so and acting as a brothel parlour-maid. She was Asian in both colouring and feature and Verity guessed she must be the young woman, Jennifer, who had been kept at the Five Points house in New York. The men certainly seemed to have had long experience of her, handling her with a vindictive familiarity. The girl, who reminded Verity of so many of her kind he had seen in India, was clearly not used to being naked with so many men, however accustomed she might be to receiving them singly. If she retained anything of Moslem belief, Verity thought, the ordeal must seem infinitely worse. As if sensing this, the men at the table summoned her, stroked and patted her thighs and loins while she filled their glasses or lit their cheroots, their eyes watching her lean across the table and their hands descending explosively on the olive-skinned cheeks of Jennifer's bottom.

At least she was still alive. But this relief was soon tempered by another girl's shrill cry. This time it was the blonde, whom Verity knew must be Maggie, her hair falling about a face that was wet with tears, her voice keening with terror, as two men dragged her past the saloon window toward some imagined horror in the cabin beyond.

Verity looked quickly at Crowe and then his blood ran chill at the most appalling sound of all. From the undergrowth behind them came a wild howl for blood. It was impossible not to turn round, to confront the dun-coloured shape and the white fangs, twenty feet away and straining toward them. The man who held the leash was a mere shadow in the darkness. Verity and Crowe reached for their guns as the bloodhound gave a snarl of fury, but there was a voice which came clearly from the deck of the *Anna*, to which they had now turned their backs.

'Oblige me by keepin' your hands where they can be seen.'

Verity had not heard that voice since three years earlier in the expensively-furnished house in Albemarle Street, yet he knew it at once.

'It ain't no hardship to blow both your heads off and have done with it,' added Dacre casually. 'Or y' may match yourselves with that brute of a dog.'

The man who held the leash stepped forward in the faint light from the saloon windows of the little steamer. The strong face, itself as surly as the dog's, identified him as Cowhide.

'Turn about,' said Dacre to his two captives, 'and follow the plank up to the deck. There are two revolvers sighted upon you and the dog at your backs, so have a care.'

Verity clasped his hands on the top of his head and followed Crowe up the plank to the steamboat's sponson. He thought with desperate haste and some confusion, though one thing was clear. This time it was Dacre who had profited by calculating Verity's likely response to the abduction of Jolly. The cracksman had deduced that Verity would solve the mystery of the escape from St Louis, and accordingly a trap had been laid at the anchorage of the *Anna*. Verity stood on the deck and faced his adversary with a confidence he did not feel.

'Right, Lieutenant Dacre,' he said solemnly, 'you got about half an hour to save your skin by acting sensible. There's a regiment in St Louis that knows where we've gone and that'll be down the river on a steamer soon enough.'

'Damme,' said Dacre, smoothing his fair whiskers with the back of his hand, 'was there ever a fellow who backed such lame nags? On a night like this, you might hear the beat of a ship's paddles ten miles off. And curse me if I hear so much as a gnat singing!'

'You'll 'ear singing all right, before this is over!' said Verity, as if hoping to overawe Dacre by his anger. 'You ain't got a fly's chance in a spider's web of getting Miss Jolly and the gold off this boat!'

Dacre gave a high-pitched, neighing laugh.

'My dear fellah! Miss Jolly ain't here! Nor any gold but what men carry in their pockets! Such fortune as I have is safe, far and away. As for Miss Jolly, she must afford a day or two of sport before being put out of her misery. But it shall not happen here.'

Crowe looked sideways at Verity.

'Drop the subject,' he said.

Verity ignored him and addressed himself to Lucifer and Bull-Peg, who now stood grinning at him from just behind Dacre.

'You men! Take your chance now and go! If you think to have them two girls below as your reward, you ain't got a hope of cheating the gallows. There ain't a dealer or a bawdy-house you can sell 'em to. They'll be watched for at every port down the river, every house in New Orleans, even in Havana or Mexico. Drop it all and run while you got the chance. Half an hour more and your goose is cooked.'

Lucifer's fat pale face creased and dimpled with a girlish snigger. Bull-Peg's mouth opened in wide, soundless mirth.

'Don't he force the pace, though?' said Dacre, appealing to the world at large against Verity's aspersions. 'And ain't I always paid my way in yaller boys – dollars or sovs? Miss Maggie and her Khan bitch ain't to be sold anywhere. There's two shallow keeping-places dug for them, just out there in the dark, to hold 'em when the sport's done. Dammit, look at the time! They ain't no business to be still alive now!'

Crowe intervened.

'Lieutenant Dacre, sir! The United States Treasury has no interest in any crime committed outside American jurisdiction. Its exclusive concern is with the preservation of confidence in the currency. Apart from that, sir, the gold is nothing to us. Name your place, sir, and the right to the gold shall be conferred upon you in exchange for the release of those three young women whom you now hold. Let the place be beyond the reach of our law, sir, where you may be safe. Let the agreement carry indemnity for any crime committed by you upon American soil. Your own part shall be merely the agreement never to reveal the fact of the robbery.'

183

Dacre shook his head, slow and wondering.

'Deuced elegant!' He turned to Lucifer, 'Damme, but ain't it a pretty sentiment, though?' He surveyed Crowe once more. 'Why, sir, you put a proposition beyond all reason. I have the whores and I have the gold. Now you propose that I shall give up half of what I own so that I might keep the rest. Plain robbery, sir, ain't it?'

Lucifer simpered and added his own explanation.

'Miss Maggie and tawny Jennifer got to be hunted presently. Naked on the little island, to prevent evasion. Dragged for with dog and whip, right to the finish. Bull-Peg ain't never done that before, not all the way. He got a right to it once, eh, cap'n? He been so worked up about it, he ain't even been able to take nourishment the last day or two.'

Verity looked at the two creatures standing behind Dacre and saw the eyes of mania in each face, Lucifer's soft with a womanly spite, Bull-Peg's with the eager fury of homicide. For the first time, he reconciled himself to inevitable death in the remote swamps of the Mississippi.

'Take them,' said Dacre, 'and do as we arranged.'

He stepped forward so quickly that Verity had no time to react as Dacre drew the Colt revolvers from his prisoners' belts, tossing them over the side of the boat and into the dark water. There was a movement behind the two sergeants, Cowhide tying their wrists, acting as escort with Bull-Peg and Lucifer.

Cowhide pushed his prisoners down the little companion-way to the engine-room at the centre of the ship. The polished steel of the pistons shone with sleek and dormant power, the faint whisper of steam indicating that the *Anna* had been kept in readiness for instant departure. At either side of the engine-room was a small iron door giving access to the interior of the paddle-boxes. Bull-Peg opened one of these and stepped through, followed by Cowhide. Dacre and Lucifer kept their guns unwaveringly on the two sergeants. Then Verity was ordered through the door. He stooped and straightened up on the other side, finding himself between Cowhide and Bull-Peg.

The space within the box was almost filled by the broad, intricate ironwork of the upper half of the red-painted paddle-wheel. The inside surface of the iron box was unpainted, a dark oval space about eight feet high. A narrow ledge, enabling a man to inspect the wheel, ran round the inner perimeter of the box, just above the black, sluggish water in which the lower half of the wheel was submerged.

Cowhide and Bull-Peg led Verity to the outward-facing round of the great wheel, the sergeant glancing about him for any means of escape. But they had tied his wrists before bringing him down and Cowhide's gun was at his back. There was hardly a way out of the paddle-box, other than through the door into the engine-room. The space between the wheel and the inspection board was so narrow that, even left to his own devices, a man would need to manoeuvre carefully to slip down into the water and dive clear of the ship.

They pushed him back against the wheel and he felt leather cuffs close tightly round his wrists and heard the tiny rattle of the chain which was attached to them. He was spreadeagled against the wet, iron ribs of the wheel, wrists and ankles held tight and immovable. He was able to lodge his heels on one of the iron ribs to ease the pain of hanging from the wrist-cuffs and anklets, but otherwise he was helpless. Cowhide's eyes directed his attention to the row of sharpened spikes, short and spaced at a distance of two or three inches. They projected inward along the bottom of the paddle-box to prevent weed or timber being carried up by the wheel. For a man tied to the wheel as it began to turn, they were the means of tearing first his clothes from his body, then his skin in deep and bloody furrows, finally inflicting wounds from which he would die quite quickly. A man who was lucky would drown from the repeated immersions. If not, the spikes would kill him, perhaps, after they had harrowed him fifty or a hundred times.

'Lis'n me!' gasped Verity to Cowhide. 'You got one last

chance. Turn approver. Be a evidence. Else it's your neck
they'll stretch.'

Cowhide looked dumbly at him with wide brown eyes,
then shrugged and edged away. Presently Verity heard
them attaching Crowe to the other side of the wheel, above
the spikes which edged the box there. His mind worked at
the problem. There would be an hour before the wheel
began its first, ghastly turn. It would take that long to
dispose of Maggie and Jennifer. But what use was such
respite to a man who could move neither hand nor foot?
And what use was it to an officer whose duty was to save
the young women's lives?

The iron door to the hull clanged shut, the last ray of
the oil lamp was extinguished. In the cavernous darkness,
every drip of water sounded like the wakened echoes of a
tomb.

16

'Mr Crowe! Can you move at all?'

'Fingers and toes,' said Crowe, gasping with the exertion.
'What about you?'

'Same here. How long do you think we got, then?'

'Sure as hell wish I knew. Not that it makes much odds
if we can't get these goddam cuffs off. They're a sight too
snug to slip off, and the bastards have fixed them so there's
nothing to work them against. They're leather with a steel
chain running through two eyelets. They use 'em in mad-
houses when necessary.'

'Do they now, Mr Crowe? Do they?'

There was a silence between the two men for a moment,
the water dripping irregularly from the iron ribs of the
paddle-wheel into the dark river below. Then they heard
shouts of laughter and the hollow baying of the bloodhound.

'Saints in heaven!' said Crowe softly. 'They really mean

to hunt those two young women naked to their deaths! Your Lieutenant Dacre isn't just a villain. He's a criminal lunatic!'

' 'ad crossed my mind, Mr Crowe.'

'There must be something. . .'

'I was just thinking about my frock-coat, Mr Crowe. Very decent sort of coat. 'ad it a year or two.'

'Oh, God!' said Crowe, as if despairing of his companion.

'Mr Crowe, they never bothered to empty the pockets.'

'They wouldn't have to, would they? Tied like this, you can't get your hand within two or three feet of the pockets.'

'Very true, Mr Crowe. All the same, I think I shall try to undo the button at the front.'

'With no hands?'

'Deep breaths, Mr Crowe. A swelling of the diaphragm and abdomen. You try it too.'

'We aren't all built the same way, Mr Verity.'

'Indeed not, Mr Crowe. All the same, you must often have wished you'd got a decent bit of flesh about you. You don't want to be skinny in this world, not if you can help it.'

There was a pause. Then the metallic resonance of the paddle-box was woken by the straining howl of Verity's exertions as he pumped the air in and out of his lungs. The button of the frock-coat, never very securely attached, creased the worsted cloth on either side. Verity paused after a few minutes, exhausted by the exertion, and then presently the howl of deep breathing began once more. Almost at once, Crowe heard a cry of triumph.

'That's it, Mr Crowe!'

In the little world which the two condemned men now shared, even the trivial defeat of a button was greeted with the jubilation appropriate to a great military victory.

'Now what, Mr Verity?'

'Well, Mr Crowe, I ain't making any promises. But in the side pocket of the coat, I got my pocket-knife. Course, I can't get a hand near it. But I might be able to wriggle against this wheel so as to work the coat up me back. All

187

right? Now, if I turn the fingers down just this minute, I can touch the top of my head. So if I could sort of work the coat into a pile on the shoulders, I might get at the pocket.'

'Go on, man! Try it!'

'Nice and easy, Mr Crowe. If I do get it over too far, that pocket'll be upside down and the weight of the knife must bring it straight out and splash into the river. A man gotta have patience over this, Mr Crowe.'

'There isn't time for patience, Verity!'

'Slow and steady wins the race, Mr Crowe. There ain't but one way now.'

Verity began to work his back up and down against the iron ribs of the paddle-wheel. At first it was easy to raise the lower part of the coat by virtue of the horizontal gathering at the back. There was enough play between the wrist-cuffs and anklets for him to raise and lower his body six or eight inches. He felt the skirt of the long coat riding about his waist.

After that, the difficulties began. His own shoulder-blades seemed an obstacle in themselves and he felt the packed folds of the coat like an immovable bundle. From somewhere outside he heard a girl's cry, not a scream but the more chilling howl of abject suffering which might precede humiliation and death. Spurred on as much by this as by his own impending torment, he worked his back desperately against the strut of iron which ran just under his shoulder-blades themselves, Despite the damp chill in the iron vault of the paddle-box, he was astonished to feel sweat running down into the cavities of his eyes. But even the sweat felt as cold to him as the touch of a melting icicle.

Pressing his back hard against the bundled cloth behind him, he could feel in general outline the firm shapes of the contents of the pocket which was deep in the side of the coat. It was possible now to wriggle it up further so that it fell forward over his shoulder. Yet this was the point of maximum danger. If the cloth slid forward and the weight of the little knife escaped, it would slither out and plop into the water below him. After that, there was no more help.

Very cautiously, he worked his shoulders to move the pocket with its hard outlines until he could feel it twisted against the back of his neck. Then he had to lower his head forward and allow the cloth to fall so that it obscured his vision as it hung over his face. Before he could raise his head and bring the folded material within range of his finger-tips, he gave a cry of anguish, quickly stifled. A small, hard shape slipped from folds of the inverted coat and, beyond the reach of his tethered hands, fell lightly into the dark water below his feet and sank at once. He heard Sergeant Crowe utter an energetic obscenity. But it was not the knife, only a pocket-compass which he had brought with him on the assumption that they might be lost in the wilderness of the Mississippi swamps.

'Now, Mr Crowe,' he said gently, as if he might be talking to himself rather than to his companion. 'Now, Mr Crowe! Not a word to be spoke. Hold yer breath and pray.'

He wrenched against the leather wrist-cuff holding his right hand above him, pulling with all his weight, and tried to invert his fingers so that they scrabbled downward to reach the top of his head, over which the coat now hung. The tips of his three middle fingers just brushed the material.

'I shall do my best to catch the knife, Mr Crowe,' he said very quietly, 'but there's bound to be a slice o' chance-medley in it.'

'Get on with it!' said Crowe impatiently. 'I never knew anything in life that wasn't chance-medley, more or less.'

Bowing his shoulders forward as far as he could, Verity felt the movement of objects in the lining of the pocket. He could do no more than use his three middle fingers as obstacles to the folded pocket-knife when it slid free, to prevent it gliding down the worsted material and falling to the water. With his left-hand fingers he could not even reach the material at all. He paused, and took several deep breaths. Then there was nothing for it but to take his chance, his right wrist twisted so vigorously that the leather at the edge of the cuff had drawn its first blood.

He felt the gentle movement and, in the intensity of the stillness, almost heard the friction of the little metal oblong against the pocket lining. He sensed it gliding toward the touch of his fingers. He felt it, cold and hard, free of the pocket. Then he lost it and then, again, somehow blocked its path with his finger-ends. It was absurd that his own life and those of four other people must now depend upon his ability to hold and lift the steel oblong with the extreme tips of his fingers.

It seemed an infinite labour, pinching the knife between his fingers, raising it as he reversed the position of his hand again, and dreading to feel the smooth metal slip inexorably from between the numbed flesh. But in a moment more, his hand was upright again and the closed knife was in the firm grip of his palm. Then he began to struggle to hold it and simultaneously, to open it by the outward flick of his thumb. It would have been difficult under any circumstances but he had always kept the hinge of the knife well-oiled and the blade itself clean. After several unsuccessful attempts he paused.

'Never call retreat, Mr Crowe!' he said fiercely. 'Ain't that what you say where you come from?'

Then he returned to the opening of the knife and, with a final effort, prized the blade out from the handle. After this, it was a matter of directing the blade downward, between the leather cuff and the skin of his wrist. To have cut through the entire cuff would have taken far too long, but Crowe had spotted the one great weakness in the equipment.

'Go for the eyelet, Mr Verity! Cut through the leather there and the chain must come free! Not more than an inch length!'

'Right, Mr Crowe!'

The little blade was sharp, but the inch of leather seemed to resist its edge for an eternity. And then Verity let out another cry.

'Done it, Mr Crowe!'

He was waving one arm triumphantly, attempting to

190

restore circulation. He turned next to his left wrist and cut the eyelet there. The leather anklets had merely strapped his feet to the paddle-wheel ribs, since he ought never to have been able to reach within six feet of them to undo them. He pulled himself on to the narrow wooden ledge running round the box, and made his way to Crowe.

'Hang on, Mr Crowe, let's 'ave your hands free!'

By the time they had finished, there were no sounds to be heard from the deck above or from the hull of the ship. Verity looked at the little iron door which led back into the engine-room.

'No!' said Crowe in a soft whisper. 'It may not open on this side. If it does, you may find a gun pointing at you when you get through. It has to be the water.'

They lowered themselves fully dressed, into the dark water and edged under the housing of the paddle, surfacing in the open night outside. Crowe managed this easily enough but Verity's bulk made it impossible for him to slip down except at the side of the great iron wheel. He thought of the spikes on the other surface and shuddered at the prospect of what he and Crowe had just escaped.

He broke surface, gasping, about ten feet from the side of the *Anna* with the hull of the little ship between him and the islet. Crowe was already paddling almost soundlessly toward the sponson and hauling himself out with a muted rush of dripping water. Verity did his best to imitate the Marine's stealth. From the dense foliage of the little island there came the baying of the dog and a man's raucous laugh. Apart from Dacre and Jolly, there were the two girls now being hunted, the hired captain and engineer of the *Anna*, and the four men at Dacre's command, whom Verity now knew to be Lucifer, Cowhide, Bull-Peg and Raoul. How many of the men were with the hunting party and how many had been left on board was mere conjecture.

The *Anna*, below decks, consisted of an engine-room amidships, the large saloon aft, and a number of small cabins in the forward part of the ship. Crowe took up his boots, which he had carried in the escape from the paddle-

191

box, laid a finger to his lips, and moved forward in stockinged-feet toward the smaller cabins. His progress was mapped by dark, wet footprints on the covered deck. With Verity just behind him, he made for a door whose little fanlight was illuminated and from which there came the voices of two men in conversation. They were, as Verity had expected, the captain and engineer, excluded from the evening's sport. Crowe cupped his hand over Verity's ear.

'Right, Mr Verity. We take one of 'em apiece. But don't move until I do – and then go like lightning for 'em. Right?'

Verity nodded energetically. Crowe braced his back against the far wall of the little passageway, inviting Verity to follow his example, as he laced his boots again. Then, with a simultaneous blow, the two men drove their heels against the fastening of the cabin door opposite them and sent it flying back. The captain and the engineer looked up in astonishment from their hands of cards. The figures in the doorway looked like nothing so much as a pair of circus clowns whose pretentious clothes had just suffered a final ignominious dowsing. Verity was about to move but Crowe motioned him back. The captain's hand shot forward to a table drawer and, in that moment, Crowe jumped, bringing the man and chair to the floor with a splintering impact. The engineer looked helplessly at Verity, getting to his feet as though in a gesture of courtesy. Verity approached, folded his fingers like a ham, and hit the man very hard under the chin. The engineer fell sideways, struck the table, and then sagged to the floor. Behind him Verity heard a muffled blow and the unmistakable click of bone, as Crowe settled his account with the captain.

'Strip 'em!' said Crowe. 'Quick as you can!'

'You nearly left it too late, Mr Crowe! That one of yours was going for the drawer!'

'I guess that's something else they never taught you at Scotland Yard, Mr Verity. We're going to need his weapon, and one sure way to find it was to give him just the chance to start moving for it. I reckon it wouldn't be much use asking him for directions in his present state.'

Crowe had opened the drawer and drawn out a clumsy-looking pistol with an elaborately-engraved butt and a barrel that seemed absurdly long.

'Hudson!' he said disparagingly. 'A toy for rich young gentlemen who fancy fighting duels without the risk of hitting anyone! Still, most guns look alike when pointing close to a man's guts!'

The cabin locker provided ample cord, used as throwing-line for the ship's main ropes. Crowe used this to truss the naked bodies of the captain and the engineer, while he and Verity did their best to struggle into the dark blue corduroy trousers and jerseys. After a quick inspection to confirm that the other forward cabins were empty, Crowe glanced down at his ill-fitting clothes.

'Not that we look much like 'em, I guess,' he said ruefully, 'but in the dark, it'll make Dacre's bullies stop just long enough to give us first chance at a shot. With four of them and two of us, we could use an advantage.'

' 'ow many bullets that thing got in it, Mr Crowe?'

'Two, Mr Verity. But they aren't likely to know that from a distance.'

They went forward as far as the engine-room. Crowe inspected several of the small iron wheels and the dials above them. He turned one of the wheels energetically to open it and closed another so tightly that the veins in his forehead were swelling with the exertion. Then he motioned Verity toward the saloon. The oil lamps on the polished table were still lit, the glasses half empty, and a fog of stale cigar smoke in the warm air. Of Dacre's accomplices and the girls there was no sign.

'I guess,' said Crowe thoughtfully, 'I guess Mr Verity we must all be hunting men at heart.'

Lucifer continued to simper, but Bull-Peg in his simple and rough manner was guffawing with sheer pleasure and with anticipation of the delights to come. Cowhide and Raoul stood back a little and watched the white men with

193

quiet amusement. Maggie and Jennifer clung naked to one another, the blonde girl's eyes wandering hopelessly with terror, while Jennifer's dark eyes flashed with a half-cowed resentment at her tormentors. Under Lucifer's supervision, Cowhide and Raoul stood the two victims side by side. With locking cuffs they joined them at their adjacent ankles. Then, by bending them, they looked each girl's outer wrist to the same cuff-chain. Lucifer giggled.

'And now, if you two beauties aim to cheat the hunt by swimming off the island, you are surely welcome to try!'

Bull-Peg untied the leash from a tree and held the straining bloodhound.

'You'll find, my dears,' said Lucifer to the two stooping girls, 'that you'll go better on elbows and knees. Now, in five minutes more we shall come for you. Cowhide and Raoul come beating and the dog come looking for his dinner. The harder you go, the longer you live. Within reason, of course.'

Lucifer nodded to Cowhide and Raoul. There were two sudden movements, two sharp reports and young women stumbled grotesquely forward on their terrified career.

'Four abreast,' said Lucifer to the others, 'dragging the ground end to end of the island. Cowhide and Raoul beat with them whips to flush 'em out if they go to ground. Bull-Peg, give that brute another good sniff at the Khan girl's things, then let it follow its nose. And remember, it's the dog that does the business. That way it looks like mis-adventure.'

'Ain't it time yet?' pleaded Bull-Peg, his large crude features contorted in an expression of genuine anxiety.

'Now,' said Lucifer reprovingly, 'ain't you been let do everything you asked with Miss Jennifer? Nothing but selfishness to spoil this for the rest of us by rushing at it now!'

Bull-Peg lowered his head submissively, not raising it again until Lucifer in his wisdom decided that the time had come for the hunters to move after their prey.

Crawling, stumbling, weeping with fright engendered by

days of ill-treatment and the promise of death, the two young women scrambled through thickets and mud. There was no sense of direction, no thought of purpose, only the insane zeal of trying to escape a death that was inevitable. Somewhere to one side of them, as it seemed, the sound of Cowhide slashing at the undergrowth with his thong was ominously clear. Behind them, the howl of the dog, though more remote, carried the chill of death to their hearts. The tawny sheen of Jennifer's hips and thighs, her ribs and upper arms, bore the fresh scars of brambles and rough twigs. Maggie's pale body was so splashed and smeared with the black mud that it was hardly lighter than Jennifer's. Despite their mutual affection, each girl now wept in her own solitary terror.

They were close to the end of the islet, with death by drowning before them and the jaws of the hound at their backs. The sound of a man's breath stilled them in their fear, knowing that it was his soft expression of triumph. Now there would be no more but Cowhide's flushing-out until the arrival of the killer-hound, and the last appalling moments. The hand which trailed the thong moved back, and the man spoke in a sharp whisper.

'Right, miss,' he said firmly, 'now you just act like a pair o' good brave girls, and these villains are going to get the shock o' their bleedin' lives!'

As they had arranged on leaving the *Anna*, it was Verity who was to guide the girls back to the little ship, while Crowe remained at large in the swampy wilderness. Maggie was, at first, too far gone in terror even to understand Verity's words, but Jennifer had begun to recover her composure and he addressed himself to her.

'Now, miss, it ain't as bad as you might fear. That blood 'ound of theirs keeps losing the scent. Having tried to abuse you by making you crawl through mud like this, o' course it do mask the scent. Villains is stupid in the end, miss. And the crueller they are, the more stupid, generally.'

The Asian girl looked at him sceptically.

'The cuffs and chains,' she said urgently, 'we can go

195

nowhere like this.'

Verity examined them.

'I'm a detective officer, miss, and I know that cuffs, like most things, can be opened if necessary. These ain't even proper police handcuffs. Good sharp bang might spring 'em.'

As the two young women crouched naked and mud-spattered, clutching one another, he found a stone with a blunted point and set to work. After several attempts the anklets still held fast.

'Miss,' said Verity, trying to rouse Maggie, 'I gotta do something more. You and your chum must wet the side o' your foot with mud and then pull as far apart as you can. There's a pistol in my pocket. What I must do is put the muzzle to the chain and fire it. The ball will go into the mud, safe enough. But there's bound to be a flash and a burn. We gotta get these things off, and quick!'

The girl nodded, the movement of her soiled blonde curtains of hair indicating that she had understood him at last. When they were both ready, Verity applied the barrel of the Hudson pistol to the centre of the stretched chain, about two inches from each girl's ankle. He chose the weakest part of the metal link, knowing that any fracture would be enough to destroy all Cowhide's careful manacling. He held his breath and squeezed the trigger. There was a roar, a flash that seemed to light the river itself, and a double cry from the two girls. With the acrid smoke in his nostrils, Verity inspected the chain, noticing for the first time the pain in his right arm from the recoil of the gun. There was a gap in the thin metal link of the little chain, quite wide enough to work the entire system of fetters loose.

As he completed this, Verity could hear shouts from the darkness, quite close by. Lucifer was petulantly inquiring which of his companions had fired a gun. Then came Raoul's voice.

'Cap'n! Cap'n! Quickly here! Here's Cowhide lying, Cap'n! Looks like he fall and break his neck!'

Verity motioned the two girls away from the voices,

196

toward the dark water of the river. He had watched Sergeant Crowe, with the effortless skill of a trapper, stalk Cowhide and bring the man down with a single, terrible blow to the neck. Raoul was now at the same spot, and Lucifer must still be with him. Only Bull-Peg with the dog was now between Verity and the *Anna*. Yet Bull-Peg would be hunting for the girls in the tangled brushwood, not in the shallows.

He led his two dishevelled charges into the water to kill any scent which the dog might pick up, and waded back, parallel to the track they had followed. They were about half-way to the *Anna* when there was a booming like distant gunfire, followed by a whistling and hissing close at hand. Verity had a brief visual recollection of Sergeant Crowe in the engine-room of the *Anna* turning the wheels of her valves. To one who had heard a ship's boilers blow, the sound was unmistakable. By the time that he caught sight of her, steam was seeping through every outlet, and Lucifer's hope of escape had taken on a significant list toward the shore.

Of Verney Dacre there was still no sight or sound. It had been Lucifer's voice which seemed to command the hunting-party. With the girls crouching to one side of him, Verity settled down in the shadows with the Hudson pistol, and its last bullet, to watch the *Anna*. So far as he knew anything about trapping, this was his snare and the crippled steamer the inevitable bait.

The sky had just begun to lighten when he saw the first figure emerge from the trees and move toward the *Anna*. He made a gesture with his hand to still Maggie's whimpering from cold. Verity had stripped himself to the waist to provide a shirt and a jersey for the girls but there was little more he could do. Peering at the newcomer again, he gave a sigh of relief as he recognized Sergeant Crowe. He was about to move forward and attract his friend's attention, when he heard a low reverberating growl. From the undergrowth behind Crowe rose the massive outline of Bull-Peg, his posture indicating the forward strain of the bloodhound on the leash.

197

The drama was being acted out fifty yards or so away, across the muddy foreshore. Crowe looked about him uncertainly and Verity rose to his feet with hands cupped and mouth wide.

'Behind you, Mr Crowe! Coming from them bushes!'

There was no way in which he could reach Crowe or Bull-Peg in time to prevent what followed. Only the bullet in the Hudson pistol would intercept the dun-coloured beast before it tore at Crowe's throat. He saw Bull–Peg slip the leash and, hardly thinking of what he proposed to do, Verity ran forward. The dog was bounding toward Crowe who half turned to meet it, though his attention was partly caught by Verity's movement. At twenty yards' range, with the Hudson pistol in a double-handed grip, Verity stopped abruptly, knowing he must shoot before the animal was too close to Crowe to make it possible. He followed the dog, his eye sighting down the barrel and, at the last opportunity, fired the pistol for the second time that night. The gun bucked in his grip and the bullet sang harmlessly over the bloodhound's back.

In an agony of failure, Verity ran on, stumbling in the soft mud and picking himself up again. Even if he had been able to reach Crowe in time, he was aware that Bull-Peg was loping forward, bellowing encouragement to the dog, on a course which was set to collide with his own. Crowe was staring at the bounding creature, as though paralysed by the menace of the fangs. The long canine body rose in a powerful dive. Crowe seemed to sag at the knees, raising his hands before him as if in a feeble attempt to shield his eyes from the savage fangs. He fell back with apparent gentleness, as if he had resigned himself to the rending torment of death and wished only to lie quietly and let the heavy beast do its work.

In his desperation, Verity took the hot barrel of the Hudson pistol and threw the gun at the dog with all his strength. Crowe was holding the animal high up on its forelegs, as its muzzle touched his throat. And then with his powerful wrists, Crowe wrenched the forelegs out and up as far as they could be forced. The hound emitted a high-pitched snarl and rolled away from its antagonist, thrashing to and fro on the ground as if in great distress. Verity supposed that Crowe must have learnt some technique for breaking the legs of a killer dog, but he had no leisure to consider the possibility. With the force of a recoiling cannon, Bull-Peg charged him in the side and knocked him sprawling.

He slithered across several yards of mud and spun on to his knees to raise himself just as Bull-Peg's heavy boot, aimed at his head, caught him on the shoulder and knocked him on his back again. It could only be a matter of a minute or less before Crowe arrived, and Bull-Peg had to finish his business fast. A second paralysing kick to the shoulder sent Verity slithering across the mud. But he had seen enough wrestling in his Cornish childhood to know when the time had come to ride with a blow and let it carry him beyond harm's reach. He spun himself as far and as fast as he could across the dark slime of the foreshore, gaining the few vital seconds necessary to get to his feet before Bull-Peg could kick again.

Bull-Peg, head lowered and fists fencing ahead of him, came at a charge. Verity caught a blow to the side of the face, which brought a flow of blood from a split gum, but he stepped back and spun, launching himself after and getting his adversary's neck in the crook of his arm. Now it was a simple matter of bowing Bull-Peg and holding him, 'in Chancery', until Crowe came to his assistance. Ten seconds more and the crop-headed giant would be done for.

Yet in that brief space several things occurred. The first was that Verity, with all his weight and strength, was unable to bow Bull-Peg's powerful shoulders. The huge man seemed, if anything, to straighten up further and threw Verity from him with a tremendous backward thrust of his doubled arms. The impact of the knuckled elbow drove like a hammer into Verity's navel, so that he fell retching on his knees. Bull-Peg was on him in an instant, holding his victim flat on his back, ham-like knees pinning Verity's

199

arms to his sides as he sat astride the sergeant's limp body.
Grunting with irritation at the delay in despatching him,
Bull-Peg set his fingers round Verity's throat and clamped
the wind-pipe tight. The blood began to roar like a torrent
in Verity's ears. His arms were immobilized and he could
not throw Bull-Peg's weight from him. Only his legs were
free to kick vainly in the air. How many seconds before
Crowe could reach him? Too many, he thought.

And then, with the greatest gentleness and consideration,
Bull-Peg relaxed the grip and allowed him to breathe again.
Verity saw the big man's head nod, as though he might be
falling gradually into a light doze. The head nodded a
second time and the heavy body turned in a casual motion
and lay beside Verity. Crowe was still twenty yards away,
running towards the scene. Verity looked up and saw fury
in a pair of beautiful Asian eyes as Jennifer raised the cone
of rock to strike a third blow at the head of her tormentor.

'No!' shouted Crowe urgently. 'Let him be! Without him
there may be no witness to send Lucifer and Dacre to the
gallows!'

The girl paused, unconvinced but uncertain. She held
the stone tightly, eighteen inches or so above Bull-Peg's
wounded crown. She was wearing only the blue jersey
which Verity had stripped off for her. The naked gold of
Jennifer's full hips and agile legs bore witness to the man's
ill-treatment of her. Crowe approached her warily.

'There's murder done, miss,' he said coaxingly. 'But one
of them must be broken before the tale can be told. Kill
this man, and the others who laughed at you during your
misery may go free to mock you still. Spare him now, and
he may live to suffer worse than death, or come to the
gallows himself.'

As she continued to hesitate, he closed his hand over hers
and took the stone from her. She looked at neither of the
two sergeants, walking back with eyes lowered to the place
where Maggie still crouched. Verity struggled to his feet.
The bloodhound lay as still as Bull-Peg himself.

' 'ere, Mr Crowe! What you done to that savage brute

then? I thought you was lying down to let it eat you up!'

Crowe looked very modest.

'I heard it worked with wild prairie dogs, Mr Verity, and I hadn't much option but to try it on this one. Never mind the fangs nor the mouth, I guess that's the mistake a man makes when he loses his sense. The legs, sir, you make 'em do the splits out and up. Breaks 'em from their sockets, I hear, and pierces the lung with the end as you turn it.'

'Well, I never, Mr Crowe!'

'Can't swear to it mind you,' said Crowe, maintaining his modesty, 'but something sure came over that vicious beast.'

Verity, naked to the waist, looked about him.

'What now, Mr Crowe?'

'Listen,' said Crowe patiently.

Verity listened. From somewhere on the far side of the islet he could hear brisk shouts and the sounds of brushwood being hacked clear. It was no more than five minutes later when, with a waving of branches to indicate their progress, Captain Oliphant and three uniformed Marine privates stepped out of the marshy thickets. Oliphant surveyed the foreshore and its occupants in the early morning light, as though he found nothing at all remarkable about the scene. Verity stepped forward.

'Sir!' he said gratefully. 'How d'yer find us?'

Oliphant looked at him with mild pity.

'A report of your direction and approximate range of patrol was left for me by Sergeant Crowe,' he said quietly. 'Your two horses were left tethered with some conspicuousness on the river bank. Pistol shots and commotion were clearly audible from the island, and that river-boat over there has created a cloud of steam that might be seen five miles away. I daresay that even your own Mr Croaker would have been here in a day or two more.'

'But you never swum the river, sir?'

'Sergeant,' said Crowe patiently, 'I cannot speak for the Metropolitan Police, of course, but when my own men face the likelihood of having to cross a river, they generally

201

provide themselves with the means of doing so.'

Puzzled and hurt, Verity withdrew, listening to Crowe and Oliphant as they continued their survey of the night's events.

'We have found,' said Oliphant in a tone of disapproval, 'one dead negro, and two prisoners still alive, a white man and a Mexican.'

'Lucifer and Raoul,' said Crowe helpfully. 'This here is a professional pugilist called Bull-Peg, hurt but living.'

Verity interrupted.

'And Lieutenant Dacre, sir? And Miss Jolly?'

There was an icy smoothness in Oliphant's reply.

'It is reported to me that the dinghy of the *Anna* has been found on the Illinois bank of the river. While you two men were amusing yourselves here with a game of hide-and-go-seek, several hours ago, the robber of the Federal Mint was slipping across the water away from you. With four hours start, by road, or rail, or even water, he could be anywhere by now within an area of a thousand square miles. Of Lieutenant Dacre, of Miss Jolly, and most important of all of the gold, there is no sign.'

17

Verity and Crowe stood conspicuously at ease, their backs to the fringe of the great crowd which had been cordoned from the parade ground by a line of New York constabulary.

'It gotta be New York, Mr Crowe,' said Verity confidently. 'You, and me, and Captain Oliphant is agreed on that. The luggage that was sent by Lieutenant Dacre's man, all them boxes, never belonged to anyone at the Continental Hotel in Philadelphia. But they was all put on the train for New York. And according to Mr Oliphant, that Bull-Peg person sung sweet as Jenny Lind to save himself from wearing a rope collar. It was New York where the 'ouse of infamy was.'

'Mr Verity,' said Crowe patiently, 'that was days ago. The gold and Miss Jolly might be over the moon by now.'

Verity stared piously ahead of him at the separate phalanxes of the American infantry regiments in their blue and gold, drawn up on the open space of the Battery. Behind them, seagulls wheeled raucously in the October sky and a moving panorama of liners, tugboats, ferries and pleasure-craft bustled in the estuary of the East River. His round pink face, under its tall hat and waxed moustaches, moved in thoughtful pursing of the lips.

'Where would you hide a leaf, Mr Crowe?'

'Leaf of what?'

'No, no, Mr Crowe! Policeman's litany!'

Crowe turned a long, suspicious face towards him.

'What *are* you on about, Verity?'

'Ain't you got the policeman's litany here, Mr Crowe?'

'I guess I never heard it.'

'Where would you hide a leaf?' recited Verity. 'In a tree. Where would you hide a corpse? In a graveyard. And now, where would you hide a ton of gold coins?'

'In a bank?'

'Very good, Mr Crowe! And where would you hide a bank?'

'In a city?'

'Go it, Mr Crowe! Ain't you the boy, though! Now, seeing as he couldn't put it all in one bank without attracting notice, where would you hide twenty banks?'

'All right,' said Crowe, 'in New York. And it still proves nothing. Where would you hide Miss Jolly?'

'Ah, well, Mr Crowe! The litany ain't really adapted to such young persons.'

'Where would you hide Lieutenant Dacre?'

'Likewise, Mr Crowe, the litany ain't really. . .'

'Then you take your goddam stupid litany, Mr Verity, and you stick it. . .'

'Mr Crowe, if you please! 'is Royal 'ighness!'

203

From all around them there rose a hoarse undulating roar of approval. The glittering mass of regiments stood fast, but there was a ripple of movement from the great crowd, from the spectators on the battery walls and the yards of ships at anchor, heads turning in the direction of Castle Garden. General Sandford, commanding the New York militia, and the Prince himself rode side by side on bay geldings. Behind them rode the Duke of Newcastle in the uniform of Lord Lieutenant, followed by General Bruce, Colonel Grey and Major Teesdale of the Prince's staff in their scarlet splendour with plumed hats. The young Prince himself seemed almost absurdly over-dressed, the slight and boyish figure adorned with the uniform of a full colonel, braided in gold and enriched by its wine-coloured sash. He bowed his cocked hat slightly, as if in acknowledgement of the cheering, and then cantered down toward the waiting regiments. When the high-stepping horse reared and pranced at the applause from the onlookers, the young Prince kept his seat with effortless horsemanship, which caused the cheers to be redoubled. Verity stamped quiveringly to attention in the presence of royalty, and the militia band struck up a complimentary tune.

Some talk of Alexander and some of Hercules;
Of Hector and Lysander, and such great names as these . . .

Where would you hide Miss Jolly, he thought, and where Lieutenant Dacre? Crowe was right, the litany ought to have an answer to such questions. Yet he knew of none.

But of all the world's brave heroes, there's none that can compare . . .

Where would you hide Miss Jolly? In a graveyard, the state she might be in by now.

With a low, row, row, row, row, row. . .

No, Lieutenant Dacre was not the man to leave the world in ignorance of such a longed for homicidal triumph.

. . . to the British Grenadiers!

Verity watched the Prince of Wales and his companions trot past each of the regiments in turn, the colours dipping and the ranks of blue-coated soldiers presenting arms with a flash of bayonets and the glint of their officers' drawn swords. The young man acknowledged these salutes too and then, at last, turned away with his escort to the open barouche and the line of carriages behind, which waited to begin the ceremonial procession down Broadway. Major Teesdale turned in the saddle and made a brief, imperious gesture to Verity and Crowe. Stepping forward smartly, they marched in step, fists swinging to shoulder-height, oddly costumed in their long civilian coats and tall hats.

Concealed in a closed carriage, they rode immediately behind the barouche, in which the Prince sat beside Mayor Wood, with Newcastle and the British Ambassador, Lord Lyons, facing him. Verity saw the same fortress-like buildings in white marble or granite, the cast-iron store fronts richly decorated and tinted to resemble bronze, which he had passed during his shadowing of Jolly and Sergeant Crowe. But now every window, balcony and roof was packed with faces as densely as the crowds upon the pavement itself. Everywhere on posts and lamp-stands the Stars and Stripes was intertwined with the Union Jack. Flags and banners drooped in the still afternoon air. But at the approach of the royal procession there was a long white ripple of waving handkerchiefs, and a tumult of hats thrown in the air. Not for the first time, Verity was uneasily aware that if Lieutenant Dacre or any of his kind chose this moment to attempt the life of the young Prince, there was virtually no protection against such an attack. It would be over before he or Crowe could reach the young man's side. It was these and other thoughts which led him, unconsciously, to scowl at the good-natured bystanders who were shouting, 'God Save the Queen!' and 'You're welcome to New York!'

'Come on,' said Crowe presently, 'nothing's as bad as that!'

'I been thinking, Mr Crowe, about the litany. It gotta

205

'ave an answer, if only we was to ask the right question.'

After lunch on the following day, Verity and Crowe stood side by side in the palatial lobby of the Fifth Avenue Hotel, where the Prince and his suite were lodged. With wondering scepticism, Verity eyed the massive chandeliers, the plate-glass, the broad stairway and the lounging chairs in rosewood and velvet. He turned to Crowe.

'Your banks over 'ere ain't much to shout about, are they, Mr Crowe?'

'Why?'

'Well,' said Verity, easing the collar away from his fleshy neck with a broad finger, 'being as I was off-duty this morning, I been to a few banks, telling 'em I was a detective officer and so forth.'

'What for?'

'Well, Mr Crowe, first off, I asked 'em if they had a list of all the boxes as might have been deposited in their vaults since the 9th of October, and if I might see same. Very abrupt they was, Mr Crowe. Sharp, even. Said they'd got such lists but that they wasn't something-well going to show 'em to me, nor to anyone short of your Secretary to the Treasury! When I asked whose authority was needed to have all their customers' boxes opened up and searched, they got quite uncivil. Said they wouldn't do that for President Buchanan himself. Two or three places I was helped to the door with a 'and on me arm!'

'How many banks have you been to, for God's sake?'

'Not more 'n a dozen or two, Mr Crowe.'

'Fat fool!'

'Easy, Mr Crowe! Easy on, now!'

'Didn't you know that banks work on trust and confidence? Let these boxes be opened and searched, they might as well put their shutters up and go out of business.'

Verity thought about this for a moment.

'Seems to me,' he said presently with portly dignity, 'seems to me Lieutenant Dacre didn't need Lucifer and Bull-Peg and that. Seems to me these banks are the best accomplices that a villain could ask for. Why, the crown jewels might be stole and hid in their vaults, and no one allowed to look for 'em! Trust and confidence! Huh!'

The Prince of Wales appeared on the stairs with Newcastle and Teesdale close on either side. Verity and Crowe fell in behind as the three men approached the hotel door and the carriage which waited beyond the long awning. There was a cheer from the waiting spectators. Then, as the Prince stepped forward, Verity caught a movement from the corner of his eye. It was a rough-looking man with the appearance of a sailor, a wild expression in his eyes, who rushed from the crowd and charged towards the royal visitor. The man's clenched fist was raised to attack and his words were hysterically shrill.

'You never shall be King of England! Not if you live a hundred years!'

The Prince stood quite still in the face of the impending blow, and the crowd seemed mesmerized. It was Verity who shouldered aside the grave, frail figure of Newcastle and grappled briefly with the man, smelling the whisky-breath. It was easy enough to seize the bony wrists of the shabby sailor and twist them sharply up between the man's shoulder-blades. The bullying shout died to a grizzle of drunken protest.

'Right, my man,' said Verity, his lips close to the culprit's ear, 'you 'ad your say for this afternoon!'

He bowed the man forward with a further twist of the wiry arms and then trundled him at a run into the privacy of the hotel lobby.

Major Teesdale, his military uniform discarded in favour of a bottle-green evening coat, stood with his hands clasped under its tails and his back to the empty grate of his hotel room.

'His Royal Highness would, of course, wish me to express his personal appreciation of your conduct in this disagreeable incident,' he said, as though finding even a reference to the matter distasteful.

Verity, smartly at attention with chin held high, gazed intently at a space on the wall, just above the mantelpiece.

'You no idea 'ow proud I feel to have been noticed by 'is 'ighness, sir! With respect ,sir!'

'Yes, yes,' said Teesdale, showing the first sign of mild irritation with his plump subordinate. 'There will, however, be no public reference to the incident. The man who insulted the Prince proves to be one Edward Moncar, second mate of the *Santa Claus*.'

'The what, sir?'

'*Santa Claus*, sergeant. More to the point, he is an Englishman.'

'Well I never, sir! And 'im carrying on like an anarchist!'

'The whole thing is to be dealt with quietly, you understand? We have trouble enough as it is.'

'Yessir. Just so, sir. 'ave the honour to request a favour, sir!'

Teesdale held a match to a cheroot, puffed energetically, and then looked up at Verity through the thinning smoke.

'What sort of favour?'

'Well, sir, it ain't exactly for meself, but someone 'igher up might be able to get a job done for me. It's them banks, sir. You no idea how uncivil they can be, sir. With respect, sir.'

'You have already been told, sergeant, that interference with private bank boxes is out of the question! Dammit, man, even the American Treasury wouldn't dare do that without a new law to authorize them!'

Verity's pink moon of a face assumed an expression of injury.

'I never meant to interfere, sir. But it don't need a new law for them banks to pick up the boxes and carry them across the vault and put them down on the other side, do it, sir? Why, they might do that in the course o' sweeping up the floor!'

Teesdale sat down slowly in a wing-chair.

'How can you find gold by moving boxes round a room?' he asked suspiciously.

208

'There's no end to what a man can do once he puts 'is mind to it, sir. Permission to stand easy and reach in me pocket, sir?'

'If you're wrong,' said Sergeant Crowe, 'they'll roast your fat hide and serve you up to the bank presidents, basted and with an apple in your mouth.'

Verity gasped with exertion as they lowered the box between them to the stone floor of the vault.

'I ain't wrong, Mr Crowe. I 'ope there's time to prove it, that's all.'

Four bank-tellers, posted in the corners of the vault, watched them with calm but hostile curiosity.

'The one thing he missed, Mr Crowe! The one thing Lieutenant Dacre must 'ave missed. P'raps he never thought we'd get so close as this. But them six boxes that he had in the Mint itself was *weighed*, Mr Crowe. They wouldn't let 'em leave else. And Mints is apt to be very particular about weights, down to the last ounce. We know from the timing that they were taken straight to the railroad depot at Philadelphia and the lieutenant would never have had time to do more than collect 'em in New York and have them fetched to the banks. 'e might chip away the wax seal or alter it. He must peel off the Prince of Wales's transfers. But otherwise the weights must match the entries made by the clerks in the Mint itself.'

'You don't know for certain,' said Crowe doubtfully.

'I'm as certain as I need to be, Mr Crowe. But I ain't going to weigh black boxes only, a-cos one thing he could do easy enough 'd be to lick 'em over with paint.'

They heaved the next box on to the weighing pontoon which had been wheeled down to the vault at Oliphant's request. But Verity and Crowe found nothing. It was one of the Treasury guards assisting them who gave the first cry.

'Mr Crowe! This is sure close enough to that last weight on the list!'

Like so many of the depositors' boxes, it was long and black. One of the tellers checked a white-painted number on the lid of the box and checked the list in his hand.

'Valerian Drummond, entered 11th October.'

Verity looked at Crowe.

'It gotta be, Mr Crowe!' He turned to the teller. 'You get this thing open sharp!'

The teller shook his head.

'Out of the question, my dear sir. You have no authority for that whatever. The boxes may be weighed but are not to be interfered with.'

Crowe intervened.

'Then you just run and find someone who carries authority!'

The teller hurried away and Crowe looked at Verity. As though by pre-arrangement, Verity moved so that his bulk screened Crowe from the rest of the room, while the Marine sergeant knelt at the box, sliding a metal bodkin with a flat blade-like end from the recesses of his coat.

'Yes, Mr Crowe,' said Verity reassuringly, 'a man gotta 'ave respect for authority. Why, a man ain't nothing but what he ain't got respect for authority.'

He began to talk more loudly to conceal the shrill protest of yielding wood.

'Why, Mr Crowe, I've known men what 'adn't respect for authority, and d'you know. . .'

The remaining tellers moved forward at the rending crack which echoed from the stone walls.

'Quick, Mr Crowe! What you got there? Is it gold, Mr Crowe?'

'No,' said Crowe flatly, 'no gold.'

'Oh dear, oh dear, Mr Crowe! That ain't half torn it! I can't say 'ow sorry I am. . .'

'What's here,' said Crowe, in the same flat voice, 'is an oil lamp, a jemmy, a pair of scales, a special drill and enough false keys to open every safe from here to San Francisco!'

' 'ere!' said Verity, craning forward reverentially. 'We done it, Mr Crowe! We bloody done it, after all!'

Valerian Drummond was remembered as an itinerant

young gentleman of good family and impeccable antecedents. On leaving for California, early in October, it had been necessary for him to deposit most of his boxed heirlooms in the hospitable vault of his New York bank, to be forwarded to him upon his instructions.

'One thing you can bet on, Mr Crowe,' said Verity as they opened the third box. 'Lieutenant Dacre's a sight nearer New York at this minute than ever he is to California. Stands to reason! Cor, 'ere! Look at them coins! Ain't they little darlings, though? Only thing is, being so new and bright, you might take 'em for plain brass!'

'Proceed with your duties, sergeant,' said Captain Oliphant gently at his back, 'and leave the numismatic observations to those who are expert in such matters.'

Verity's plump face creased in an honest frown of incomprehension as he stepped back and allowed two of the Treasury officials to close the box and apply their own seal.

The black-lacquered boxes, as well as those which Dacre had had waiting in the little house on Juniper Street, had been distributed in the vaults of eight banks. Detection was made easier by the fact that though under different names, the initials of the depositors always corresponded with Dacre's own. The deposit boxes of Vincent Dowd, Vivien Dickson, Vane Duport, Villiers Deene and Valmont Damien, yielded up their treasure.

'I don't get it,' said Crowe, shaking his head, 'I don't get it at all. After so much trouble to get the gold, he made it so easy to find.'

'Easy to find once you was given a start, Mr Crowe.'

'But to put his own initials to the names! Like a signature! Almost as if he wanted us to catch him, to prove to the world that he'd done it.'

'Mania,' said Verity knowledgeably. 'What medical men calls a mania, Mr Crowe. In Lieutenant Dacre's case it do take the form of showing himself off. I s'pose every man got his mania, one way or another.'

'And what might your mania be, Mr Verity?'

211

'Dunno, Mr Crowe. Funny that. I reckon a man p'raps can't tell his own. 'as to have it pointed out to him.'

He lapsed into a long and dissatisfied silence, as though the recovery of the gold still troubled him.

'Mr Crowe, would you have any objection to going back to that first treasure-vault, where the business began?'

'There's nothing else to be found there, old friend.'

'I ain't so sure, Mr Crowe. There was a box there, long and black, what never corresponded to any weight nor to Lieutenant Dacre's initials. But I been getting a sort of picture of that box all afternoon, and I can just see something in that picture now which tells me why.'

Crowe looked at him, sharing a thought which the two men preferred not to speak. They made their way back to the gothic porch with its steep flight of steps in the cavernous shadows of Wall Street. The Treasury officials had escorted the gold coins off the premises and were just clearing up as the guards admitted Verity and Crowe to the vault below the level of the street. One of the bank's vice-presidents, with a bundle of keys, was looking forlornly at the rows of boxes awaiting return to their niches.

'That one!' Verity nudged Crowe. 'Been on my mind all afternoon. See that graining – sort of flame pattern in the wood? Dead ringer for the one you opened and found Lieutenant Dacre's cracksman tools in. Them two boxes must a-bin made of the same wood, the same time.'

'Oliver Baynham, Esquire,' said Crowe, reading the name on the lid. 'Ain't likely, Verity, the initials don't fit.'

'Course not. This one wasn't to be opened even if we found the gold. What's in there could 'ang a man. It's Lieutenant Dacre's box, however. Look at it, Mr Crowe! See for yerself!'

The man with the collection of keys came forward, deprecating the noise.

'My good sir, this bank has been more than willing to assist the servants of the Treasury in recovering the stolen coin. But it will not be party to breaking faith with its customers by prying into their secrets. You have your gold, sir. There is no more to be said.'

'You open that box, my man!' said Verity, his large head thrust forward in the manner of a fighting cock.

'Quite out of the question, sir!'

'Then what you'll be,' said Verity darkly, 'is a necessary after the fact.'

'The word, sir, is *accessory.*'

'No it ain't!' Verity's voice quivered with the deep menace of it. 'The word is *murder!*'

Crowe separated the two men.

'More important than the gold,' he said, 'is a young person, Miss Jolly, abducted by Lieutenant Dacre for criminal purposes. Now, sir, the boxes made to order for Lieutenant Dacre were of the same wood as this. There could hardly be a more convenient coffin than this nor a more secret vault than yours.'

'Claptrap!' said the banker shrilly. 'My first duty is to the property of my clients.'

'You client ain't going to like the appearance of his box so well once I've 'ad it open on the hinge side!' said Verity in pink anger.

'Be quiet!' snapped Crowe, and turned again to the banker. 'Now, sir, that box will be opened. Be sure of it. It may be done discreetly now, or with some publicity by the New York Police Department. What we find now shall not be made known. But where police officers go the press must follow.'

The banker looked about him helplessly and then adjusted a key to the lock. It failed. He tried another, and then another. After half a dozen attempts, he turned the iron shaft and there was a click. He raised the lid and the vault seemed to fill with the fragrance of orange and spice. Verity and Crowe stepped forward to look. Preserved in the dry air by the tight seal of the lid, the face of Joey Morant-Barham stared with gaping mouth and sightless eyes at the plaster mouldings of the bank ceiling.

CIPHER
British Embassy
Washington
17th of October 1860

Further to his telegraph of last evening, Lord Lyons is able to confirm the recovery, almost in full, of the gold coin reserve removed from the Federal Mint at Philadelphia on the 9th instant. The perpetrator of the outrage is assumed to be Lieutenant Verney Dacre, a British subject, who remains at large. Lord Lyons considers that this continued evasion, though lamentable in the strict moral respect, may not be unconducive to British diplomatic interests. Where there is no arrest and no trial, the outrage against United States security cannot be brought home to one of Her Majesty's subjects.

It is perhaps fortunate that the United States Treasury should have employed as an agent a young woman of British nationality, though of doubtful moral reputation. This young person has been abducted by the suspected robber and her fate gives cause for concern. However, in the apportionment of blame as a whole, Her Majesty's ministers must insist that the American authorities accept their share for the manner in which a young Englishwoman was sent to her fate by them.

Lord Lyons is also obliged to add that since Lieutenant Dacre is certified by a coroner's inquest to have died in 1857, any approach by the United States government might first be answered by this evidence and by the suggestion that the robbery at Philadelphia must be the work of an impersonator, probably an American citizen.

As matters stand, the United States government seems intent on maintaining financial confidence by complete secrecy over the entire unfortunate incident. Three minor conspirators, all of them American, are to be tried on capital charges not directly related to the robbery or requiring public disclosure of it. Lord Lyons is strongly of the opinion that Her Majesty's government should now withdraw from participation in the matter, since further involvement can only exacerbate a problem already too delicate. In conclusion, Lord Lyons begs to remain etc.

The Right Hon. Lord John Russell
Secretary of State, Foreign Office, London, W.

18

'Course I knew 'im!' said Verity scornfully. 'So'd you have done, Mr Crowe, if you'd had a beat down Haymarket. And then calling himself Major Morant! Prime give-away that was! 'e was young Mr Morant-Barham, dragoon officer. Ran a plump young doxy who did plastic poses on the stage and called herself Janet Bond the Female Hussar. That's a-cos she wore them very tight things. Dark hair all piled on her head, and them tights! Talk about smuggling a couple of jellies in a sack!'

He sniggered, and then coloured slightly, as if conscious of his own vulgarity. The two sergeants gazed out from their curtained alcove into the grand ballroom which had been made in the theatre of the New York Academy of Music. The auditorium with its tiers of boxes, red plush and cream paint, was gaudily fresco'd and resembled the opera house at Philadelphia. But on this occasion, the improvized ballroom floor was jammed with New York society in all its reckless magnificence. On the silk dresses of the women in the stalls, boxes and galleries, a profusion of diamonds sparkled like dew-laden banks of flowers in bright sunlight. The mass of men and women surged and seethed toward the far end of the room, where the Prince and his party were virtually besieged in the small space roped off for them by crimson cord. The floor had already given way at the centre under the weight of the crowd, and the grand ball was interrupted while carpenters repaired the damage. Now, to the strains of a Strauss quadrille, the Prince was to open the dancing with Mrs Morgan, wife of the Governor of New York.

The two sergeants watched through the chink in the curtains, Verity frowning with disapproval at the arrangements as he once more realized the impossibility of getting to the Prince's side in the event of danger. Presently, the little door behind them opened and Major Teesdale appeared. There was an envelope in his hand.

215

'Sergeant Verity,' he said waving the envelope irritably, 'what the devil is the meaning of this?'

'Meaning o' what, sir? With respect, sir.'

'The meaning, dammit, of having your billet-doux delivered here as though you might be some society belle?'

'Billy dues, sir?'

'Letters!' snapped Teesdale. 'Correspondence! I shall not expect a repetition of this, sergeant, do you understand me?'

'Yessir. Very sorry, sir. No idea 'ow it could have happen, sir. Ain't in the habit of receiving letters meself.'

Teesdale held out the blue envelope at arm's length, as though it might be contaminated, and Verity took it. Immediately he drew himself up at attention, as if waiting to receive the remainder of Major Teesdale's reprimand. But Teesdale swung round and closed the door noisily after him.

'Did I understand you to tell me, back in Philadelphia, that you were a free man?' inquired Crowe sceptically.

'Mr Crowe, 'oo in 'ell would be writing letters to me? I don't know a living soul in this place.'

He tore open the envelope and drew out a small white card. His eyes widened as he read it and his face assumed an expression of plump consternation.

'Oh Lor', Mr Crowe! 'ere, you have a read of this, quick.'

> *'The Passing of Miss Jolly'*
> *The performance of this amusing melodrama*
> *will commence tomorrow evening at 8 sharp*
> *and will be prolonged until a little after*
> *midnight. An unrepeatable spectacle.*

' 'e's a bloody murdering lunatic, Mr Crowe! 'e ain't half-way rational! And didn't I tell you he gotta be somewhere in New York?'

Half an hour later, Crowe turned again to his companion.

'For the tenth time, Mr Verity, you were taken off the case, your people want no more to do with it, and you'd best keep your nose out.'

'Mr Crowe, there's murder to be done tomorrow evening!

Ain't it plain to you? And not only murder. He's going to kill that young person as slow as he knows how!'

Crowe shrugged defensively.

'You don't know for certain that the card came from Dacre. It could be someone's notion of a joke.'

'Joke, Mr Crowe? You got a lot of people in New York with that sense of fun, 'ave you? You got any idea how many of 'em could tell you enough about this whole caper to write a note like this? 'ave some sense, Mr Crowe! It gotta be Dacre. And he ain't a few miles away from us! 'e could be dancing with all them swells this minute, for all we know.'

Crowe gave his friend a moment to cool down. In his mind, Verity heard the sounds of a nameless room. He heard Miss Jolly's voice, high and fluting, almost childlike in its clear lilting. He heard the monosyllables drawn out in protest or dismay, the first cries and the soprano frenzy of her last ordeal.

'Look,' said Crowe reasonably, 'the card's from Dacre, all right? But can't you see, for God's sake, that it's no job for you?'

Verity glared at his friend.

'No I can't, Mr Crowe. I fought Lieutenant Dacre and his kind before, and I ain't going to show 'em me backside now by running from danger.'

'You goddam fool!' Crowe slapped one fist into his other palm. 'That's all he wants! Miss Jolly could be dead days ago, or she might have come to terms and spread her legs for him. The only use of that card is to get you coming after him where he can lie in wait. He sure as hell needs you dead, even more than he needs Jolly!'

'He never does, Mr Crowe!'

'Verity,' said Crowe softly, 'how long is it since that little matter on the after-deck of the *Fidèle*?'

'Not the same thing, Mr Crowe, with respect. I might be killed or I might not. But that young piece Jolly got under his skin somehow. If you'd a-seen how he made his bullies in London take off her things and bend her over that

217

rocking-horse, and then tan Miss Jolly's bottom for her, you'd understand.'

Crowe sighed.

'No, Verity. I guess it's you that can't understand. It's not a secret that Miss Jolly was a whore, like most of her kind. She mayn't have liked what Dacre did to her, but if he beat her like a puppy-bitch she might still whimper and make up to him like one. It's you he's after this time. Think it through. With Jolly bought, and you dead, there's not a living soul that could ever identify Dacre as being the cracksman who was in Albemarle Street three years ago and in Philadelphia this month.'

'Then what's the game we must play, Mr Crowe?'

'The game,' said Crowe firmly, 'is for the Treasury to play. We hired the girl, and we must get her back if anyone does.'

He held out his hand for the white card.

'Oh, Mr Crowe!' said Verity, as if deeply disappointed by his comrade, 'Oh, Mr Crowe!'

'I think you'll be glad I came along this far,' said Verity cheerfully on the following morning. They crossed the road in front of the massive Pharonic structure of the Tombs prison.

And this is as far as it goes,' said Crowe quietly.

'I dunno, Mr Crowe. I felt I owed this much to the Bull-Peg person. After all, 'e ain't got much to sing about. He may have turned evidence for you over poor young Captain Moore, but there's all them other little matters.'

'Ten minutes,' said Crowe sternly, 'that's all. I'll be stood outside the cell. And Miss Jolly is Treasury business now. See?'

'Why, Mr Crowe, 'oo could worry himself over Jolly when he might have this Bull-Peg person in prospect?'

The damp cell, with its opening like a furnace door, was in the very row where Verity had been held on his first night in America. Leaving Crowe outside, he closed the door after him and confronted Bull-Peg. The massive body seemed more blubbery than Verity remembered it, as the prisoner crouched in one corner, his back to the wall, his wrists and ankles chained. He glared at Verity and made a sound that was midway between a bellow and a whine. Verity sat down on the wooden ledge of the bed.

'Right, my man,' he said, 'I'm 'ere as your friend. I ain't got no reason to like you but I'm bound for old England again in a day or two more. I got no cause to make things worse for you than they are.'

'I'm a evidence!' The voice was a booming grizzle.

'Course you are,' said Verity reasonably, 'in the matter of Captain Moore's death. They can't touch you for that. Just the matter of ravishing Miss Jennifer. . .'

'Plantation girl!'

'British subject,' said Verity grandly, 'ravished by you in the state of Missouri.'

'Looked like plantation girl.'

'Looks is sometimes deceptive, Mr Bull-Peg. And now o' course, 'ere in New York, the murder of Mr Morant-Barham. Bullet in the back of the neck. . .'

'I never . . .'

'Pulled the trigger, Mr Bull-Peg? No! Course you didn't! Accomplice is all you are. They 'angs you just as hard for it.'

Bull-Peg struggled to his feet. He gave an outraged howl.

'I'm a evidence!'

'Course you are, Mr Bull-Peg, in the case of Captain Moore. In the cruel ravishing of Miss Jennifer, however, and in the murder of Mr Morant-Barham, you're just a plain defendant, like the rest of 'em. Most unfortunate you should have ravished Miss Jennifer in Missouri. Other side of the river might be different.'

'Uh?'

Verity leaned forward, confidential and helpful.

'Mr Bull-Peg, I come here as your friend, in a way of speaking. You'll be tried here with the others for Mr Morant-Barham's murder. In due course, you'll be convicted as accomplice for being Lieutenant Dacre's man, who did it. They'll keep you here a while and then hang

219

you in the yard out there. But what's worse is you being took to Missouri first of all to answer the ravishing of Miss Jennifer.'

'What's worse than hanging?'

Verity gave a frown of serious concern.

'Mr Bull-Peg, you do know the law of ravishing in Missouri? Once you been tried, you'll be took out and gelded, same as a stable-groom do with a frisky young stallion.'

Bull-Peg's eyes were suffused with deep horror and disbelief.

'Course,' said Verity reasonably, 'you don't have to take my affydavy for it. You ask them that knows the law in those parts. By the time they fetch you back here to stand trial for murder, you'll be a public curiosity. And you have no idea how docile the gaolers shall find you, even until they takes you out to hang six months later.'

Verity's calm exposition of the horrors awaiting the criminal carried conviction to Bull-Peg's heart as no melo-dramatic recital would have done. The big man bellowed and shook his chains.

'I'm a evidence!'

'Don't seem right for a man to lose his privates over a tawny young piece like Miss Jennifer,' said Verity sym-pathetically, 'and her egging him on all the time.'

'Right!' bellowed Bull-Peg enthusiastically. 'That's right! That's just how it was!'

'I could be a real friend to you, Mr Bull-Peg. Best friend you ever had. You tell me about Mr Morant-Barham and them houses of Lieutenant Dacre's. One in Five Points I seen, another somewhere else I want to hear about.'

Bull-Peg gulped and shook his head.

'I never was there, I swear it, mister! I never so much as heard of Mr Barham!'

'That ain't the way Lucifer and Raoul tells it, Mr Bull-Peg.'

'Then they told you lies, mister! Bad things! I never done murder! I never was there!'

Verity noticed that Bull-Peg was beginning to sweat and his face was trembling slightly. The conversation was moving admirably to its climax.

'Mr Bull-Peg,' he said gently, 'you was seen coming and going from that house in the Five Points square.'

'Couldn't be. Never was near it. Swear!'

'Tell you what, Mr Bull-Peg. We offered hundred dollars reward for anyone in the neighbourhood who could identify you as being seen there. Now, we got a lady keeps a pie-stall on the corner of that little square opposite the bawdy 'ouse. For one hundred, she's going to swear to seeing you. . . .'

'There ain't a pie . . .' squealed Bull-Peg, and then he stopped.

'Oh dear, oh dear, Mr Bull-Peg, you went for that like a 'ungry mouse for the trap-cheese, didn't yer? How long you think you'd last in court. once they really got into you?'

Bull-Peg slithered down to an abject squat in the corner of the cell. Verity rapped the door and Crowe's face appeared.

'Got all that, didn't you, Mr Crowe?'

'Yes,' said Crowe uncertainly, 'oh, yes. Sure did, Mr Verity.'

Verity turned again to Bull-Peg.

'Right, my lad,' he said briskly, 'you got five minutes. I want to know where that other house is. It ain't twenty miles from here and I reckon it was used to kill young Mr Morant-Barham, the bawdy house in Five Points being too risky by then. You tell me the truth and I'll do my best to have you made a evidence for Mr Morant-Barham, and I'll have Miss Jennifer's charges stopped. You might even walk free from here in ten years more. Cross me, and you shall be the sorriest wreck of a man that ever walked this earth. And if Miss Jolly is murdered too because she couldn't be found in time, Mr Crowe and me has seen you here this morning. If that young person is tormented and dies, we're witnesses for you being accomplice again by refusing to say where she might be found. And if you really

221

don't know where the other house might be, you ain't half unfortunate, my man.'

Verity, accustomed though he was to interrogations, had never expected to see a man of Bull-Peg's physique shaking so visibly. The cropped head nodded and the voice began to croak. Several minutes later, Verity beamed down on his terrified protégé.

'Why!' he said proudly. 'Mother, father, brothers and sisters never been a better friend to you than I been this morning!'

'I don't care to see a man broke in such a fashion, that's all,' Crowe remarked with dignity, as though concluding the discussion.

'No more don't I, Mr Crowe. But then, I had to choose between that creature in his cell and Miss Jolly getting the hiding of her life from Lieutenant Dacre, and a noose round her neck or a knife in her belly to follow it. A man gotta have a sense of values in such things, Mr Crowe.'

The tail-board of the wagon, its hinges well-oiled, had been let down. A dozen armed officers in rope-soled shoes eased themselves silently down and moved like ghosts in the darkness towards the grand entrance-gate of the villa garden. There had hardly been time to locate the house from Bull-Peg's description before the hour stipulated in Dacre's note. Yet this suited Verity's purpose.

'I want to catch him there, if I can, Mr Crowe. And if he's going to put paid to that young doxy between eight and midnight, no sense in us frightening him off before by showing a whole regiment of Marines around the place, is there?'

Captain Oliphant and several men were already in position, standing at a distance from the imposing house but well able to survey the exits and entrances.

'Nothing,' said Oliphant as Verity and Crowe approached him. 'No movement, no sign of life, not a glimmer of light. I begin to fear, sergeant, that our client Bull-Peg sold you a pup.'

Verity frowned.

' 'e didn't look as if he was doing that, did he, Mr Crowe? Why, bless you, sir, 'e almost bust himself trying to be helpful when we put the matter to him good and straight.'

Oliphant shrugged, as if the affair were no concern of his. Behind its screen of trees and beyond the semi-circular sweep of the sandy drive, rose the darkened façade of River Gate. Verity could just make out Tudor casements and chimneys in red brick. The outline of the house suggested the front of an Oxford college, absurdly scaled down, with a squat and square little tower above the main door, and a pair of wings which hardly projected more than ten feet from the front wall of the building.

With Crowe at his side, he moved soundlessly across the springy turf of the well cared-for lawn. The windows of the ground floor were uncurtained and he could just make out the interiors as his eyes grew accustomed to the darkness. Not only were the rooms unoccupied at the moment, they gave every sign of having been recently stripped of their contents. Bare floorboards and dusty walls met his gaze on every side. He turned to Crowe and spread out his hands in incomprehension. At the back of his mind was a growing anxiety that Dacre had foreseen the discovery of his hiding place and would have evacuated it in ample time. If that were so, Jolly's last hours would be spent at the hands of a tormentor, far beyond any help that her rescuers could bring.

Verity cursed himself for having pinned everything on the hope that Dacre would still be at his riverside mansion. Of course the cracksman would know that Bull-Peg or one of the others could be made to turn evidence Now, following in Crowe's footsteps, he edged round the side wall of the dark building The narrower windows of the servants' quarters were also uncurtained and the rooms deserted. It was only when they had reached the yard at the back of the house that he heard the first faint animal sounds. Crowe laid a hand on his arm to still him. The silence was broken by a distant mewing, almost exactly like a kitten in distress. If the house itself had offered any sign of occupation, Verity would have dismissed this plaintive keening and given his attention elsewhere. Now, with Crowe listening intently beside him, he tried to distinguish the direction from which it might be coming.

Set back from the rear of the house, facing it across the yard, was a stable building whose wooden door stood half-open and derelict. The stable block, built of stone rather than brick, looked as though it might be part of a farm which had stood on the site before the riverside villa had taken its place. The two sergeants moved toward it and Crowe, for the first time, slid back the shutter on his dark lantern. Verity followed his example and they moved cautiously through the opening. Behind them, the rest of Captain Oliphant's party spread out to surround the stone building.

Inside the stable block the same scene of dereliction was repeated. The whitewash had peeled from the stalls and the rotting straw on the floor was black with the slime of decay. But now the mewing was louder and more frantic, coming from somewhere above their heads. Facing them, and dividing the stable block into two, was a wooden partition, about six feet high. Above this, the building was open from end to end, but the partition separated the animals from the store of fodder. A cottage door with a latch was set in the centre of the partition to allow access. Verity raised his lamp, looked up toward the rafters beyond the wooden division and emitted a long breath of horror. There was another sound which was now audible, a gentle hiss like a tap with an ill-fitting washer. But it required no sound to demonstrate the hideous details of the death which Dacre had prepared for his traitress.

Attached by four bonds at wrists and ankles, Miss Jolly hung from the high beam, her body twisting and arching in terror, an urgent mewing penetrating the cloth which filled her mouth. The hissing came from a speck of red light, rising slowly in the dark to the place where she hung. At first Verity thought she was entirely nude. Then his lamp caught the burning tail of the slow fuse, now hanging only a few inches below the base of her spine. Dacre had sheathed part of the fuse and left other sections open, to burn against her with appalling effect. He had trussed Miss Jolly with it as though harnessing her for some erotic game. It ran several times round the smooth gold of her slim nude waist, then following the intimate clefts and sensitive buds of her body. The final length of cord ran to a wooden keg on the beam itself, apparently containing enough powder to give the victim her quietus and blow the entire building to pieces.

When he positioned Jolly and lit the fuse, several hours before, Dacre had calculated Verity's reaction. In the horror of the moment, Verity could think only that the glow-worm spark of the fuse would touch the back of the girl's bare waist in a few seconds more. She was already arching up her belly frantically, as though this would postpone contact with the sputtering fire. There was no time for reason, no time for anything other than action.

Verity sprang forward, half-turning to smash his shoulder into the flimsy latch-door of the partition and burst the fastening. He was in mid-stride when Crowe's voice rang in his ear at the pitch of a scream.

'*Stop!*'

At first he thought that Crowe had misunderstood his intention and that the alarm in his voice was unwarranted. Then he had a glimmer of recollection: the after-deck of the *Fidèle* and Verney Dacre, apparently sitting with docile resignation on the upturned life-raft. He checked his stride. Crowe shouted again.

'Not the door!'

And then Crowe was beside him. The Marine cupped his hands as a stirrup. Verity lodged his foot, snatched the top of the partition and was over it in a second. He fell to the floor on the other side, picked himself up, and turned round to where Crowe was just landing.

'Knife, Mr Crowe! On my shoulders with it! She ain't more 'n twelve feet up! Just reach that smouldering cord!'

225

He dipped again, to let Crowe crouch with his feet on the plump shoulders. Then, using every resource of his powerful body, Verity straightened up, lifting the crouching Marine until Crowe could balance sufficiently to stand upright, knife in hand as his arms reached for the slow burning fuse. Verity gripped Crowe's ankles to give him purchase and heard the girl's stifled cries of urgency above him. At last Crowe gave a gasp.

'Right, Verity. Safe enough. Now she can be fetched down.'

Verity helped his companion down, then turned to the door in the wooden partition. Attached to the bar of the latch on the inner side was a black metal cylinder, the size of a large tankard. From it, a short length of cord hung down into an iron pot below. Now that he was facing it, Verity saw that the open top of the cylinder cast the faintest wavering light on the roof above. It was this which Crowe had seen and he had not. Now it was easy enough to imagine how the movement of the latch, had he tried to open the door, would have upset the flame in the cylinder, igniting the oiled fuse and carrying fire down into the big iron pot below. With extreme caution, Verity dipped a hand into that pot and felt the dry grains of powder run through his fingers.

'Easy!' said Crowe, meticulously detaching the cylinder with its concealed flame, while Verity dragged away the pot. 'One finger on that latch outside, one good thump on the door, and you'd have been accompanying the heavenly choir. There's enough powder in that thing to take you, me, Miss Jolly and the entire building up to the stars and back.'

'That's it, Mr Crowe! He knew we'd find our way here! He was sure of it! And he'd have got us all in one go!'

Forgetting even to thank Crowe for his timely warning, Verity strode to the stable entrance and ordered the guards to remain outside. He and Crowe took down the long stable-ladder from its hooks and began to climb to the beam. Preparing himself for shrill squeals of terror or muted sobs of gratitude, Verity detached the gag with great gentleness. The dark eyes slanted savagely and he froze at the volume of obscenities which the girl emitted. Even though they were directed, as a form of hysterical relief, against her absent tormentor, he was shocked by them. He detached the cord of the dead fuse where it ran round the slim thighs, the waist, between the legs and buttocks, over the belly and breasts. Prepared though he was for Dacre's homicidal cruelties, he was reduced to speechlessness by this.

'Now, miss,' he said at length, 'I gotta take you on my shoulder, fireman style. Just let your head and arms hang down my back, and don't worry. All set then?'

He held her by the slim brown waist, as though she had been no more weight than a child, and laid her over his right shoulder, his arm crooked protectively round her legs. He was uneasily aware of the smooth warmth of Miss Jolly's bare hip against the side of his face. She wriggled a little.

'I don't need a hand just there, *thank* you!' she said shrilly, and then, 'Make him stop touching me like that!'

Sergeant Crowe, descending the ladder a few feet below, looked up.

'One more word,' he said angrily, 'and you'll get something that'll make you wish you were back with Lieutenant Dacre!'

This provoked the final release from shock, a deep ascending wail which burst into violent sobs. As they reached the ground and she was set on her feet, the trim dark beauty threw herself, howling, into Verity's arms. Instinctively he reached round her to hold her.

'Now, now, miss,' he said reassuringly, 'it ain't so bad as that. It's all done and over with.'

His left hand was against the back of her waist, his right palm lying round the left cheek of her bottom. Suddenly aware of this, he tried to withdraw, feeling her wriggle determinedly after him.

'Now, now!' he said, allowing himself the luxury of reproving her wantonness by an affectionate little pat. 'Now, now! There ain't no call for that at all!'

227

19

Sergeant Crowe stared out across the steamer's rail at the thin red and black strata of the tall cliffs of the Pallisades. As the cheers of New York faded on the morning air, the *Harriet Lane*'s paddles beat up-river, carrying the Prince of Wales to the grand military review at West Point.

'Should have done it,' said Crowe bitterly. 'All the powder taken out into the open space behind, a torch set to it, and a blaze in the sky that Dacre could have seen wherever he was. That way, he'd count you, and me, and Miss Jolly as dead. And there might have been an end of the matter.'

'Best as it is, Mr Crowe,' said Verity firmly. He was standing with his big barge-shaped boots planted firmly astride, his plump face set grimly under the stove-pipe hat, as he scowled at the passing scenery of the Hudson.

'Best for who?' Crowe inquired.

'Mr Crowe, you having had less to do with Lieutenant Dacre than some, p'raps all you want is to see the back of 'im. For some of us it's different. Three years since, I was bloody near dismissed in disgrace and tried for murder in Mr Dacre's place. You saw, last night, what he tried to do to that unfortunate young person. I saw what he *did* to her three years ago. More stripes 'n a zebra. I want 'im Mr Crowe – and I'm bloody going to have him too! The only way that can be is if he knows his devilish tricks at River Gate never worked and that he's gotta try again. Just let 'im, Mr Crowe, that's all!'

'You think he'll follow you back to England?'

'Risky, Mr Crowe. Risky. More like he'll try it here.'

'Not a chance, my friend. Every last place for the rest of the tour is checked tighter than a virgin's honour. They've got West Point sealed off at the landward end of the promontory. As for the two places where a man could come ashore across the river, there's not a chance for him there. On top of which, there's three or four hundred troops and cadets on the post!'

Verity frowned in disapproval.

'Mr Crowe, it 'as been observed before that there's no time for making fools of men so good as when they think themselves safe beyond question.'

As the mountains closed in on either side of the river and the current ran faster in its narrower channel, the paddles of the *Harriet Lane* beat hard and loud. Majestic cliffs crowned with woodland echoed the sound as the steamer broke the deep silence of the hills. Ravens, hawks and buzzards, startled from their wilderness, rose and wheeled high above the mastheads. Brown and ruby-coloured foliage seemed almost to reach the wisps of low October cloud, through whose haze the dimmed sun turned the light and shade of the hills to gold and purple. The calm mirror of the Hudson reflected and deepened the gorgeous tints. Sergeant Verity, deep in thought, glowered at the passing beauty.

It was just after one o'clock when the steamer came in sight of a promontory, above whose steep cliffs there appeared rows of buildings, the ground behind rising still higher to what looked like a ruined fort. Sergeant Crowe made signs of preparation as the telegraph bell rang for half speed and the steamboat nosed gently toward the little mole, which marked the southern landing of the United States Military Academy at West Point. Distantly and far above them, they heard the deep booming reverberation of a cannon which signalled the opening of a royal salute.

Taking their place in the rear of the party as usual, Verity and Crowe went ashore, standing well back, as Colonel Delafield, the commandant, welcomed his young visitor at the landing. The guard of honour, in cadet grey with frogged tunics and bell-crowned black caps, snapped into the drill of presenting arms with smacking precision. At this signal, the military band opened a preliminary drum roll and struck up a clash of cymbals.

God save our gracious Queen . . .

During the two anthems, Verity stood rigidly to attention, only his eyes moving as he took a survey of the place. High above the rest rose the casemented strongpoint of Fort Putnam. Lower down, on a plateau, were the main blocks, grouped round the parade ground. The cadet mess and the cavalry stables, as well as the riding hall, accompanied these. The impression was one of granite solidity and absolute control. Yet Verity had put himself in Dacre's position, and he could almost predict what must happen now.

Apart from motionless formations of the cadets, grey uniforms on a grey windy space, the breeze whipping and snapping at the flags of two nations, the central area was bright with the green and pink dresses of the young men's mothers and sisters, the dark suits of fathers and brothers, who were privileged guests on this grand occasion. With Crowe beside him, Verity once again stood back, keeping unobtrusive observation as the young Prince, in company with the commandant, rode forward on his bay horse. The cadet formations marched and countermarched with a balletic precision, swinging at last to pass the Prince in a formal salute.

The parade ended and the Prince accompanied his hosts to the superintendent's house, with its verandah and the deep richness of its creeper. Verity and Crowe assumed their places, at ease, with their backs to the building, on either side of the front door. They were to remain in position while the royal party took tea with the commandant, the superintendent, and the professors of the academy. It was about ten minutes after the two sergeants had taken up their guard that Crowe saw Verity killed.

It happened with such speed, and so little warning, that there was nothing which could have been done to ward off the attack. This time it was Crowe who heard the ominous *whizz! whizz!* of flying metal, and the rapid pattering of shot as it pitted the rendering on the wall behind him. He saw Verity thrown back against the wall, arms and legs out, as though by some invisible force. He watched the limp body slither down the rendered wall and topple over so that it lay on its back, arms flung out and eyes fixed glassily on the grey sky above.

Shocked into immobility for a moment, Crowe stared at the fallen sergeant and then sprang forward to the iron railings which separated the leafy garden of the house from the roadway beyond. There was no sign of the assassin, merely a few family groups in which individual cadets in their full dress strolled nonchalantly with proud mothers or adoring sisters. Regardless of his own safety, he ran across the road into the trees beyond and looked helplessly about him. It took no more than a few seconds before he was racing back to where the corpse of Sergeant Verity lay. He stooped over his fallen friend.

' 'ere, Mr Crowe!' said the corpse, still glassy-eyed. 'Did I do all right, Mr Crowe? Don't let yer lips move! Talk like I'm doing. 'e gotta think I'm dead, Mr Crowe. I twigged it as soon as I heard that shot in the air.'

'Damnation!' said Crowe, stiff-lipped and breathless with relief. 'What sort of game is this, for God's sake?'

'Into the house, Mr Crowe! Board and sheet! Let 'im see me carried in with a shroud over me. Bet yer a penny to a pound he'll be watching from somewhere!'

The tall Marine looked about him uncertainly. Then he moved quickly into the house. He reappeared in a few minutes with Major Teesdale and several officers of the commandant's staff. Verity was lifted on to the board with brisk precision, and then the procession entered the house once more.

'Right then,' said Teesdale irritably as Verity got to his feet, 'explain these absurd theatricals!'

'Bullet-marks on the wall outside, sir,' said Verity rapidly. 'Same caper as all along. Only this time I heard the shot pinging in the air and, like a flash, I thought I'd better show him what he wanted to see, sir. I'll lay odds it was Lieutenant Dacre. It can't be anyone else. They got no reason. After the *Fidèle* and the other night, I half expected it, sir, so I went and threw meself down, like as if I'd been mortally hit.'

Teesdale regarded him sceptically.

'With what object, sergeant? A man fights back at his enemy! He doesn't fall down and sham dead at the first sound of battle!'

Verity coloured perceptibly at the imputation of cowardice.

'You never dealt with Lieutenant Dacre, sir, with respect, sir. We got one chance and once chance only. Take 'im off his guard, sir. He thinks he got me. Now there's only Miss Jolly that's held safe on the steamer. If Mr Crowe and the American officers got no objection, we might use her as bait again. Only this time we gotta be sure.'

'You have no reason to suppose Lieutenant Dacre to be alive or in America!' snapped Teesdale, but Oliphant intervened.

'I guess you might just tell us what you have in mind, sergeant.'

'Yessir. First off, sir, 'ow did Lieutenant Dacre get into West Point?'

'Not through the cordon,' said one of the commandant's captains. 'No one but family of cadets met by the cadets themselves came through. As for the two landings, the guard on those has been even stricter. Your Lieutenant Dacre wouldn't last two minutes before being recognized once he got here.'

'No sir,' said Verity dutifully, 'once he got here he was safe enough. Reg'lar villains' paradise you got 'ere, sir. With respect, sir.'

The West Point captain's eyes widened.

'Sergeant,' said Teesdale coldly, 'you will explain that!'

'I reckon I seen Lieutenant Dacre today, sir. I reckon we all have.'

There was a chill silence in the room.

'Sergeant?'

'Where would you hide a leaf? In a tree,' said Verity softly, almost as though talking to himself. 'Where would you hide Lieutenant Dacre at West Point? Not in any hole or corner. Walking bold as brass in the full light o' day, dressed in a smart grey uniform and black cap, looking just the same as several hundred other young gentlemen!'

'Impossible,' said the West Point captain. 'He would never get in dressed like that. He would be held for being beyond the Academy limits in the first place.'

'No sir,' said Verity patiently, ' 'e never come in dressed like, of course. It's just how he was able to move round unchallenged when he got in. Easy enough to get a uniform tailored, being as famous as it is. Or p'raps there's some poor young gentleman lying senseless and stripped somewhere. What I gotta know quick is 'ow he could a-got in.'

'He couldn't,' said Teesdale peevishly, 'we have established that.'

'And them bullet-holes in the wall outside establish something else again, sir. With respect, sir.'

Verity turned to the West Point captain.

'Sir, you being a military gentleman, p'raps I might take advice from you. Supposing you was besieged here, as you might be, with a cordon round the limits, how would you get away?'

'My boat from the landings.'

'No, sir,' said Verity patiently, 'there's enemy guns there.'

'I might swim the river.'

'No, sir. There's marksmen watching it.'

'Then I don't see how.'

'So what 'd you do, sir.'

The captain laughed helplessly.

'I guess I'd telegraph New York for reinforcements.'

'Would you just do that, sir?' asked Verity solemnly. 'Right away.'

With a frown of incomprehension, the captain went away and spoke to one of his subordinates. There was a delay of several minutes before the man came back from the telegraph office close by. The captain returned to Verity and the others.

'Unfortunately, gentlemen, the line to New York seems to be temporarily out of order.'

233

'Out of order, sir?'

'Dead.'

'And what about the line to other places, sir?'

'The line across the river to Cold Springs is not responding either.'

Verity's eyes brightened.

'This telegraph, sir. Where is it and what's it like?'

'Why,' said the West Point captain, 'it was laid ten years ago from New York along the east bank of the Hudson. At the request of the Academy it extends across the river just below us.'

' 'ow, sir?'

'Where the river is narrowest and the cliffs at their highest it is carried across between two posts. It is the normal practice with telegraphs, sergeant. It comes ashore on this bank where the cliffs are wooded and then is carried through the trees to the telegraph office of the Academy.'

Verity stared incredulously at them all.

'Then there's a line across the river where any man could get at it?'

There was general laughter.

'Sergeant,' said the West Point captain kindly, 'you are not to imagine that we have strung a tightrope across the river for Lieutenant Dacre's benefit! The telegraph wire is copper, quarter of an inch thick. I doubt that our man would trust his life to that. Even though there be eight wires, they are spaced parallel over a three-foot width. A man could grasp only two of them at a time.'

'What I imagine, sir, is a lot o' things,' said Verity softly, 'I imagine Lieutenant Dacre with a broad stout strap fast to both wrists and going over all them wires as he pulls across, hanging beneath. He may hold two, but his weight is spread over all. I daresay I'd trust meself to four-inch thickness of copper, and I ain't nearly his weight, sir. Then again, I imagine Mr Dacre knocking out the insulating cups on the top of one pole and taking his time to shoot 'em off the opposite one. Don't have to be accurate, sir, not when you got all day to do it. Once the wires lie slack, he

234

might twist them into a cable almost before he started. Course, I don't know about 'im being a tightrope artist. One thing we do know, however, about the caper in Philadelphia. He got from that attic in Juniper Street to the roof of the Mint on the far side of the road. And if he was that high in the sky he must have done it by rope, unless he sprouted wings, sir! With respect, sir!'

'Sergeant!' snapped Teesdale reprovingly.

The West Point captain raised a soothing hand.

'We need hardly take your word for it, sergeant. By simple electrical measurement we can tell where a line is broken. The higher the insulation, the shorter the length of line left intact. The higher the capacity on a galvano-meter reading, the shorter the length. Both tests are being made. We pride ourselves here on the practical and scientific quality of our education.'

'So do Lieutenant Dacre, sir,' said Verity sullenly.

Presently, the telegraph officer arrived.

'Through the roof, captain!' he said excitedly. 'Both readings! Far side of the river, I'd guess.'

'Well, Sergeant Verity,' said the West Point captain, 'I guess that's cards, spades, and trumps to you!'

'Sir, 'ave the honour to request to be allowed to make a suggestion, sir!'

'By all means, sergeant.'

'Sergeant Crowe to be got across the river to the far side where he may head off Lieutenant Dacre just at the post where the telegraph do come ashore there, sir. 'im to take Miss Jolly, and her to be displayed by the post so that if Lieutenant Dacre should be hesitating, he'll be over in a flash and Sergeant Crowe and party may fall upon him, sir, them being concealed. Since Lieutenant Dacre can't escape on this side, request I be allowed to track after him to the telegraph post over here, sir, just to make sure we got the scent. I can follow him by the route of the posts from the office, sir. That way, if I'm wrong, it's only Sergeant Crowe, the young person, me and a few others that'll be wasting our time, sir. The rest can search the

235

grounds and see 'is 'ighness safe. Ain't no reason why it should ever be made into any kind of public scandal.'

Teesdale shrugged and looked at Oliphant and the West Point captain.

'Sergeant Crowe!' said Oliphant. 'You have your orders, it seems!'

'Sir!'

Crowe hurried away and Verity turned to Teesdale, holding his tall hat under his left arm as he came to attention.

'Permission to proceed in accordance with suggestion, sir!'

'Oh,' said Teesdale ungraciously, 'very well then!'

Verity was uneasily aware of the amount of time that had been lost in arguing his case. But he had certain advantages denied to Dacre. The cracksman would have to make a sedate withdrawal, strolling casually toward the woods in order not to draw attention to himself. Verity ran. Dacre presumably had to dispose of the uniform in which Verity supposed he had disguised himself, and must dress once again as a casual visitor to Cold Springs or one of the towns on the far side. Moreover, Dacre might have to wait before crossing the river if there were strollers in the woods or even a steamboat passing underneath. Nothing was certain, but Verity believed that he could catch the cracksman as he had never believed in his abilities before. At the worst, he stood an excellent chance of catching Dacre suspended above the cliffs and the river, Crowe waiting on one side and Verity on the other. It had been different on the *Fidèle*, even at River Gate, where he had so nearly been destroyed by his unseen adversary. Now he had learnt his lesson from the lethal jokes played by Dacre and by the example of Sergeant Crowe's lithe skill.

Underfoot, the ground, as he passed the last buildings of the Academy and turned into the trees, was soft and deeply-carpeted with russet drifts of fallen leaves. It was impossible to walk silently but he recalled something Crowe had said

236

about walking with an irregular pace which might some-how be confused with the rustling of the branches in the wind. He found that it was impossible to accomplish and he resumed his loping plod. At every tree he expected Dacre to lunge out upon him from behind its gnarled trunk. But the choice was between safety and circumspec-tion or catching the cracksman before he reached his lifeline across the river. Crowe might or might not gain the opposite cliff in time. It hardly seemed to matter in the grand scheme of things. Verity knew that he, and he alone, must be the man to seize Verney Dacre. He thought of the expressions on the faces of superior officers who had sworn to the cracksman's death three years before. Even as he ran, he chortled breathlessly.

Something was wrong. As the chortling broke into a heaving laugh, he realized that he was gripped by mounting excitement, looking forward to the final struggle as a child looks forward to a game. The growing exhilaration over-came his sense of caution or self-preservation. It crossed his mind that in the hunt for Dacre he had caught some-thing of the cracksman's own careless frenzy in his lust to be revenged upon Jolly. Yet Verity felt as he ran that he wanted to shout with the triumph of the chase.

The line of telegraph posts came out on the cliff and followed the river. Verity glanced down at the rocks and currents below. The prospect of Dacre meeting his death in a final plunge had a sobering effect even on his enemy. Downstream he could see the faint spider thread of the cable but no sign of the posts on either bank, nor of Dacre or Crowe. It seemed a long path to follow but, at the back of his mind, Verity knew this was to his advantage. The further the distance, the better his chance of overtaking the fugitive. Every minute that the hunt was prolonged brought Crowe and his companions closer to cutting off the cracks-man's retreat on the far cliff.

As he panted closer to the crossing he saw that his likening of the cables to spiderwork was more apt than he had supposed. On both sides of the river, they had been dislodged from the white porcelain of their individual insulating-cups at the head of the posts and jumbled together. Looking again, he saw that Dacre had chosen his route with a skill that was admirable. The post on the far bank stood slightly higher than the nearer one. In consequence, Dacre had only to hold whatever rudimentary harness he employed so that it spread his weight over the wires above him. Hanging by this, he must have been able to glide forward and downward as effortlessly as a bird. Nor was that all. Attached to him in some way there had evidently been the end of a thin strong rope, uncoiling from its drum to the far shore as his body's moving weight pulled upon it. Now its nearer end was fastened to the head of the post, and the further end to the base of the post on the far side, so that it was taut and level.

Verity stood motionless. Ahead of him, in a space between the trees, he saw the tall, unmistakable figure of Verney Dacre, the fair head bowed as he bundled a grey tunic up and scooped fallen chestnut leaves over it. Whatever suit of his own he might have was evidently on the far side of the river, for the cracksman was dressed in the uniform of his profession: a pair of tight black trousers, a black jersey, and a black Balaclava which he pulled over his head and round his chin, unaware of the hunter behind him.

Verity took a step forward, knowing that he could hardly expect to get closer with Dacre hearing him. Better, then, to take advantage of the shock.

'Right, Mr Dacre,' he said loudly. 'Seems you and me is both ghosts with an account to settle then!'

Dacre spun round. The visible portion of his face seemed all the paler by contrast with the black woollen helmet. His dismay lasted for no more than a second or two.

'Oblige me,' he hissed softly, 'oblige me by standin' exactly where you are! I care more for what's on the far side of this river than for whether you live or die. You may have it either way!'

The barrel of the hunting rifle was levelled at Verity

as Dacre backed toward the telegraph post, and Verity
knew there was no more to lose. He guessed that the
cracksman would hardly have had time to reload the gun.
If he was wrong, a man who had already attempted to
shoot him dead once was hardly likely to leave him alive
now. He remembered stories of fairground performers who
were alleged to catch bullets between their teeth and he
wondered if such things were really possible.

'Stand fast!' shrieked Dacre, the barrel of the rifle
coming up.

Verity ran to one side, gaining the cover of a tree, and
heard Dacre curse. No! Of course it was unloaded. Had it
been otherwise the first shot would have been fired already.
The one hope was to go straight for him, before he had a
chance to slip a round into the breach. Verity emerged
from behind his tree and charged like an overheated bull
at his tall, disdainful tormentor. Dacre reversed his grip
on the gun, swinging the butt wildly at Verity's head. The
plump sergeant felt the wind of the blow fan his cheek and
then he was upon his man. But the strength in Dacre's
thin wrists was beyond anything he had imagined. Verity
felt himself whirled round with such force that the button
of his coat and a fragment of cloth ripped away in Dacre's
hand. He staggered back, just within reach of the gun, and
picked it up. But he knew what he must do. Unarmed, he
could settle with Dacre, but if the weapon were to change
hands again there might be a different outcome. He ran
to the edge of the cliff and whirled the rifle out into the air.
It fell with apparent gentle grace, sailing like a bird's
wing to smash at length in the rocks and currents below.

With victory in his heart, he turned to meet Dacre's
attack. And as he did so, his right foot slid from under him
on the slime of rotting leaves. Rising, he took Dacre's boot
full in his stomach and a blow to the back of the neck as
he fell. In the bright daze of nausea he knew that he was
about to be killed. But there was no more than a deep
silence and the awareness that he was alone. He pulled
himself up and saw, far out over the vertiginous drop

between the cliffs, the black figure of Verney Dacre, hanging by his hands from the rope, working fist over fist with frantic speed to reach the far side.

There was still no sign of Crowe and his men. Verity ran for the post and began to climb stumblingly, extemporizing his plan as he did so. He must catch Dacre, nothing less would do. Even if he could cut through the rope on this side, the cracksman might be close enough to the far shore to survive by holding fast. Indeed, it would provide him with a ready-made escape down to the river itself. Dacre had the advantage of a start but Verity swore to himself that he was the stronger and faster of the two men, despite his bulk. If he could overtake Dacre on the rope, that would do. If Dacre should reach the far side a little ahead, he would hardly have time to attend to the rope, even if Crowe were not already there to meet him. As the thoughts flashed one by one through his mind, Verity was already hanging by his hands, the coarse fibre of the rope burning his palms as he snatched his way hand over hand.

It seemed an absurd parody of the Niagara acrobatics, though the penalty for miscalculation was in every way as grisly. Verity looked down once, seeing the ribbon of water shining far beneath him. Even the black wings of a bird, turning as slowly as burnt paper in the air, were so far below his feet as to make his stomach heave at the chasm of air which seemed almost to draw him down. Resolutely he turned his eyes upward to the bright afternoon cloud and the breeze which cooled his face. His plump arms going like pistons, he raced after the slim and agile figure of his enemy.

He thought that it would be best not to confront Dacre on the rope. Even at a distance, he could see that the cracksman held something between his teeth which glinted like a knife. Best to be so close behind him that Dacre would have time to scramble for the far post but not time to attack the rope. They were well placed for this. Dacre was some two-thirds of the way across. Verity was hardly half-way, but he knew that he was gaining on his prey and could choose his time for attack.

It was while he was thinking this that he saw Jolly, the figure in the pink silk, unmistakable by the distant post. Dacre had seen her already and was scrambling on his way with redoubled energy. Verity looked for Crowe and the others, but he saw no one. There was something in the girl's attitude, even at this distance, that conveyed the flashing hatred of the dark eyes and the pitiless vengeance which animated the sharp young features. Verity saw her stoop and he knew why Dacre was struggling like a madman to reach her. Miss Jolly was cutting or prying loose from its post the rope to which the two men clung for their lives.

Dacre was too far gone to get back to the other bank. For Verity it was his only hope. With even greater frenzy than he had given to the pursuit of the cracksman, he now began to haul himself desperately in the opposite direction. He glanced once at the appalling drop below him and almost wept with despair as his blistered palms snatched the coarse rope, without seeming to bring the safety of the cliff much closer. He glanced once over his shoulder. Where was Crowe? Probably he could not even see what the girl was doing as she crouched carefully with her back to the men of the ambush. How much longer before the terror of feeling the rope slack in his hands, and the last dizzy moments of falling?

But his strength might save him. By the hackneyed perspective of fear, the cliff was now approaching with greater speed. He glanced back and saw Dacre still dangling and jerking, hopelessly short of the other side. And then the moment came. Verity felt the tension go and seemed poised, for an instant, above the drop. But the fall of the rope saved him, carrying him toward the cliff as well as down. He landed ten feet below the ridge, knocked breathless on a slope where grass grew in the crevices between the rock. But though the incline of the ground and the glassy smoothness of the footing would certainly have precipitated him helplessly over the edge, he had hugged the rope to him and his grip withstood the jarring of the impact as he broke the worst of the fall with his feet. He lay against the rock for a moment, feeling the moisture between his palms and the hairy texture of the rope, until he realized that it was his own blood.

He clung there, coughing and dizzy from lack of breath, his eyes blurred by perspiration and tears of relief. For the first time since it had all begun, he thought that he was going to live to see Bella and Paddington Green again. There were figures at an enormous distance on the far cliff, a splash of pink silk among grey and brown. There was no rope, and no cracksman, not even a head among the rocks and the foam.

'Lord 'ave mercy,' said Verity softly to himself, ' 'e's gone at last.'

There were voices above him now and someone was pulling gently at the rope.

'All right!' he cried, 'I'm 'ere! I'm hanging on!'

They helped him over the edge and he lay down among the smell of sweet, decaying leaves.

'I never saw,' he gasped inquiringly, 'I never saw the end. 'ad me back to it.'

There were grey, frogged jackets, and fresh young faces.

'He's gone, Mr Verity, sir,' said one of them. 'Couldn't even keep the end of the rope as it fell. Went smash among the rocks in the middle. Guess he didn't even live long enough to drown.'

20

The hills of Maine were blue with the haze of a bright October afternoon, the nearest height overlooking Portland harbour black with people. The cheering spectators of the Prince of Wales's progress through the town had scrambled for this higher ground to watch the embarkation of the heir apparent on HMS *Hero*. Already the ugly squat stacks of the *Hero*, the *Nile* and the *Ariadne* were funnelling their columns of black smoke upward through the tall graceful rigging. As the noise of the crowd blended in a single roar of farewell, hats waving and handkerchiefs fluttering, the young man who was the centre of so much approbation stepped into the admiral's barge. The oars of the blue jackets cut the waters of the bay and the little boat pitched and bucked its way across a rising swell toward the anchored flagship. From the *Hero* and her consorts the first booming of a royal salute and the plumes of white gun-smoke carried across a darkening sky. Two signals fluttered out from the *Hero*'s yards, the Prince's standard and the 'boats' recall'. Straining to starboard under the force of the rising sea, the three great ships steamed majestically in line astern between the Cape Elizabeth light and the hills beyond. Their guns still boomed, answering the salutes of the American forts, as with banners of black smoke trailing in the wind they made for the open sea and England.

Sergeant Verity, leaning on the rail of Her Majesty's supply auxiliary *Galloper*, watched them go. Tied to the wharf, where she had been loaded with the impediments of the royal tour, the *Galloper* slopped against the harbour swell. At every wave, the commissariat supply vessel wallowed like a dying whale.

'You never were in the least danger, I assure you,' said Crowe beside him. 'We made pretty sure you could reach the other side before we let her cut the rope.'

'Pretty sure, Mr Crowe? I was bloody near ten feet short of it, that's all!'

Crowe clapped him on the back.

'Come on now, Verity! Care might kill a cat! Look to the future! There!'

Crowe pointed to the open port of the lower deck, where the *Galloper* was made fast. Approaching it was an intriguing little procession. At the head moved the bustling figure of Miss Jolly in turquoise silk, followed by Maggie in black bombazine with a veil. Jennifer, in white cotton, walked beside her young mistress, her hair arranged in an elegant coiffure.

243

'What's it to me?' asked Verity suspiciously.

'Well,' said Crowe, 'I guess it's this. Miss Jolly has done the job that the Treasury asked of her. So she goes home. Miss Maggie is, after a fashion, part of the conspiracy to murder Captain Willson Moore. However, she never knew murder was intended and so there's no cause to do more than deport her back where she came from. But then there's that Moslem Venus there, our sultry Jenny.'

'I understood, Mr Crowe, that the young Khan person was no more to do with us and wasn't to come aboard.'

'She sure is, Verity,' said Crowe gently. 'Seems, one way or another, she turned out a regular slave after all. Her master being dead and his possessions forfeit, I suppose she becomes almost the property of the Treasury. However, she must be given to someone.'

'Set 'er free!'

'To starve in the streets of a country she hardly knows? To be took up by traders and sold into the fate we just saved her from? No. She knows the master she wants and the papers of transfer have been completed.'

' ''oo, Mr Crowe?'

'You, Mr Verity. You may not have slavery in England, nor do they in Maine, but she swears to be your woman, follow you, serve you, sleep at the foot of your bed at night . . .'

'You lost yer bloody reason, Mr Crowe? The bed I sleep in is in Paddington Green with Mrs Verity!' The awfulness of the crisis threatened by Jennifer's dutiful attachment to him sank deeper into his mind. ' 'ere, Mr Crowe, I can't go back to Paddington Green, to Mrs Verity and her old father, taking this young person with me! What'll they say? What'll the 'ole street say?'

'I guess they'll say you're a pretty lucky fellow, Verity.'

'I ain't doing it, Mr Crowe. She goes where Lieutenant Dacre's belongings go. That's an end of it.'

Crowe sighed.

'No one knows Lieutenant Dacre, my friend.'

'Not know him?' squealed Verity. 'He fell off a bleedin'

rope over the Hudson in front of you a few days back. Ask Jolly!'

'Miss Jolly,' said Crowe innocently, 'though full of natural resentment against her assailant, felt that she could not finally identify him as Lieutenant Dacre, when the matter was put to her yesterday by the Treasury investigators.'

Verity was aware of a second procession coming aboard, made up of porters carrying valises, hat-boxes and band-boxes, all of them coloured and ribboned in such a way as to suggest the presence of expensive feminine garments within.

'No,' he said bitterly, indicating the immaculate luggage, 'I bet she couldn't, not the way it was put to 'er. Well, Mr Crowe, I identify him as Lieutenant Dacre.'

'You and who else, Verity?'

Verity thumped the ship's rail with his fist.

'Can't you see, Mr Crowe? It's all to save people's faces? The truth is being bent corkscrew to save 'em? Young Jolly been bribed with a few baubles, and I'm to be paid off by 'aving that young Khan doxy to warm me bed at night! That Captain Oliphant of yours, he's no better than Inspector Croaker.'

'He's cleverer, Mr Verity.'

'So's Lieutenant Dacre, come to that, or was. I s'pose you was under instruction that he wasn't to be took alive. Save everyone's face by pretending it never was Dacre!'

Crowe shook his head.

'The rope was cut to save you. You'd have caught him on it, and fought him, and he'd have killed you. Anyone could see that. As for it being the same Lieutenant Dacre you knew in London three years ago, if you say so, it's good enough for me.'

'You tell Captain Oliphant, Mr Crowe, tell 'im that so soon as this boat gets to England, the Khan girl shall go with her Miss Maggie. Don't tell me she ever wanted anything else. And if I gotta shout from the 'ouse-tops that it was Lieutenant Dacre done the Philadelphia Mint, I bloody will. Tell 'im that, Mr Crowe. There ain't no quarrel between you and me.'

They parted at length, Crowe standing on the wharf as the ropes of the *Galloper* went slack. Verity leant on the rail, talking to his friend.

'I'd give something,' he said, 'to show 'em up. Parade Mr Dacre in front of 'em.'

Crowe nodded.

'The time may come,' he said vaguely.

A stretch of dark water had begun to open up between the ship and the wharf.

'Whatcher mean, Mr Crowe?'

'Something I could be shot for telling you, old friend!'

'Whatcher mean? Quick, Mr Crowe! Quick!'

'You two on the rope performed a miracle!'

'Quick!'

'The rope,' bawled Crowe, 'when recovered and measured, was twenty feet shorter than the distance between the two posts.'

His face broadened in a final grin as, in the gathering twilight, he raised his hat to salute his friend for a last time.

The voyage of the *Galloper* was an unhappy interlude in Verity's life. The weather alternated between an oppressive yellow fog and violent storms. He struggled on deck during the calmer periods only to find the universe enveloped in a yellow cloud which seemed to insulate the *Galloper* from all light and sound beyond a few yards distant. The ocean itself was dumb, only a huge, silent fog-swell rocking the ship slowly with its mute undulations. From time to time there was a creaking of the masts and cordage as the vessel drooped from side to side, and the occasional shrill alarm of the fog-whistle. Here and there, the fog-lights emitted their dim yellow glare which carried no more than a few yards even at midday.

Verity thought about Crowe's final remarks, as he paced through the wet, dun haze of the deck.

'No,' he said to himself, 'they must a-measured it wrong, that's all. Something o' the sort.'

He went back to his cabin on the lower deck, next to that occupied by the three young women. It was no more than an open space which had been divided into separate quarters by the erection of painted canvas 'walls'. Every sound from one 'cabin' could be clearly heard in the next. If one of the girls happened to lean against the intervening canvas, her shape appeared in the 'wall' of Verity's own sleeping quarters. Lying awake, as the ship rolled and creaked, he heard the warm sighs and murmurs, Jennifer's voice calling Maggie in muted urgency, the soft and silken whisper of flesh against flesh. Then there would be Miss Jolly's giggling, a furtive spoken exchange, snorts of laughter, and languorous spoken entreaties. Irritably, Verity jammed his fingers in his ears and thought of England.

On the next night, the fog cleared and the gale hit them, rising by the hour, the sailors taking in reef after reef of canvas in the face of the storm. As the sea struck the ancient supply vessel in a series of squalls, clouds of hail began to ring and spin on the decks like salvoes of small shot. Now the soft exchanges beyond the canvas wall gave way to piteous wails of sickness and fear. Verity decided that he preferred the gale to the fog.

Day after day passed in this fashion. Then there was a rumour that Galway had been sighted, though no one whom Verity asked could confirm having seen it. There was a growing body of opinion which put the ship's position somewhere in the northern half of the Bay of Biscay. The *Galloper* hove to, taking soundings. These produced coarse gravel at eighty-three fathoms, which was said to put her off Ushant. That night there appeared in the sky several bursts of red rockets, answered by others from a considerable distance. The *Galloper*, under full steam, made for the spot and found the *Himalaya* riding at anchor and awaiting her rendezvous with the *Hero*. By a freak of the storms, aided by the delays to the other ships who were supposed to keep in convoy, the supply vessel had crossed the Atlantic as rapidly, though in less comfort, as her seniors.

247

The next morning, the *Hero* and the *Ariadne*, followed at a proper distance by the *Galloper*, sighted the Cornish coast, the rocks rising black in the grey dawn. Verity, from the deck of the supply ship, gazed with affectionate nostalgia upon the county of his boyhood. He was still looking toward it for a last time when he heard the booming salute of the Citadel guns as the Prince's flagship entered Plymouth Sound.

'Mr Verity?' the chief petty officer of the watch appeared at his side. 'Telegraph from the *Ariadne*. Escort for you, from Plymouth to London. You'll be put off in the first boat.'

Verity's pink face looked round and blank.

'Escort, Mr Scott? 'ang on, I haven't done anything to be arrested for, 'ave I?'

The petty officer shrugged.

'Couldn't say, Mr Verity. There's police matrons waiting for them young tits as well. Only you're the one that's to be sent under escort.'

As the whaler tossed and rolled across the grey water from the weed-hung side of the *Galloper*, Verity looked at the quay ahead of him. There was no sign of a police uniform, but he hardly expected that. It was as he struggled up the steps, his box manhandled after him, that a cheery face with red mutton-chop whiskers peered down at him.

' 'ello, Verity!' said Sergeant Albert Samson. 'I'm yer escort!'

The journey on the hard wooden seat of the third-class carriage was a test of physical endurance beyond anything he had known on the *Galloper*. Exeter, Bristol and Bath, the mock-gothic stations of Brunel's Great Western line passed with agonizing slowness. Discomfort, numbness and the aching cramp of returning sensation, formed the cycle of Verity's personal misery. At every station, Sergeant Samson would position himself with his head poking from the carriage window. Verity heard him addressing hopeful passengers.

'Police escort in here, ma'am . . . Lots o' places in the carriages further along . . . No place for a genteel young person like you, miss, not in 'ere . . . Got address in London, 'ave yer? Ever in the penny gaff down Monmouth Street? Cider Cellars? Samson, miss, just ask for the name . . .'

On the subject of the escort duty, Samson remained taciturn.

'Couldn't say, Mr Verity. Mr Croaker's orders. Course, I never been told you was under arrest or anything like that. Just that you gotta be took off that ship and fetched to 'im direct. P'raps he thought you might make a run for it without me to watch over you.'

'Mr Samson, I been out o' the country! I ain't been 'ere to do anything, right or wrong!'

Samson leant forward confidentially from the opposite seat of the wooden carriage.

'All I can say, my son, the way Mr Croaker was carrying on, I reckon he's going to have you on the biggest charge since the Heavy Brigade at the field of Balaclava.'

'But, Mr Samson, I ain't done nothing!'

Samson shrugged. They crossed green meadows and saw the broad gleam of the Thames below Oxford, the first red-brick villas rising near its banks.

'Here,' said Samson, 'them three doxies on the boat! You must have heard a thing or two through that canvas, Mr Verity. Go on! Let's 'ave the tale told. What I can't make out is whether it was that blonde Miss Maggie and that Indian piece jigging round together with Jolly watching, or whether Jolly took one of the others and left one in the cold, or whether all three was head to tail like snakes in a circle. What was it then, old son?'

Verity glowered at his colleague.

'Mr Samson, you got a simple mind ain't yer? Young persons don't indulge themselves like that.'

Samson laughed.

'Much you know, Verity! Ain't we broke into bawdy houses and such places? And ain't we seen two doxies loving one another as if their lives depended on it?'

249

'Like I said, Mr Samson, you got a simple mind! You think what poor fallen creatures do in front of men to earn a guinea is what they want to do? You never 'ave understood the female sex, 'ave you? If you had, you'd know that such things don't happen. It's debauched men, not unlike you, Mr Samson, that forces 'em into such displays. As for doing it voluntary, it ain't in feminine nature. And I ain't particular to discuss the matter further.'

'Tribades,' said Samson.

'Eh?'

'It's what it's called by men of learning.'

'Then you get a proper Latin-and-Greek gentleman's education, Mr Samson, and p'raps I'll listen to you. Until then, I hope you won't mind keeping such nastiness to yerself.'

At the Great Western terminus, Verity looked wistfully toward the chimney-pots of Paddington Green. But there was a black cabriolet waiting. He and Samson, and even Verity's box, were loaded into it. As they rattled toward Whitehall, he gazed out on the familiar beats of central London which seemed by now almost to belong to another life. Down the long Regency bow of Nash's Quadrant, the whores were parading in pink or green crinolines and pork-pie bonnets with waving feathers. They stood like statues or like waxwork models, painted and wide-eyed, among the pushing throng of silk-hatted swells and the sporting 'aristocracy' of the night-houses. In the winter afternoon, the first bright glare of gas lights had appeared by the time that the cab turned down the Haymarket. Verity watched the coffee-stall with its tall steaming urns and saw the coquettish twirl of parasols, held slanting above eyes that sparkled with the excitement of cheap spirits. The raucous laughter, the glow of painted cheeks, the jostling of race-course 'snobs' in their loud clothes, passed before him like the easy reassurance of home. For all the exhilaration of the royal presence, it was to this seething mass of rowdy tricksters and hard-faced women that he belonged, not to the retinue of kings or princes.

Approaching Whitehall, and the office of 'A' Division, Metropolitan Police, in Scotland Yard, his eyes surveyed the old familiar territory. The ragged child with a broom taller than himself stood alert on the pavement, ready to sweep a crossing through the mud and filth of the road for anyone who might tip him with a small coin. The raddled whores from the Westminster slums, wearing the shabby cloaks and grimy feathers which had once been the pride of Regent Street, sidled out from their ramshackle lodgings to ply their trade in the dark alleys close to the great Parliament buildings, where their ravaged beauty was concealed by the shadows and the night. Here and there, the homeless poor huddled in pathetic family groups of three or four in the doorways of buildings, seeking an archway for the night where they might rest, undisturbed by the footsteps of Verity's uniformed colleagues on their beat.

They turned into Whitehall Place, where stood the old house which had been a gentleman's residence with views of the Thames over Westminster Bridge, until it had been acquired by the police commissioners for their own purposes. Verity entered the door which led from the police office yard. He heard the drunken voices from the cells, smelt the familiar carbolic which overlaid more offensive odours, and felt a deep sense of foreboding.

'Sergeant Verity! I trust I still have your attention!'

'Yessir! Course, sir!'

From the swivel chair behind his oak desk, Inspector Croaker looked up at the plump, hatless sergeant who stood at attention with chin up, facing his superior. The gleam in Croaker's dark little porcine eyes might equally well have been anger, or triumph, or a combination of both. With his frock-coat buttoned up to his leather stock, his face the sickly yellow of a fallen leaf, and his dark whiskers finely trimmed, his appearance was an enduring image in Verity's mind. 'Sour as vinegar and mean as a stoat', Verity had described him to Bella. The dry, withered tones of Croaker's voice were expertly adapted to the flights

251

of official irony with which he lashed his subordinates. Verity held himself rigidly at attention, his gaze directed over Croaker's head to the dark river beyond the uncurtained window.

'You would make a fool of me would you, sergeant?' said Croaker, his words hardly more than a whisper. 'You would make me a laughing-stock in America, would you?'

'Sir? Ain't sure what you mean, sir. With respect, sir.'

'Are you not, sergeant?' Croaker was swallowing greedily in anticipation of his vengeance. 'You are seconded from this detail to guard His Royal Highness. On your first day you break into a New York police office, commit aggravated assault upon two officers, and have to be extricated from a prison cell to the embarrassment of the Prince and his staff. You then persuade the United States Treasury that Lieutenant Dacre, who died three years ago in London, has robbed the Federal Mint! Were you not aware, sergeant, that I and the other responsible authorities had already given our word to the Treasury that the man was seen dead?'

'No, sir. No one told me what you said.'

'Do you choose to lie to me, sir?' squealed Croaker, gripping his desk as if in a desperate attempt to restrain himself from violence. 'I tell you, this is some plan of yours! Would you play the lawyer with me, sir?'

Verity eased his neck gently free of the sharp edge of his collar.

'Stand still!' shouted Croaker. 'I will have you at attention till tomorrow morning, if I choose. I will keep you here till you take root, unless I am afforded satisfaction over your conduct!'

' 'ave the honour to state, sir,' said Verity firmly, 'that I seen Lieutenant Dacre three times in America. Once on the steamboat *Fidèle* at St Louis. Second time on the little boat, the *Anna*, near Sulphur Springs Landing. Third time, by the river at West Point. That's facts, sir. With respect, sir.'

'Ah,' said Croaker sardonically, 'I thought we should

come to this. It rests on your own word, does it?'

'And Miss Jolly's, sir.'

Croaker's dark eyes glittered with animal delight.

'Yes, sergeant. The United States Treasury had already made arrangements to employ that young person before I was able to assure them of Dacre's death three years ago. That brave young woman saw more of the villain on this occasion than you ever did. She is prepared to swear on her oath that it was not Verney Dacre.'

'Bleedin' little liar, sir. With respect, sir.'

'Really, sergeant? Are we to believe instead the word of a man who was nearly killed on the after-deck of the *Fidèle* because he could not tell the difference between Lieutenant Dacre and a wire clothes-frame?'

'Wasn't like that, sir.'

'The word of a man who was so stupid that at Niagara Falls he arrested his own colleague instead of the supposed criminal?'

There was a pause. Verity's face glowed a deeper port-wine shade.

'I been put up, sir!' he said furiously. 'But I ain't going to be seen off!'

'On the contrary,' said Croaker, 'the Metropolitan Police is very probably going to see you off, as you put it.'

Verity's face tightened in alarm.

'Sir?'

'I did not bring you here this afternoon, sergeant, for the pleasure of hearing your American reminiscences. My duty in another matter requires me to decide whether to suspend you from duty pending investigations, or to have you arrested forthwith to face criminal charges.'

'Sir?'

Croaker sniffed and glanced at a paper lying before him.

'In July, sergeant, while investigating the death of Lord Henry Jervis, you and Sergeant Samson had occasion to escort a young person, Cox, from Brighton to London by railway. That young person now alleges that you and Sergeant Samson removed her clothes during the course

253

of the journey and – ah – performed certain acts.'

Verity's cheeks puffed out with indignation.

'Lies, sir!'

'Really, sergeant? Young women seem to tell lies rather a lot about you, to judge from your protests this afternoon.'

'Sir,' said Verity firmly, 'she can be proved a liar. She and Mr Samson nearly missed that train, sir. They scrambled into the last carriage by the luggage-van while I was further up. There's two gentlemen in my carriage I could find again if I 'ad to, who'd swear to the truth of it. I never was with that young Cox person. And if she lied about me, then she'd lie about Mr Samson too.'

The inspector pursed his lips.

'Very well, sergeant, then we need only proceed against you for a serious breach of discipline.'

'Sir?'

Croaker held up a worn volume, bound in dark brown cloth.

'Where detective officers are obliged to escort a female suspect, they are to ensure that the suspect is never privately alone with less than two officers. You have, therefore, just pleaded guilty to a flagrant breach of that regulation. The penalty would lie somewhere between six months' loss of seniority and dismissal.'

'What I saw in America, sir, I saw. The Mint robbed by Dacre, sir.'

'What robbery, sergeant? The United States is no longer complaining of one. Gold may be erroneously delivered to banks without anyone being robbed. It was held safely enough by the banks themselves.'

Verity stared incredulously at his antagonist as he sensed Croaker's trap closing upon him. Croaker wagged the brown book again.

'The penalty, in the other matter, is to apply with equal severity to your colleague, Sergeant Samson.'

Verity fell silent. The gas light hissed steadily in the stillness. At last Croaker spoke again, his voice hardly a murmur.

254

'Box clever with me, sergeant, and I will have you! Yes, damn you, sir! Cross me, and I will see you broke for it!'

The glitter in the dark little eyes was now one of unambiguous triumph. At a gesture from the inspector, Verity stamped about and marched smartly from the room.

'Off 'ome now, are yer?' asked Samson cheerfully. 'Conquering 'ero? Half a minute. This come for you, day or two back.'

He gave Verity an envelope. Too full for speech, Verity thrust it into his pocket.

The cab turned into the shabby little street beyond the Edgware Road. Half-way down the row of houses was a wide archway in the façade, filled by a wooden door. It marked the stable where Stringfellow kept his own cab and the ancient horse Lightning. Above and around the stable were the rooms of the little dwelling where the old cabman lived with his daughter, Bella, and Verity, once his lodger but now his son-in-law. Weary of everything but the prospect of seeing Bella and the two infant Veritys again, the sergeant got down from the cab and approached the little door at the side of the stable entrance. He knocked and waited, guessing that the bolts might be across it on the far side by now. He heard them drawn back. Prepared to gather Bella in his arms, he stepped back in dismay.

The door had been opened by a stranger, a girl of about sixteen, small and pretty with large brown eyes, a halo of cropped fair curls and an attractively solemn little face. Verity's heart beat faster at the certainty that some disaster had overtaken his little family while he was away. He thought at first that, in his weariness, he had gone to the wrong door, but the little passageway beyond it showed the familiar green wash upon its walls and the cracked wood of the stairs. Fearful of the answer to his question, he gasped,

' 'ere! Where's Mrs Verity?'

The girl gave him a wide-eyed look and bobbed a half-curtsey.

'I'll see if madam is at home.'

The absurdity of the pretentiousness and the relief from his worst apprehensions struck him equally.

'I'm Verity,' he said sternly, 'and I'm home!'

The girl stood back uncertainly as he shouldered past. There was a movement at the far end of the passage, against a flush of oil light, and the sound of the wooden leg which had served Stringfellow since the loss of his own at the siege of Bhurtpore, thirty-seven years before. The old cabman lurched forward, grasping for his son-in-law's hand.

' 'ello, Verity, me old sojer!'

'What's all this, then, Stringfellow?' Verity nodded at the door.

'Only Lilruwfie,' said Stringfellow. 'Don't pay no notice.'

'Who?'

'Little Ruthie!' said Stringfellow with toothless deliberation. 'Name's Ruth, in other words.'

'What's she doing here?'

'Earning her keep, o' course. What else should she be doing?'

And then there was a cry from the stairs as Bella, with her plump little figure and blonde curls, scuttled toward Verity's open arms.

'Servants!' said Verity indignantly. ' 'ow I shall be able to look the rest of the street in the face, I don't know! We *are* servants, Mrs Verity. Least, I was before I went for a sojer. Superior servant, of course, but in service all the same.'

He and Bella lay side by side in the ancient bed, to which Julius Stringfellow had brought his young bride quarter of a century before. The Veritys lay on their backs like two figures on a tomb. There was an air of resentment and ill-temper.

'Speak for yourself, Mr Verity,' said Bella crossly, 'I ain't a servant, and shan't be. Any case, it's Pa's house and he shall do as he likes. With you away and poor Pa crippled, it ain't easy to manage them two either, with no help.'

She jerked her head at the two cradles at the foot of the bed, where Billy and Vicky slumbered with the round red faces and the black hair of Verity himself.

'It ain't right for Mr Stringfellow to have that young person sleeping like a cat in front of the kitchen fire all night,' said Verity in his most magisterial manner.

'She ain't in front of the fire,' said Bella sharply. 'She got a proper attic servants' room.'

'But Mr Stringfellow got that!'

'Pa got one of them. He done the next one out special for little Ruth. She got nowhere to go, once she came to London from the country.'

Verity sat upright with a start.

'Your Pa up there with that young person?' It was perhaps from the next house in the terrace, beyond the lath and plaster of the flimsy partition wall, that he heard the creak of boards, low voices and the familiar slap of a hand on smooth bare flesh.

Bella sat upright as well.

'William Clarence Verity!' she wailed. 'I never took you for such a unnatural, ungrateful creetur! Pa give you a 'ome! 'e give your offspring a roof over their 'eads! And all you do to thank him is to think nastiness about him behind his back. I – hoo-hoo-hoo!'

There was an angry wail from one of the cradles.

'Now, now, Mrs Verity!' said Verity hastily. 'I never said that!'

This time there was no doubt that the sound came from above them. It was Stringfellow's fruity chortle and a growl of appreciation.

'See what you done!' howled Bella. 'You started little Vicky off and you woke poor Pa! He gotta be up five o'clock to see to the 'orse and get to Langham Place cab-stand!'

Verity temporarily abandoned the moral warning he had prepared for Bella about her father's behaviour and the awful danger of finding herself with new brothers and sisters younger than her own children.

'I got a great respect for your old father,' he said sternly,

257

trying to close his mind to the muttering overhead.

Bella subsided into uncertain silence. Verity swung himself out of bed and walked over to the little window of the room. After the mist and smoke of the day, the November night was clear and cold, promising one of the first frosts of the winter. From Paddington Green to the horizon south of the river, from the gardens of Bayswater to the steeples of Aldgate and Bow, the city was lit by the faint, luminous beauty of a thousand stars. He thought of the letter which Samson had given him, forgotten in the disagreeable discoveries awaiting him on his return to Stringfellow's little house. It was still in his coat pocket, as he fumbled his way toward the garment and drew it out. He slit open the envelope and felt for the paper inside. There was none. He touched a round hard shape, like a large coin, with something soft attached to it. Even before he drew it out, he knew what it must be. It was the button torn from his coat in the struggle beside the rope. He had last seen it in the hand of Verney Dacre, the only man, surely, who could have known to whom it belonged.

Verity's heart leapt with exultation, despite the momentous implications of the message.

'I'll show 'em!' he said fiercely. 'I'll have Mr Croaker flayed and salted for this when the time do come! And all them that's in it with him! Dead, was 'e? Huh! I'd wager he ain't dead now!'

'Mr Verity?' the voice came softly from the bed. 'What you on about?'

He was bursting with the news, but he realized in time that the full truth would lead her to worry and fret for his safety.

'Nothing, Mrs Verity, dear,' he said, easing himself into bed once more, 'only some meanness of Mr Croaker's again.'

The reconciliation soon began.

'It was for you, Mr Verity,' said Bella softly. 'You being part of His Highness's household. And it was only to be little Ruthie, no more 'n that.'

258

'There, there, Mrs Verity! Bella!'

'And you wouldn't want her sent to Mrs Rouncewell's, along with them other unfortunates, would you?'

Verity thought of the burly ex-police matron and her leering appreciation of Ruth's naked charms.

'No,' he said hastily, 'course not.'

'And Pa says she won't be no inconvenience to you. 'e says . . .'

'Yes, Mrs Verity?'

'Pa says he won't have her in your way or anywhere that you might get a chance to give her a bit of a touch-up.'

There was a pained silence. Presently Bella said,

'Mr Verity?'

'Yes, Bella?'

'What's a touch-up?'

'What did your Pa say it was, then?'

'Dunno. All he said was that when you arrested un-fortunate young persons, 'e bets you give 'em a good touch-up.'

'Oh, that,' said Verity, improvising rapidly. 'That ain't nothing but a slum phrase what's used for officers arresting people. An officer that nibs someone, arrests 'em. If he snaps the darbies on, he arrests 'em. If he feels their collars, he arrests 'em. And if he gives a good touch-up, he does the same.

'So you gave Miss Jolly a good touch-up?'

'Likewise,' said Verity, 'that ain't a real name. A jolly is slum talk for a girl what causes bother. She soon got called Miss Jolly for that. What she was called before, if she ever had a name, no one knows.'

'If you arrested me, then, ' said Bella innocently, 'I s'pose I'd get a good touch-up?'

'In a manner o' speaking, Mrs Verity.'

He felt the bed begin to shake with her suppressed laughter.

'William Clarence Verity!' she gasped happily. 'You ain't 'alf a bloomin' liar.'

'That's what a jolly is,' he said with a giggling snort.

259

'Ask anyone down Paddington Green.'

Wearying of the joke, she turned toward him and nudged him with her plump little elbow.

'Welcome 'ome, Mr Verity,' she whispered knowingly. 'Welcome 'ome!'

>>> If you've enjoyed this book and would like to discover more great vintage crime and thriller titles, as well as the most exciting crime and thriller authors writing today, visit: >>>

The Murder Room
Where Criminal Minds Meet

themurderroom.com

www.ingramcontent.com/pod-product-compliance
Ingram Content Group UK Ltd.
Pitfield, Milton Keynes, MK11 3LW, UK
UKHW040434280225
455666UK00003B/65